The Black Swan of Paris

The Black Swan of Paris

Karen Robards

THORNDIKE PRESS
A part of Gale, a Cengage Company

Thorndike Press, a part of Gale, a Cengage Company.

Thorndike Press® Large Print Basic
The text of this Large Print edition is unabridged.
Other aspects of the book may vary from the original edition.
Set in 16 pt. Plantin.

LIBRARY OF CONGRESS CIP DATA ON FILE.
CATALOGUING IN PUBLICATION FOR THIS BOOK
IS AVAILABLE FROM THE LIBRARY OF CONGRESS

ISBN-13: 978-1-4328-8048-4 (hardcover alk. paper)

Published in 2020 by arrangement with Harlequin Books S.A.

Printed in Mexico
Print Number: 02 Print Year: 2020

For my three sons,
Peter, Christopher and Jack,
with all my love.

What is the use of living, if it be not to strive for noble causes and to make this muddled world a better place for those who will live in it after we are gone?

— Winston Churchill

Chapter One

May 15, 1944

When the worst thing that could ever happen to you had already happened, nothing that came after really mattered. The resultant state of apathy was *almost* pleasant, as long as she didn't allow herself to think about it — any of it — too much.

She was Genevieve Dumont, a singer, a *star.* Her latest sold-out performance at one of Paris's great theaters had ended in a five-minute standing ovation less than an hour before. She was acclaimed, admired, celebrated wherever she went. The Nazis loved her.

She was not quite twenty-five years old. Beautiful when, like now, she was dolled up in all her after-show finery. Not in want, not unhappy.

In this time of fear and mass starvation, of worldwide deaths on a scale never seen before in the whole course of human history, that made her lucky. She knew it.

Whom she had been before, what had almost destroyed her — that life belonged to someone else. Most of the time, she didn't even remember it herself.

She refused to remember it.

A siren screamed to life just meters behind the car she was traveling in. Startled, she sat upright in the back seat, heart lurching as she looked around.

Do they know? Are they after us?

A small knot of fans had been waiting outside the stage door as she'd left. One of them had thrust a program at her, requesting an autograph for Francoise. She'd signed — *May your heart always sing, Genevieve Dumont* — as previously instructed. What it meant she didn't know. What she did know was that it meant *something:* it was a prearranged encounter, and the coded message she'd scribbled down was intended for the Resistance.

And now, mere minutes later, here were the Milice, the despised French police who had long since thrown in their lot with the Nazis, on their tail.

Even as icy jets of fear spurted through her, a pair of police cars followed by a military truck flew by. Running without lights, they appeared as no more than hulking black shapes whose passage rattled the big Citroën that up until then had been alone on the road. A split second later, her driver — his name was Otto Cordier; he worked for Max, her manager — slammed on the brakes. The car jerked to a stop.

"Sacre bleu!" Flying forward, she barely stopped herself from smacking into the back of the front seat by throwing her arms out in front of her. "What's happening?"

"A raid, I think." Peering out through the windshield, Otto clutched the steering wheel with both hands. He was an old man, short and wiry with white hair. She could read tension in every line of his body. In front of the car, washed by the pale moonlight that painted the scene in ghostly shades of gray, the cavalcade that had passed them was now blocking the road. A screech of brakes and the throwing of a shadow across the nearest building had her casting a quick look over her shoulder. Another military truck shuddered to a halt, filling the road behind them, stopping it up like a cork in a bottle. Men — German soldiers along with officers of the Milice — spilled out of the stopped vehicles. The ones behind swarmed past the Citroën, and all rushed toward what Genevieve tentatively identified as an apartment building. Six stories tall, it squatted, dark and silent, in its own walled garden.

"Oh, no," she said. Her fear for herself and Otto subsided, but sympathy for the targets of the raid made her chest feel tight. People who were taken away by the Nazis in the middle of the night seldom came back.

The officers banged on the front door. "Open up! Police!"

It was just after 10:00 p.m. Until the siren had ripped it apart, the silence blanketing the city had been close to absolute. Thanks to the strictly enforced blackout, the streets were as dark and mysterious as the nearby Seine. It had rained earlier in the day, and before the siren the big Citroën had been the noisiest thing around, splashing through puddles as they headed back to the Ritz, where she was staying for the duration of her Paris run.

"If they keep arresting people, soon there will be no one left." Genevieve's gaze locked on a contingent of soldiers spreading out around the building, apparently looking for another way in — or for exits they could block. One rattled a gate of tall iron spikes that led into the brick-walled garden. It didn't open, and he moved on, disappearing around the side of the building. She was able to follow the soldiers' movements by the torches they carried. Fitted with slotted covers intended to direct their light downward so as to make them invisible to the Allied air-raid pilots whose increasingly frequent forays over Paris aroused both joy and dread in the city's war-weary citizens, the torches' bobbing looked like the erratic flitting of fireflies in the dark.

"They're afraid, and that makes them all

the more dangerous." Otto rolled down his window a crack, the better to hear what was happening as they followed the soldiers' movements. The earthy scent of the rain mixed with the faint smell of cigarette smoke, which, thanks to Max's never-ending Gauloises, was a permanent feature of the car. The yellow card that was the pass they needed to be on the streets after curfew, prominently displayed on the windshield, blocked her view of the far side of the building, but she thought soldiers were running that way, too. "They know the Allies are coming. The bombings of the Luftwaffe installations right here in France, the Allied victories on the eastern front — they're being backed into a corner. They'll do whatever they must to survive."

"Open the door, or we will break it down!"

The policeman hammered on the door with his nightstick. The staccato beat echoed through the night. Genevieve shivered, imagining the terror of the people inside.

Thin lines of light appeared in the cracks around some of the thick curtains covering the windows up and down the building as, at a guess, tenants dared to peek out. A woman, old and stooped — there was enough light in the hall behind her to allow Genevieve to see that much — opened the front door.

"Out of the way!"

She was shoved roughly back inside the

building as the police and the soldiers stormed in. Her frightened cry changed to a shrill scream that was quickly cut off.

Genevieve's mouth went dry. She clasped her suddenly cold hands in her lap.

There's nothing to be done. It was the mantra of her life.

"Can we drive on?" She had learned in a hard school that there was no point in agonizing over what couldn't be cured. To stay and watch what she knew was coming — the arrest of partisans, who would face immediate execution upon arrival at wherever they would be taken, or, perhaps and arguably worse, civilians, in some combination of women, children, old people, clutching what few belongings they'd managed to grab, marched at gunpoint out of the building and loaded into the trucks for deportation — would tear at her heart for days without helping them at all.

"We're blocked in." Otto looked around at her. She didn't know what he saw in her face, but whatever it was made him grimace and reach for the door handle. "I'll go see if I can get one of them to move."

When he exited the car, she let her head drop back to rest against the rolled top of the Citroën's leather seat, stared at the ceiling and tried not to think about what might be happening to the people in the building. Taking deep breaths, she did her best to block out the muffled shouts and thuds that reached her ears and focused on the physical, which, as a performer, she had experience doing. She was so tired she was limp with it. Her temples throbbed. Her legs ached. Her feet hurt. Her throat — that golden throat that had allowed her to survive — felt tight. Deliberately she relaxed her muscles and tugged the scarf tucked into the neckline of her coat higher to warm herself.

A flash of light in the darkness caught her eye. Her head turned as she sought the source. Looking through the iron bars of the garden gate, she discovered a side door in the building that was slowly, stealthily opening.

"Is anyone else in there? Come out or I'll shoot." The volume of the soldiers' shouts increased exponentially with this new gap in the walls. That guttural threat rang out above others less distinct, and she gathered from what she heard that they were searching the building.

The side door opened wider. Light from inside spilled past a figure slipping out: a girl, tall and thin with dark curly hair, wearing what appeared to be an unbuttoned coat thrown on over nightclothes. In her arms she carried a small child with the same dark, curly hair.

The light went out. The door had closed. Genevieve discovered that she was sitting with her nose all but pressed against the window as she tried to find the girl in the darkness. It took her a second, but then she spotted the now shadowy figure as it fled through the garden toward the gate, trying to escape.

They'll shoot her if they catch her. The child, too.

The Germans had no mercy for those for whom they came.

The girl reached the gate, paused. A pale hand grabbed a bar. From the metallic rattle that reached her ears, Genevieve thought she must be shoving at the gate, shaking it. She assumed it was locked. In any event, it didn't open. Then that same hand reached through the bars, along with a too-thin arm, stretching and straining.

Toward what? It was too dark to tell.

With the Citroën stopped in the middle of the narrow street and the garden set back only a meter or so from the front facade of the building, the girl was close enough so that Genevieve could read the desperation in her body language, see the way she kept looking back at the now closed door. The child, who appeared to be around ten months old, seemed to be asleep. The small curly head rested trustingly on the girl's shoulder.

It wasn't a conscious decision to leave the car. Genevieve just did it, then realized the risk she was taking when her pumps clickety-clacked on the cobblestones. The sound seemed to tear through the night and sent a lightning bolt of panic through her.

Get back in the car. Her sense of self-preservation screamed it at her, but she didn't. Shivering at the latent menace of the big military trucks looming so close on either side of the Citroën, the police car parked askew in the street, the light spilling from the still open front door and the sounds of the raid going on inside the building, she kept going, taking care to be quiet now as she darted toward the trapped girl.

You're putting yourself in danger. You're putting Otto, Max, everyone in danger. The whole network —

Heart thudding, she reached the gate. Even as she and the girl locked eyes through it, the girl jerked her arm back inside and drew herself up.

The sweet scent of flowers from the garden felt obscene in contrast with the fear and despair she sensed in the girl.

"It's all right. I'm here to help," Genevieve whispered. She grasped the gate, pulling, pushing as she spoke. The iron bars were solid and cold and slippery with the moisture that still hung in the air. The gate didn't budge for her, either. The clanking sound it made as she joggled it against its moorings made her break out in a cold sweat. Darkness enfolded her, but it was leavened by moonlight and she didn't trust it to keep her safe.

After all, she'd seen the girl from the car. All it would take was one sharp-eyed soldier, one policeman to come around a corner, or step out of the building and look her way — and she could be seen, too. Caught. Helping a fugitive escape.

The consequences would be dire. Imprisonment, deportation, even death.

Her pulse raced.

She thought of Max, what he would say.

On the other side of the gate, moonlight touched on wide dark eyes set in a face so thin the bones seemed about to push through the skin. The girl appeared to be about her own age, and she thought she must be the child's mother. The sleeping child — Genevieve couldn't tell if it was a girl or a boy — was wearing footed pajamas.

Her heart turned over.

"Oh, thank God. Thank you." Whispering, too, the girl reached through the bars to touch Genevieve's arm in gratitude. "There's a key. In the fountainhead. In the mouth. It unlocks the gate." She cast another of those lightning glances over her shoulder. Shifting from foot to foot, she could hardly stand still in her agitation. Fear rolled off her in waves. "Hurry. Please."

Genevieve looked in the direction the girl had been reaching, saw the oval stone of the fountainhead set into the brick near the gate, saw the carved lion's head in its center with its open mouth from which, presumably, water was meant to pour out. Reaching inside, she probed the cavity, ran her fingers over the worn-smooth stone, then did it again.

"There's no key," she said. "It's not here."

"It has to be. It has to be!" The girl's voice rose, trembled. The child's head moved. The girl made a soothing sound, rocked back and forth, patted the small back, and the child settled down again with a sigh. Watching, a pit yawned in Genevieve's stomach. Glancing hastily down, she crouched to check the ground beneath the fountainhead, in case the key might have fallen out. It was too dark; she couldn't see. She ran her hand over the cobblestones. Nothing.

"It's not —" she began, standing up, only to break off with a swiftly indrawn breath as the door through which the girl had exited flew open. This time, in the rectangle of light, a soldier stood.

"My God." The girl's whisper as she turned her head to look was scarcely louder than a breath, but it was so loaded with terror that it made the hair stand up on the back of Genevieve's neck. "What do I do?"

"Who is out there?" the soldier roared. Pistol ready in his hand, he pointed his torch toward the garden. The light played over a tattered cluster of pink peonies, over overgrown green shrubs, over red tulips thrusting their heads through weeds, as it came their way. "Don't think to hide from me."

"Take the baby. Please." Voice hoarse with dread, the girl thrust the child toward her. Genevieve felt a flutter of panic: if this girl only knew, she would be the last person she would ever trust with her child. But there was no one else, and thus no choice to be made. As a little leg and arm came through the gate, Genevieve reached out to help, taking part and then all of the baby's weight as between them she and the girl maneuvered the little one through the bars. As their hands touched, she could feel the cold clamminess of the girl's skin, feel her trembling. With the child no longer clutched in her arms, the dark shape of a six-pointed yellow star on her coat became visible. The true horror of what was happening struck Genevieve like a blow.

The girl whispered, "Her name's Anna. Anna Katz. Leave word of where I'm to come for her in the fountainhead —"

The light flashed toward them.

"You there, by the gate," the soldier shouted.

With a gasp, the girl whirled away.

"Halt! Stay where you are!"

Heart in her throat, blood turning to ice, Genevieve whirled away, too, in the opposite direction. Cloaked by night, she ran as lightly as she could for the car, careful to keep her heels from striking the cobblestones, holding the child close to her chest, one hand splayed against short, silky curls. The soft baby smell, the feel of the firm little body against her, triggered such an explosion of emotion that she went briefly light-headed. The panicky flutter in her stomach solidified into a knot — and then the child's wriggling and soft sounds of discontent brought the present sharply back into focus.

If she cried . . .

Terror tasted sharp and bitter in Genevieve's mouth.

"Shh. Shh, Anna," she crooned desperately. "Shh."

"I said *halt*!" The soldier's roar came as Genevieve reached the car, grabbed the door handle, wrenched the door open —

Bang. The bark of a pistol.

A woman's piercing cry. *The girl's* piercing cry.

No. Genevieve screamed it, but only in her mind. The guilt of running away, of leaving the girl behind, crashed into her like a speeding car.

Blowing his whistle furiously, the soldier ran down the steps. More soldiers burst through the door, following the first one down the steps and out of sight.

Had the girl been shot? Was she dead?

My God, my God. Genevieve's heart slammed in her chest.

She threw herself and the child into the

back seat and — softly, carefully — closed the door. Because she didn't dare do anything else.

Coward.

The baby started to cry.

Staring out the window in petrified expectation of seeing the soldiers come charging after her at any second, she found herself panting with fear even as she did her best to quiet the now wailing child.

Could anyone hear? Did the soldiers know the girl had been carrying a baby?

If she was caught with the child . . .

What else could I have done?

Max would say she should have stayed out of it, stayed in the car. That the common good was more important than the plight of any single individual.

Even a terrified girl. Even a baby.

"It's all right, Anna. I've got you safe. Shh." Settling back in the seat to position the child more comfortably in her arms, she murmured and patted and rocked. Instinctive actions, long forgotten, reemerged in this moment of crisis.

Through the gate she could see the soldiers clustering around something on the ground. The girl, she had little doubt, although the darkness and the garden's riotous blooms blocked her view. With Anna, quiet now, sprawled against her chest, a delayed reaction set in and she started to shake.

Otto got back into the car.

"They're going to be moving the truck in front as soon as it's loaded up." His voice was gritty with emotion. Anger? Bitterness? "Someone tipped them off that Jews were hiding in the building, and they're arresting everybody. Once they're —"

Otto broke off as the child made a sound.

"Shh." Genevieve patted, rocked. "Shh, shh."

His face a study in incredulity, Otto leaned around in the seat to look. "Holy hell, is that a *baby*?"

"Her mother was trapped in the garden. She couldn't get out."

Otto shot an alarmed look at the building, where soldiers now marched a line of people, young and old, including a couple of small children clutching adults' hands, out the front door.

"My God," he said, sounding appalled. "We've got to get —"

Appearing out of seemingly nowhere, a soldier rapped on the driver's window. With his knuckles, hard.

Oh, no. Please no.

Genevieve's heart pounded. Her stomach dropped like a rock as she stared at the shadowy figure on the other side of the glass.

We're going to be arrested. Or shot.

Whipping the scarf out of her neckline, she draped the brightly printed square across her shoulder and over the child.

Otto cranked the window down.

"Papers," the soldier barked.

Fear formed a hard knot under Genevieve's breastbone. Despite the night's chilly temperature, she could feel sweat popping out on her forehead and upper lip. On penalty of arrest, everyone in Occupied France, from the oldest to the youngest, was required to have identity documents readily available at all times. Hers were in her handbag, beside her on the seat.

But Anna had none.

Otto passed his cards to the soldier, who turned his torch on them.

As she picked up her handbag, Genevieve felt Anna stir.

Please, God, don't let her cry.

"Here." Quickly she thrust her handbag over the top of the seat to Otto. Anna was squirming now. Genevieve had to grab and secure the scarf from underneath to make sure the baby's movements didn't knock it askew.

If the soldier saw her . . .

Anna whimpered. Muffled by the scarf, the sound wasn't loud, but its effect on Genevieve was electric. She caught her breath as her heart shot into her throat — and reacted instinctively, as, once upon a time, it had been second nature to do.

She slid the tip of her little finger between

Anna's lips.

The baby responded as babies typically did: she latched on and sucked.

Genevieve felt the world start to slide out of focus. The familiarity of it, the bittersweet memories it evoked, made her dizzy. She had to force herself to stay in the present, to concentrate on *this* child and *this* moment to the exclusion of all else.

Otto had handed her identity cards over. The soldier examined them with his torch, then bent closer to the window and looked into the back seat.

She almost expired on the spot.

"Mademoiselle Dumont. It is a pleasure. I have enjoyed your singing very much."

Anna's hungry little mouth tugged vigorously at her finger.

"Thank you," Genevieve said, and smiled.

The soldier smiled back. Then he straightened, handed the papers back and, with a thump on the roof, stepped away from the car. Otto cranked the window up.

The tension inside the car was so thick she could almost physically feel the weight of it.

"Let them through," the soldier called to someone near the first truck. Now loaded with the unfortunate new prisoners, it was just starting to pull out.

With a wave for the soldier, Otto followed, although far too slowly for Genevieve's peace of mind. As the car crawled after the truck, she cast a last, quick glance at the garden: she could see nothing, not even soldiers.

Was the girl — Anna's mother — still there on the ground? Or had she already been taken away?

Was she dead?

Genevieve felt sick to her stomach. But once again, there was nothing to be done.

Acutely aware of the truck's large side and rear mirrors and what might be able to be seen through them, Genevieve managed to stay upright and keep the baby hidden until the Citroën turned a corner and went its own way.

Then, feeling as though her bones had turned to jelly, she slumped against the door.

Anna gave up on the finger and started to cry, shrill, distressed wails that filled the car. With what felt like the last bit of her strength, Genevieve pushed the scarf away and gathered her up and rocked and patted and crooned to her. Just like she had long ago done with —

Do not think about it.

"Shh, Anna. Shh."

"That was almost a disaster." Otto's voice, tight with reaction, was nonetheless soft for fear of disturbing the quieting child. "What do we do now? You can't take a baby back to the hotel. Think questions won't be asked? What do you bet that soldier won't talk about having met Genevieve Dumont? All it takes is one person to make the connection between the raid and you showing up with a baby and it will ruin us all. It will ruin everything."

"I know." Genevieve was limp. "Find Max. He'll know what to do."

Chapter Two

Is it my fate to die tonight? Lillian de Rocheford's blood ran cold as the question pushed its way into the forefront of her mind. An owl hooting on the roof of a house brought death to the one who heard it — everyone said so. It was silly, pure superstition. She did not for one moment believe it. But last night an owl had landed on the Château de Rocheford's steep slate roof almost directly above her attic bedroom, waking her with its mournful hoot. Today the summons had come: they were needed. She had wanted to refuse. The circumstances were such that she could not.

Arrangements had been made, a rendezvous point set. And now here they were.

And I'm jumping at everything that moves because of that damned owl.

"They should be here by now." She didn't realize she was fretting aloud until Andre Bouchard, who'd moved a few paces ahead to peer out into the fog, looked back at her. His shadow, distorted by the gray diffusion of moonlight filtering through the trees, stretched back toward her like a skeletal hand.

"If there was trouble, we would have heard something. Shouts, gunfire." He spoke in a whisper, as she had done.

It was true, what Andre said: war was rarely silent. In the last four years, since the Germans had done the unthinkable and broken through the supposedly impregnable Maginot Line to overrun France, the noise, like all the other horrible things the invaders had brought with them, had been unrelenting. First, the desperate evacuation from nearly every port along the Atlantic coast of the French army and the British and Czech soldiers whose combined efforts had failed to keep France safe. Next, the resulting firestorm as the Germans had launched their attack against the retreat that had left thousands upon thousands dead. Then came the surrender, the declaring of the city of Cherbourg open to the Nazis by their own city council, followed by the ominous rumble of trucks bringing in the despised Wehrmacht to live among them. After that, the growl of the British and, later, the American aeroplanes streaking over her beloved Cotentin Peninsula, the whistle and boom of the bombs they dropped, the staccato rat-a-tat of the entrenched Germans' return fire, had begun. By now all of that had become so much a part of the fabric of an ordinary night that its absence made her skin prickle with dread.

It was because of the fog, the thick swirling fog that glinted silver as the searchlights sliced through it, that the night sounds were muffled and the planes did not come, she knew. But knowing did not make her less afraid.

There was a curfew in place. Merely to be found outside at this hour would result in arrest. Far worse to be caught where they were, in the supposedly impassable marsh that cut off the beaches from the rest of the Cotentin, and was so prized for its defensive value that the Vikings had once called the area Carusburg, or Fortress of the Marsh. It was also a key part of the Germans' defensive strategy in the event of an attack launched against the Normandy beaches. For them to discover that she knew a way through the marsh would, she had no doubt, result in her instant execution.

Ordinarily she would have simply refused to think about it, but — the owl.

A cold finger slid down her spine. *Only a fool would be unafraid.*

The damp chill of the fog caressed her cheeks, brushed salt-tinged fingers across her mouth like a passing ghost. The faint smell of decay that was part of the marsh drifted by with it. She clenched her teeth in an effort to stop shivering and tightened her hand in its knit glove over Bruno the pony's muzzle to keep him quiet. The searchlights were closing in. Mounted in the boats of the Kriegsmarine patrolling the harbor and the adjacent coastline, their sweep was as punctual as sunrise.

With one last anxious glance at the approaching beams, she ducked her face against the warmth of Bruno's shaggy brown neck to prevent them from catching on her eyes, inhaled the pony's familiar musky scent and counted down the seconds until it was safe to look up again.

. . .5 . . . 4 . . . . 3 . . .

"Baroness. There."

Andre's relieved whisper brought her head up prematurely, but it was all right, the searchlights had moved on. Useless to remind him that for tonight she was simply Lillian, that using her title even in this place, where with luck only the beavers could hear, was to endanger her. A lifelong tenant farmer on Rocheford, her husband's once grand estate, wiry, balding Andre was unable to bring himself to address her so familiarly even now, when the world as they had known it was being ground to bits beneath the filthy boots of the *boche.*

"Be quick." Some of the tension left her shoulders as the *chaland* sliding noiselessly toward them through the glinting black water took on shape and form. Andre left the narrow spit of solid land on which they waited to squelch out to meet the small, flat-bottomed boat. The sucking sound of his boots in the mud made her heart knock in her chest.

"The Germans are far away," she murmured to Bruno, though whether to comfort the pony or herself she couldn't be sure.

Bruno threw up his head unexpectedly, dislodging her grip, as her husband Paul, Baron de Rocheford, slid out of the boat to help Andre pull it the rest of the way in. Lillian barely managed to clap her hand over the pony's muzzle again in time to prevent him from whickering a greeting at the man he must be able to recognize by smell alone, because the distance made him no more than a denser shape in the fog. Once tall and elegantly slender, her handsome Paul was gaunt and stoop-shouldered now. He would turn sixty — impossible to believe — this year, but age was not the culprit. It was the brutally harsh conditions under which they were forced to live. At fifty, for the same reason, she herself had become bony and sharp featured, with haunted hollows beneath her eyes and hungry ones beneath her cheekbones. Her once luxuriant black hair was now thin and mostly gray. Her trousers, purchased before the war, had to be belted tightly around her waist to keep them from dropping straight to her ankles. Her once formfitting sweater hung on her like a sack. Like her much-patched black coat and the threadbare black scarf twined round her head, she had seen far better days.

Unable to call out, Bruno stamped his feet in frustration. The splash of his hooves on the soggy ground, and the jingle of his stirrups, sent her stomach shooting into her throat. The concrete abomination that was the Atlantic Wall with its pillboxes full of machine guns and soldiers was not that far away. It would be foolish to trust their lives to the muffling effect of the fog.

She gave a sharp tug on Bruno's bridle and growled "Stop, you" into his ear.

Her heart knocked so loudly now that she could hear its beat against her eardrums. Still she stood fast, holding the grizzled pony that was the sole survivor of Rocheford's once proud stable, the pony that, long ago, in happier times, had been a gift to her daughter on her birthday.

The sixteenth of May.

Tomorrow.

"For me?" She could still hear the incredulous delight in her five-year-old's voice, still see her slight figure in the blue party dress as she let go of her hand to fly down Rocheford's front steps toward a much younger but still placid Bruno, who'd just been brought round by a smiling Paul.

"Papa, he's beautiful!"

The voice, like the memory, was forever

preserved in her heart.

Lillian's chest tightened. Every cell in her body quivered with the sudden onslaught of fierce sorrow.

Her fiery little daughter, lost to her these many years.

Ça suffit. Put it out of your mind.

"Any problems?" Paul's lowered voice reached her through the mist. He was talking to Andre.

"No, none," he replied.

The two men were close now, sloshing toward her through calf-deep water.

Besides Paul, and Jean-Claude Faure, a bookkeeper from the town who had accompanied him to the rendezvous point, the boat carried two other men, who were helping to propel it by use of long poles. They were strangers to her, as far as she knew. As they were members of a different cell she had no need, or desire, to know their identities, just as they had no need to know hers. In this new world where no one could be trusted and collaborators were everywhere, anonymity was the key to safety.

Lying awkwardly in the bottom of the boat was the reason they were all taking such a risk: an injured British pilot. His plane had been shot down over the harbor two nights previously. He and his crew had managed to parachute out. What had happened to the others she didn't know. This man was a particular problem because he was injured to the point where he was unable to walk. He had been rescued and hidden at great risk. Even now the Germans were conducting an all-out search for him and his crew. Getting him out by sea was judged impossible: the harbor and shoreline were closely patrolled. Moving him overland by vehicle was determined to be equally impossible, as every road out of the valley was blocked, every train stopped and searched.

Since the tide of the war had started to turn against them, the Germans had become increasingly vicious and volatile, like angry wasps defending their nest. The rumors of an imminent Allied invasion somewhere along the coast seemed to have whipped these local ones into a frenzy. They were going house to house, business to business, farm to farm, ransacking homes, boats, shops, even the schools and churches, in search of the downed airmen. To be caught aiding any of them meant summary execution. Even to be suspected meant torture and imprisonment. Many had already been taken in for questioning. As a result, fear lay over the surrounding countryside like the heavy fog.

A solution to the difficulty had been found. Tonight they would walk the pilot out, strapped to Bruno's back, through the swamp paths that had once been used by smugglers. She knew those paths like she knew the many rooms in her house. Since she had married Paul at the age of eighteen and come to Rocheford to live, she had haunted the estuary, fascinated by the birds, the wildlife, the plants. The mushrooms she had gathered in the marsh and cultivated in the far reaches of the château's cave-like cellars supplemented the household's meager diet now that the tightly rationed food supply had all but run out and mass starvation had become a grim reality.

Paul had teased her about her mushrooms once. He did not laugh at them now.

Her knowledge of the paths was why, despite the owl, she had insisted on coming. The danger to the men would be far greater without her to guide them. Paul had wanted to leave her behind.

"The trip will be too hard," he'd told her. "Too long, and too dangerous."

Yes, but one wrong step off the ribs of solid ground that snaked across the marsh, invisibly weaving a walkway through the swaying grass and tangles of trees and scrub and fingerlet waterways, and all would be lost. The ground was deceptive. It looked firm where it was not. In many places water beneath the tall grass was more than two meters deep, and the mud below that was silt, oozing and liquid. Unwary animals got trapped in it and died all the time. The same could, and did, befall unwary humans.

"I am coming," she'd said. His eyes were the color of coffee, while hers were a clear, pale, aquamarine blue. They met, a clash of the dark and the light.

She rarely argued with him. After all these years, they were attuned in most things. But he also knew her well enough to know when she meant what she said. He looked into her eyes, saw that this was one of those times and gave up the fight as lost before it began. A smart man, her Paul.

"Bring her in," he said to the men in the boat. "Hurry."

The bow pushed through the last of the reeds to bump dry land. Lillian led Bruno as close to the water's edge as she dared. Andre held the small craft in place while Paul and the others lifted the pilot out.

The man groaned, a low, pained sound.

"Take care. His leg is broken." The caution came from one of the men she did not know. "And perhaps some ribs, as well."

"Sergeant Pilot Ronald Nash," the pilot said clearly in English as the men heaved his tall, lanky form into the saddle. Even as Lillian felt a thrill of fear at how loud his voice was, she realized that he was rotely identifying himself. He slumped forward over the pommel. "Three Squadron —"

"Merde."

"The drug's worn off."

"Here." Amid the jumble of alarmed voices

and hurried movements, one of the new arrivals pressed a cloth to the pilot's face. When he took it away after a minute or so, the pilot had fallen the rest of the way forward so that his head rested on Bruno's neck.

"Drug?" Lillian asked. She did her best to hold Bruno still as the men tied the pilot's now limp body in place. His flight suit had been replaced with ill-fitting civilian clothes. His splinted leg stretched stiffly toward the ground.

As the men finished, a blanket was tossed over him. Its purpose was both to shield him from the elements and to hide him from view.

Although if, say, a German patrol should chance to see them, she didn't think a blanket over the airman would be enough to get them waved on their way.

"Chloroform." Paul came up beside her. At the same time, the boat shoved off and the men with the poles got to work again, heading back the way they had come. "They thought it was best to keep him quiet and to combat the pain."

"Much risk for nothing if he dies," Jean-Claude grumbled. A dour man of near her own age, he lived with his elderly mother and was one of the last Lillian would have expected to chance all for such a cause.

"We must make certain he does not, then," Paul replied perfectly pleasantly, but with the ring of a leader. Lillian felt a surge of pride in him. From the time he'd heard the little-known general Charles de Gaulle, in the wake of France's surrender, speaking over the radio from London to call on all Frenchmen to refuse to accept defeat and continue to fight, that's what he had done. Living meekly day by day under the iron fist of the occupying Nazis, swallowing the shame of France's surrender and the collaboration of the Vichy government was not something he could stomach.

"Did you *have* to get into the water?" Lillian scolded under her breath as she turned Bruno about and headed inland. Left without his rider now for lo these many years, the pony had grown unaccustomed to the saddle and the weight on his back and moved reluctantly, unhappy with his burden. She *tch-tched* at him under her breath, pulled harder on the rein, got him going at an acceptable pace. "Is there a *reason* why Jean-Claude, perhaps, or one of the others couldn't jump out and pull the boat in?"

"I'm taller?" Paul grinned at her. For a moment she caught a glimpse of the charming young man she'd first met shortly after she'd turned thirteen, when, as the aristocratic son of a prosperous landowner, he'd come to visit her physician father's clinic in Orconte to observe the effects of an administration of smallpox vaccine, which had just become obligatory in France. At that young age, they'd both been starry-eyed about the future, with no idea that it could hold such things as poverty or hunger or death or war. "You worry too much, *ma choupette.*" He leaned down to whisper confidentially, "Besides, I stole a pair of Henri Vartan's work boots."

Formerly their farm manager, forced to find other work once the hard times hit in the thirties, Henri still lived in his cottage at Rocheford but now worked for the railroad, which as it happened served as a valuable cog in the Resistance network. Lillian glanced down, saw that Paul was indeed wearing a pair of unfamiliar rubber boots that reached almost to his knees, and harrumphed her opinion of that.

"I'm all right, Lil." His voice gentled. "Everything is going to be all right."

"I'm glad you think so." Her tone was tart, but the truth was his words soothed her. She knew it was stupid, knew he could no more predict the future than she could, but still his reassurance went a long way toward calming the nervous flutter in her stomach. Usually she was better able to keep the fear at bay. Even the high-risk work they'd been doing in preparation for the major operation that was coming had not unsettled her like this.

All because you heard an owl.

Yes, and also because taking photographs of the tall, mine-topped poles, called Rommel's asparagus, as they were being set in place to bristle up around the shoreline, and mapping the antipersonnel mines that had been laid down to repel an amphibious landing, and gathering samples of sand from the beaches to make sure they could support the weight of insurgent tanks, which was what they had been doing for the last few weeks, were all easier to explain away than being caught smuggling a British pilot out through the supposedly impassable marsh in the middle of the night.

The searchlights swung past, but thankfully they were now beyond the reach of the beams.

"We must go single file." Glancing around, she repeated it for the benefit of the others as the spit opened out into a sea of shoulder-high grass that stretched endlessly into the night. With the patrols out, she didn't dare use a torch. Instead she would navigate by memory, and landmarks, such as the abandoned beaver dam dead ahead. "The path is narrow."

Some three hours later, they walked out of the marsh into a wood, then paused just inside a line of trees to cautiously survey what lay on its other side: the narrow paved road that led into Valognes.

A blackout was in effect, so no lights marked the town's location. Farmhouses dotted the surrounding land, Lillian knew, but they were as good as invisible in the dark.

Stepping into the road, they started toward the town.

"How are you doing?" Paul asked, coming up beside her.

Lillian managed a smile for him. "Fine." It was almost true. Except for the fact that she was so hungry the sides of her stomach were practically stuck together, and her arm ached from dragging Bruno along, and her feet in their sturdy brogues were freezing. The layers of newspaper with which she'd lined her coat were failing miserably in their task of keeping out the cold, so the rest of her was freezing, too. Even the small garnet heart she wore on a chain around her neck — all her other jewelry had been sold or traded long since, but this particular piece had been too precious to give up — felt cold against her skin. Worse, her nerves were on edge in a way that was both unpleasant and unfamiliar. But there was no point in regaling Paul with any of that: he would only worry. With a hint of humor she added, "You couldn't have had them meet us at the edge of the swamp?"

He took the rein from her, and she relinquished it gladly.

"Better that they don't know we came through it." His voice was pitched so that it reached her ears only, and he looked ahead as he spoke. She thought he was searching for landmarks to guide them just as she had done. "The Germans think the marsh is impossible to cross, and we don't want anyone to tell them differently."

"You're right, of course." This reminder of what, when the invasion came, she would be called upon to do made her pulse quicken.

His expression changed, and she followed his gaze to find that he was looking at a small pile of stones beside a corner fence post. It was clearly the sign he'd been watching for.

"We're close now." He glanced around, raised his voice so the others could hear, pointed. "Up this way."

On the other side of the road, what looked like a cart track led uphill between parallel fence rows. They turned onto it, trudged over the rocky, uneven ground. At the top of the rise was the dark outline of a barn. Their destination, Paul told them; then he gave a soft, three-noted whistle.

The barn door slid open with a rusty rumbling sound. Peering through the floating wisps of fog into the impenetrable black maw of the barn's interior, Lillian felt a quiver of unease.

A man walked out of the barn, beckoned to them urgently. A gray shape against the darkness behind him, he was impossible to identify.

Paul's step slowed. He said, "They should have whistled back." At his tone she experienced a sensation that felt very much like a spider crawling across the nape of her neck

— or a goose walking over her grave. To her alone, he added under his breath, "Turn and walk down the hill. Now. If something happens, run."

Sucking in her breath, Lillian glanced at him. At what she saw in his face her heart stampeded.

Before she could answer, before she could even begin to comply, the night exploded into chaos.

The sound of charging footsteps accompanied a blinding explosion of light from the barn as a trio of powerful searchlights switched on, catching them full in their beams.

"Halt!" Soldiers pointing rifles burst through the open doorway.

Frightened, Bruno whinnied and reared, jerking the rein from Paul's hold as he bolted with a thunder of hooves. The blanket dislodged, revealing the slipping body of the pilot. Andre and Jean-Claude yelled and jumped aside to get out of the way.

Paul's hands slammed into her shoulder, shoving her violently to the ground.

The soldiers opened fire.

"Ah!"

For Lillian, that one cry pierced the tumult like an arrow lodging in her heart. The voice was Paul's. She saw him fall. He landed on his side on the muddy track, rolled onto his back. Bathed in the garish brightness of the searchlights, he writhed, ashen faced.

"No!" On hands and knees, she scrambled toward him. Blood stained his coat, spurted from a wound in his chest. *"No!"*

She reached him, saw at a glance that it was worse than bad. Snatching off her scarf, she tried to stanch the blood.

He looked at her, sucked in a shuddering breath. Already his lips were taking on a bluish tinge. She could feel the warm wetness soaking through her scarf and gloves.

No. No. No.

"Paul." It was all she could say. A lump lodged in her throat. Her chest felt like it was caught in a vise. She pressed both hands down hard on his wound, praying that it would be enough to stem the bleeding.

"Lil." His eyes closed, then opened again. Heart thudding, she leaned close to catch his words. "Last night — did you hear the owl?"

Horror turned her blood to ice.

"I —" There was no time for more. Rough hands closed on her arms. A trio of rifles were thrust in her face. Screaming, crying, fighting like a madwoman to get back to him, she was dragged away.

Chapter Three

"All right. You've had enough."

Max's low-pitched warning as he came up behind her spurred Genevieve into tossing back the champagne remaining in her delicate crystal flute like it was a shot of neat whisky.

"It's never enough."

His arm snaked around her waist. He yanked her back against him.

"Hey! You almost made me drop my glass." Not bothering to struggle, she glared at him over her shoulder.

"Pull yourself together." He spoke into her ear. His voice was harsh. They were alone in the hall, or he never would have grabbed her like that. In public Max always exhibited the deference that was due her as the star around which his life supposedly revolved.

"Let go of me."

"What we're doing here is too important for you to jeopardize it with your stunts."

"Are you calling rescuing that child last night a stunt?" The outrage in her voice was in no way diminished because she had, of necessity, to keep the volume low. After Otto had taken her to Max — at an illicit nightspot in the place des Vosges — and left her in the car while he'd gone in to get him, Max had come out and climbed into the back seat, his grim expression making it clear that Otto had already briefed him about what had occurred. He'd taken one look at her face and obviously picked up on the desperate resolve with which she'd been clutching the baby. Instead of scolding her or launching into a diatribe about her foolishness in getting involved, he had been as soothing and reassuring as only Max at his best could be. And, just as she'd been certain he would, he'd known exactly what to do. He told her all about the Oeuvre de secours aux enfants, also known as the Children's Aid Society, or OSE, even as Otto had driven them to a house in the Bastille. Assuring her that the clandestine organization had been set up by the Resistance for exactly that purpose and the child would be protected from the Nazis and well cared for until she could be restored to her family, he'd persuaded her to hand Anna over to him when they'd stopped in front of it and taken her inside. When he'd returned, alone, he reassured her some more as Otto drove them to the Ritz. Genevieve had spent the hours since *not* sleeping and *not* thinking about Anna or the girl or any of the associations the encounter had dredged up. Oh, and drinking.

"It was a good thing to do. It was also stupid. What if you'd been caught? Do you know what they would have done to you?" His breath tickled her ear. She could almost feel the movement of his lips against the delicate whorls. She *could* feel the firmness of his body pressed up against her back and the hard strength of his arm around her waist. She fought the urge to close her eyes — until she realized that her arm was wrapped on top of his, holding it as he held her. Instantly her arm fell away, and she stiffened into rigidity.

"I'm sure you're going to tell me."

"They would have arrested you. Then they would have tortured you. Do you have any concept of what torture is like? They might, for example, have begun by breaking your fingers, one by one. You'd give up Otto and me and the whole bloody network the minute they started in on you, believe me."

"It didn't happen, did it? So why are you worrying?"

"Because now you're drunk. And that makes you a liability."

"I am not drunk."

"You stumbled over the carpet back there. There's too much at stake here. We can't afford any cock-ups."

"I do my job."

"And you need to keep doing it. No more haring off to rescue children. No more getting drunk. Just do what you're supposed to do."

"Since when do you get to dictate my every move?" She shoved at the arm wrapped around her waist. It wouldn't have worked, but a waiter carrying a tray came around the corner just then — his attention fortunately on the tray's load of freshly filled champagne flutes rather than the little drama playing out between her and Max farther along the hall — and, seeing him, too, Max released her.

Without another word, Genevieve walked on as if nothing had happened, deposited her empty flute on the tray as the waiter passed and grabbed another full one, more to annoy Max than because she really wanted it. Ostentatiously sipping at the champagne, she continued to make her way along the narrow hallway that led from the dressing rooms to the stage. Tall and intimidating despite the old injury that made him walk with a pronounced limp and the aid of an elegant black stick, Max lengthened his stride until he loomed beside her.

"Feeling full of yourself, are you?"

To hell with sipping. She gulped a mouthful of champagne. "Feeling sick of being ordered around by you."

"Sure it's not the amount of booze you've consumed making you feel sick?"

She shot him a fulminating look. "You can —"

She was interrupted by chorus girls in their elaborate costumes rushing past, as they sped on their way to get into position for the finale. Others, exiting the stage, hurried toward the greenroom where the after-show party was already getting started. With Max now half a step behind her, she made her way toward the stage, dodging performers and stagehands alike as they got caught up in the crosscurrents of the backstage in flux between numbers. A welter of low-voiced chatter cut through the frenetic music of the closing bars of the evening's second-to-last act, the ever popular cancan, currently onstage. So many bodies in such close proximity made the enclosed area overwarm, which she supposed many might consider a blessing on this cold May night in Paris, where, as a result of the Occupation, coal and heating oil were almost as impossible to obtain as food. The smell, a mix of heavy perfumes, cigarette smoke, cosmetics, unwashed costumes and musty carpet, would probably be considered unpleasant by some. To her it was familiar and comforting, the scent of home.

"You should already be in position." There was a definite edge to Max's voice. She took that as a win, because he rarely lost his patience, and drank more champagne. "You're on in a matter of minutes."

"Whose fault is that? *You* delayed me."

"Being late is unprofessional. Take that as a word of warning from your manager."

Genevieve made a scoffing sound.

Besides being what the *Pariser Zeitung,* the propaganda-filled, German-instituted Paris daily, described as the "brilliant impresario behind the dazzlingly successful international tour," she, "the achingly beautiful star with the voice of an angel" was embarked upon, Max was indeed, officially, her manager. Unofficially, and whether she liked it or not, he was, quite simply, the man who could tell her what to do.

She didn't like it. She didn't like *him.* Most of the time.

Max was black haired, strong chinned, with a tanned, lived-in face, hard dark eyes and a straight blade of a nose above a surprisingly beautiful, sensitive mouth. Handsome? Her girl singers seemed to think so. While she might once have agreed, her opinion had changed radically since she'd become more closely acquainted with him. His papers said his name was Maximillian Georges Bonet, a now forty-four-year-old French citizen who was medically unfit for military service. It was in that guise, three years previously, that he'd inserted himself into her life. It was all a lie, as she'd learned to her cost far too late to do anything about it. The truth was that he was thirty-four, nine years her senior. The even more terrifying truth was that he was a British agent. A spy. Major Max Ryan, Special Operations Executive. SOE.

And he was using her, her French nationality, her fame, the gift that was her voice, to run an espionage network that encompassed the length and breadth of Occupied Europe.

With no regard at all for the fact that he might very well get her — get them all, the entire unknowing troupe — killed. The Germans had no mercy for spies. The Führer himself had ordered that the Geneva convention was to be disregarded for them. If they were captured, their lives could be spared only for the purpose of interrogation. As soon as the interrogation — torture — was over, they were to be shot. No exceptions.

The knowledge made for peaceful, nightmare-free nights.

Max had befriended her in Morocco, where she had fled in the face of the German invasion. He'd taken advantage of the one thing they genuinely had in common, music, to make her like him, make her trust him, deliberately, as she now knew. Then, when she'd turned to him for help in a moment of direst need, he'd snapped the trap shut on her.

Instead of finding a shoulder to lean on, as she'd thought, she discovered that what she'd really done was make a deal with the devil.

Not that she'd figured it out right away.

He'd "helped her out" at the beginning, arranging first one tour and then a succession of them for her, in increasingly glittering venues. Gradually he'd assumed total control. He'd streamlined her operation, taken over her publicity, dictated where and when she performed, implemented the steps needed to cement her status as a true international star. Soon he'd had her touring nonstop, had her songs all over the radio, had her appearing alongside the greats, until now she was acknowledged far and wide as the toast of Europe.

Also now, appearances to the contrary, the truth was that *she* worked for *him*.

"Afraid I'll miss my cue?" Knowing it was getting under his skin, she sipped more champagne. Mouth tightening, he plucked the flute from her hand, sloshing the cool liquid all over her fingers in the process, and thrust it into the hands of a chorus boy heading in the opposite direction. The young *choriste* looked affronted until he saw who had thus accosted him. The resulting change in his expression would have been comical had she been in the mood to be amused.

Max scowled at her as the boy skittered away with the flute. "Afraid you'll pass out onstage. Or on that perch contraption you come down on. In which case you'll probably break your neck."

"It's a swing." Knowing he was watching,

she slowly and deliberately licked the sticky sweetness of the drying drink from her fingers. "That *would* be inconvenient, wouldn't it? Whatever would you do?" She made big, mocking eyes at him.

"Mademoiselle Dumont, there you are! We must get you into place!" Pierre Lafont, the theater's resident stage manager, came panting up. Around fifty, short and flush-faced with a shiny bald head and a suit that, by the way it hung on him, revealed that he had once been a much heavier man, he seemed to be perpetually sweating.

"I know, Pierre. I was delayed." The quick smile she gave him was apologetic. If anything went awry, it was he, not she, who would suffer reprisals.

"Herr Obergruppenführer Wagner is once again honoring us with his presence." Pierre's tone was carefully neutral: it was dangerous to say anything that was not extremely complimentary about any of the Nazi officers clogging Paris, but Wagner, the SS's most notorious interrogator, inspired more fear than most. Pierre's eyes, however, revealed his true state of mind: they were round with nerves. "He is in his usual seat."

"How lovely," she said. Including tonight, they had five nights remaining in their three-week run at this, the Casino de Paris, one of the city's most famous music halls. She had first become aware of Wagner's attendance on the night of her second show, when he'd had an enormous bouquet of flowers along with a note of extravagant praise for her performance carried to her onstage during curtain calls. He hadn't missed a show since.

"You've acquired quite a notable admirer, it seems." Max's expression matched his voice: bland as an almond.

She wanted to slay him with a glance. Instead, mindful that they weren't alone, she smiled.

"It seems I have," she agreed, and had the satisfaction of seeing his eyes narrow. She swept ahead of him into the backstage area, careful to stay out of the way of the girls in the wings as they ran in two at a time to join the high-kicking double chorus line revolving onstage. She was in costume, in a tight, strapless black bustier-style bodysuit glittering with sequins that lent her slender figure a voluptuousness it didn't actually possess and a full, trailing skirt composed of dyed-black ostrich feathers that made opulent swishing sounds as they brushed across the stage's wooden floor. The skirt parted in front to showcase her long, slim legs in sheer black stockings that were attached to the bodysuit by black satin suspenders. Black peep-toe shoes, a black velvet ribbon worn as a choker, and a headdress of three tall black ostrich plumes completed her ensemble, which was designed to play off both a repeating line in her finale song about waiting for a lover who would return as surely as birds come home to their nest and the nickname Max and his team had bestowed on her.

Inspired, she assumed, by her coloring — black hair, milky skin and changeable blue-green eyes — they had dubbed her the Black Swan. At this very moment the nickname, along with her image on the aforementioned swing, adorned large posters plastered all over Paris: The Black Swan Sings! The Black Swan Swings! Come See the Black Swan in *Seasons of Love* at the Casino de Paris, April 29 to May 21!

"Mademoiselle. If you will." Pierre scurried around her to gesture anxiously at the ladder-like staircase that led to the catwalk high above.

"Afterward we go to the party at the Spanish embassy," Max reminded her in an undertone as she put a foot on the first of the rung-like steps. Ah, yes, the Spanish embassy, where she would be expected to once again put her life on the line by helping him with his spying.

"I'm feeling a little under the weather. Perhaps I'll be too ill to attend." She threw the riposte over her shoulder. Her words were purely an attempt to irritate him. Refusing was not an option, she knew.

"By then the effects of the champagne will have worn off."

She was already climbing and used that as an excuse to pretend she hadn't heard. Her head swam unexpectedly. Maybe she really had overdone it with the drinking — all right, she had — but her encounter with baby Anna combined with today's date had just been too much to bear. Max was right — it was important that she keep a clear head, but the pain had been so searingly intense that if she hadn't found something to dull it, she wouldn't have been able to function at all. Max should be thankful she'd managed to get through the show, she thought, and took a firmer grip on the iron safety rails and paid extra attention to how she placed her feet. If she were to fall . . .

She had a lightning vision of an open window, of curtains fluttering in the breeze.

Her mind reeled. Her heart took a great leap in her chest. She froze in place, utterly unable to move.

For the briefest of moments, it felt as if time and space had dissolved.

With a major effort of will, she banished the horrifying snippet of memory.

Gritting her teeth, she forced herself to keep climbing.

When she reached the top — a breath-stealing height — she stepped out onto the narrow metal catwalk. Keeping a tight grip on the rail, she glanced down to find that, while Pierre had gone, Max still stood at the foot of the stairs where she had left him. His head was tipped back as he watched her. A swirl of color and activity surrounded him as the chorus girls, in their jewel-toned bird costumes, hurried to line up for the closing number, jostling one another and the exiting cancan dancers, but he remained unmoving, a study in austere black.

"Mademoiselle Dumont, forgive me, but we must hurry. The overture is beginning."

Startled by the whisper — she hadn't heard anyone approach — she looked up to find one of the stagehands at her elbow. His name was Yves, she remembered, and yes, he was right, there were the opening violins. Carefully gripping the guardrail, she followed him along the catwalk to where the elaborately gilded and flower-festooned swing awaited her. He helped her get into position on the narrow velvet seat, then spread the long feathers of her skirt out behind her so that they would fall just right. She adjusted her headdress and the front of her skirt to show her legs to best advantage and listened as the rest of the orchestra joined the violins. The idea with this number was that she was supposed to be a bird on the kind of arched swing typically found in bird cages. Suspended high above the audience, she would sing the popular love song that was almost always a showstopper.

"Ready, mademoiselle?" Yves asked.

At her nod he signaled the stagehands who worked the crank that would swing her out into the darkness high above the audience and then lower her until she was in the center of the cavernous open space. He unhooked the tether that had held the swing in place and gave her a push, and she was away.

The first movement of the swing was always the worst, a wide arc that was dizzying at the best of times. Tonight the effects of the champagne magnified the vertiginous feeling until she couldn't be quite sure whether the room was spinning or her head was. Holding on tightly, she took in the horseshoe shape of the vast auditorium, the tiers of boxes rising nearly to the domed ceiling, the orchestra seats far below. Once, as a starstruck eleven-year-old, she'd sat in one of those seats with her family, practically vibrating with excitement. Her mother sat on her right, her sister on her left and her father on her sister's other side. They'd been happy then, the four of them, with no idea at all of what the future held. She and her sister clasped hands, rapt, as they watched Josephine Baker on that very same stage where she now performed. The trip to the theater had been a surprise treat that their parents had arranged, despite the slightly risqué nature of the show, because she and her sister had been such fans. She could still remember the glittering costumes, the live doves released onstage to fly out over the audience — and how electrified she'd been by the singer herself, with her easy charisma and bright, jazzy voice. That was the first time she'd known: *I want to be a singer.* But such a thing then, had seemed ridiculous, impossible. She'd been part of a family, part of a world, and as such had carried the weight of expectations and hopes and dreams that were not necessarily her own, even though, at the time, she'd never even thought to question them.

Ironically, in the end she'd gotten what she'd wished for that night, but the cost had been — everything. Everything she'd loved. Everyone she'd loved. That world she'd inhabited — precious in retrospect — ripped asunder. The realization was almost more than she could bear.

The ache in her chest was crushing in its intensity.

Her suddenly blurry gaze swept over red velvet upholstery and gilded moldings and the gorgeous arched stained-glass window that was the Casino de Paris's trademark — where she found the slap in the face she needed to bring the present back into focus. Tonight, just as it had been every night of her run and presumably every night of the last four years, the iconic window was defaced by the giant swastika banner draped across it.

Her stomach clenched as she stared at it. It seemed to take over the space, just as the

Germans had taken over everything else in Paris. Shops, bookstores, cafés, restaurants, theaters, music halls, even brothels, were overrun with them. They filled the buses, the trains, the sidewalks, the streets. Swastikas hung from the Eiffel Tower, the Arc de Triomphe, Notre-Dame: the conquerors' silent crow of victory. The Louvre was empty of paintings, the schools were missing students, shops were closed, houses left empty. Their occupation of the city had devolved into a reign of terror, but from the beginning they had made a point of promoting and protecting the arts. Even while they imposed untold suffering on millions, they seemed determined to show the world that the cultural life of Paris was flourishing under their rule. Although nearly everything performance related required approval from the Propaganda Staffel, artists of all description were given tremendous leeway by the otherwise brutally restrictive regime. Composers, playwrights, musicians, actors, dancers and singers were celebrated. In Germany, Paris was touted as the new holiday resort for the *Herrenvolk.* The Nazi motto of *Jeder einmal in Paris,* "Everyone once in Paris," promised each German soldier at least one month in the City of Light. The soldiers, particularly the officers, flocked to visit, bringing their wives and children with them to shop and sightsee and be entertained.

Looking down as she was lowered into place, Genevieve saw that seats were filled with a sea of gray-green uniforms. The Nazis continued to turn out for her in droves.

She thought of her Aryan certificate, which she was required to possess to appear onstage, tucked away in a drawer in her dressing room.

She thought of Anna — and Anna's mother.

She thought of —

She felt suddenly nauseous. And it had nothing at all to do with the champagne.

Her hands gripped the chains so tightly she could feel, through their velvet casing, the metal links digging into her skin.

The familiar whoosh of the curtains opening revealed dozens of chorus girls in their bright bird plumage pirouetting across the stage. Soon more would enter from the back of the auditorium and dance down the aisles, twirling chiffon scarves above their heads to simulate birds in flight. Beautiful staging for a beautiful song.

The spotlight hit her. Its warmth was welcome. Its brightness was blinding.

The audience looked up as one. Genevieve took a deep breath.

You can do this. One more time.

Swinging languorously above their heads, Genevieve smiled down at the upturned faces and began to sing.

"J'attendrai . . ."

Chapter Four

They started first on Jean-Claude. Both he and Andre had been stripped to their skivvies, then chained to metal chairs bolted to the stone floor. The chairs were perhaps six feet apart, with a spotlight on a stand between them. The spotlight was turned so it pointed at Jean-Claude. He blinked nervously and licked his lips, trapped in a pool of bright white light.

Without so much as asking him a question, one of them grabbed his smallest finger and pulled the nail off with pliers.

Jean-Claude screamed. A stream of his urine hit the floor, puddling under the chair. The ammonia stench instantly overrode the dank smell of the cellar where the three of them had been taken.

Lying in a bloody, bruised heap on the cold floor in the shadows near the wall, Lillian retched, a dry heave that brought up nothing. That was because she'd already vomited up everything in her stomach when they'd beaten her for trying to get away from them, for fighting to reach Paul.

Oh, Paul. By now, some eighteen hours after the blood had come spurting out of his chest, reality had set in. He was gone. She was riven with grief. She could not live. Death was no longer something she feared. It was something she longed for, so she could continue on with him. Images of the past, happy images — her with Paul, her with her little girls, the four of them together, gathered around the table for a meal, splashing in the surf at the beach, laughing together always as the loving, close family they'd been in the good days before the world fell apart — flashed in and out of her mind. They were both a comfort and a torment.

"Now we will talk, yes?" The interrogator leaned in, smiling amiably as he picked up Jean-Claude's damaged hand. With his forearm chained to the chair so that his hand dangled over the end of its arm, Jean-Claude could only curl his uninjured fingers in a futile attempt at protecting them.

The German continued, "You know the penalty for what you have done is death, do you not? But perhaps I will be merciful. If you tell me what I want to know. But I warn you — do not lie to me."

"No, no, I would not lie," Jean-Claude gasped.

"Are you a loyal subject of the regime?" He

stroked a caressing thumb over the back of Jean-Claude's hand.

"Y-yes," Jean-Claude quavered. He panted rather than breathed. Fear had rendered his eyes round as coins.

"You lie." The interrogator's tone turned vicious. Grabbing Jean-Claude's ring finger, he yanked off another nail.

Jean-Claude screamed and flailed to the extent he could while bound so tightly to the chair. Eyes closed, Andre poured sweat and muttered prayers under his breath. Lillian lay where they had dumped her, broken in body and soul.

For Jean-Claude and Andre, she felt a profound sadness. They still wished to live. She doubted they would, any of them, beyond this night.

They asked Jean-Claude his name. Where he lived. He answered both questions in a trembling voice. Who lived there with him. He hesitated to answer that one. Lillian completely understood. He was devoted to his old mother, and he feared for her. The Nazis were known to ruthlessly torture and execute whole families if one member was discovered to belong to the Resistance.

They took the pliers to another nail. He screamed out his mother's name as they yanked it off, then dropped his head and between sobs moaned, "Mother, forgive me."

"Who do you know in the Resistance?" The

interrogator was a German officer, a small man with a pale, pinched face. Another German officer, arms crossed over his chest, looked on. He was taller than the other man, tall enough so that his head came close to brushing the low, beamed ceiling. His back was turned to Lillian as he focused on Jean-Claude.

Jean-Claude stuttered in his haste to name names. He gave up everyone in the Resistance that he knew. Fortunately, he knew by name only her, Paul, Andre and one other. That was their way, their rule. One's own cell, and a contact. In case of an arrest, it prevented the whole network from being brought down.

The contact he named — Eugene Ingres — had been killed the previous week in a botched attempt to blow up a train trestle. The Nazis knew that and repaid Jean-Claude for his proffering of useless information by ripping off another nail.

Lillian knew that, too, because Paul had been informed of Ingres's death, and Paul had shared what he knew with her as naturally as he breathed. It was she who kept secrets, while he was as open as a sunny day.

Had been. Paul *had been* as open as a sunny day.

Acknowledging the past tense left her gutted.

"This attack they say is coming, this invasion by the Allies —" the interrogator sneered as he said the word "— what do you know of it?"

Lillian tensed at the question. Jean-Claude knew nothing of the planned invasion beyond the rumors that were flying through the general population. Neither did Andre. The whole world seemed to know an attack was coming, but in France only a select few at the highest levels of the Resistance had been told anything concrete. Those few who had been briefed included — *had* included — Paul. And because Paul had known, so did she.

It was why they had been gathering samples of sand: to test if they contained enough rock particles to enable the beach to bear the weight of tanks and other heavy equipment when they rolled ashore. If the beach sand could not stand up to the weight, the tanks and vehicles would bog down in sand that was too fine and be rendered useless. It was why they had been taking photographs and mapping minefields. The Allied invasion *was* near, just as the Nazis feared, and contrary to what they were being led to believe — misinformation was being planted everywhere — it was to begin here, on the beaches of Normandy.

When the bastards got to her, how long would she be able to keep silent? She would not, *could not,* reveal what she knew.

But this horror they were perpetrating on

Jean-Claude . . . She was human. She did not think she could withstand such torture for long.

She began to tremble. Even that tiny degree of movement hurt, but there was nothing she could do to stop it.

She did not fear death. She did fear pain, mutilation, abasement. Almost as much as she feared betraying her country by giving up the secret that had been entrusted to Paul.

Paul, you have to help me. Please come for me. I want to go with you.

But despite her fervent plea, her heart continued to beat, and she continued to breathe.

Voice faltering, Jean-Claude said, "I know nothing. Only what I have heard. Rumors, you understand. That an invasion is coming. Perhaps. No one can say for sure."

The interrogator leaned closer, moving the pliers threateningly up and down centimeters from Jean-Claude's body. Jean-Claude panted and shook as he followed the movement of those pliers with his eyes. Four of his fingernails were gone now. Those fingers ended in raw stumps that dripped blood. Beneath the glaring spotlight, he looked skeletal, his bones showing through his skin, which was the grayish-white of a corpse.

Darting in with fiendish swiftness, the pliers latched onto his right nipple, squeezed and twisted. Jean-Claude shrieked.

The pliers was withdrawn, only to hover threateningly over Jean-Claude's other nipple.

"You will tell me where this invasion is coming, and when."

Chest heaving as he sobbed, Jean-Claude tried to shrink away from the tool's bloodied metal tip. The upright chair was unforgiving, holding him in place.

"I know nothing —" Jean-Claude's voice went shrill as the pliers touched his skin, caressed it. "No, no, wait, I have heard — Pas-de-Calais. We have all heard it is to be at Pas-de-Calais."

Pas-de-Calais was wrong, a deliberate piece of misinformation spread through double agents and suspected informers so assiduously that it was being whispered everywhere. As he said it, she saw the light: when they turned to her, Pas-de-Calais was the answer she must school herself to give, in extremis, no matter what.

God grant me strength.

"How do you know this?"

From the corner of her eye, Lillian saw that Andre was shaking in his chair.

"I — I —" Jean-Claude faltered. "As I said, it is a rumor. I —"

The pliers darted in, grabbed Jean-Claude's other nipple, twisted and yanked, pulling off a bloody chunk of flesh. His shriek hurt her eardrums, caused her heart to leap into her throat and turned her stomach inside out with a terrible mix of pity and fear.

Blood ran down his chest, tracing a bright red line through the dark hairs that grew there. He sobbed in great hiccuping gasps.

"I have no time to waste on rumors. Who would know the truth?" The pliers returned to grip the first nipple, now red and engorged. *"Who?"*

"No, no, do not, I beg you! I will tell you all! Madame!" His eyes shot desperately in her direction. Lillian caught her breath. The tiny hairs on the back of her neck catapulted upright in horror at what he might be about to say. He knew how she and Paul had been. "Madame, forgive me —"

He broke off, choking on a sob. Tears poured down his cheeks.

The pliers twisted.

"She knows!" Jean-Claude arched screaming in his chair. The sound bounced off the stone walls, the ceiling, the floor, so loud and horrifying it made even the interrogator wince.

And then it stopped, just like that, cutting off from one second to the next. Jean-Claude gasped, only once. His eyes rolled back in his head. His face went pale and slack. Mouth still open wide, he slumped sideways in his chair. Drool spilled from the corner of his mouth.

There was a moment of shocked silence. Even Andre ceased his muttered prayers.

"You — what have you done? He was talking!" The second German shoved the first out of the way as he leaped toward Jean-Claude, checking his pulse, lifting his eyelids. He'd reverted to German, but she knew enough of the language to pick up the meaning. "His heart has stopped! You've killed him, you fool!"

"Is it my fault that he was weak? That his heart was weak?" The interrogator slapped Jean-Claude's face, slammed his fist into his chest. "Wake up, *blöder Hund*!" Then, urgently, to his compatriot, he said, "Help me get him on the floor." Cursing each other, shouting for reinforcements from upstairs, they got Jean-Claude out of the chair and laid him out on the floor. A quartet of soldiers clattered down to join them, but it was soon clear that there was nothing to be done.

Jean-Claude was dead. His heart had given out, from fear or pain or some combination of the two.

Lillian could not help thinking that, of the three of them, he was the fortunate one.

Dizzy with sorrow and fear, she closed her eyes as his limp body was carried upstairs. Sweat drenched her. She was cold, so cold.

When they came back . . .

Please, Paul, please come, please, please, please.

"Baroness!" Andre whispered. He had to

repeat her name twice before his voice broke through the haze of despair that gripped her.

She opened her eyes. They were alone in the cellar.

Andre said, "In the corner. The bleach. Baroness. Can you reach it?"

Lillian frowned, then followed the direction of his eyes to a small table in the corner. Flanked by a bucket and mops, it held what looked like cleaning supplies. The ever meticulous Germans were prepared to tidy up after torturing their victims, it seemed.

"The blue container. Bring it to me. Hurry."

The urgency of Andre's voice communicated itself to her. Enlightenment dawned. She didn't need to ask him why: she knew.

It was a way out. *My God, how has it come to this?* She took a deep, steadying breath.

Alone of the three of them, she'd been left unbound, whether because she was a woman and was therefore not considered a threat or because of the extent of the injuries they had inflicted on her, she didn't know.

"They'll be back at any minute." Andre's hoarse warning came as she dragged herself to her feet. Her coat was gone. Her sweater and trousers were torn and filthy. She could hardly stand and had to lean against the wall, scooting along it to reach the table. Moving brought shafts of pain. She gritted her teeth and kept going. Her right arm — was it broken? It didn't matter. She picked up the container of bleach with her left hand, then shuffled toward Andre.

"Lord, have mercy on me, a sinner," Andre prayed as she reached him. His eyes opened. To her he said, "Hold it so I can drink."

She got the lid off, managed to get the container to his lips. Their eyes met. His were cloudy with tears, dark with desperation.

Afraid. Just as she was afraid.

But what choice was left to them?

He tilted his head back, bade her continue with a gesture.

"God be with you, my friend," she whispered, and tilted the container so that the contents poured into his open mouth. He gulped mightily once, twice, as the bleach fumes assaulted her nose and made her eyes burn. Then he jerked his head away and began to choke and struggle, fighting the terrible effects of the chemical. White foam bubbled from his mouth, dripped down his chin. He made horrible sounds as his body spasmed, fighting the chains, convulsing in the chair.

She fell back, overcome with horror, with fear.

I can't —

The sound of booted footsteps on the stairs made her glance around.

"What the hell . . . ?" The interrogator, with the other officer behind him, came into view. He stopped halfway down the stairs, his expression changing ludicrously as he took in the situation with a glance.

Her eyes met his. For the space of perhaps a heartbeat, an image arose in her mind of her girls, not grown as they were now, but the little ones they had been, one fair, one dark, each reaching out to her.

Maman —

Goodbye, she told them silently. *I love you.*

Tears stung her eyes. Her heart slammed in her chest. She lifted the bottle.

"Stop!" he shouted at her, leaping down the remaining stairs. With the other officer barreling after him, he hit the floor running.

Summoning every last bit of courage that remained to her, Lillian put the bottle of bleach to her lips and drank.

Chapter Five

"Smile," Max hissed in Genevieve's ear as they walked in the door. The servant who'd admitted them had turned away to open the door to someone else, so they were essentially alone in the entry hall. "You're one of them, remember. Part of the elite group. That's how we get this done."

By *them,* he was referring to the collaborators, those with whom the Germans socialized, who cozied up to them, who were living high off their association with them while the rest of the country, the rest of Europe, suffered. In other words, including the Germans themselves, who were even worse, practically everyone at the party.

"I am smiling."

"You look like you sucked on a lemon."

"I told you I don't feel well. It's the best I can do."

"Try harder."

Drawing back her lips, she bared her teeth in an enormous grin. Just to show him.

"There you go. Beauty personified." He chucked her under her chin, which he knew full well would annoy her. Then he left her to see to the safe disposal of their coats. She scowled after him before turning to brave the party on her own. As she was greeted by their host, the Spanish consul, General Eduardo Castellano, and his wife, Sophie, and drawn into the small group of guests nearest the foyer, Genevieve managed to put the true purpose of her presence out of her head. Despite a headache that beat like a drum against her temples, she summoned up a dazzling smile that she hoped looked more genuine than it felt and set herself to being charming.

"We were enchanted by your wonderful performance. My wife was in tears, I give you my word!"

"Where did you train, my dear? Such an extraordinary voice!"

"Can you believe this weather? So cold this week, and now this terrible rain!"

"After Paris, where does your tour take you? Will you leave France?"

"If she is lucky, it will be someplace warmer."

Feeling like her smile was growing more rigid by the minute, Genevieve circulated, exchanged air-kisses, answered questions, made small talk and held on as if for dear life to the smooth, hard stem of the champagne flute someone had thoughtfully provided her with a few minutes before. The possible effects of overindulgence she'd experienced earlier had faded, leaving her feeling as sober as a park bench. Which was good, because the only way she was going to make it through the rest of this night was with the help of liquid fortification.

She glanced around for Max and failed to find him. Whatever he was doing — and she doubted it was limited to supervising the bestowal of their coats — was taking him far too long. Tonight of all nights she needed him with her to parry the questions, to deflect the curious stares, to stand between her and the effusive interest bombarding her on all sides. The glittering star persona she assumed for such gatherings was firmly in place, but inside she was a quivering mess. Not because of Anna, or what had happened the previous night or even the danger of this job he had coerced her into, or at least not primarily because of those things. There was still an hour remaining in what was for her this most dreaded of days: May 16, the date of one little girl's birth, and another little girl's death.

She would dearly love to be able to blot both events from her consciousness, but she was beginning to think that no matter what she did, forgetting was never going to be possible. On this of all days, the past would not leave her alone. Her wound was buried deep, but it was still there, still raw and painful. Holding Anna in her arms had been the equivalent of rubbing salt in it. The only thing that made her grief even remotely bearable was that no one who was in her life now knew anything about it, so there was no one to note the significance of the day, no one to mark it or remind her. The memories, and the pain, were hers alone.

Just a little longer, and she would be through it.

"Mademoiselle Dumont, I was fortunate enough to hear you sing at Neue Burg in Vienna last summer."

"He cherishes the photograph he took with you there, showing it to all of us whenever he wants to feel superior."

The German officers in front of her were large, blond and bucolic, very polite, as were all the invaders: the Wehrmacht had been ordered to treat the French with dignity to avoid arousing the hatred of the populace. Even now that the war was going less well for them, with North Africa fallen to the Allies, Sicily conquered, the Russians routing the Germans on the eastern front, massive bombing raids on German cities and whispers of a looming Allied invasion of France being bandied about everywhere, their good manners did not fail.

The second officer was laughing at the first, who reddened. Genevieve laughed, too, said something along the lines of *Vienna is so beautiful, one of my favorite cities,* and moved on. The truth was she remembered that night well. At Max's instigation, she'd had her picture taken with dozens of concertgoers. There'd been a reason: a prominent scientist and his family on the run from the Nazis had been hidden among the crowd, and the photos taken of them that night had been used to forge travel documents that had allowed them to make their way out of the country to safety disguised as part of her troupe's entourage.

"Traveling as you do sounds so exciting! Tell me, what is it like being on tour?"

"I heard you over the radio earlier today. The song you sang — so lovely — and then to know that I would see you perform it in person tonight —"

Being on tour is terrifying, because we're often risking death by smuggling someone or something across some border or another. And that lovely song I sang over the radio today? It was a signal to an agent.

But of course she couldn't say that. Instead she murmured platitudes and smiled. What people saw when they looked at her was Genevieve Dumont, the singer, the star. That's what they wanted to see, what they expected to see. They thought they knew all about her, about her success, her happiness, her life that seemed charmed in this time of madness. But the face she showed the world was not who she was inside.

She excused herself and continued through the room. The Spanish embassy was a large mansion constructed of smooth, pale stone. Protected by a black iron fence and large gates, it stood on the right bank of the Seine in the eighth arrondissement. For the occasion of tonight's party, it was guarded by a contingent of tightly wound German soldiers who had searched everyone as they entered, with only a handful of exceptions. They were on edge because Paris was experiencing more unrest than usual. On April 1, the Waffen-SS had massacred 86 innocent civilians in Ascq in retaliation for the explosion that had derailed a train carrying the Twelfth SS Panzer Division Hitlerjugend. Resistance activity had heightened as a result. The cross of Lorraine, that symbol of the Resistance, was appearing everywhere, painted on the sides of buildings, carved into train trestles, erected and set ablaze in the center courtyard of the Sorbonne. A little over three weeks ago, an Allied bombardment had killed over 670 people in porte de la Chapelle in the eighteenth arrondissement. Last week an explosive had been hurled into a Montmartre restaurant packed with German soldiers, killing a number of them. The 5:00 p.m. curfew imposed on the city as a result had just been reextended until the more usual 9:00 p.m. After that hour, the whole of Paris went dark, and from the outside at least, the embassy was no exception, party or no.

Once the lights were out, the sound of jackboots on pavement sent whole blocks into hiding, in cellars and closets and under beds. Like the one she had witnessed the previous night, most raids occurred during the curfew hours of 9:00 p.m. to 5:00 a.m. Anyone caught outdoors without a pass during those hours was subject to arrest. Citizens who had business outside their homes after curfew scurried through the streets like rats, heads down, intent on their destinations, hoping to avoid the patrols that had the power to stop anyone at any time and demand to see their papers. And if those papers were found to be not in order, or if for any reason suspicion was aroused, the patrols arrested as they pleased. People went out and never came back.

Because of her fame, Genevieve had a pass that exempted her from being searched — she was one of the handful who had been permitted to enter the embassy unmolested — which was why Max had insisted she come tonight despite her continued (perfectly true) protests that she was feeling unwell. In her evening bag was information to be passed on to his contact in the embassy and from there carried out of France. Its mere presence on her person was enough to keep her heart knocking in her chest and her stomach in a permanent knot. It was also enough to get her killed: the Nazis were ruthless in dealing with anyone who dared oppose them, and in this atmosphere of heightened tension, they would be merciless even, she feared, to one such as her.

"Everyone who has seen it praises your show to the skies," a gentleman stopped her to say. "Alas, it is sold out! Who do I have to know to obtain tickets?"

"Jacques, do not pester Mademoiselle Dumont," his wife beside him said. "Do you think she carries extra tickets in her bag?"

In involuntary reflex, Genevieve's hand went to the bag in question, clutching it close to her side, excruciatingly aware of what was tucked inside the beaded satin pouch that hung from her shoulder by a delicate silver chain.

Realizing the telltale nature of what she had done, she smiled, sipped from her glass to combat the sudden dryness of her mouth, and dropped her hand. After a few more words exchanged, she walked away, only to be intercepted by two other people.

"My dear, your dress is simply exquisite!"

"You must tell us — is it a Lanvin?"

Her long gown of slinky, clinging silver lamé was indeed by Jeanne Lanvin, who was one of the few couturiers still working in

Paris. It was cleverly slit up the front to reveal one leg, but only when she moved. Dangling diamond earrings sparkled against the loose, cascading black waves that tumbled around her shoulders. Her lipstick was crimson, her high heels silver. In the process of becoming Genevieve Dumont, *the star,* she had become adept at transforming her rather ordinary prettiness into a dazzling facade as required. Tonight she looked, as her dresser Berthe, who had helped her change from her stage costume into this evening ensemble, had told her, "like a million Reichsmarks. I would have said francs, but we all know those aren't worth anything anymore."

Although no lights were visible from the outside due to the tightly drawn blackout curtains, inside the mansion the party was shifting into high gear. Music, laughter and much animated conversation filled the air as the Spaniards played hosts to more than a hundred favored Parisians along with a smattering of guests of other nationalities and a full complement of high-ranking Germans, all of whom seemed anxious to meet her.

Beautiful furnishings, rich carpets and valuable paintings formed a lavish backdrop for bejeweled ladies in evening gowns and gentlemen in tuxedos or military uniforms. But the real luxuries were the heated rooms and the abundance of food and drink, all of which were in desperately short supply in Paris, and indeed throughout France and the rest of Occupied Europe. Spain was officially neutral but had demonstrated a marked partiality for the Axis powers. Its calculated flirtation with the Nazis had not only kept it from being invaded but had resulted in its being able to obtain items completely unavailable to anyone except the Germans themselves.

Such as, for example, the ingredients used to create the small but succulent curl of meat-stuffed pastry on the tray of canapés currently being offered to her by a bowing waiter. Paris seemed to be one of the few places on earth that still had plenty of food — and such food! — although only for the Germans and their hangers-on. Which now, to all outward appearances at least, included her. The canapé was mouthwateringly alluring, and if she didn't eat it, someone else at the party would. Genevieve popped it into her mouth, guilt pangs about the deprivations being suffered by her less fortunate fellow citizens notwithstanding. She needed to eat if she was going to drink, and for the next hour or so she was definitely going to drink.

"Mademoiselle, would you care for more champagne?"

"Thank you, yes." Genevieve accepted another waiter's offer with a wag of her empty glass and replaced it with one that was not.

Laughing gaily at some witticism uttered by a prosperous-looking Belgian that she didn't even entirely hear, she moved on only to be pulled into conversation with a knot of admirers that included several more Wehrmacht officers. She nodded and smiled, replied as necessary, and sipped her champagne, enjoying the smooth, cool slide of it over her tongue and the way the tiny bubbles in the golden liquid glistened as the light passed through it. Her talent as an actress was not even in the same galaxy as her talent as a singer, but now she was operating mostly on autopilot, which made things easier. The party, the other guests, the soldiers were starting to go a little fuzzy around the edges. The feeling of disassociation from her surroundings she was experiencing was actually good. It was easing the worst of her nerves. Her heart rate was almost normal now, and the knot in her stomach had loosened. The party, which she had dreaded as she did all such fraught-with-peril events, was starting to seem not so terrible after all.

"Mademoiselle Dumont." Someone touched her elbow. "If I may be so bold — I was told that you would be willing to honor our small gathering with a song? I would not presume to bother you, but as you know, it is the anniversary of the marriage of our consul general and his wife."

Genevieve knew who he was: the Spanish press attaché, Bernardo Santaella, a small, dapper man with brilliantined black hair and a swooping mustache. She suspected that he was Max's contact in the embassy, but not only did she not know for certain, she didn't *want* to know for certain. In ignorance lay some small measure of safety. Or at least so she told herself.

"Yes, of course. The honor is mine. I've even brought a song with me especially for the occasion." Responding as instructed by Max, Genevieve drank rather than sipped at her champagne as she followed Santaella through two arched doorways and across meters of polished marble toward the grand piano. Gleaming black, with a closed lid, the magnificent Steinway was situated sideways before a large, heavily curtained bow window at the far end of the most imposing of the crowded reception rooms. Above it a chandelier glittered and gleamed.

Smiling in response to the stream of compliments and comments directed her way by those she passed, she did her best to focus on the performance and nothing more. Before Max — where *was* he? — she had never considered herself to be of a particularly fearful disposition, but despite the deadening effects of the champagne, knowing the true purpose of what she was about to do made her hands sweat.

Which was not so good for someone who was getting ready to accompany herself on the piano as she sang.

"Can I get you anything, Mademoiselle Dumont?" Santaella pulled out the piano bench for her and bowed. A detachable microphone was affixed to the fallboard, and a selection of bound sheet music waited on the music desk. It was clear that the piano was regularly used to entertain the embassy's guests. He nodded at her nearly empty glass. "More champagne?"

"Yes." Smoothing her skirt beneath her as she sat down, she sipped at the fresh champagne that a waiter brought at Santaella's gesture, then placed the tulip-shaped glass on the piano's satin-smooth lid. "Thanks."

As Santaella bowed and moved away, she pulled her bag into her lap. Snapping open the clasp, she fumbled to extract the folded booklet of sheet music she'd brought with her. It held, among others, the song she'd been asked to perform. Since her arrival at the party, she'd been on tenterhooks waiting for this moment. Now that it was here, she tried without success to ignore the butterflies taking flight in her stomach.

Folded, the booklet of perhaps a dozen songs was several centimeters thick. She managed to get it out, unfolded it so that the title — *Enter Springtime* — was uppermost and propped it on the music desk. A prolonged, exuberant finish from the roving accordion players who'd beguiled partygoers for the past quarter hour crescendoed to a triumphant flourish as she flexed her fingers, stretched them silently over the keys, made herself ready. A semicircular arrangement of chairs was being placed for special guests around the side of the piano that faced the room.

Santaella was over near the chairs now, conferring with another member of the embassy's staff. He would be announcing her at any minute, she knew.

You have only to sing and play, and it's over. You can go back to the hotel and go to bed.

Conscious of how tense she was, she relaxed her shoulders, her arms, her wrists, her fingers.

"Mademoiselle Dumont, well met!" The male voice with its guttural German accent was accompanied by a heavy hand dropping onto her shoulder. She barely managed not to jump, glanced around to see who would approach her at such a moment and found herself looking up into a clean-shaven face with squinty blue eyes, a fleshy nose and a thin-lipped mouth above a jutting chin. The gray-green SS officer's uniform he wore had gorget patches of pips and oak leaves and glittering hardware that indicated his high rank. The swastika pinned to his tie glittered in the light. Fortyish; short fair hair shiny with hair tonic, worn in a slicked-back, middle-parted style; stocky build. Not unhandsome but — chilling. It was, she thought, something to do with his eyes.

Her heart lurched: they hadn't met, but she knew who he was.

A smile cracked his face, stretched his mouth until she saw that he had twin dimples in his cheeks.

He beamed down at her. "I was hoping to encounter you here! If you will permit me to introduce myself, I am Obergruppenführer Claus von Wagner. I have greatly enjoyed your performances, as I hope you have enjoyed my small tributes to them?"

He meant the huge bunches of flowers he'd had carried up to her during every one of the last week's curtain calls. Genevieve did her best to arrange her face into an expression as close to delight as she could contrive.

"Herr Obergruppenführer of the beautiful flowers." She shifted on the bench so that she could more easily look up at him. "I have so enjoyed them. Their perfume has filled my dressing room for days. Thank you for your kindness in sending them."

"Not at all. It has been my pleasure. I understand that you will be honoring us with a private performance tonight. What song have you chosen? I hope I may have the privilege of turning the pages for you as you play?" He reached past her to pick up the booklet of songs she'd just placed on the music desk. His expression indicated that he had no doubt about her agreement.

Genevieve's smile froze in place as he began to casually flip through the pages. Her heart thumped. Her stomach turned inside out.

Besides the usual musical notations, each page of the booklet he was thumbing through was scribbled over with information on German troop, ship and munition movements, ship and rail cargoes and their routes, and other material intended to aid the Allied forces in targeting their attacks. She was to leave it behind when she finished; it would be picked up and passed on. The fact that the information was written in invisible ink and could not be seen until exposed to direct heat or some other reconstituting agent did nothing to ease her burgeoning panic.

Especially as he trailed his fingers — his *warm* fingers — down the page he was looking at. Even beyond the degree of heat given off by his hands, was it possible that he might be able to feel the hidden writing? Could a telltale roughness be there on the paper?

Anxiety squeezed her chest.

Her gaze was riveted on the booklet in his hand, she realized, and she jerked it up to his face just as he glanced at her questioningly.

He was waiting for her to reply.

What could she do? What could she say? To deny him might raise suspicion. Alternatively, if he discovered the secret writing . . .

Cold sweat broke out across the back of her neck.

There was no help for it. She was going to have to say that she preferred to turn the pages herself and get it away from him.

Around the sudden tightness in her throat — not good for a singer — she began, "Herr Obergruppenführer . . ."

Chapter Six

"I'm afraid if you want to turn the pages, you'll have to settle for doing it for me." Max's voice was the most welcome sound Genevieve had ever heard. It was all she could do not to melt from gratitude as he walked past her. Pulling the Gauloise he was smoking from his mouth, he strolled up to Wagner with outward ease and added, "I'm the piano player tonight. The sheet music is for me. Genevieve doesn't need it. She knows every song in the world by heart."

"Oh, but I thought — Mademoiselle Dumont is known to accompany herself on the piano. I have heard she plays beautifully."

"Not tonight."

Max was smiling. Wagner wasn't.

"I'm very tired." Smiling apologetically up at Wagner even as her heart raced, Genevieve threw herself into the breach. "From my show, you understand. I have only enough energy left to sing."

As Wagner looked from one to the other of

them, Max shrugged, an excellent rendition of the ubiquitous Gallic gesture: *Women, what can you do?*

Genevieve forgot to breathe as Max returned the cigarette to his mouth and held out his hand, oh so casually, for the booklet. Rangy and handsome in his white dinner jacket, looking every bit the typical Frenchman with his dark hair and eyes and perpetual tan, Max would have been the taller of the two if it hadn't been for the slight twist to his body from leaning on his stick.

It was clear Wagner didn't like being thwarted. His eyes narrowed. His lips pursed.

"Ladies and gentlemen, if you will gather around, we have a wonderful treat in store for us!" Santaella's voice boomed, startling Genevieve into glancing in his direction. The room was crowded now, with more people pouring in through the arched doorway. The consul general, his wife and special guests were being escorted to the chairs that had been set out for them. "As you know, we are here tonight to celebrate the wedding anniversary of our esteemed consul general and his lovely wife. In honor of this most festive occasion, Mademoiselle Genevieve Dumont, the incomparable Black Swan, has consented to sing a very special song for us!"

All eyes were suddenly on her. Genevieve could only pray that the tension stretching her nerves to near breaking point didn't show on her face. Lifting a hand, she smiled and waved from her spot on the piano bench. People began to applaud. The consul general, his wife and guests settled into their designated chairs. Out of the corner of her eye, she saw Wagner grudgingly hand the booklet to Max and felt the smallest soupçon of relief: at least the incriminating thing was out of his hands.

As the applause swelled, Max stubbed out his cigarette in a nearby ashtray and slid onto the bench. He was on the side nearer the rich blue of the curtains, his damaged leg stretched out stiffly, while she was on the side nearer the audience. They were so close their bodies brushed.

Returning the booklet to the music desk, he flipped it open and settled down to play. Without so much as a word to her, he began to pick out the intro, taking it slow, drawing it out, infusing the notes with plenty of bluesy heat. His fingers, long and tan against the ivory keys, moved with practiced grace.

Watching his hands, Genevieve experienced a moment of déjà vu: this was how she had first seen him, as an itinerant pianist in a smoke-filled bar.

Max flicked a look at her.

"Distract him." He spoke under the cover of the music. He was referring to Wagner, she knew: she could feel the other man's gaze boring into her. Max's lips barely moved as he said, "You know how. Vamp it up, angel."

Her heart thundered. Her chest felt tight. Max hadn't called her angel since that never-to-be-forgotten night when she'd found out who and what he really was — and for him to give her an instruction like that, the danger must be more acute even than she feared.

The lights went out, except for the chandelier over the piano. She, Max and the piano were effectively spotlighted.

It took every bit of self-control she possessed to ignore the tremor that slid down her spine and simply concentrate on the music.

Max continued to play. The seductive notes of the intro swirled around her, around the now raptly waiting audience, drawing them in, catching her up. With her innate performer's sensibility, she knew what they saw: the golden circle of light spilling down over the polished ebony of the grand piano; her, slender and elegant in her gleaming silver gown, her head tilted so that the black silk of her hair hid part of her face as she watched Max's hands on the keys. Him in his dinner jacket, unsmiling and intensely masculine, his head bent so that a lock of his hair fell over his forehead. The two of them, seated close together on the bench.

He hit the segue into the vocal.

Supremely conscious of everyone's eyes on her — of Wagner's eyes on her — Genevieve detached the microphone with a smoothly practiced movement and kicked up her legs as she turned sideways on the bench so that she was facing the audience. Her skirt fell away, baring slim legs in their sheer nylon stockings to midthigh. She crossed them, arched her back and let her head fall back so that it rested on Max's shoulder. She could feel the solid strength of it supporting her.

"Bésame . . . bésame mucho . . ."

The love song poured out in a silky purr that entwined with Max's bluesy playing so that the two seemed like parts of the same whole. In honor of the consul general and his wife, the lyrics were in Spanish.

Straightening away from Max, she came to her feet and moved behind the bench to trail her fingers across the width of his shoulders as she sang. The smooth wool of his dinner jacket was stretched taut over heavy muscle as he bent over the keys.

She then began a slow slink toward the audience. Her voice slid from a purr into a growl as she begged her lover to kiss her like it was the last time they would ever meet. She put every ounce of provocation she could summon into her movements and let the song do the rest.

She could feel the electricity in the room, feel the heat her performance was generating, feel the eyes of the audience fastened on her every move. Wagner stood just outside the circle of light, in the shadows at the front of the gathering near the semicircle of chairs. He watched her with frowning concentration, his arms crossed over his chest, his booted feet planted apart.

Her skin prickled a warning under the weight of his gaze. There was something in his expression that was not quite right, that made her feel cold all over — what was it? Could he suspect? Was he perhaps thinking about the songbook, realizing that she had carried it into the embassy with her, and considering the possibilities inherent in that? Or could there have been a telltale look or feel to the paper that was even now working its way to the surface of his consciousness?

Her heart galloped. Her pulse kept pace.

Distract him.

Back at the piano, Max steamed up the bridge.

Stopping in front of Wagner, Genevieve swayed in time to the music, looked into his eyes, summoned a come-hither smile and sang directly to him.

"Bésame mucho . . ."

As her voice and body language lent the words a languorous heat, the taut muscles of his face relaxed. His lips stretched into a slow grin as he watched her. Gliding away at last, she felt reassured. He was still watching her, but in a way that she no longer had any trouble interpreting.

She finished the song as she had begun it, slinking back to the piano, sinking onto the bench, letting her head drop back onto Max's broad shoulder as he blazed through the closing notes.

When it was done, she came to her feet, as energized as she was frightened now. Moving out in front of the audience, bowing and blowing kisses, she accepted their enthusiastic applause, gesturing at Max to include him in the acclaim.

Max looked at her, said something she couldn't quite hear. She cupped a hand around her ear and leaned toward him in an exaggerated way as he raised his voice to be heard over the clapping that was growing louder rather than dying away.

Across the top of the piano he called to her, "One more?"

"What do you think? One more?" She repeated his question to the room, tilting the microphone toward them to amplify their reply.

The roar she received in response had her laughing and retreating to confer with Max, who was, she saw with a stomach-clutch of understanding, rearranging the songbooks on the desk as he sought a new song.

Their eyes met in a quick but speaking glance.

" 'Lili Marlene'?" He tapped the open page in front of him, which was in a different booklet from "Bésame mucho." Sleight of hand with the sheet music — it wasn't much protection from the murderous arm of the SS, but she was willing to embrace anything that might work.

She nodded and turned back to the audience as Max began to pick out the plaintive notes of the intro. Enormously popular after having once been banned from the airwaves by Joseph Goebbels himself for not being militaristic enough, the song was in German. Max's choice was designed to signal unity with the occupiers and was another way of throwing Wagner off the scent, she knew, but a patriotic kernel lodged deep within her soul swelled in objection. Still, she knew the lyrics, it was a beautiful song and she didn't want to end up dead or in a concentration camp, so she sang the tale of the woman left behind when her man went off to war in a way that, when she finished, had everyone in the room on their feet clapping wildly.

After that it was over. The lights came on. With a flick of her eyes at Max, she picked up her champagne and walked away from the piano to join the group around the consul general and his wife.

"You speak German. I am most impressed." Stopping beside her as she graciously accepted compliments on her performance, Wagner spoke in a voice pitched for her ears alone.

"I speak lyrics." She looked up at him with a smile that belied her fraying nerves. His expression was admiring. She had expected him to follow her, hoped he would follow her: anything to get him away from that songbook. Which didn't mean she felt comfortable in his presence. The look in his eyes was now all too easy to read: it was carnal, almost predatory, in nature. That kind of sexual aggression made her skin crawl, but she kept her smile in place and did her best to appear warmly interested in what he had to say. Her hand tightened on her flute, but she didn't follow through on her urge to drink from it. With danger so close at hand, she needed to keep her wits about her, and damn the date.

Immediate risk trumped past sorrow.

He said, "Spanish ones, as well. But I understand you are French."

"I am." Shooting a quick glance past him, she saw that Max had left the piano. Was the songbook still there? She couldn't see the music desk. There was no way to tell. "If we are to speak of languages, your French is very good. I compliment you."

"I've made something of a study of languages. I find it — occasionally — very useful."

In his line of work. Genevieve experienced an inner shiver as she made the connection but managed to keep her smile undimmed.

"It is good to have you with us again, Herr

Obergruppenführer! How long do you stay in Paris this time?" The consul general's genial entry into the conversation saved her from having to answer.

"My stay is open-ended."

"Until you find who sent the villains who scuttled the barges in the Seine, eh? Don't worry so much, my friend. The French character is very adaptable. In the end, these small pockets of resistance will amount to nothing."

"That is only one of my reasons for being in Paris." The sudden glint in Wagner's eyes warned of his dislike of that line of conversation. Sophie Castellano cast a quick look of reproach at her husband, who hastily changed the subject.

"Well, well, you no doubt have much to occupy you. Have you had the pleasure of attending one of Mademoiselle Dumont's shows? I assure you, they are not to be missed."

"I have had that pleasure. And you are right. They are not to be missed."

Genevieve smiled her thanks.

"Paris has much to offer in the way of amusements," senora Castellano said, clearly bent on steering the conversation away from controversial subjects. "We feel very fortunate to have been sent here. Tell me, what sights have most impressed you?"

"I've seen very few."

"What of our restaurants? I hope you've had a chance to sample the best of those."

"I have, but, alas, I find I don't enjoy dining alone." He looked at Genevieve. "Indeed, if you could spare the time, Mademoiselle Dumont, I would count myself most honored if you would accompany me to one of my favorite dining establishments some evening soon."

Genevieve continued to smile while her mind worked feverishly. Encouraging Wagner was the last thing she wanted to do, for a host of excellent reasons. But offending him would be a mistake, and under the circumstances embarrassing him in front of their hosts might well prove catastrophic. In five days, she and the troupe would be leaving Paris. Whatever she promised now, she could surely keep him at bay for five days.

"It would be my pleasure," she said.

He beamed. The dimples she'd found so incongruous appeared, lending a sudden flash of boyish charm to a face that was neither boyish nor charming.

"Excellent." He started to say something else, to set a date for their outing, she guessed, but was interrupted by the arrival of a junior officer at his elbow. The young man had his hat tucked under his arm, smelled of the outdoors and wore boots wet with the rain that poured outside, which told Genevieve he had just arrived. His body language made it clear that he had something of importance to impart: he was big with news.

"With your permission, Herr Obergruppenführer —" The officer's voice was low with deference but urgent nonetheless.

Wagner looked at her and said "If you will excuse me" with punctilious courtesy, and stepped aside to listen to what seemed from his darkening expression to be unpleasant tidings.

Genevieve's pulse started to race anew as she watched the exchange. No doubt her guilty knowledge about what was concealed within the songbook was affecting her reactions, but she couldn't help but worry that whatever the young man was saying had something to do with her and Max.

A moment later Wagner returned to her side.

"Nothing too terrible, I hope?" The consul general asked before Genevieve could say anything. He cast a concerned glance at the young officer, who stood waiting at attention a few feet away.

"An administrative matter merely." Wagner's tone was dismissive, but his eyes were bright with what looked like anger, and a small muscle jumped in his jaw. The dimples that had been on display earlier were nowhere in evidence now. He looked at Genevieve. "Forgive me, but I must go. If I may, I will do myself the pleasure of calling on you very soon."

"I look forward to it."

He bowed with a click of his heels and strode away with the younger officer trotting behind him.

"Trouble," the consul general said with a knowing look at his wife.

"Nothing to talk about while we are having a party," she scolded, and turned her attention to Genevieve, who found herself torn between relief and trepidation. She was beyond glad Wagner had gone, but fear that the reason might have something to do with the song booklet made her cold with dread. She cast a slightly desperate glance around for Max: nowhere in sight.

"Mademoiselle Dumont, I understand that you are staying at the Hotel Ritz? How are you liking your accommodations there?"

"It's a very beautiful hotel." She'd stayed there before, in the summer of 1931 when her parents brought their daughters to Paris to celebrate her sister's fifteenth birthday. The highlight of that trip had been seeing Josephine Baker, but in retrospect the entire five days had been magical. Her mother had taken the girls shopping along the rue de la Paix, the entire family had climbed the Eiffel Tower to marvel at the view and they'd gone rowing on the Seine. She and her mother had been in one small boat, her sister and father in the other, and the excursion had devolved into a race with her and her sister at the oars. Her sister, older and stronger, had won, which had only slightly marred her enjoyment. Later, looking back, she'd thought of that as the last of the good times, coming as it had just before the terrible economy had overtaken her family along with everyone else and such treats had become a thing of the past. She had found the hotel infinitely more beautiful then than now, and not only because it had not been, as it was currently, packed with Germans. "I am embarrassed to tell you that within its walls I am spoiled with every luxury."

"And so you should be spoiled," senora Castellano replied, patting Genevieve's arm in a motherly way. "Your voice brings light to our lives in these dark times. Come, let me introduce you to more of my friends."

Chapter Seven

"Ready to go?" Max asked when he caught up with her some time later, as she emerged from the powder room. How much time later Genevieve couldn't really say. Call it two glasses of champagne later. She was feeling much better, more relaxed, almost calm. She credited that to the fact that Wagner was still gone and she hadn't been arrested. Oh, and the champagne.

She smiled at Max, strictly for the sake of anyone watching.

His eyes narrowed at her. They were, she noted with a critical look at them, actually more hazel than brown, with a hint of green in their depths.

He looked more closely at her. "Is something wrong?"

Realizing that she'd been staring, her brows snapped together. "Where have you been?"

"Around. Come on, let's get our coats."

"I have to say goodbye to our hosts first." She started walking toward the closest of the crowded reception rooms, where she had last seen the consul general and his wife. Max caught her elbow.

"Probably better not."

They reached the foyer, and Max asked the servant on duty for their coats.

"Mademoiselle Dumont and Monsieur — Bonet?" the man asked, and when Max replied in the affirmative, he went away.

"But I haven't said goodbye to anyone," Genevieve protested. She made an effort to head for the reception rooms but Max retained his hold on her arm, preventing her.

"I said goodbye for both of us. Anyway, you don't want to be here when our good friend gets back, do you?"

Genevieve stopped trying to pull away and stood still, frowning. She knew who he was talking about: Wagner. "*Is* he coming back?"

"I don't know. He could."

"You're just trying to scare me."

"I wouldn't do that."

The look she gave him said it all.

He smiled. Annoyingly.

She scowled at him. "I never want to be put in a position like that again. He was watching us like a fox would a pair of chickens the whole time."

"He was watching you."

"He asked me out."

"*Did* he?" From Max's expression, Genevieve saw that the revelation interested him.

He was, she realized, turning it over in his mind, working out ways in which he could use it — use *her* — to his advantage. As always.

"You know what — sometimes you can be a real shit."

"Only sometimes?" His tone mocked her. "We're making progress."

Before she could do more than blister him with a glance, the servant returned with their coats. The man helped Genevieve into hers, custom made to go with her dress in a gorgeous silver brocade shot through with gold threads, while Max, juggling his stick, shrugged into his plain black overcoat all by himself. The servant then opened the door and bowed them out. They found themselves on an imposing covered portico with a soldier stationed on either side.

As the door closed behind them, the resultant darkness made it impossible to see very much at all. A strong gust of wind blew in from the river, catching Genevieve unaware and making her stagger sideways.

"Careful." Max caught her with an arm around her waist. She leaned against him gratefully for a moment, regaining her balance while letting him shelter her from the wind, afraid that the shock of the cold, damp air after the warmth of the rooms inside might blow away some of the pleasant wooziness she was feeling.

It was past midnight now, and the date she'd been dreading for weeks was safely behind her. All she had to do was get to the hotel, go to bed and fall asleep, and when she woke up, it would be a new day, a new year, and she could look forward instead of back.

The Citroën waited at the foot of the steps, its motor running. The pass permitting it to be on the streets after curfew was displayed prominently on the dashboard.

"Ready?" Max asked as one of the soldiers reached them, and Genevieve nodded.

They started down the short flight of steps. The soldier escorted them, holding an umbrella over their heads, lighting their way with a covered torch.

Rain spattered on the umbrella and the pavement and fell all around with a soft rushing sound. The smell of it was fishy, like the scent of the nearby river. A sliver of moon peeped out from behind the clouds, providing barely enough light to enable her to see the car and the steps. Even with her coat, she found herself shivering. Max held tightly to her arm, and for once she was glad. The steps felt slick, and that would be because they were wet with rain and her soles were leather. Leather was a valuable resource and reserved almost exclusively for the war effort, but she was allowed to have leather shoes instead of the wooden or cork soles with cloth uppers most people had to make do with.

Just as she had access to real rather than ersatz coffee, special meals in special restaurants when all around her people were starving on a diet of little more than potatoes and leeks, and all kinds of freedoms unavailable to ordinary French citizens, which with more and more frequency lately she fiercely wished she was.

Resplendent tonight in a chauffeur's uniform, Otto was once again behind the wheel. An Austrian whose real name she had never discovered, he'd been with Max since long before that first night in Morocco, when she'd made one of the many life-altering mistakes that pockmarked her existence and walked right up to that piano in that bar and started singing along to Max's playing.

"Below-stairs gossip had it that Wagner was here tonight," Otto said as the car pulled away from the steps. He cast a glance in the rearview mirror at Max, who had climbed into the back seat beside her. "Did you see him?"

"We did," Max said. "Genevieve sang to him."

"Did she?" Otto's next glance was aimed at Genevieve, who shot Max a sideways look but didn't otherwise bother to respond. She was feeling rather pleasantly floaty now, and the last thing she wanted to do was engage in a verbal sparring match. "He must have enjoyed that."

"He certainly seemed to," Max said.

"Castellano satisfied with his present?" Otto asked.

"He was."

Genevieve frowned. "What present?"

Max said, "A quarter million pounds deposited in a Swiss bank. Keeping Spain open for business is expensive."

"Oh." That the British government paid millions of pounds to Spain and various Spanish officials to sweeten the pot of continued neutrality was an open secret, and she promptly lost interest. The worry that had been niggling at her for the last twenty-four hours niggled again. She didn't want to — she wanted to forget the whole experience because of the associations it dredged up — but she had to ask. "Did you find out anything about what happened to Anna's mother?"

"Anna?"

"The baby. From last night."

"Oh. The woman's alive," Max said. "Wounded, but alive. Her name is Rachel. Rachel Katz. She was taken to Drancy."

Genevieve sucked in air. Located in a suburb of Paris, Drancy was an internment camp for Jews slated to be deported to Germany. Everyone knew about the abysmal conditions prevalent there. For someone who was wounded, being taken to Drancy was the next thing to a death sentence.

There's nothing to be done. She did her best to force the memory of big, dark eyes, of terrible desperation and fear out of her head. The baby — was she being looked after properly? Little ones were so helpless, so utterly dependent on the adults in their lives . . .

She had to clear her throat before she could speak again. "What of Anna?"

"You don't have to worry. She's being cared for."

"Did you leave word —"

Max shook his head before she could finish. He knew what she was asking: Did he leave word in the fountainhead about where Anna had been taken?

"The building is being watched. To try something like that now would be too great a risk. The best thing we can do for Anna and her mother is keep our heads down and do our jobs," Max said.

Difficult as it was to accept, it was the truth, she knew. She closed her eyes, opened them again.

The interior of the car was dark and warm. It smelled of fine leather, cigarette smoke and rain. Fat droplets spattered the hood and slid down the windows. The motor purred, the heater hummed, the wipers swished, and the effect was surprisingly cozy.

"Looks like they're being extra thorough."

The tension in Max's voice as the Citroën

pulled in line behind another car waiting to be allowed out through the big iron gates instantly brought her back to full alertness. She peered anxiously ahead through the windshield to see what was happening. Soldiers who'd spent the evening in a truck parked alongside the entrance as backup for the pair of guards in the small gatehouse were out in the rain in force with their shielded torches, courteously holding umbrellas over the heads of the resplendent guests as they stepped out of their cars for inspections of their papers and persons. More soldiers examined the car, looking inside it, opening the trunk, running a mirror beneath the chassis. Citizens were subject to search at any time, and those entering or exiting areas like the Spanish embassy, which was considered the sovereign territory of another nation, were heavily scrutinized, but this seemed more extreme than usual.

"They've got invasion fever," Otto said. "It's almost as if they're afraid enemies might be hiding in their midst."

"God forbid," Max said.

Knowing what was in her evening bag as they'd arrived, Genevieve had been nervous even though her pass allowed her to escape inspection. Still, as she frequently pointed out to Max, it took only one soldier to disregard the pass or not understand the scope of it and she was done for. Minus the incriminating songbook now, she watched with more interest than concern as the people in front of them were frisked, had their papers checked and their cars examined before they were allowed to leave.

"We're up." Otto pulled forward, rolled down his window and raised his voice to be heard above the rain as he spoke to the guard. "We are not subject to search. We have a pass. I am driving Mademoiselle Genevieve Dumont."

"The Black Swan?" The soldier pushed his head almost all the way through the open window and shone his torch into the back. The light danced over Max and then hit Genevieve. She blinked once at its brightness, then smiled and waggled her fingers at the guard. He goggled.

"Mademoiselle Dumont," he gasped, straightening away from the window so fast he knocked his hat askew. Righting it, he waved them on. "Proceed!"

"Of all the possessions of this life, fame is the most useful," Max murmured once they were moving and Otto had the window rolled up again. Genevieve knew a misquote when she heard one, although she couldn't quite place it.

"Don't you mean *noblest*?" Otto asked.

Ah, there it was: *Of all the possessions of this life, fame is the noblest.* It was a quote by — she couldn't remember who, but Max had said it to her before. Actually, he'd needled her with it before. More than once.

"That, too," Max replied.

Pulling slowly through the gates as they opened, Otto turned onto the street, heading for the first arrondissement and the Ritz. Because of the blackout, the Citroën's headlights were fitted with slotted covers that directed their beams downward to the ground. Wet, the pavement gleamed as shiny black as the nearby Seine.

"There's another reason they're being so careful," Otto said as the Citroën sped up. "Word is, a few hours ago someone tossed a grenade into a truck full of German soldiers on the quai des Grands-Augustins. Six died. Just about everybody in the vicinity got rounded up and hauled off to Fort Mont-Valérien."

"Oh, no," Genevieve said. Fort Mont-Valérien was a notoriously brutal prison the Nazis had established in the western suburbs of Paris.

"There's been some rioting in retaliation." Otto sounded grim. "You can be sure there'll be more. And it won't end well."

Max said, "At least now we can make an educated guess about why Wagner left the party the way he did." He looked at Genevieve. "When he was talking to you, did he say anything about trouble in the city?"

Genevieve shook her head. That made her

vision go fuzzy, so she rested her head back against the smooth leather seat behind her and blinked in an effort to clear it. "He wouldn't tell me something like that."

"I bet you'd be surprised by what you could get him to tell you."

Fuzzy vision or no, her head came up. "No," she said.

"I didn't ask you anything."

"I know what you're thinking. I won't do it."

"Won't do what?"

"Date him so I can milk him for information for you."

"Such a thought never crossed my mind."

"Just like such a thought never crossed your mind about Ernst Goth, or Ryszard Zelewski, or Hans Conti, or —" She wasn't even halfway through the list of Nazis in various occupied territories whom Max had strong-armed her into meeting for coffee, or dinner, or dancing, or a drive, or anyplace, really, where she might be expected to be able to get them to talk.

"Not the same thing at all." Max remained imperturbable. "They had information I needed. As far as I know at this point, Wagner doesn't."

"Whether he does or not, you can forget it. He scares me. It's something in his eyes."

"So what did you tell him when he asked you out?" Max said.

Her answer was reluctant. "I said it would be my pleasure."

Max didn't say anything. He didn't even change expression. He didn't have to. She *knew* him.

Her voice grew heated. "What was I supposed to—"

A loud boom rent the air.

The sound was muffled, distant, but unmistakably an explosion. Two more equally muffled detonations followed in rapid succession. Genevieve sat up in time to watch in shock as a pillar of flame shot skyward from the general direction of the Champs-Élysées. Blindingly bright in the darkness, high enough to be seen above the area's gabled roofs and church steeples and monuments, it threw off sparks like fireworks and bathed the interior of the Citroën in a seething orange glow.

Chapter Eight

"Hell," Max said. "That's too close for comfort."

"Not a grenade," Otto said. "Dynamite, probably. Wonder what they blew up."

Max shook his head. "Whatever it was, the Krauts will go nuts."

"Retaliation for the arrests, do you think?"

"Probably."

None of them had any doubt that the explosion was the work of the Resistance, whose members were growing increasingly bold as the rumors of an upcoming invasion multiplied.

Even as the blaze shrank out of sight, multiple police sirens went off almost as one. Their strident two-note wail filled the air.

"They'll be out in force now," Otto said. "Setting up roadblocks. Searching everything and everyone."

There was something in the way he said it — Genevieve frowned at the back of his head.

"Probably not a good time to be pulling up

to the Ritz," Max agreed.

The Luftwaffe had taken the hotel over, using it as their Paris headquarters. Genevieve thought of the guards stationed around the entrances, of the lobby and restaurant where the Germans ran tame, of the high-ranking officers lodged permanently on the Vendôme side of the property. It was, however, still being operated as a hotel, though it was accessible to only the most high-level guests, most of whom had rooms on the rue Cambon side. She, in fact, was staying in a VIP suite, one of the few that overlooked the square. As far as she knew, they'd gotten rid of any incriminating evidence when they'd left the songbook behind at the embassy. They had a pass permitting them to be out after curfew. So why would returning to the hotel, even under enhanced scrutiny, be a problem?

"Why is pulling up to the hotel a problem?" she asked.

"Lousy timing," Otto said. "They'll be arresting people left and right."

Max said, "One thing's for sure — we need to get off the street. Our best bet's to head for the rue de la Lune."

They'd rented a rehearsal studio in a building there, on the sixth floor. A studio was necessary because, to save costs, the Casino de Paris was stingy about making heat and electricity available during the day. Chorus run-throughs were routinely held in the studio in the mornings, and featured performers might be put through their paces as necessary afterward. The rest of the time, it was Max's lair.

"Tonight?" Otto flicked another look at Max. His tone was uneasy. "With her?"

"You have a better idea?" Max asked.

"I know it's a brothel, if that's what's worrying you," Genevieve said. Since the Wehrmacht had come to town, brothels were almost as common as cafés and nightclubs. Heavily promoted for the "comfort" of the German soldiers, they were even listed in a guide to the city's amusements issued to all newly arrived military. "I might have picked somewhere else to use as rehearsal space if it had been up to me, but then I wasn't consulted."

"It has dependable heat. Not many buildings do anymore. And a lot of people coming and going, especially at night. Nobody's going to notice a few extra." Max glanced out the window. A distant popping sound puzzled Genevieve for a moment until she realized: gunfire. Probably the Milice in pursuit of the bombers. The French police were arguably more vicious and more hated even than the Germans.

Otto had changed directions, and the Citroën glided smoothly through the rain toward the second arrondissement. Few cars were on the streets and speed limits had been drastically lowered in an effort to prevent accidents in the dark city, but a pair of big black sedans raced by. They were clearly official and headed toward the site of the disturbance at great speed. Running without sirens and with their slotted headlights making them difficult to see, they were upon them with no warning. The whoosh of their passing was unexpected enough to make Genevieve jump.

She stared after them uneasily. "Do you think they'll catch whoever did it?"

Max said, "I think they'll catch somebody."

None of them said anything more for a few minutes. The atmosphere in the car was somber.

"What do we do about the, um . . ." Otto broke off, but the significance with which he did so was not lost on Genevieve. His lack of specificity was for her benefit. It was clear he expected Max to know what he was referring to, just as he expected her not to.

"Nothing we can do except sit tight," Max said. "Anything else is too risky right now."

"Should we try to get word to them?"

"They'll know when no one shows up. And they'll know why."

"Best laid plans." Otto's shrug was philosophical.

Genevieve said, "Do either of you want to tell me what you're talking about?"

Otto grunted, a negative sound if she'd ever heard one.

Max looked at her. "Do you really want to know?"

"Yes."

"No, you don't. Trust me."

Her brows snapped together, which made her head hurt, which added an extra degree of sharpness to her voice. "Have you ever met a secret you didn't like?"

"Here we are," Otto interrupted as the Citroën turned a corner and slowed. The words La Fleur Rouge were scrawled in giant neon letters above a modest entrance. Because of the blackout, the sign was unlit. Their destination was at the end of a block, one of four buildings abutting one another and facing off with four more across a section of narrow, cobblestoned street. The lower levels were occupied by commercial establishments, including a restaurant, a cobbler, a patisserie — and the brothel. All were completely dark. Not so much as a sliver of light showed through the doors, or the windows behind the wrought iron balconies that marched up the smooth stone facades.

Inside was a different story. Thanks to the Germans, Paris's fabled nightlife was alive and well and more decadent than ever. The curfew had simply driven it behind heavy curtains and closed doors.

Max said, "You can let us out around the side."

Otto nodded. "Then I'll find a place to park."

The car stopped and Max got out. She sat blinking against her exhaustion in an effort to get her eyes focused properly as he came around to open her door for her, then slid out under the protection of the umbrella he held. Her head swam as she stood up. She had to grab hold of his arm to keep her balance.

"Steady," he said. "You all right?"

She nodded. Despite that initial wobble, she made it the short distance across the sidewalk to the door without mishap and under her own steam, and even managed to hold the umbrella over them both to shield against the rain as Max used his tenant's key. The cold, damp breath of the wind made her shiver, while the unrelenting wail of the sirens and the whiff she got of something burning made her stomach knot.

At least the gunfire had stopped.

A burst of music and light and warmth enveloped them as they stepped inside a long corridor. The gaiety in the air was palpable. It was such a stark contrast to what was going on outside that it was briefly disorienting.

She was often in the building during daylight hours, so she knew what to expect even if she hadn't actually experienced *la maison close* in full nighttime swing. Lush tapestries and enormous gilt-framed mirrors and chandeliers dripping jewel-colored crystals hung everywhere. To the right were the parlors, where scantily clad women waited on red velvet sofas for men to choose one to accompany them to the lavishly themed bedrooms upstairs. At first glance she could see only a sliver of one of the parlors through the beaded curtains that hung in the doorway, but as the beads swayed from the draft created by their entry, she got a better look. A knot of soldiers stood chatting with someone she couldn't see, and a buxom blonde wearing a filmy negligee over a white brassiere and drawers rose from the far end of one of the sofas where she'd been seated with two other similarly clad girls. She smiled coquettishly at an officer with his hat tucked under his arm, who put his hand on her waist and led her away.

Collaboration horizontale was what it was called, and it was engaged in not only by prostitutes but by many French women. Those women were scorned, but Genevieve could not find it in herself to blame a girl for using the only assets available to her to take care of herself and possibly her family. Often fraternizing with the enemy in such a way was the difference between food on the table and a roof over one's head, or not. Sometimes it was the difference between surviving or not. She was all for surviving.

Max's hand slid around her elbow.

"Come on," he said under his breath. Leaving the wet umbrella in the bin beside the door, she went with him toward the lift at the far end of the hall.

"Turn up the collar of your coat." He spoke in an undertone as he jabbed the button for the lift. "One thing we don't need right now is all the attention that goes along with somebody recognizing you."

Obediently flipping up the collar of her coat, she scrunched her shoulders to bring it up even higher for more protection. "Do you think anyone's going to come this way?"

"Probably not. The girls have their own lift."

He'd no sooner said that than a trio of negligee-clad girls, each with a soldier in tow, erupted through the beaded curtain. Giggling, admonishing the men to be quiet, they hurried along the hall toward the lift. The wooden soles of their high-heeled slippers clickety-clacked over the marble floor.

Taking one look at them, she turned rounding eyes on Max. There was nowhere to hide.

"Don't make a sound," he said, and without warning bent to scoop her up over his shoulder. She barely repressed a squeak at the unexpectedness of the move as he straightened, which left her hanging head down with her face against the damp wool of his coat. It was a movement of easy strength, accomplished without apparent effort on his part. Realizing the purpose behind it, she let her hands and arms dangle as the three couples arrived breathless and laughing beside them.

"— beat them upstairs," a soldier said, amid murmurs from all of them acknowledging Max's presence. "I've got a dinner riding on it."

"They were still in line for the other lift, weren't they? We'll beat them," a different soldier replied. "Because Mademoiselle Delphine here knew another way up."

A girl gave a coquettish giggle. Genevieve had her eyes squeezed shut, but a number of clicking sounds in quick succession made her think someone was repeatedly pressing the lift button.

"Don't worry, *Liebchen,* it will take us straight up to the party," one of the girls said. "Even if your friends get into the other lift, that one always stops on every floor."

"Madame said we were only to use the lift in the parlor." A different girl sounded worried.

"The line was too long. She also told us to be flexible," the first girl replied.

"I'm looking forward to seeing *you* be flexible." From the soldier's tone, Genevieve could almost see the leer on his face.

The lift dinged. A rattle announced the opening of its door. Holding her firmly in place, Max walked into the lift and turned to face the front while the others crowded in behind him.

The space was small, her position undignified. She hung over Max's shoulder like a couture-clad rag doll. His hand curled around her hip and his arm pressed into the backs of both thighs. He had a close-up view of her rear, and what made it worse was that she suspected he found the situation amusing. There was no help for it, though. She could do nothing but lay unmoving as the lift chugged upward. She had to admit that it was an effective way of hiding her identity, but some combination of the movement of the lift and the combined scents of Max's damp coat, the Göring-Schnapps from the open bottle that the nearest soldier intermittently guzzled from and the girls' cheap cologne was making her nauseated. It didn't help that the hard shelf of Max's shoulder pressed right into her stomach.

There was something else digging into her stomach, too — a flat, stiff, rectangular shape. Actually, more than one. Since her evening bag was a lump in the vicinity of her hip bone, and Max's shoulder was a smooth, muscular ledge running the width of her body, there was only one place they could be: inside her coat.

"She all right?" a girl asked. Genevieve realized the *she* in question was herself, got the impression that she was being peered at and did her best to project a drunken stupor.

"A little too much fun." Max's reply was

easy, convincing. For what must have been the millionth time since she'd met him, she marveled at how convincingly he lied.

The lift shuddered to a stop, the door opened and the girls with their soldiers spilled out, clattering away as the door closed.

"Put me down," Genevieve said with arctic dignity as the lift lurched into motion again.

"Certainly."

She'd been right about the amusement. It was there in his voice.

She found herself sliding down the front of his body until her feet were planted firmly on the floor. She pushed away from him.

"Oh."

To her surprise the walls of the lift swirled around her. She staggered and had to grab onto the front of his coat to steady herself.

"All right?"

"No."

"Next time you might want to think twice before you go getting drunk," he said.

"Next time you might want to give me some warning before you go flipping me upside down. And I'm not drunk." Her retort was completely overshadowed by the small but embarrassing burp that interrupted it.

"Precisely."

Still hanging on to his coat, she tried for a frown but had the feeling the look she gave him was more of an unfocused squint. The lift stopped and the door opened. Wrapping his arm around her waist, he swept her out with him into what, except for the light spilling from the lift, was pitch blackness.

In a testament to the building's thick walls and sturdy construction, a sibilant hiss from the radiators was the only sound. The lift door rattled shut at the same time as he flipped a wall switch. Two small ceiling fixtures came on, illuminating the space.

The studio took up the entire sixth floor. They stood in the large open area used for rehearsals. It had hardwood floors, heavy curtains over the windows, a ballet bar and mirrors across one wall, a Bösendorfer piano against another, and a sofa and small dining table against a third. Hanging racks overflowing with costumes were lined up near the piano. Several chairs were scattered around. A partitioned-off corner that wasn't quite a room because it lacked a fourth wall contained a bed, a chest and rudimentary cooking facilities. A bathroom opened off that.

"I feel sick," Genevieve announced. The floor seemed to be undulating beneath her feet. She tightened her grip on him.

"I'm not surprised. Do we need to head for the bathroom?"

"I need to sit down."

"Come on, then." He shepherded her over to the sofa, then undid the quartet of large silver buttons that fastened her coat with his usual annoying efficiency and started easing her out of it. "Here, let's get your coat off first."

That reminded her. She blinked up at him. "There's something inside it."

"What?"

His mild response didn't fool her. It was there in his face: he knew. She grabbed at her coat when he would have lifted it away from her and hugged it tight. She could feel the solid rectangular shapes. As she'd suspected, they were inside her coat, inserted between the brocade and the silk lining.

The look she gave him was accusing. "While I was in the embassy. That's why you were so keen to look after the coats. You had something put in there."

He tugged the coat out of her hands. "Sit down."

She wasn't usually that compliant, but her head was spinning. Or maybe the room was. She sat. "Tell me."

"Spanish citizenship documents." He laid the coat carefully over a chair and took off his own, throwing it down beside hers. "Twelve sets."

Her eyes widened. Such documents were more valuable than gold. Literal lifesavers, they were a shield that could protect vulnerable individuals from the Nazis while enabling them to travel openly throughout France and the occupied territories and cross the border into Spain and safety. On the other hand, being caught smuggling them out of the embassy was an almost guaranteed route to getting tortured and executed. And she'd been the one smuggling them.

Her voice was an indignant croak. "Who are they for?"

He shook his head. Of course he wasn't going to tell her. If she'd been slightly more clearheaded she wouldn't have asked. Max played things close to the vest, always.

"Why wasn't I told?"

"Because it's much easier to act innocent when you are innocent." He pulled one end of his tie to undo the neat bow, then undid the top button of his shirt.

"If I'd been searched . . ."

"You would have been astonished at the discovery, as any innocent person would be. And you would have said, 'I have no idea how they got in there.' And you most likely would have been believed, because you are who you are, and because your reaction would have been genuine, and because once you took it off, anyone could have had access to your coat." He moved away. "Anyway, you weren't searched. You have a pass, remember?"

She made a scoffing sound. "You keep saying that. One day some soldier is going to ignore it."

"I doubt that. The Black Swan is far too famous."

"I hate that stupid nickname. Swans don't

even sing."

"Some say they do. When they're dying."

"Wonderful."

"It's about crafting an image. Differentiating you from the other girl singers. Which you've got to admit we've done. Everybody from here to Zanzibar knows the Black Swan."

"Maybe that's because I have a three-octave vocal range." This time her hand made it over her mouth in time to stifle another embarrassing burp.

He threw her a glimmering half smile. "Could be."

"Where are you going?"

He was halfway across the room. He never stepped out of character enough to abandon the limp or the stick, but as she'd observed before when he was out of public view, his damaged leg didn't slow him down at all. The leg *was* badly scarred, which he claimed was from a motorbike accident. But she had her doubts about how debilitating the injury actually was.

"To make coffee. You need it."

"Real coffee?" There was longing in her voice.

"Close enough."

Close enough meant ersatz coffee, made from something like roasted chestnuts. Real coffee was almost impossible to get anymore, unless you were a high-ranking German or someone who hobnobbed with high-ranking Germans. She fared better in that and most other regards than the majority of Occupied Europe's increasingly desperate citizens. She felt guilty about it, even though staying at the Ritz and having access to things such as real coffee was part of her job and, as Max had told her countless times when her conscience assailed her, ultimately for the greater good. Her thoughts were so muddled and her feelings so conflicted on the subject that she gave up on both and merely watched while he busied himself with a kettle and cups. He made coffee as he did everything else, with no wasted movements.

The rain had picked up again, drumming against the windows, its steady rhythm soporific.

"It feels like it's been weeks since we've seen the sun," she said.

"I like the rain. Reminds me of home."

He played the louche Frenchman so well that sometimes it was hard to remember that he was actually a Brit.

"Do you miss it? England?" she asked. To her certain knowledge, he hadn't been back to his home country in at least three years, and as she had met him in Morocco, it had been longer than that, probably since the war began. Despite how well she knew him, she actually knew very little about him. Well, very little that was true. All the things he'd told her about his past during the first, blinders-on part of their association had turned out to be lies, and since she'd discovered who and what he actually was, their conversations about his background had been almost nonexistent. She'd been furiously angry at him for a long time, but gradually her anger had faded until it was now more in the nature of resentment that bubbled uneasily beneath the surface of their working relationship. Time had given her the perspective to acknowledge that all he had done had been in service of his country, and as for his lies to her — well, she'd told him lies, too.

"Sometimes." His back was turned as he filled the kettle with water and put it to heat on the single burner. "Usually when I feel like popping down to the pub for a pint." He shot her a quick smile over his shoulder. "Which is most days."

With a sniff of faux disdain she said, "We French, we prefer wine."

"You also prefer coffee to tea. And eat snails."

For a moment, one moment only, she succumbed to a reluctant smile.

A few raindrops still glistened in the black waves of his hair, she noticed, and noticed, too, how well evening clothes became the long, lean lines of his body. He looked handsome, and urbane, every inch the violence-eschewing musician turned businessman he pretended to be. Ordinarily the sheep's clothing that covered what she had learned the hard way was the wolf beneath was impenetrable, but there was something about him tonight, a kind of electric energy, a restlessness, that made her wonder if perhaps there was more going on than she knew. Probably. But she wasn't going to worry about it, or think about Max, or anything else, because worrying about something you could do nothing about was useless; in Max's case she'd already made that mistake once, and right now merely thinking at all made her head hurt. The sofa was comfortable, and she let her head drop onto its cushioned back just as she had in the car.

"Hungry?" he asked. He was opening cabinets in the kitchen area.

"No," she said to the ceiling, revolted by the thought of food.

He laughed.

She was smiling again, she discovered. The homely kitchen sounds as Max rattled around were comforting. Almost, *almost,* she could let go of the grief and regret and fear and all the other bad emotions that had been plaguing her so badly for the last twenty-four hours.

Her lids felt heavy. They kept wanting to close. If she could only rest them for a second . . .

On the thought, her eyes closed.

And, finally, Vivi caught up with her.

Chapter Nine

Somewhere a woman screamed, over and over, world without end. Shrill, heartbreaking screams full of terror and dread. They split the air, split her heart.

Her chest ached, her throat burned. She ran as fast as she could, heart jolting.

A flutter of white silk. A splash of crimson on gray stone ground.

Too late.

It was only as she acknowledged it, faced it, that she realized that the screams tearing apart the once bright afternoon were hers.

The pain woke Genevieve with a jolt, as it always did. Where it always did. Before she *knew,* before the horrible cold finality of it descended, before she was forced to confront the hideous truth that Vivi — that her child, her baby daughter — was dead.

Before what had to be the worst agony a human being could suffer slashed her heart to ribbons and forever scarred her soul.

She'd tried all day to outwit the dream,

tried to ward it off, tried to escape it.

She hadn't succeeded. It had her in its clutches now, inflicting its torture, flaying her with guilt, regret, grief. Impossible to believe that so much time had passed, that she'd existed in this world for *seven years* without Vivi in it. Her arms ached to hold her little girl just one more time; the glimpse she'd had of her in the dream had been so real that it seemed impossible that it was not. She'd seen her riot of black curls and chubby little body and wide smile; she'd felt her, in her heart and her soul, truer than a memory, more vivid than any dream.

Right now, in this foggy gray moment between sleep and wakefulness, the anguish felt new again. She had to remind herself that the past was the inalterable past, and she was Genevieve now. The eighteen-year-old she'd been on that day, her birthday, had nothing to do with the woman she was now.

If only she never had to go through another damned birthday again.

Genevieve lay perfectly still, struggling to breathe, while the weight of what felt like a thousand heavy stones crushed her chest.

She tried her best to thrust the dream away. A beloved phantom lingered.

Vivi, Vivi, Vivi.

I'm so sorry.

Hot tears leaked from the corners of her eyes. She did her best to escape the memories, the pain, by turning away from them and striking out into the clouds of groggy gray, fighting through the mist toward consciousness.

Nearby, voices. Men. She kept fighting, concentrated on them.

"— betrayed. Both cells are lost."

That voice belonged to a stranger. A native-born Frenchman, she thought: his accent was from Picardy. His voice was low and harsh with urgency. She stayed perfectly still — she wasn't sure she could have moved if she tried — as it penetrated the lingering miasma of the dream.

More details registered: she lay on her side, her head on a pillow, her knees bent. The surface beneath her was soft, and the softness curved up behind her. Her back pressed against it. Except for a slight headache, she was physically comfortable, warm. Safe.

"When?" The reply was a single terse word, but it was all she needed. That voice belonged to Max. She grabbed onto it like a lifeline, let it pull her the rest of the way toward the surface, away from the past, from the pain.

"Two nights ago."

Max swore. "What happened?"

"They were trying to get an injured British pilot out. There was an informer."

"Arrested? Dead?"

"Five arrested. One dead. The Crimson Cell leader. Killed in the ambush, before they could arrest him."

"Name?" Max asked.

"De Rocheford. Baron Paul de Rocheford."

The name hit Genevieve like a slap to the face, snatching her breath and rendering her fully aware in the same instant. Her eyes flew open. She was, she discovered, on the sofa in the studio with the quilt from Max's bed spread over her. A single lamp on the dining table lit the space, leaving the majority of the room, including the sofa where she lay, in deep shadow. Max was there. From the papers spread out across it and the pen lying on top of them, she could see he'd been using the table as a desk. Minus his jacket and tie now, his hair mussed and tired lines bracketing his eyes, he was seated in front of it. He looked up at the stranger, an old man with stooped shoulders and a gray beard. A stubbed-out Gauloise still smoldered in an ashtray at his elbow.

Had she heard the man right? Had he really said Paul de Rocheford?

Dead?

Goose bumps raced over her skin. Instinct told her not to move, not to make a sound, if she wanted to hear more.

"Who was the informer?"

"We aren't sure. Yet. We'll find out." The man's tone promised a grisly end for the guilty one.

Max asked, "What do they know, the ones

who've been arrested?"

"We're not sure. De Rocheford was briefed, because his help was needed to prepare for the operation. None of the others were."

From their attitude, Genevieve got the impression that theirs was a long-standing relationship, and the meeting a scheduled one. At a guess, it was the explanation for Otto's reluctance to bring her to La Fleur Rouge tonight. Max being visited by strange men at odd hours was nothing new. In Belgium, Austria, Poland, Denmark, Norway, Czechoslovakia, Africa, Spain — everywhere they went, everywhere she performed, there were always strange men dropping in at strange hours on Max. What they spoke of, what they planned, she knew only from overheard fragments of conversations: a bridge blown up in Austria, a factory burned to the ground in Norway, an assassination in Czechoslovakia.

The less she knew, Max assured her, the better.

She hadn't argued. Acutely aware of the terrible fate in store for her if Max was compromised and they were exposed, she hadn't wanted to know.

Now she did. Quite desperately.

"Who was arrested?" Max's tone was all business. No emotion there. Genevieve, on the other hand, was a seething tangle of emotion. So tangled, in fact, that she couldn't quite sort out what she felt.

The man reeled off names. Genevieve recognized none of them. Then he added, “And possibly the baroness. We’ve had conflicting reports on whether or not she was with them.”

“Lillian de Rocheford?” Looking thoughtful, Max drummed his fingers on the tabletop while Genevieve’s stomach turned inside out. Everyone knew what the Nazis did to prisoners. “How is it we don’t know?”

“She wasn’t supposed to be part of the mission,” the man said. “De Rocheford didn’t like her to be involved in anything too dangerous, which this definitely was. It came up last-minute, with no time to plan. But she hasn’t been seen since. Some say she was captured. Some say she was injured but escaped. We haven’t been able to confirm anything yet. It’s also possible that, upon learning what happened to her husband and the others, she’s gone into hiding.”

“We need to find out. Quickly.”

“We’re doing everything we can. Of course, you will appreciate that it’s difficult right at present. We must be very careful.”

“I understand. But this is of the utmost importance.” Max’s voice was coolly authoritative.

He lit another cigarette. If she’d been hoping she was still asleep and this was just another nightmare, that hope was dashed.

No dream cigarette could re-create the distinctive burnt-rubber smell of a Gauloise.

The man said, "Getting anyone else arrested will do none of us any good."

Max drew on the cigarette. "Where are the other cell members being held?"

"Cherbourg. They've rounded up dozens of locals, too. It's bad."

"What happened to the pilot?"

"He's being kept separately from the others. He'll be interrogated, then shipped to a POW camp. We've already confirmed that his briefing went no further than the run he was on."

"Well, that's something. How certain are you that de Rocheford had no chance to tell the Germans anything?"

"Absolutely certain. There is concern in some quarters about what he might have told the others in his cell, however. Particularly the baroness. It seems he had a distressing tendency to confide in her."

"Damn it." There was the briefest of pauses, and then he said, "I want a message sent to Baker Street. Today. Wait for the answer." Turning, he stubbed out the barely smoked cigarette in the ashtray and picked up his pen.

"I'll bring it as soon as I have it," the other man promised as Max tore a sheet of paper in half and scribbled on it. While he waited, the man looked around. His gaze probed the shadows, sliding over Genevieve where she lay on the sofa. Her eyes were tightly shut again by the time his gaze reached her, and she'd drawn her head down into the quilt like a turtle into its shell. The light from the lamp barely touched the sofa, and she wasn't sure he could even tell that anyone was huddled there. But every instinct she possessed shouted it would be a mistake to let him know that she had overheard.

"Any word from Gunner?" Max asked, still writing.

"Nothing. I fear something may have gone wrong. It's been almost three weeks."

"The Krauts are running scared." There was a note of grim satisfaction in Max's voice. "I wouldn't write him off just yet. He may have had to lie low for a while."

"If we were smart, that's what we all would do."

"If we were smart." Finished writing, Max folded his note and handed it to him.

The man twisted the paper into a tight coil, doubled it, pulled a packet of cigarettes from his coat pocket, tapped one out, pinched out the apparently false plug of tobacco in the top, and inserted the paper into what was clearly a hollowed-out middle section. He then put the plug back, restored the cigarette to the pack and put the pack into his pocket.

"I hear Huntsman is being sought far and wide," the man said. Huntsman was Max, his code name, and the casual warning sent a thrill of fear through Genevieve. Ordinarily she didn't feel acute rushes of fear, or, indeed, any emotion at all. It was part of how she had survived. But the date always left her feeling especially vulnerable, and combined with Anna and the dream and what she had just overheard, this bit of bad news packed a punch.

There were so many of them, the Nazis. So many who collaborated with them, too. Their spies were everywhere. All it took was an unwary word, a piece of bad luck, the wrong Resistance fighter captured, and it was over. The average life expectancy of an SOE agent working behind enemy lines was five months.

"I hear that, too." Imperturbable as always, Max got to his feet and reached for his stick. Of course, being searched for by the Germans was merely business as usual for him; nothing to worry about at all. She told herself that, and let that particular fear go as the hideousness of the rest overwhelmed her. The two men moved away, their voices too low now for Genevieve to overhear. A moment later the rattle and ding of the lift announced the stranger's departure.

Max knew nothing of her life before. Why should he? She'd been Genevieve Dumont for nearly four years when they'd met, already established as a singer, her name legally changed to the stage name she'd assumed from the time when she'd put France behind her, as she'd thought, forever. No longer able to survive as the girl who had been Vivi's mother, she'd fled her country, her old life, everything and everyone she'd loved, after her daughter's death, because all of that was inevitably associated with Vivi, and she could no longer bear to be in any part of that world without her daughter in it. The person she was now, the person Max knew, was a totally different creature from the girl she'd been then. The only part that survived was her singing voice — and that damned haunting, hellacious dream.

Dashing a hand across her eyes to eliminate any lingering trace of tears, Genevieve pushed the quilt aside and sat up. Her head throbbed and her stomach still wasn't back to normal, but the rampant fear stampeding through her veins trumped everything else.

Max's brow was furrowed and he seemed to be lost in thought as he turned away from the lift.

"What was that about?" She pushed a hand through her hair, lifting the curtain of black curls away from her face. She still wore her evening dress, but her shoes had been removed, she assumed by Max, to whom she also gave credit for the quilt and pillow. Her stockinged feet encountered the cold floor. Given the blackout quality of the curtains it was impossible to be sure, but her impression was that she'd slept for a few hours and it was close to dawn.

At her question he looked up quickly, and his expression changed. A second later the overhead light came on and she blinked.

"How long have you been awake?"

"Long enough to hear that —" Her voice wanted to break; oh, God, she wouldn't have expected to feel so devastated. The trick was to approach what she really wanted to know sideways rather than head-on. "The Nazis are searching for Huntsman."

His grimace dismissed that as unimportant.

"Oh," she continued, "and some baron's been killed and his wife is missing. Or did I get that wrong?"

His eyes narrowed. "You shouldn't listen to what doesn't concern you."

The clipped quality of his answer made it clear: she had not misheard. It was all she could do to fight off the wave of dizziness that assailed her.

"You shouldn't talk about what doesn't concern me where I can listen."

"Touché." He stood over her now, looking down at her closely. "You feeling all right?"

She must have paled, she realized. Certainly she was sweating.

"My head hurts." She closed her eyes and let her forehead drop into her cradling hand, the better to hide her face from him. Her answer wasn't a lie. It just wasn't why she was suddenly feeling sick as a dog. That tangle of emotions she was experiencing was unraveling strand by strand.

"I believe it's called a hangover." His voice was dry. He was walking away from her. A moment later she looked up at the sound of running water to find that he was in the kitchen filling a glass.

She said, "That man — have you worked with him before? Is his information usually reliable?" The tiniest sliver of hope that someone might have got it wrong burned inside her.

"Reliable enough. Why all the interest?" He came back toward her carrying the glass; it held a cloudy white liquid that fizzed. Alka-Seltzer, if she had to guess.

"He saw me." If her mind hadn't been clogged by burgeoning panic, she would have artfully gone to work to tease all the details out of him. But artfully was, she feared, beyond her for the moment.

"No, he didn't. At least, not so he would ever recognize you again. It was too dark. And you were bundled up to your nose in a quilt." Max stopped in front of her, handed her the glass. "Drink this."

She took it, looked at the mixture, made a face. "I'm really more of a 'hair of the dog' kind of girl."

"Not anymore, you're not. Drink it."

"Fine." Maybe it would help. She raised the glass to her lips, drained the contents, shuddered.

"Good job," he said.

Still grimacing at the chalkiness of it, she shot him a narrow-eyed look. "Don't pat yourself on the back just yet. I could still puke."

He smiled.

The rattle of the arriving lift claimed their attention. Otto stepped out of it, bundled to the eyeballs in overcoat, muffler and hat. In one hand he carried a leather valise.

"So?" Max greeted him.

Otto replied with a terse nod.

At the sight of his familiar figure, Genevieve was both relieved and disappointed. She'd dreaded the arrival of another operative almost as much as she'd hoped for it. One with more information about the fate of the de Rochefords.

Information she found herself craving like an addict craves morphine, even if some tiny remaining clearheaded part of her warned that maybe she really didn't want to know.

Through the unraveling strands of anger and betrayal and bitterness, she'd broken to the hard nugget of truth at the tangle's core.

The person she used to be was still there, alive inside her after all.

Genevra de Rocheford.

And, despite everything, she quaked with shock and fear over the fate of her estranged parents.

Chapter Ten

Genevieve — because she *was* Genevieve, she reminded herself fiercely — couldn't believe how terrible she felt. She was cold all over, and shivery with it. Her head pounded and her heart raced and her stomach felt like it was full of writhing snakes. And she was *not* suffering from a hangover — or at least, only a very small one. This was all because of *them.*

Since Vivi's death, she'd excised them from her life, just as she'd excised everything that was Genevra, everything from before. She'd stood there, listening to the dolorous church bells tolling for Vivi, and wept. Alone in every way that mattered despite the people gathered around her, she watched the tiny casket that held her daughter being lowered into her grave. Her heart hadn't simply broken; it had crumbled into dust and disintegrated. As it did, every connection she'd ever had to her past had shattered. She'd thought never to see, or speak to, or even think of, her family again.

They hadn't wanted Vivi. From that moment on, she hadn't wanted *them.*

Over the ensuing years, nothing about that had changed. How, then, was this affecting her so? Her emotions must still be raw from the dream, she decided. Otherwise, surely, the news would not have thrown her into such a tailspin.

"Any loose ends?" Max asked Otto.

"Taken care of." Otto set the valise on the floor.

Genevieve forced herself to concentrate on the pair of them. On the present, the here and now, this studio, these men. Falling apart did no one any good, and might well incite an unwelcome curiosity in Max.

Otto said, "Was that Hippolyte Touvier I saw leaving?"

"Careful." Max jerked his head toward her. His tone was semi-jocular. "Our little songbird just warned me that we shouldn't talk about what doesn't concern her where she can hear."

Otto turned a questioning look her way.

"My God. If you can't trust me by now, then maybe we'd better call this whole arrangement off." Her tone was far sharper than Max's teasing called for. She couldn't help it. She was rattled, on edge, off balance. "You think I care about all your secrets?"

"You don't know all my secrets." Max gave her an appraising look, then glanced at Otto. "You have something for me?"

From the pocket of his overcoat Otto produced a broadsheet promoting what looked like, from the illustration of a bottle on it, some kind of tonic. Max took it, plucked the empty glass from Genevieve's hand and headed for the kitchen.

"He's trying to protect you. The less you know, the safer you are." Otto lowered his voice to reach her ears alone as Max turned on the stove's burner and held the paper over it. That's when Genevieve realized: the broadsheet must contain a message written in invisible ink. *Quelle surprise.*

"He's worried about my safety *now*? That's rich."

Otto took off his hat, hung it on a peg built into the wall for that purpose and unwound his muffler. "He's been worried about your safety from the beginning. But he's got a job to do. We all do, you included."

"I never *wanted* this job."

He put his muffler on another peg and unbuttoned his coat. A quick look around told Genevieve that her own coat had disappeared. For nefarious purposes, she had no doubt.

"Some of us volunteer, some of us are drafted," Otto said.

"Easy for you to say. You're one of the

volunteers." She cast a dark glance at Max, who was carefully moving the paper this way and that centimeters above the flames. "Like him."

"He's a *soldier.* We all fight in our own ways. And sometimes we do things we might not want to do." Otto hung his coat, then turned to look at her. "What you have to ask yourself is where you would be right now if he hadn't been there when you needed help. Remember Morocco?"

That brought Genevieve up short. She did, indeed, remember. She'd been back in Paris on a tour slated to take in several of Europe's capitals when the Germans had broken through the much-touted series of defensive fortresses that formed the Maginot Line. In the wake of France's stunningly unexpected defeat, she, like so many others clogging the roads and trains, had fled south with not much more than the clothes on her back, escaping Paris steps ahead of the Nazis. Taking a harrowing route overland, she'd ended up trapped in Africa's largest Atlantic port city, Casablanca, while she tried to obtain the immigration, exit and transit visas that would allow her to leave.

The process had been unbelievably slow and difficult.

By February of 1941, she'd been stuck in Casablanca for seven months. Desperately afraid, all alone, cut off from everyone and everything she'd known, she'd been down to her last few francs and reduced to singing for her supper wherever she could find a gig. Once a week she'd finagled herself a slot onstage at the Rialto Theater, the owners of which tended to prefer burlesque and vaudeville acts to singers. Other times she sang in hotel lounges or at private parties or smoke-filled bars, often teaming up with Max on the piano. The pay was low, often just tips, but it was enough to allow her to survive. Morocco had recently come under the control of Vichy France, which had sworn its allegiance to the conquering Germans. Britain and France were both in the area, fighting it out, with British torpedo boats attacking a French battleship in the harbor and French bombers strafing the city in retaliation. Most days, all anyone had to do to die was step out into the street at the wrong moment.

"I do," she said. "It felt like the most dangerous place in the world."

"It was something, though." Otto sounded faintly nostalgic.

Her reply was tart. "If you like choking dust and camels and villains."

But in retrospect, it had been something. With its blazing heat, gleaming white buildings, majestic Moorish architecture and swaying palm trees lining wide colonial boulevards, Casablanca was beautiful, exotic — and in turmoil. By an accident of geography, it had become a way station for thousands of weary, frightened refugees. It was crowded to the bursting point, thick with criminals from pickpockets to smugglers to murderers, a place where loyalties were fiercely divided and nearly anything could be had for the right price. It was also a teeming nest of spies and intrigue, with calamity awaiting the unwary around every corner.

"Lucky you ran across the one guy who wasn't a villain, huh?" Otto's voice was soft but full of meaning. "Otherwise, I wouldn't have wagered a shilling on your chances of making it out of there alive."

Genevieve's lips thinned. Much as she might want to, she couldn't actually disagree. Max had saved her. But . . .

"You're a cheerful-looking pair. What's the subject?" Max was back, glancing from one to the other of them. The broadsheet was nowhere in sight. From the slightly scorched smell in the air, she guessed that he'd burned it, as was the usual fate of such documents once their message had been received.

"You," she said.

"Old times," Otto said at the same time with a dismissive shrug. Clearly he didn't intend to enlighten him any further.

Max's eyebrows went up.

"Charles Lamartine." Genevieve's tone was brittle as the man's face popped into her mind's eye. It was her night for dealing with ghosts.

Her grievance with Max stemmed from that night — the night when the character of their budding friendship had changed. She'd thought . . . she'd thought that, maybe, in Max, she'd found someone special. She hadn't realized then that she was stepping right into the jaws of the trap he'd been laying for her since they'd met.

"Ah," he said, as their eyes held. He didn't need to say anything more: she knew he knew exactly what she was referring to.

Well-known Nazi collaborator and man about town Charles Lamartine had been sniffing around her for weeks before he heard her sing a defiant "La Marseillaise" from the stage of the Rialto. She'd chosen the song in response to a conversation she'd overheard by a group of Nazi sympathizers who'd compared defeated France to a cowed dog. Lamartine had smilingly told her that her choice had certainly severed any chance she might have at official protection, then followed her back to her rented room above a deserted shop. After knocking on her door, he'd muscled his way in when she answered and tried to force himself on her, covering her face and throat with slobbering kisses, ripping her dress, shoving her down onto her bed. She barely managed to save herself as he dropped down on top of her by grabbing and shooting him with his own Rubis revolver. With a choked gasp rather than a cry, he'd reared up, rolled off the bed, hit the floor and died before she could do more than scramble to her feet to stare down at him in horror. The wild, unthinking panic that had given her the strength to save herself devolved into a shaking fit that had her sinking down onto the floor beside him as her knees gave out. When she finally, finally accepted the fact that he was really dead and she had killed him, she was appalled by what she had done. Then, as the ramifications slowly sank in, she was seized by fresh panic as she realized the true enormity of what she now faced.

She was already a well-known singer, though not nearly as famous as she'd since become. Even if she'd possessed her present degree of fame, however, it wouldn't have been enough to save her. Lamartine was known to work closely with high-ranking members of the German spy network, the Abwehr. His killer would be looked on harshly, especially in the aftermath of her partisan-rousing song. If she reported Lamartine's death to the local police, she could expect at the minimum a lengthy interrogation. Even if they believed that she'd acted in self-defense, she was unlikely to escape arrest. Perhaps she would be freed at trial, but more likely she would be convicted and executed for murder.

In extremis, she'd managed to pull herself together enough to go out into the night in search of Max, the one acquaintance she had in the city who she thought might be able to deal with such a crisis. Explaining what had happened in disjointed whispers, she'd brought him back to her room. One look at the corpse on her floor and she'd once again started to shake. The knowledge that she'd *taken a life* felt horrible. Max had come through for her magnificently, wrapping her first in his arms and then in a blanket, giving her brandy, calming her down. He'd disposed of the body, then as questions had started to circulate about what had become of Lamartine, he'd managed to get her out of the country, obtaining an almost impossible emergency certificate allowing her to travel by emphasizing to the Reich the public relations importance of a series of performances he'd quickly arranged for her across Europe. Of course, afterward he'd used her to further his own agenda as a British agent, and in hindsight she saw that he'd been grooming her for inclusion in his spy network from the moment they met. But by the time she'd worked that out, she'd been so hopelessly involved in his schemes that there was no escape. She'd become his, in the worst possible way.

"How about we leave the past in the past?" Max said.

Genevieve didn't reply.

"Good plan." Stepping into the breach, Otto glanced at Genevieve and gestured at the valise. "I brought you some clothes. Berthe packed them. Max thought you might not want to go back to the hotel in last night's evening gown."

"How thoughtful of him." The edge in her voice was aimed at Max. "By the way, I see my coat is missing. I'm quite fond of it, actually. Am I ever going to see it again?"

"I'll bring it back later," Max said. "Why don't you go get changed?"

Her lips compressed. But she really, really needed a moment to herself, and lashing out at Max wasn't going to fix anything. She took the valise and headed for the bathroom, conscious of Max's gaze following her the entire way. It didn't require someone who knew him as well as she did to divine that something in her manner was striking him as a little off. *Well, let him wonder.*

Some fifteen minutes later, she adjusted the belt around the snug waist of her brown tweed suit, slid her feet into a pair of brown pumps, checked to make sure her stocking seams were straight and took a final look in the small mirror over the sink. She'd pinned her hair away from her face in soft rolls and made judicious use of the cosmetics Berthe had packed, but she still looked pale and hollow-eyed.

Haunted was the word that came to mind.

She picked up the trench coat Berthe had included and the valise that now contained her discarded evening clothes and left the bathroom. Max was half sitting, half leaning on the edge of the table, shirtsleeves rolled up, arms crossed over his chest, engaged in a low-voiced conversation with Otto. They broke off as soon as they saw her.

"Otto's going to take you back to the hotel now. He says the streets are safe." Max's gaze assessed her. It occurred to her that he knew her as well as she knew him, and she felt a niggle of unease as she wondered what her face might reveal. The version of her past that she'd given him was far different from the truth, which she would not, could not share.

"Relatively safe," Otto said.

Straightening away from the table, Max stepped up beside her to take her coat from her. He helped her into it as Otto moved away to hit the button for the lift.

"Why don't you skip this morning's rehearsal and rest today?" Max's voice was low. "You look like hell."

"Thank you."

At the acid in her tone, Max flicked her cheek with a long forefinger.

"Beautiful hell," he amended. "If you're feeling guilty about Lamartine again, don't. He was a bad man. He was going to hurt you, and you did what you had to do."

"I know." But she felt guilty anyway.

He studied her face. She would have turned away, but she was afraid of what he might read into *that.*

"If it's not Lamartine, then what is it? What's the matter, angel?"

Angel: there it was again. In a voice that was almost — tender.

"You tell me." She gave him a searching look. They stood very close, so close she had to tilt her head back to see his eyes. "You haven't called me that since —"

She broke off. She didn't like to remind him of those first months after he'd gotten her out of Casablanca. She didn't like to remember them herself. As the itinerant entertainer cum new manager cum knight in shining armor she'd thought she was getting to know, he'd been irresistibly charming. She'd sung in the venues he'd arranged for her, explored various cities with him, eaten nearly all her meals with him, had fun with him. Relied on him for protection and advice and companionship. Until, on the last night of their stay in Oslo, she'd taken shelter in his hotel room during a terrible bombing raid, fallen asleep in his bed (he, like the gentleman she'd thought he was, had slept on the floor) and then awakened not to the sound of more bombs exploding but to find a British agent, too injured to be discreet, slipping through Max's hotel room door. Thus, abruptly, she had discovered who and what Max really was, along with the ulterior motive behind his pursuit of her. Since then, their relationship had been strictly business.

"Oslo, wasn't it?" he said. "I remember. Nice to know you do, too."

Something indefinable passed between them.

They'd spent two weeks in Oslo before she'd learned the terrible truth. They'd shared so much — including a searing, heady kiss that, much as she tried to banish it from memory, came back to her in moments of weakness. She'd thought they were headed to something special — something like falling in love. But the revelation that Max Bonet was actually Major Max Ryan, SOE, was followed by a rejected apology, a blazing if low-voiced fight and finally her attempt to walk out the door.

He'd grabbed her before she could leave the room.

"Where do you think you're going?" His voice was a harsh whisper.

"Away from you." She tried to jerk free. He didn't let go.

"Keep your voice down." Out the window, the moonlit night was just beginning to lighten to gray. The bombing had stopped, but sirens still wailed. On the bed, the badly wounded agent, patched up to the extent possible by Max, lay rigid and panting rather than writhing in pain as he had been doing earlier. "You're not going anywhere."

"Oh, really? You just watch me."

"You're going to help me get this man out of the country. I can't do it without you."

"I wouldn't help you cross the street. You *lied* to me. You —"

"They'll kill him if they catch him. They'll kill us, too."

"Us?" She shook her head vehemently. "Oh, no. I'm not involved. I had nothing to do with this."

"You've been helping smuggle people through checkpoints and across borders since we left Morocco. The playbills that get passed out at your shows? They contain coded messages. Right now a dozen radios are hidden beneath false bottoms in your costume trunks."

Her jaw dropped.

"You're in too deep to get out." He held her in place, looked down into her eyes. Except for the moonlight filtering in through the window, it was dark in the bedroom, but not so dark she couldn't see him. The handsome face with the beautifully carved mouth, the long-fingered pianist's hands, the tall, lean body — she was achingly familiar with them. With him. Only, she realized with a blinding flash of fear-fueled anger, nothing about him was what it seemed. She didn't actually know this ruthless man who was gripping her arms so tightly — any part of him — at all.

The man she'd thought she was falling in love with didn't exist.

Furious, she said, "I will get out. I'll walk right out this door. You can't make me stay. You can't make me help you."

"You're right. I can't. But I'm going to try to get my guy out regardless, and without you in the car with us, our chances of getting caught are sky-high. I won't give you up, but once they have me and realize I'm your manager, they'll come looking for you."

"My God." The truth of it was appallingly obvious.

"The only chance you have is to go, right now, to the Nazis — their headquarters is at Møllergata 19 — and turn me and that chap there in. We'll be tortured and executed, but you — you'll be a heroine of the Reich. If you want to do that, I won't stop you." He let go of her, stepped back, gestured toward the door. "The choice is yours."

She was so angry, so hurt, so scared, so shocked that she could barely think. The magnitude of the betrayal stunned her. She stood glaring at him, her hands clenching and unclenching at her sides.

One thing was crystal clear: she might not know him, but he knew her. And he knew as well as he knew it was cold outside that she wouldn't turn him in to the Nazis.

It killed her to say it. "What do you want me to do?"

In the end, with the help of Otto — who up until then she'd thought was strictly their driver — they'd loaded the wounded agent into the secret compartment in the car that was revealed by pulling out the back seat, then drove through numerous checkpoints and across the Norwegian border into Sweden. At each stop Genevieve's heart was in her throat, but their papers and her travel pass and status as an increasingly popular star got them through.

Once his agent was safe in neutral Sweden, Max, exhibiting no shame whatsoever for what he'd done to her, was prepared to return to the business of espionage under the guise of being her manager. She had shows already scheduled in Denmark, the Netherlands and Belgium, he reminded her.

"Cancel them," she told him. "I'm not going anywhere with you."

He'd gone away, and when he'd come back, it had been to say goodbye. She let him into her hotel room because she didn't want to chance prying ears overhearing whatever he had to say. Sweden was officially neutral, but the Nazis had spies everywhere.

"You should be all right here," he said. "Whether we win or lose, Sweden is probably as good a place as any to ride it out. If it can be ridden out. But if the Nazis win, not even

Sweden will be safe."

She gave him a stony look.

He continued, "Or you could help us win. You could use your talent, your unique position as a marquee artist, and join the fight. The threat is so enormous we need every advantage we can get. Aren't you the girl who sang 'La Marseillaise' in front of a theater full of Nazis? Do it for France."

"Goodbye, Max," she said.

"You might also want to consider that my guy saw you. Got a real good look, and you're hard to forget. He's lying low, recovering, but he's still here in Stockholm until he does. The Nazis almost caught him in Oslo, and they don't give up easily. He's a good man, but even good men have been known to talk under the right circumstances, and if he were to be arrested . . ."

"You are such a *bastard.*" It was a wrathful exclamation, because her eyes had been well and truly opened, and she now recognized he was just trying to manipulate her into doing what he wanted.

His smile was wry. "We leave in an hour. The car will be around front if you change your mind."

In the end, of course, she had changed her mind. Because she loved her country. Because she had one gift, and she could use it to help in the battle against the horror that was the Third Reich. Because Sweden suddenly felt gray, and cold, and so lonely. And also because, despite the fact that she'd recognized his attempt at manipulation for exactly that, he'd succeeded in planting the thought that she wasn't safe anywhere.

"From here on out this is strictly business," she'd informed Max in a hostile undertone as she'd yanked open the door and slid into the back seat of the waiting car. Both he and Otto looked around at her from the front seat.

"I wouldn't have it any other way," Max said, and climbed out of the front passenger seat to oversee the bestowal of her luggage in the trunk.

That was the scene unspooling in her mind when the ping of the arriving lift brought her back to the present, to the studio in the rue de la Lune, only to discover that her eyes were still locked with Max's.

Despite everything, her pulse gave a wayward flutter at the memory of what Max had been to her before she'd found out what a dirty liar he was. Clamping down on it, she frowned at him and said, "Bad memories are unfortunately often the hardest to shake."

He smiled. "Not all of them are bad."

"Now there's where you're wrong," she said.

Without another word she stepped away from him and into the lift with Otto.

Chapter Eleven

The early morning air was cold but dry. Only a few puddles remained on the cobblestoned square of the place Vendôme as evidence of the previous night's downpour. A pinkish sun crept above the Ritz's roofline, painting everything from the building's arched doorways and peaked dormers to the monolithic Vendôme Column to the surrounding stone buildings in shades of rose gold. A half-dozen long black cars waited, engines running, hood to trunk in front of the hotel. From the hustle and bustle surrounding them, Genevieve deduced that one or more high-status guests had either just arrived or were imminently departing.

As Otto let her out as near as possible to the Ritz's front entrance, Genevieve spent a wasted moment speculating on who said guests could be. Everyone who was anyone, from the highest-ranking German officers to royalty to stars of the stage and screen to playboys and heiresses to famous artists of various persuasions stayed at the Ritz, the only luxury hotel allowed to continue operating as such in the city. The soldiers guarding either side of the massive front doors seemed even more interested in the goings-on than she was, which she appreciated because it meant they accorded her scarcely a glance as she walked beneath the domed awning and entered the hotel.

The subtle scent of amber, which was unique to the hotel and never seemed to fade, greeted her as she strode into the lobby. Bellhops laden with luggage scurried about. A nod to the receptionist at the front desk, a glance at the lift that was being held and was clearly not available for immediate use, and then she turned a corner and headed up the curving steps of the marble-and-steel *grand escalier.*

Four flights later, she let herself into her suite. It was ornate, as was everything at the Ritz. High ceilings, crystal chandeliers, gilded wall sconces, cream paneling, tasteful paintings and a fireplace provided an elegant backdrop for exquisite furnishings, including an antique Louis XIV sofa beneath a portrait of the Sun King himself placed between a pair of tall, heavily curtained windows.

"There you are! I was worried when you didn't return last night." Berthe bustled out of the adjoining bedroom as Genevieve dropped the valise and took off her coat.

Around Genevieve's own height, thin as everyone these days but raw-boned and sturdily built, forty-four-year-old Berthe Krawiek slept in the auxiliary maid's room that was part of the suite. She had nut-brown hair worn in long braids wrapped crown-like around her head and soft brown eyes set in a round, heavy-featured face that, unlined and smooth, bore no trace of the traumas she had endured as a result of the war. Despite the early hour, she was fully dressed in one of the high-necked, long-sleeved black dresses she wore every day.

"There was trouble in the streets." Genevieve handed Berthe her coat.

"That's why I was worried. I wouldn't have, otherwise, because I knew you were with M'sieur Max." Berthe knew nothing of Max's true identity, or his work for the SOE, but she adored him. He had, quite literally, saved her life. When Max had found her, in Warsaw on one of the early tours he'd arranged after Genevieve had left Stockholm with him, Berthe had been starving and living in the ruins of her bombed-out home. Her husband had been killed in the fight for Warsaw, and the theater she'd worked in had been destroyed at the same time. In the aftermath, as the Nazis had consolidated control of the city, she'd been hanged as part of one of many mass executions. The only reason she'd survived was because the rope broke, and in all the confusion she'd been able to crawl away. She still bore the marks of that horror on her throat, which was why she never wore anything but high-necked dresses. Max had hired the former lady's maid turned theatrical wardrobe mistress even though, at first, Berthe had been so weak and traumatized that she'd barely been able to communicate. With food and care and kind treatment she'd recovered, physically at least, although her face still lapsed into melancholy when she thought no one was looking, and shadows darkened her eyes.

"That is a reason not to worry," Genevieve agreed, crossing the room to draw back the gold silk curtains and stare pensively out at the place Vendôme, where the black cars still waited, sending up white puffs of exhaust. The wrought iron wonder that was the Eiffel Tower was visible in the near distance, not far from the muddy brown waters of the Seine. Behind her, Berthe hung up her coat and rang downstairs for coffee — the Ritz's guests were served the real thing — and croissants, a decadent luxury that accompanied the coffee as a matter of course. As she watched, a rotund man in a long fur coat puffed out of the hotel. He was bowed into the lead car by his Nazi-uniformed entourage, who then piled into the following cars. Moments later the motorcade pulled away.

"Someone very important is leaving. I wonder who?"

A male voice said, "It is Reichsmarschall Göring, Mademoiselle Dumont. He has been recalled to Berlin, for an urgent conference with the Führer."

Genevieve turned to find that Berthe had admitted the white-gloved waiter, a wizened old man named Albert, who in different times would have long since sought the comforts of retirement. He placed a silver tray with her breakfast on a low table in front of the sofa.

Inhaling the guilt-inducing smell of coffee and fresh bread, she said, "Thank you, Albert."

"He says he will be back within a week. He is a fan of our steak with truffles." A naughty twinkle. "And our bathtubs."

Which were opulently king-size, having been upgraded after Britain's portly Edward VII got stuck in one while cavorting in it with his mistress and was forced to endure an embarrassing extraction by hotel staff.

Genevieve smiled in response and sat down as Berthe shooed the waiter out.

"I'm just going to put these things away." Berthe picked up the valise. "Call out if you want me."

Taking a sip of the strong, bitter coffee — oh, she needed that — Genevieve nodded. Berthe took herself off.

After supplementing the coffee with a few

bites of buttery croissant, Genevieve pushed the tray aside and stood up, too restless to eat. The curtains hung open from her earlier perusal of the courtyard, allowing pale sunlight to pour in. She crossed to the window, pushed a cool silk panel farther to one side and looked out again. The place Vendôme was livelier now as Paris woke up, busy with bicyclists and pedestrians and street vendors as well as cars.

She watched the activity without really registering any of it until her attention was caught by a woman holding a little girl by the hand as they hurried across the square toward a waiting bus. The child was three, maybe four years old. Beneath a bright blue beret, black curls bobbed.

Genevieve closed her eyes.

When she opened them again, she knew what she had to do.

Turning away from the window, she walked to the closet and selected a coat. Not one of her own: Berthe's big black box coat. She tied on Berthe's black-and-gray plaid head scarf and traded her pumps for the pair of sensible flats with corrugated wooden soles she wore for walking outside in inclement weather. Then she picked up the cloth bag Berthe used for shopping.

She strapped on her wristwatch, dumped the contents of her everyday handbag into the shopping bag, added her papers, called

"I'm taking a walk" to Berthe and left the suite.

She took a bicycle taxi to the place de la Bastille and got out in front of the Colonne de Juliet, a tall column with the golden statue *Génie de la Liberté* at its top, which paid tribute to those who had died in labor uprisings a hundred years before. From there, she walked to her destination: the house where Max had taken baby Anna.

The street bordered a leafy park. So early in the day, there was almost no traffic, vehicular or pedestrian. The house itself was narrow, four stories tall, stucco with a blue-painted front door.

The woman who opened the door to her knock regarded her with narrow-eyed suspicion. Fortyish, with a long, narrow face and smooth bands of sandy hair pulled back into a neat chignon, she stood in the opening as though to block the visitor's view of the interior of the house.

"Yes?"

Of course she would be wary. Genevieve was surprised at herself for not having expected that.

"I —" Genevieve broke off as, beyond the woman, she saw a dark-haired baby girl left sitting on the hall floor as her minder answered the door. Her breath caught — as she knew so well, one moment of inattention was all it took — but a swift glance around found no obvious hazards. Meanwhile, the baby crawled over to a chair nearby and pulled herself into a standing position, looking around with a delighted grin as she succeeded: Anna.

Genevieve's heart turned over even as she smiled.

Glancing around to see what Genevieve was smiling at, the woman looked back at her, her expression less welcoming than before.

"What can I do for you?"

"The baby — Anna — I brought her —" the woman's expression had her hurriedly correcting herself "— I gave her to the man who brought her here. Huntsman."

"Come in." The woman pulled the door wider. Genevieve stepped inside. Anna cruised from the chair to a nearby low table, obviously getting close to taking her first independent step. Genevieve remembered . . .

The pain was sharp as a knife.

"I wanted to see if she was all right. Her mother —"

"Her mother has died in Drancy. We just received word last night." The brusqueness of the woman's voice softened slightly at what must have been the stricken expression on Genevieve's face. "*L'enfant* will be taken care of, you may be sure."

The woman had not offered her name, and Genevieve had not given hers. These were dangerous waters, the taking in of children such as Anna a serious crime. To be caught doing so was punishable by death.

Genevieve's throat was tight as she watched Anna moving gleefully along the front of the table, oblivious to what she had lost, to the darkness swirling around her. The sounds of other children deeper inside the house told her that Anna was not alone.

Genevieve looked at the woman. "She will stay here?"

The woman shook her head. "We are waiting for her papers. When they arrive, she will be taken to the Catholic sisters in Vère, where she will be among many sheltered in the school they run there."

The papers she referred to were false, lifesaving identity cards that would hide Anna's Jewish heritage.

Before Genevieve could reply, Anna lost her grip and sat down with a hard plop, toppled back and hit her head on the floor.

Instinct had Genevieve rushing over and scooping her up almost as soon as the child began to cry.

"Shh, Anna. Shh, shh." Bouncing and patting, she cuddled the little girl close as her initial wails subsided into sniffling sobs. The weight of her, the soft baby smell of her hair, the little hands that clutched at her neck — it was too much. Genevieve's eyes closed. She sucked in air.

"Here." As the memories threatened to

overwhelm her, she thrust Anna at the other woman, who took her with a flicker of surprise.

Hiccuping more than sobbing now, Anna strained back toward Genevieve, stretching out small, plump arms beseechingly.

"Mama," she said, tearstained eyes wide on Genevieve's face. "Mama."

A boulder dropping on her chest couldn't have caused a more crushing agony. She could feel the blood draining from her face.

"I have to go," she said. "Please . . . watch her carefully." Somehow she managed to get herself out of the house.

She made it as far as the park, and no farther. Sinking down onto an iron bench, she bent forward and dropped her head between her knees.

Memories, so many memories, an ocean of them, a universe of them, sent her tumbling head over heels, catching her up in a vast whirlpool of images: Anna with Rachel; Vivi, darling Vivi, in her own unworthy arms; herself with her own *maman.*

When the dizziness subsided, when the waves that buffeted her withdrew, Genevieve was left with one certainty. The tie that bound mothers and daughters was like no other. It was eternal, stronger even than death.

Anna would never have a chance to know Rachel. Genevieve would never in this life hold Vivi again.

But her mother was still out there.

The love — the bond they shared — it was still there, too.

Finally, she acknowledged what for the last seven years she had willfully refused to face: angry and hurt and destroyed by Vivi's death as she had been, she had missed her mother, her family, every day they'd been apart.

She stood up, dashed a hand across her eyes to vanquish any lingering tears and started walking.

The need that drove her was so strong that it was nothing short of a compulsion.

She was going to find her mother.

She was going home.

Chapter Twelve

Except for the German occupiers, Paris had become a city of women. Everywhere Genevieve looked, she saw women queuing in line, hurrying along sidewalks, pedaling away on bicycles, crammed into buses, staffing cafés and shops and working at every imaginable job, all against a backdrop of soldiers in the ubiquitous gray-green uniform.

A large portion of France's men had lost their lives in the Great War. The new generation of Frenchmen had either gone off to fight, been imprisoned or killed as France fell, or had fallen victim to the Service du travail obligatoire. The STO swept up hundreds of thousands of workers and sent them to Germany as forced labor to compensate for the lost manpower of the soldiers at the front. By and large, the only French males left were either too young or too old for combat, or were members of the Milice, or, like Max, had been deemed medically unfit.

The city itself had turned Kafkaesque: the

familiar distorted in a way that was almost nightmarish. The clocks had been set back an hour, so that Paris ran on Berlin time. The streets were quiet, as the usual traffic noises were greatly reduced because of the shortage of gasoline. Hunger was rampant. The average Parisian had lost more than a stone of weight since the Germans had taken over. Everything from food to clothing to medicine was almost impossible for the ordinary citizen to obtain. What little was available required a coupon to purchase, giving rise to a flourishing black market. Signs in German above the cafés spoke to the occupiers: *Wehrmachts Speiselokal; Soldatenkaffee.*

Sudden noises — sirens, screams, the pounding of running feet, the droning of aeroplane engines overhead — produced an exaggerated fear reaction in a traumatized population conditioned to expect calamity. In this new reality, disaster could, and often did, overtake anyone at any time.

From 1942, Jews had been forced to wear a six-pointed yellow star on their clothing so that they could be easily identified, and they were singled out for the harshest possible treatment. In the windows of nearly every commercial establishment hung signs that read *Les Juifs Ne Sont Pas Admis Ici* — No Jews Allowed Here. The *statut des Juifs* banned Jews from any kind of civil, commercial or industrial job. Jewish-owned businesses almost without exception had fallen victim to Aryanization, the forced transfer to non-Jewish owners. Jewish artists were not allowed to perform, and it was forbidden to sing songs by Jewish composers or stage plays by Jewish playwrights. Books authored by Jews were banned or burned. The arrests had begun by targeting foreign-born Jews. Then the horror that was the Vél d'Hiv roundup resulted in more than thirteen thousand Jews being forced without warning from their Paris homes and confined in the stadium for days before being shipped off to German internment camps. From that time, more were arrested every day, and those few who remained lived in fear. Drancy was a name to strike dread into the souls of those for whom it loomed as a constant threat. Its prisoners were regularly packed into trains bound for Germany to serve as forced labor in the work camps. Whispers that the trains — that the majority of France's Jews — were really bound for death camps were rife, but no one seemed to know for sure. Or if they knew, they were too afraid to speak openly.

The Nazis reigned supreme. Red, black and white swastika flags adorned iconic monuments and public buildings. Across the front of the National Assembly building a huge banner hung that read *Deutschland Siegt An Allen Fronten!* — Germany Is Victorious on All Fronts! The Germans had set up their headquarters in the Le Meurice on the rue de Rivoli right in front of the Tuileries Gardens. The Wehrmacht regularly goose-stepped down the Champs-Élysées.

Outwardly Paris was still Paris, her beauty largely untouched by war. But her gay, bright, defiant spirit — her joie de vivre — had been stolen. The City of Light had turned drab and gray — and afraid.

After paying off the bicycle taxi she'd hired, Genevieve took the metro to the Montparnasse train station. The platform was packed shoulder to shoulder: soldiers, schoolchildren, clergy, tourists, many women armed like her with shopping bags as they sought to leave the city in an effort to obtain items that rationing had put out of reach. Food was limited to a maximum of eighteen hundred calories per person per day, fewer for children and the elderly. The allocation of meat was a scant six and a half ounces a week, and still it was almost impossible to obtain. Poultry, eggs, cheese and vegetables were more easily acquired in the countryside. French policemen, the Milice, their allegiance pledged to the occupiers, roamed the crowds, eyeing first this one and then that one with suspicion, demanding to see papers as they chose. Undercover officers of the Geheime Feldpolizei, the Wehrmacht's secret military police, could be anywhere, searching for spies.

In Berthe's shapeless, oversize coat, with

the shabby scarf pulled well forward to hide her face, Genevieve attracted no notice. She was simply one among the crowd.

Careful to keep her head down, she boarded one of the last cars — the very last car was designated Jews only and the platform had a separate cordoned-off section for them to wait — and took a seat beside a window. A tired-looking woman and her adult daughter sat down next to her, talking in hushed voices about the younger woman's husband, apparently interned in a POW camp in Germany, and the hardships facing her and their two young children with him gone.

The car continued to fill up until people were sitting in the aisle and no more could cram on. Then the train rumbled out of the station, jerking and rocking as it picked up speed.

Pulling the scarf closer around her face, Genevieve did her best to block out the motion, the racketing of the wheels over the rails, the buzz of many disparate conversations and all the unpleasant smells that resulted from too many people stuffed into too small a space. German soldiers patrolled the train, appearing without warning at the end of the car to pick their way down its length while closely eyeing the occupants before moving on to the next. After a single unwary glance, she kept her gaze averted from the unappetizing sight of a Wehrmacht officer and his

French ladylove kissing and pawing each other in the seat in front of her and thus earning shocked mutters of "Shame" and "No decency" from the women beside her.

Instead she looked out at the passing countryside. At first she concentrated on the sights of the city, and then the just-greening fields and small villages and farms. Soon enough, though, she was staring blindly through the glass as everything outside herself faded away.

Her mother, her father, her sister: their faces were all she could see. Their voices were all she could hear.

She had been the little one, the quick-tempered one. The rebel of the family, while her sister had been the perfect child.

"Pretty is as pretty does." She could hear her elegant, aristocratic mother scolding her for some transgression, using the rebuke that had become an oft-repeated refrain from the time she had entered her teens. She could see the reproving look in the aquamarine eyes that in shape and color were so like her own, the despairing shake of Baroness Lillian de Rocheford's well-coiffed head.

"You can't *do* those things, *bébé.*" Emmy — Emmanuelle, her sister, four years older and fair-haired like their father but with those same aquamarine eyes, the unspoken beauty of the family — chimed in, always on their mother's side, scandalized by yet another breach of propriety on the part of her junior.

Paul, her handsome, easygoing father, defended her: "It is good that she is high-spirited. What, would you have her be boring?"

"I would rather her be boring than a scandal," her mother answered grimly, and her father laughed, and Emmy looked serious, and she — she would toss her head and do just as she pleased and think that her mother was stuffy and her sister a bore and nothing bad could ever happen to her. Until something bad did.

"Cherbourg!"

The conductor's bawling announcement of the train's arrival brought Genevieve back to the present with a thud. Her breathing came too fast and her pulse raced and she felt — undone.

Leave the past in the past, she warned herself, repeating the words Max had said to her and growing impatient at herself for remembering them so well, then felt a chilly frisson of foreboding as she realized how impossible that now was. Cherbourg was the past, and she was here.

Disembarking, hurrying toward the bus that would take her the rest of the way to her destination, Genevieve was glad of the sunlight and the gentle caress of the wind blowing in off the sea. It was warmer here than in Paris, as it tended to be except in the dead of summer, when it was the reverse. Inhaling deeply of the briny-scented air, she tasted salt on her tongue and felt her stomach clench at the familiarity of it.

I'm almost home.

The smell and taste of the sea formed the backdrop of her childhood. It was ingrained in her memory just like the endless beaches and the big houses lining the boulevard by the bay and the tall hedgerows that served as living fences between even the most insignificant properties. The fifteenth-century walls, the bridge arching over the Divette, the narrow streets and small shops, the green parks, the stone houses, all were unchanged.

What had changed was that the town was now thick with Germans, civilians as well as soldiers bearing insignia of all ranks and service branches. Military trucks rattled through the streets. The docks where local fishermen had once cast their nets had been turned into a fortress of huge concrete walls dotted by manned lookout towers and a host of antiaircraft guns. A stopping point for large transatlantic ocean liners, including the doomed *Titanic,* Cherbourg during the Great War had been a major arrival and departure point for American and British troops. Now as the only deepwater port in the region, and with England only 112 kilometers away directly across La Manche, the English Channel, the town was of vital strategic importance to this second wave of murderous Germans. It was, therefore, heavily defended. Every weaponized aquatic vessel from torpedo boats to destroyers, including one the approximate size of a stadium, bobbed at anchor in the harbor.

As the bus trundled through each successive neighborhood, Genevieve saw more and more damage, houses burned to their foundations, whole blocks reduced to rubble, craters in the streets. Anger filled her, and she was silently cursing the Germans when she heard a pair of fellow passengers damning the Brits and the Americans for the destruction, blaming them for blitzing the town with almost nightly air raids.

"The bombs will stop soon enough," one of them, a graybeard in a tattered overcoat, consoled the other. "They will attack once too often with their waves of aeroplanes, and Göring and his Luftwaffe will be waiting. Rommel is here, too, to beat them back if they try to land along the coast. The Tommies and their friends stand no chance of winning against those two. They will be defeated in the air and on the land. The war will be over before you know it."

"The whole world is turning upside down," his stooped and bespectacled companion said, and sighed. "What can you do? We must all adapt as best we can."

This sense of fatalism, the certainty that

the military juggernaut that was Germany could not be defeated, was widespread among her fellow citizens. The many who took that view looked with horror and rage on those French who were in the Resistance, who actively worked to undermine the Reich. The fear was that the rash actions of a few would bring hideous reprisals down upon them all.

The bus was well out in the countryside now, one of the few nonmilitary vehicles on the road that skirted the vast salt marsh where she had passed many a pleasant hour exploring during her childhood. Cool and dark, mysterious and dangerous, the swamp was avoided as a matter of course by most, although it nevertheless managed to claim fresh victims every year. Taught to respect it by her mother, Genevieve had also been taught its secrets. She had missed it, she realized as she caught fleeting glimpses of brackish water glinting among tall reeds, missed the sense of freedom she had found there, missed its wildness and its magic.

Through the windows she began to spot familiar landmarks. The hollow tree where bees often swarmed in the summer, the bog that had trapped the Paquets' horse, the Cheviots' now tumbledown barn — they brought the past alive again for her in a vivid rush of nostalgia. Then the one in particular she had been watching for came into view, and she jumped up and pulled the rope to request a stop.

Chapter Thirteen

The narrow stone bridge that arched across the stream running parallel to the road had a gravel path twisting uphill through a thick wood on the other side of it. It was there that Genevieve left the bus to continue her journey on foot. The bridge was hand built in the previous century of local stone. As she crossed it, the creek, brown and shallow, babbled over the rocks as it had always done. In the summers she and Emmy had waded in that creek, their shoes off and their skirts tucked up. Sometimes they'd been alone, sometimes they'd been joined by Phillippe Cheviot, son of the farmer who'd owned the aforementioned barn. In those later summers, Phillippe, who was Emmy's age exactly, had seemed to spend a lot of time fishing that creek. She realized only later that he'd done so because he'd been crazy in love with Emmy — all the boys, it seemed, had been crazy in love with Emmy, but he'd had an advantage because he lived so close. She, of course, had followed the little-sister script by falling crazy in love with Phillippe. The heartbreak that had resulted — there'd been so much heartbreak, too much heartbreak, she couldn't bear remembering.

If we'd only known what was to come.

But the terrible truth of life was that it was never given to anyone to know what the future held.

Thrusting the shade of her younger self, their younger selves, from her mind, she concentrated instead on what lay ahead as she followed the familiar path that twisted this way and that through a medley of beeches and oaks and pines and hawthorns.

The branches, some thorny, some budding with newly green leaves, some evergreen and heavy with needles, interlaced above her head, forming a dim tunnel. Climbing, she took in the smell of resin and pine and broom, listened to the chatter of birds and squirrels, and realized she was running only when she burst out into the clearing at the bottom of the final rise and looked up past the final ten meters of sheer granite cliff that rose like a wall in front of her — and there it was.

Rocheford.

She stopped where she was, breathing hard, as her heart swelled and her throat choked tight.

Situated on a promontory that jutted out

over a rocky beach and crashing waves far below, with unparalleled views of the harbor and the sea in one direction and the estuary and its surroundings in the other, the château was four stories tall with a soaring slate roof. Built in the seventeenth century in the Louis XIII baroque style, its facade of stone and brick had faded over the centuries to a soft rose-and-cream coloration. Heavily decorated with stone carvings of gargoyles and related otherworldly creatures above the eaves and around the innumerable arched windows, it bore the de Rocheford coat of arms embedded in the pediment above the front door. The gardens and grounds encompassed the five plus hectares at the top of the promontory. The home farm and the fields used in the cultivation of the Melon de Bourgogne grapes that were the estate's lifeblood spread out at the base of the cliff for another two hundred hectares.

Looking up at the house, a thousand memories swirled through her head in an instant: not the later years, when the economy had crashed and they'd had to sell Maman's jewelry and then the furniture piece by piece to survive, but the earlier ones, the happier ones. Running into Emmy's room at night when storms raged and thunder boomed so close above the château that the very walls seemed to shake, jumping into her sister's bed and huddling under the covers with her until the night grew still again; singing, always singing, especially Maman's favorite, "Ca c'est Paris," in duet with Emmy as Maman played the Mistinguett tune on the piano in the green parlor; hanging over the banister, first with Emmy and then, as Emmy grew up, alone, watching the girls in their swirling dance frocks, the boys with their slicked-back hair and correct evening clothes that made them look so grown up. She remembered Emmy, sixteen at the time, beautiful in a white party dress, looking up to find her there behind the banister where the two of them used to watch the partygoers together. Emmy had smiled and waved, just a small wave, not enough to give her little sister's presence away, and whispered, *"Je te tiens, tu me tiens."* It was their catchphrase — *I've got you, you've got me* — taken from a nursery rhyme in a book their mother used to read to them, and it immediately made Genevieve feel better, reassuring her that the twosome that had been her and Emmy was unbroken. Then, later, Emmy had brought up a selection of delicacies from the refreshment table that they'd shared, giggling at the tales Emmy told about the boys she'd danced with, before Emmy went down to rejoin the festivities. Genevieve felt a stab of nostalgia for those long-ago days, for the way things had been, for the glittering parties she had never, in all the years she had lived there, been officially old enough to attend — not that that had stopped her. Nothing and no one had ever been able to stop her from doing anything she chose, although her mother had certainly tried.

Maman. Papa. Emmy. How she longed for them.

Despite the way it had ended, despite the darkness and the pain, all she wanted to do in that moment was race the rest of the way to the top of the cliff, race up the imposing stone staircase that led to the front door, race inside to *them.*

But they're all gone. The shaft of pain that accompanied the thought was agonizing.

A flag had been mounted beside the front door. The wind caught it, set it to waving. Red, white and black: a swastika.

Her mind recoiled. She took an instinctive step back.

Papa would never permit . . .

But they said he was dead.

A German soldier came out the front door. An officer in a peaked cap and greatcoat, calling a cheerful *"Auf Wiedersehen"* to someone behind him in the house.

Genevieve melted into the shadow of the trees as two soldiers came running around the side of the château to stand at attention while the officer descended the steps. At the same time, a big black Mercedes-Benz, its tires crunching over the gravel drive, came round from the back where the garages and stables were located. One of the soldiers opened the rear car door. The officer got in, the soldier slammed the door shut and the car drove away.

The soldiers then went up the steps and into the house. She could only assume they were quartered there.

Her heart gave an odd little kick. With a real effort of will she managed to shift a mental gear that put her immediate visceral reaction behind her. That there were Nazis living at Rocheford was simply one more blow she had to accept, one more desecration wrought by war.

Turning, she walked swiftly through the trees along the path that wound through this last heavily wooded part of the cliff.

If her mother was in hiding, she would not be in the house anyway.

But Genevieve had a good idea where she might be.

That knowledge was the reasonable part of what had prompted her headlong rush to Rocheford. The other part was pure unreasoning emotion.

Leaving the path, pushing through a tangle of hollies and gorse overhung with vines, she reached the fissure in the rock that would be invisible to anyone outside the curtain of plants and slipped inside. The passage was narrow and crooked, a tight fit in places even for someone as slender as herself. The stone on either side was the rough, cold granite of the cliff that supported the house. Barely enough light filtered through to enable her to see the wooden door at the end — and, beside it, the knee-level gash in the stone that was just wide enough for a woman's smallest finger to probe inside.

She crouched, probed and found it, stashed away in that crack where it had been kept for the whole of her life, and longer: a key.

Fishing it out, she unlocked the door, then tucked the key safely back inside the gash. Doing so had been drilled into her by her mother, whose spare key it was, until the action became as automatic as breathing.

She pushed the door open. The heavy panel moved without making a sound: no creak, no groan. Which told her that the door had been used recently and had been cared for to prevent the rust and swelling with which the damp sea air afflicted all things wooden and metal.

No sound, either, from inside what was in essence a small natural cave that opened through a door on its other end into the outermost of the château's labyrinthian cellars.

Genevieve found herself hesitating on the threshold, peering cautiously into pitch darkness as a pungent fishy odor rolled out to envelop her.

She knew that smell: mushrooms. It brought her mother back to her as vividly as if Lillian stood before her. All her life, her mother had studied mushrooms, collected them, cultivated them.

Her hopes soared: she had not been inside the cave in years, but it was obvious from the ease with which she had opened the door, from the smell — living, growing mushrooms — from the very quality of the air, that someone made frequent and familiar use of it.

Who could it be, except —

"Ach, look, it's the BDM!" That taunting cry — the BDM was the League of German Girls, the distaff segment of the Hitler Youth — made her jump. The voice belonged to a man she could only assume was a soldier. It floated down from above, from the château grounds. A second soldier, clearly indignant at being jeeringly called a girl, shot back, "Shut your mouth, imbecile, and get moving."

A shiver of warning slid down Genevieve's spine as she was reminded of exactly how close the Germans were. She closed her lips, which had been parted to call out to her mother: she dared not, lest she bring the soldiers down upon them.

Cursing herself for not having thought to bring a torch, she walked cautiously inside the cave, looking about her as she traversed the well-worn stone underfoot. It was warmer in here, and the air was heavy and moist. The shaft of dim light from the open doorway allowed her to see only so far: the high curved ceiling, the uneven corners, the nooks and crannies shrouded in gloom. Her mother, unsurprisingly, was nowhere to be seen.

If Lillian was in hiding, logic dictated that she would have whisked out of sight at the opening of the door. If she was injured, she could be lying on the floor, tucked into a corner, curled up anywhere, concealed by darkness.

Narrowing her eyes, Genevieve tried probing the shadows: she could see nothing.

Only then did it occur to her to wonder what she would do with her mother if she found her. *Save her* had been the impetus that had driven her to Cherbourg, but exactly how that was to be accomplished she hadn't questioned. Now she did. The logistics were daunting: she had to be back in Paris, at the theater and prepared to go onstage, for a six o'clock show. Attempting the return journey in the company of a woman being actively hunted by the Nazis would be beyond risky. If Lillian was wounded or injured, the task of getting her to Paris became that much harder. It was also possible that Lillian would be too injured to travel. Then what?

I'll worry about that when I find her.

Everything else must fall into place from there.

Walking deeper into the cave, ears straining to separate the outside noises from any possible sounds coming from the darkness in front of her, she saw the shadowy outline of the wooden table where her mother was accustomed to sit while she cleaned the mushrooms, sorted them or removed the pores from the undersides of mushroom caps, which was a delicate, tedious procedure.

Placing a hand on the smooth, cool surface, Genevieve glanced down to find her mother's curved knife with the scarred beechwood handle and brush on one end resting mere centimeters from the tips of her fingers. There was no mistaking that the knife was the same, that the table was the same.

Her throat tightened. Despite everything, despite all that had happened, it seemed impossible that she had stayed away so long.

Lillian had taught her the fine art of handling mushrooms at that table, with that knife. A vision of her younger self, in her oldest frock with a kerchief tied around her head to keep out the dirt that might sift down from the ceiling, seated there while her mother, similarly attired, lifted the mushrooms they had collected together from a basket as she explained how to tell the ones that were good to eat from the poisonous ones replayed itself in her mind's eye.

She had always loved to go into the marsh to gather mushrooms with her mother, then bring them in here to sort and clean. Possibly, she saw with the wisdom of hindsight, because Emmy had wanted nothing to do with it. Fastidious Emmy had hated the marsh, and the cave, and mushrooms.

This was a place and an interest that she and Lillian alone had shared.

A heavy ache radiated out from the middle of her chest.

Remembering how close the four of them had been once upon a time hurt.

She would never have suspected that in the deepest recesses of her heart, beyond the chasm created by Vivi's death, they remained her family still.

The years of estrangement had felt long and hard. At times she'd been so lonely, and missed them so terribly, that it was a physical ache inside her. But to reach out to them would be to open a door to the past, and that she couldn't do.

The past held so much pain. Rejection, shame, loss — closing herself off from it had been the only way she'd been able to survive.

Shuddering, Genevieve thrust the memories from her mind.

She glanced down. Besides the knife there was also an oil lamp on the table — no electricity in here.

Wait. She heard something — she thought

she heard something — at the far end of the cave. Her gaze snapped up. Was something — some*body* — there?

Loath to move completely beyond the reach of the triangle of light, she stayed where she was. Her eyes having grown more accustomed to the darkness, she peered intently toward where she thought the sound had come from. She saw nothing, heard nothing more.

After a moment of concentrated listening with no result, the tension in her body eased. She turned her attention to assessing everything she could see. Years before, shallow tiers of earth and growing medium had been built terrace-style up the walls. Now a variety of mushrooms filled the tiers. The cèpes with their spongy undersides; the reddish-tinted sanguins; the pied de moutons, so called because they looked like a sheep's foot; the large and small amethysts; the grisettes; the common funnel caps: all those and more she recognized. Trowels and rakes and watering cans hung from their accustomed hooks. Wicker baskets were stacked on shelves. As far as she could tell, nothing had changed since she had last entered this place at the age of fifteen.

She had no doubt at all that this was still the workroom, and the work, of her mother.

Beyond the end of the table, from the area where she thought the sound had come, the darkness remained impenetrable. If Lillian was there, she gave no sign. Of course, even if Lillian was there and saw her, she would appear to her mother as no more than a dark silhouette against the light filtering in through the door. Lillian almost certainly would not recognize that silhouette as her younger daughter. After all this time, she had to be just about the last person her mother would expect to see.

There was no help for it.

Taking a breath, all too conscious of the danger of being overheard, Genevieve whispered, “Maman.”

A rustle of movement was the only warning she got before someone leaped on her from behind.

Chapter Fourteen

A thick arm snatched her off her feet, yanking her painfully back against a large male body. Even as a scream tried to blast its way out of her throat, a rough hand clapped over her mouth, stifling any sound.

"Be quiet." The warning was fierce for all that it was whispered. His grip shifted, and something cold and sharp pricked the delicate skin of her neck.

Genevieve froze, her struggles dying stillborn, stopped instantly by the feel of a knife pressed to the soft place just below her chin. Her blood thundered in her ears. She hung motionless in the hold of her captor, listening to his harsh breathing, tasting the saltiness of the ungloved palm that crushed her lips, smelling the scent of — was it smoke? — that clung to him. His arms were big and his body was thick and his legs were like tree trunks.

"The throat — it cuts like butter." There was no mistaking the deadly nature of the threat growled into her ear. She could feel his chest heaving against her back. As the door swung silently closed and pitch darkness overtook them, fear curdled her stomach.

At the same time, on the far side of the table, a match flared. Grappling with the toe-curling realization that there were at least two men and possibly more in the cave with her, she watched with horrified fascination as the lamp was lit.

The wick caught, sending up a tongue of flame to combat the darkness. As the flickering light spread, the man replaced the lamp's glass chimney and straightened. Shaking out the match he'd used and dropping it onto the floor where he crushed it beneath his foot, he scowled at her across the table. He was a big man, fiftyish, grizzled dark hair, large triangular nose, jutting chin and —

Familiar.

Even as she squinted at him, cudgeling her memory in an attempt to place him, he appeared to examine her face. She realized her scarf had fallen back so that her hair and features were exposed. Would he recognize the Black Swan?

"You —" He broke off, eyes widening, then finished in an almost reverent tone, "Mademoiselle Genevra?" That he knew her for who she had been was worse. Or better. She couldn't decide. Without waiting for her to respond, he continued in a rush, "My God, it is you! Thank God, thank God! You are come with Mademoiselle Emmy? I sent word to her as soon as I found out what had happened, but I was afraid she might be too late." Seeming to choke up, he shot a hard look at the man holding her. "Let her go, you fool. It's them. They've come."

Genevieve found herself instantly released with a muttered apology. Off balance after being unceremoniously dropped back onto her feet, she grasped the edge of the table to steady herself. Behind her, the man who'd grabbed her folded his knife and restored it to his pocket, which she found at least a little bit reassuring. With her peripheral vision she registered a third man, clearly the one who had closed the door, approaching the table from that direction. Average height, sinewy looking, bald: she didn't know him. Realizing that he must have been hiding behind the door the whole time she was in the cave gave her the shivers.

"I knew Mademoiselle Emmy would come as soon as she got my message," the first man said. "Or she would get the SOE to send somebody else if she could not — to save the baroness."

Mademoiselle Emmy? Was expected to come with the SOE? Her sister was working with the SOE? Calm, careful Emmy? It seemed impossible — but then, so did so much else that had befallen them all. Emmy had fled to England with her new husband in 1939, at the very beginning of the war, but she had lost track of her after that. She tabled her confusion for the moment and instead focused on what most concerned her.

"Where is the baroness?" Zeroing in on that one vital piece of information, she kept her focus on the man who had lit the lamp.

"She's been arrested. They're holding her at a house in town. Under heavy guard. No one's been able to get near her." He rubbed a weary hand over his face. "You're only just in time. Word is they'll be moving her tonight. In my opinion, that's the best chance we'll have to attempt a rescue. How many do you have with you? Where is Mademoiselle Emmy?"

Something clicked in Genevieve's mind.

"Monsieur Vartan?" She knew she was right even before his expression confirmed it. While she was growing up, Henri Vartan had been as much a part of the landscape of Rocheford as the sea. Often he would come to the house to confer with her father. Always she saw him about the estate. Now, clearly, he was involved in the Resistance, as were these other men. And her parents. And Emmy. For the briefest of moments her mind boggled at this further proof of the previously unimaginable places the war had taken them. Then her other urgent concern asserted itself. "My father — what do you know of him? I've heard that —

that he is dead."

"Yes." Vartan's face creased with sorrow. "Two nights ago, from gunshot wounds. He died quickly, you understand. A hero. Betrayed by a filthy collaborator."

The last bud of hope she'd been cherishing withered in her chest. Grief pierced her heart. She had to steel herself against the pain.

"My mother was with him? Was she wounded?"

"She was with him. As far as we know, she was not injured."

What lay unspoken between them was the meaning of that *was.* The Nazis were notorious for the brutality with which they treated captured members of the Resistance. Once they had her in custody, their treatment of her would be harsh. Trying to push away the images thus conjured up, Genevieve swallowed hard.

"How many do you have with you?" Vartan repeated his previous question, his tone urgent now. "For our part, there is only myself and one other left. These two —" he indicated the men with him "— have been betrayed to the Nazis. They're being searched for as we speak and are hiding here as they wait to be transported out, so they can be of no use in this matter. We will need at least six to attempt a rescue if they try to move the baroness by car, which I feel is the most likely way. If they should decide to use the train instead, the thing becomes much more difficult. Our best chance in that case would be to try to stage an assault on the car on the way to the station, but we would have little advance notice and only a brief opportunity in which to act."

"Whatever you do, the reprisals will be great," the man who'd held the knife on her said. The deep rumble that was his voice matched his oversize build. He had shaggy salt-and-pepper hair and a full beard. His clothing suggested a shopkeeper. "At some point, the cost becomes too high."

"It is the *baroness.*"

"Hers is just one life."

Vartan stared hard at him.

"I know your brother was one of those taken in for questioning, Tomas, and I am sorry for it, but he knows nothing, and I am sure they will release him in due course. Setting aside the fact that we all are greatly indebted to both the baron and baroness for many, many acts of kindness, the fact that they are moving the baroness should alarm all of us. It says they suspect she has information they want, and, believe me, whatever information she has they will torture out of her. At the very least, they will learn our names. For the sake of us all, she must be rescued if there is any reasonable chance of accomplishing it." Vartan held the other man's gaze until it dropped in defeat, then looked at Genevieve. "Where is Mademoiselle Emmy?"

"She isn't here," Genevieve said. "I'm alone. I was in Paris when I heard and I came as quickly as I could. We must wait for Emmy, if indeed I understood you correctly that she is with the SOE and they are coming?"

Vartan's expression changed. She could read the sudden wariness in his eyes.

"It may be that you have no business knowing that," he said slowly. "Or knowing anything about any of us."

The man with the knife — Tomas, Vartan had called him — took an audible breath and drew himself up as if in readiness to grab her again. The third man stepped sideways, blocking her path to the door. The rising air of menace that emanated from them as they stared at her confirmed how perilous her situation was. In these difficult times, to plot against the Nazi occupiers was to risk death, and collaborators anxious to curry favor with the new overlords were everywhere. If Vartan and the others thought she might run to the Germans with what she now knew about them, they would be foolish indeed to ever let her leave the cave alive.

In their minds, it was her life or theirs.

Her heart started to pound under the weight of those basilisk stares, but she kept her composure and focused her attention on Vartan.

"Emmy and I are not together, it is true. But we both — we all —" her glance encompassed the three men "— want the same thing — to rescue the baroness. My *mother.* You have known me all my life, Monsieur Vartan. I am a de Rocheford, don't forget. And I am part of the Resistance, too." She said that last quietly, with a kind of defiant pride. It was the first time she had ever claimed such a thing out loud.

"Alone, you cannot help us." Vartan's tone was grim, but the suspicion with which he'd regarded her was gone. Following his lead, the aggressive stances of the other men relaxed. "We do not have the numbers. We must still wait upon the arrival of the SOE."

"What makes you think they'll come?" Genevieve asked.

"Mademoiselle Emmy will have received my message. She regularly visits the baron and baroness, not only out of affection but to coordinate their activities with the needs of the Allies. She will come now, with what I pray is a team of sufficient size to allow us to do what needs to be done. The question is will they arrive in time."

"And if they don't?"

"We're better off doing nothing than trying and failing. Once —"

A quick rap on the door, followed by three carefully spaced knocks, interrupted. They all glanced around, Genevieve startled and the three men as if the sound, which she realized must be a prearranged signal, was not unexpected.

At a nod from Vartan the third man, who was closest, moved to the door and opened it.

The man who entered was perhaps fifty, small and dark in the way of the Basques. His step was quick, his manner intense.

"We must go." He glanced around, made a hurry-up gesture. "All the soldiers who've been manning the checkpoints have been called into town. We have this small window. *Vite, vite.*"

"What's to do?" Vartan asked, as Tomas and the third man rushed into the darkness at the far end of the cave.

"There's to be a public execution."

The news hit Genevieve like a shot to the heart, rooting her to the spot. Her lips parted, but no sound came out. Instead, like a landed fish, she gulped futilely at the air.

Maman.

"The extra soldiers are needed to control the crowd. We will never have a better chance than this to get these men away," the newcomer added, motioning impatiently for the men, who reappeared carrying rucksacks that she could only guess contained their belongings, to walk past him and exit the cave, which they did. "The search for them is intensifying."

She was afraid, sorely afraid, to ask, but she had to know.

"Who's to be executed?" Her voice was hoarse. Cold ripples of dread raced over her skin.

The newcomer gave her an appraising glance.

"This is?" he asked Vartan, who had stopped to blow out the lamp.

"One of us." Vartan's answer, with its pointed lack of an introduction, was meant to protect both her and the newcomer, Genevieve realized. She realized, too, that after what had been his clearly inadvertent use of Tomas's name, Vartan had never named the third man. This indicated not so much a lack of trust in her as a hard-learned caution, and she accepted it as such: people could not betray what they did not know.

Vartan's reply seemed enough for the newcomer, because he turned away.

Without answering her question, an answer she had to have. She was hideously, horribly afraid she already knew it anyway. Dry-mouthed with fear, she hurried after the man as he walked out the door and barely remembered to pull the scarf up around her face before she caught up with him. Not that she really expected any of these men to recognize the Black Swan in Berthe's shapeless coat, with the shabby scarf concealing her hair and shadowing her features. Especially when she considered that without her stage makeup she looked like any ordinary girl, and people pretty much saw what they expected to see and no one would expect to see the so-called toast of Europe here under these conditions. Still, it was best to be careful. The last thing she wanted was to be identified as Genevieve Dumont, which would not only put her in danger but in the wrong hands inevitably lead back to Max and his network, endangering them as well.

"Who is to be executed?" she demanded as she caught up to the newcomer, who because of his larger size was slower in negotiating the narrow fissure than she was. As important as it was to attract as little attention as possible to herself, in that moment it felt even more important to get the answer. If it was indeed her mother — what would she do? What could she do?

Something. Flutters of panic took wing in her stomach as she sought vainly for a course of action.

"I don't know." A shrug accompanied his reply. The sense she got from him was that he was indifferent, because it wasn't part of the job he'd come there to do. Before she could question him further, he was through the fissure, slipping behind the curtain of vines and out of sight.

Vartan, who'd been locking the door with what was apparently his own key the last glimpse she'd had of him, had caught up with them in time to hear the exchange. He gave her a quelling frown.

"Even if he knew, he wouldn't tell you. He doesn't know you. And he has learned to be suspicious of strangers, as have we all. If he were to consider you a threat in even the smallest degree, he would see it as his duty to kill you. You want to stay away from him."

"I have to know —"

"What good will it do?" The heaviness of Vartan's voice underlined her deepest fear: if the Nazis were planning to execute Lillian, there was nothing she, or any of them, could do to stop it.

"I have to know," Genevieve repeated stubbornly. Turning her back on him, she slid out from behind the curtain of vines into the cold green dimness of the forest.

Chapter Fifteen

The newcomer waited with the others. He gave her another of those hard, appraising looks as she emerged to join them. It made her nervous.

"Follow me. Be quick and quiet," he said to the group in general as Vartan appeared behind her, and with the two others following, he loped off down the path in the opposite direction from the way she had come up.

Acutely conscious of the too-fast beating of her pulse, Genevieve fell in behind the three men, with Vartan bringing up the rear. Remembering the soldiers on the château grounds earlier that for all she knew were still there, she didn't speak, nor did anyone else. The only sounds the small party made were their quickened breathing as the leader set a bruising pace and the hurried slither of their footsteps on the path, which was steep and slick with fallen leaves.

Finally, winded, they emerged just above a

dirt road where an ancient-looking farm truck waited in a turnout, blocked from the view of anyone passing on the main road by the sheltering woods. In front of her, on the other side of the road, were the hectares of land where Rocheford's vines had been lovingly tended for more than a century. Now the fields lay muddy and forlorn. Row upon row of broken, shriveled clumps of dead sticks and blackened leaves were all that remained of the grapes that had been the estate's primary source of income. Even when that income had dropped to a pittance and Papa had been forced to take a job in town so that they could survive, the pride had remained. Papa had cared for the fields and the vines with his own hands, fighting to keep what he called the heart and soul of Rocheford alive.

Shock stopped her in her tracks. She could only gape. Winter was the primary time for pruning the vines. In spring they burst forth renewed. By now the sap should be rising, the buds breaking and the perfect flowers — so-called because they didn't need bees for pollination — appearing in delicate white clouds. Instead there was ruin.

As Vartan caught up to her she gestured, stunned, at the fields. "The vines —"

Stopping beside her, he gave a mournful shake of his head. "We tried to save them, all of us, the old hands, even in the last years working side by side with your father for no pay. It was no use. When our army retreated toward the coast after the fall of France, the Germans followed with their panzers. Their tanks went right through these fields. Their soldiers bivouacked here. The vines were crushed, trampled. Then came the Allies with their air strikes. The vines were bombed, burned. So many times, I've lost count. Until there was too much damage. In any case, for many months now there has been no one left to care for them. They are destroyed, just like everything else we valued."

Genevieve felt sick to her stomach. Her first thought was how upset her father must be — must have been.

I should have returned sooner. I should have been here to help him bear the burden.

A lump formed in her throat, and the topic she had been avoiding became impossible to hold at bay any longer.

"He was happy?"

"Your Papa?" Vartan shrugged. "Who is happy, in these times? He was surviving, and that was enough."

"Where is he? His — body? Do you know?" She could hardly get the words out.

Vartan's mouth thinned. "They took him. Dumped him in the sea like trash."

She closed her eyes, let the anger and the hate and the pain wash over her. Damn the *boche.* Then, *Maman is alive. I must think of her.*

I never want to see you again. Those were the last words she had said to her mother. At the time, she'd meant them with every cell in her body. Now her insides shriveled when she thought that they might be the last words she would ever speak to her in this life.

She opened her eyes, squared her shoulders and walked on down the hill. Vartan followed.

The newcomer had pulled back the tarpaulin covering the truck bed. As she approached, Genevieve saw that it was loaded with carboys filled with a golden liquid. With a rattle and a creak of hinges, he lowered a narrow wooden panel beneath the floor of the truck bed to reveal a hidden compartment.

"Climb in." He gestured to Tomas and the other man.

"I'm too big," Tomas objected, hanging back and eyeing the space with misgiving. Meanwhile the other man, with a resolute expression, shoved his rucksack into the opening, stuck his head in after it, and followed that with his shoulders and chest before wriggling the rest of his body inside.

"There is no other way," the newcomer said to Tomas. "Get in or stay behind."

"If he's going toward town, could you ask him to give me a ride?" Genevieve spoke to Vartan in an undertone as Tomas, with much kicking and squirming and under-the-breath cursing, both on his part and that of the newcomer who was rather brutally assisting him, managed to squeeze into the secret compartment despite his doubts. Her voice was steady, but she feared the desperation she was feeling must show in her eyes. The thought of waiting for the bus made her want to jump out of her skin. If transport could not be arranged soon, she would run every step of the way if she had to, to get there. Each minute of delay was agony.

Vartan went up to the newcomer, who was closing the panel and locking it in place, and said something. The newcomer responded with a sour glance in Genevieve's direction and then a shrug.

Vartan beckoned her over. "Our friend here has graciously agreed to give us a ride to town. I must just get my bicycle."

Genevieve registered that *us* with a twinge of relief: at least she would not have to face what was coming alone. Without a word to Genevieve, the newcomer turned to walk toward the truck cab. Determined not to be left behind no matter what, Genevieve did not wait but climbed up into the cab as the newcomer got behind the wheel.

A moment later, the bicycle having joined the carboys in the back of the truck, Vartan heaved himself in beside Genevieve. The truck jounced onto the road and headed out.

"I'm not going all the way into Cherbourg. I can take you only as far as where the road branches off for Valognes," the newcomer warned them.

"That will do," Vartan said. Genevieve said nothing. Her heart bumped against her ribs. It was all she could do to sit still.

Hurry, hurry, hurry.

Though she bit her lip to keep from saying them aloud, the words beat a tattoo through her head.

The truck pulled over at the edge of town.

"You will send word?" Vartan asked.

"I will," the newcomer answered.

Vartan nodded and got out. Genevieve slid out behind him.

Perhaps if she went to whoever was in charge and told them she was the Black Swan and Lillian was her mother, she could persuade them to spare her.

It was a nearly impossible hope, she knew, and it came with a host of inherent problems, not the least of which was that it might well turn the eyes of the Nazis toward Max. But she could think of nothing else that had any chance of succeeding.

Desperation knotted her stomach.

I can't just let her die.

Genevieve rode through town seated on the handlebars of Vartan's battered old bicycle, fingers locked around the cold metal, teeth clenched against the jolting as the tires bumped over pavement pockmarked with craters left from the bombs, chest so tight with anxiety that she found it difficult to breathe. With gas almost impossible to obtain, bicycles had become the most common mode of transportation throughout France, and they attracted no attention now.

The civilian population was sadly diminished. Genevieve remembered a bustling city of forty thousand people. From what she could tell, only a fraction remained. Shops were closed and houses were shuttered. Thin, shabbily dressed women hurried along the streets clutching shopping bags and holding small children by the hand, their heads bowed as they did their best to avoid notice.

Soldiers stood on every corner, far more of them than she had noticed earlier. She realized with a fresh burst of fear that they must have been ordered to take up their positions in case of trouble. A repeated announcement blasting from military trucks rolling through the streets advised that there would be a public execution in the square at Old Town at one o'clock. All adult citizens who were not at that time engaged in vital work were required to attend. Knowing that the Germans were sticklers for punctuality, she glanced at her watch: it lacked thirteen minutes of the hour.

A crowd of about a thousand was already gathering around the square, which stood almost in the shadow of Fort du Roule. Built high atop a rocky hill overlooking the harbor and the city, Fort du Roule was a coastal fortress freshly armed and outfitted by the Germans to ward off attacks by sea. As formidable as it was, the fort itself was nothing new: it had stood in that spot since the seventeenth century. Genevieve's eyes focused instead on the massive concrete wall that stretched out along the harbor and beyond. Newly built, ugly and raw, bristling with troop pillboxes, machine guns, antiaircraft weapons and searchlights, it dominated its surroundings. Such an overwhelming display of military might sent goose bumps racing over her skin.

She remembered the old men in the bus. Were they right? Was Germany's ultimate victory inevitable?

With difficulty she tore her gaze away. Her heart sank as she registered for the first time how overwhelming the military presence truly was. How would it be possible for the Allies to prevail against that? For that matter, how would it be possible for her, alone, or even with Vartan's help, to get her mother away?

Perhaps I can trade with them for her life. Max had said the Reich minister of armaments and war production had just personally contacted him, declaring himself a fan and inquiring about the possibility of her doing a concert in Berlin.

If they would only release her mother, she would perform a dozen concerts.

But who would she even see to make such a deal? She had no idea, and there was *no time.*

She wished Max were here.

Rising panic quickened her breathing, dried her mouth.

The streets around the square had been closed to vehicular traffic. They were packed with people. Vartan's bicycle wound its way among them, slowing repeatedly as it avoided pedestrians and bumped over holes in the cobblestones. Genevieve gritted her teeth as she clung to her precarious perch.

A brisk salt wind blew in from the bay, kicking up whitecaps and sending wispy clouds scudding. Pale sunlight slanted down to gleam on a metal gutter here, a glass window there. Against a background of teal blue sea and ice-blue sky, Old Town, rising up from the docks in layers like a wedding cake, retained at first glance much of the charm it held in her memory. Stone buildings with elaborate wrought iron balconies wrapped around a maze of narrow, cobbled streets. The parklike square, once well kept and beautiful, was in the center of the uppermost layer.

Now, though, the trees were gone, and what grass remained was sparse. All that survived of the central fountain was its broken concrete pool. The cathedral at the far end had fared little better: one of its crenellated towers had been destroyed and a tarpaulin covered the resulting hole in its roof. The buildings around the square likewise bore visible marks of war damage.

As they reached the square, her heart sank. Armed soldiers ringed the perimeter, facing outward, standing shoulder to shoulder with their rifles in their hands to form a bulwark against the crowd that, because of the pressure from those pouring in from behind, surged ever closer to them. More armed soldiers hunkered down on roofs. Still more were positioned on balconies and in upper windows of the buildings. The numbers were staggering. The silent message was clear: any wrong move on the part of the citizenry would result in a massacre.

When the bicycle could go no farther, Genevieve slid off the handlebars onto legs that were unsteady. With fingers stiff from holding on so tightly, she adjusted her scarf, making sure it was pulled far forward enough to hide her face. Shifting from foot to foot, barely able to contain her agitation, she had to fight to hold her ground next to Vartan in the midst of the jostling crowd. A steady hum composed of countless low-voiced conversations rose above the muffled thuds and booms and hammerings of the busy harbor, where what sounded like a hundred projects were currently underway. Except for a few disjointed fragments that reached her ears — "retaliation," "damn the Brits," "pilot," "all their fault," "how many?" — the individual voices were so intermingled that it reminded her of the buzzing of a swarm of bees. A glance around confirmed what she already knew: dismal resignation was the prevalent mood. Some jaws were clenched in anger, some eyes glittered with outrage, but most of those in attendance stood with shoulders hunched and faces blank. Sickened, maybe, but helpless in the face of what was to come and unwilling to do anything to attract the attention of those who held over them the power of life and death.

"What can we do?" she whispered.

Vartan didn't reply. The bleakness of his expression made her stomach drop straight down to her toes. It told her as clearly as words might have done how desperate he considered the situation to be.

"Could Emmy —" she didn't want to be any more specific; she was whispering, but even a whisper could be overheard "— be here somewhere? Or . . . or someone?"

Vartan would know what she meant: someone from the SOE or the Resistance, anyone whose purpose it might be to stage a rescue.

She could barely hear his reply. "It's possible. We won't know until . . ." He hesitated, scanning the crowd. "Until we know."

She knew what he was saying: until a rescue attempt was launched. She moistened her lips. But what if it wasn't?

"We have to —" she began.

His fierce whisper interrupted. "Alone, we can do nothing, do you understand?" His eyes gleamed a warning at her. "Do you not see that they have an army? Getting ourselves arrested or killed won't help the baroness."

He was right, she knew. But, dear God, she couldn't just watch in silence while her mother was murdered in front of her eyes!

I have to do something. There has to be something . . .

He must have seen the distress in her face, because he grabbed her arm. "Maybe it's better you leave now. You came by train? I'll take you to the station. We can slip away if we go now. Anyone watching will think we are looking for a better viewing spot."

"No! No." Whatever happened, she had to be here. To witness Lillian's death would be an unimaginable torture. To walk away and leave her to die with no one of her own present was unthinkable.

His fingers dug painfully into her flesh. "Then you must promise me —"

Three military transport trucks roared into the blocked-off street on the opposite side of the square and squealed to a stop. Genevieve's eyes riveted on them, and everyone else's must have, too, because the crowd fell silent. She scarcely noticed when Vartan's hand dropped away from her arm. Spine straightening until she stood tall and stiff as a mannequin, one hand gripping the handlebars for support, she watched with a pounding heart as a contingent of German soldiers poured out of the covered back of the last of the trucks. Surrounding the other trucks, they stood guard as what looked like maybe thirty civilians were forced out of them and marched at gunpoint into the square.

Chapter Sixteen

The civilians looked tired and dirty. They wore everyday clothes, as if they had been snatched from their jobs or whatever they had been doing without warning. Some of them stumbled as they walked. They had suffered injuries: one clutched an apparently broken arm to his chest, another's leg dragged, a third's shirt was black and stiff with what Genevieve was sure, from his bruised, swollen face, must be blood. As they drew nearer, forming a line down the middle of the square facing the crowd at the soldiers' direction, her mouth tasted sour with fear. Her gaze darted along the line. Quickly she scrutinized each one. They were all men. Her mother was not among them.

Her relief was so profound that she actually felt light-headed.

An officer stepped in front of the line of prisoners. From his uniform she knew that he belonged to the SS, and her skin prickled with foreboding. Facing the crowd, he lifted a bullhorn to his mouth. His booming voice drowned out every other sound.

"I am Sturmbannführer Walter Schmidt. It is my unpleasant duty to inform you that several days ago some of your fellow Cherbourgeois participated in a crime against the Third Reich and all loyal French citizens. They attempted to rescue and smuggle out of the country a downed British aircrew. The British pilot has already been captured. Most of the traitors who assisted him have likewise been taken into custody. Our interrogation of them has already yielded much fruit. Two members of the British aircrew and the remaining French traitors who assisted them are still being sought. They will, I assure you, be found. The city of Cherbourg has been judged guilty of harboring such traitors. For that, there is a punishment, which will be visited upon these men, who have been selected from the population at random, as a lesson to your community. They will be shot."

The silence after Schmidt finished speaking was electric. It reminded Genevieve of the charge in the air right before a thunderstorm hit.

"No! No!" The outburst from the depths of the crowd came as Schmidt turned and gestured to the soldiers behind him, who responded by shoving the condemned men to their knees. A woman, middle-aged and thin, dressed in a ratty overcoat, with graying hair flying from an untidy bun, burst through the wall of soldiers lining the square to dart toward the prisoners. "You cannot! He has done nothing! I beg of you —"

"Maman —" One of the prisoners staggered to his feet. He was gangly and tall but clearly very young, with long dark hair straggling around a face that was all bones and angles. A soldier standing behind him clubbed him brutally in the back of the neck with his rifle butt. With a cry he fell to his knees again before keeling over onto his side, where he curled moaning into a fetal position.

"Karl! Karl!" The woman, wailing, had almost reached the prisoner before two soldiers, who'd broken out of the line surrounding the square to give chase, grabbed her and started dragging her away. "Please! He has done nothing, I tell you! In the name of common decency, you cannot! He is only thirteen!"

Mingled pity and horror clutched at Genevieve's chest. Thirteen! A child.

Schmidt snapped, "Fire!"

The bang of thirty sidearms discharging almost simultaneously made Genevieve jump and clap a hand to her mouth. The echoing crack was loud enough to hurt her ears, to scatter, screaming, a flock of seagulls flying overhead, to wrench the most heartrending cry she had ever heard from the throat of the now bereaved mother, still being dragged away.

The rest of the prisoners pitched forward to lie sprawled alongside Karl in the withered grass. In that first terrible instant, a fine red mist hung in the air above the fallen bodies. Then it fell, covering the inert forms with a lacy pattern in vivid scarlet, disappearing into the darker red puddles beginning to roll across the ground.

A collective gasp from the crowd preceded the most awful silence Genevieve had ever experienced. A smell — gunpowder, raw meat, other things too awful to contemplate — was borne toward them on the wind.

My God. But she didn't say it aloud. Instead she hung on to the handlebars as nausea roiled her stomach. If she hadn't had the bicycle to cling to, she didn't think she could have stayed on her feet.

Schmidt faced the crowd again, lifted the bullhorn to his mouth.

"That is all. You are dismissed," he said.

Under the watchful eyes of the soldiers, the crowd began to melt away. The noise that would have been expected as part of the breakup of such a large gathering, the chatter, the calling out, the slapping of shoulders and shaking of hands, all that was absent. Except for the rustle of clothing and the clomp of many feet on pavement, a heavy silence prevailed. It was composed, Genevieve thought, of equal parts shock and shame.

Without a word Vartan turned the bicycle around and, with her beside him, walked it back the way they had come. They walked because operating a bicycle seemed almost unbearably frivolous now, and besides the crowd was too dense to permit anyone to ride. Head lowered, she trudged along among the shuffling mass of her mute fellow witnesses to the horrific slaughter of innocents. Were they complicit, in their silence, their lack of action? But what could they have done? There was nothing, she knew. But still.

It was all she could do to continue to put one foot in front of the other, to keep from looking back at the limp, bloodied bodies that were now being thrown with sickening thuds into the back of one of the trucks that had been driven onto the grass to collect them.

When they were out of sight of the square, Vartan was approached by another man and stopped to talk, heads together, the conversation low and grave. Shaken to her core, Genevieve sank down on some nearby steps that led to the stoop of one of the pretty stone houses lining the street and clasped her hands tightly together in her lap.

The crowd streamed past. The weight of what they'd witnessed rode visibly on slumped shoulders. Sorrow and despair hung in the air like the salt smell of the sea.

Vartan finished his conversation and came to stand in front of her.

"They are monsters," Genevieve said. Her voice, thin but clear, hung in the air. Vartan's brows snapped together in quick alarm. Reminded by his expression of the danger of speaking out, she clamped her lips together lest another unwary word escape.

"We must go." There was a strain in his voice that hadn't been there before. "Come, we will walk together to the train station."

Genevieve stood up. The train station was not far away. Despite her fear for her mother, despite the bone-deep horror of what she had just witnessed, there was no choice: she had to go. She had to return to Paris, and she had to be there in time to take the stage. To miss her show was unthinkable. It would raise too many questions. There would be such an uproar — she grew tense thinking about it. She had never missed a show. She could not miss a show, especially not now. To do so would be to focus a pitiless German spotlight on herself and her troupe — and Max and his activities.

They walked with the bicycle between them, without speaking, until the crowd had thinned enough so that there was no chance they would be overheard. The station — a low stone building with a green tile roof — was within view. A train waited rumbling behind it: her train, the 2:10 to Paris, she was almost sure. Another train whistled a warning as it chugged in. The plume of gray smoke from the engine stretched back over the long line of passenger cars. The sulfur-like smell of burning coal that accompanied it made her grimace.

Vartan cleared his throat, slanted a look at her. "Mademoiselle Genevra . . ."

His voice triggered the angry, hushed words she'd been choking back. "You heard that bastard. My mother is one of those he was talking about. They are interrogating her. *Torturing* her. I must go, but you must launch your rescue. Perhaps Emmy will come in time. Whether she does or not, you must go ahead, do you understand? With the SOE or without them. If you can get her away and hide her, I will come back in the morning and —"

He shook his head. "No. It is too late. The baroness — she is not here. That is what my friend told me just now."

"What?" She stopped walking, frowned at him.

He stopped, too. "The gestapo came for her. They have already taken her away. We think perhaps to Paris, to Fort Mont-Valérien or Cherche-Midi or even to eighty-four avenue Foch."

"Oh, no." Genevieve's breath caught. The prisons Fort Mont-Valérien and Cherche-Midi were bad, but 84 avenue Foch! It was the gestapo headquarters in Paris, and the most dreaded address in the city. The interrogations that took place there were notorious for their cruelty. Few prisoners left the premises alive.

"Are you sure?" Her voice cracked.

"That she was taken? Yes. About her destination? Not so much. Although Paris is what we hear."

"Dear God." She swallowed hard. "When did they leave?"

"About an hour ago. In a convoy of three cars. My friend saw them go. They may have suspected we were planning something." He glanced around, his expression furtive. "There are wagging tongues everywhere. Come, we must walk."

They were already the object of curious glances from some of those who were quickly forming queues in front of the reopened shops in hopes of using their coupons to obtain a baguette or bit of meat for supper. Up ahead, a group of soldiers who'd been manning one of the barricades blocking traffic into Old Town were taking it down. The last thing she wanted was to attract their notice. Heart pounding, trying to look as though the most important thing on her mind was the lack of fresh vegetables, she moved over to walk closer to the buildings with Vartan as the streets reopened to what were mostly military vehicles. Her hands trembled, she discovered, and balled them into fists.

All too conscious of the proximity of the shoppers, she kept her voice scarcely louder than a breath. "What of those who were captured with her? Were they taken away as well?"

"They are dead."

"Killed — during interrogation?" Genevieve's blood ran cold.

"That is what we think."

"And my mother? What kind of shape is she in?"

"The baroness had to be carried to the car."

She felt as if she were choking. "How long do you think she can survive?"

"I don't know. They will do their best to keep her alive. Until they get what they want."

Anguish twisted her stomach. "In the end, they will kill her."

"I am afraid — yes."

So many thoughts ran through her head in such rapid succession that it was impossible to untangle them. She had to force herself to stay calm, to try to think, to keep moving steadily past the watchful soldiers toward the train station. A bus pulled up in front of it, disgorging a full complement of passengers, who walked up the steps to the terminal.

She said, "When we get to Paris, there are people you can go to for help, are there not? They can tell you where —"

"I am not going to Paris."

"What do you mean? You have to! You can't simply abandon her!"

"She will not be abandoned. But I must disappear for a while. My friend warned me — at this moment there is a search party on its way to my house."

"Oh, no . . ."

"It may mean nothing, a routine search like many others, but it may mean I am betrayed. I dare not chance it. I should have gone with —" he almost said a name, caught himself; she knew he meant in the truck with the newcomer "— the others. I stayed only to help the baroness, but I can do nothing for her now."

Incipient hysteria bubbled to life inside Genevieve. In the final analysis, she was a singer, not an agent, not an SOE operative. To have all the responsibility thrown back onto her — fright galvanized her. Lillian would be killed and there was nothing she, alone, could do to stop it.

"But what of my mother? Is there someone else who can come with me? Your friend you were talking to, perhaps?"

He grimaced. "You have to understand there are rules. Even if there was no search party, I wouldn't be going with you. I don't operate in Paris. Neither does my friend. I have no knowledge of the cells there. Each group of us works within our own area. For security's sake, we know only the identities of those in our own cell, and perhaps an outside contact or two. That way, if one is arrested, the whole network is not destroyed."

"But my mother —"

"There are other people who know about this, and now it is up to them to decide what course is best regarding her."

"What other people?"

"Higher up the chain of command than I."

"They don't know her! They might not —"

"When she left Cherbourg, the decision was taken out of my hands. I am sorry."

"You said yourself she must be rescued."

"Let us pray that is what happens."

"*Pray.* We need to do more than pray!"

His voice roughened. "Listen to me. You've put yourself in grave danger already. Merely knowing my identity and something about the cell here makes you a threat in the eyes of some. I have vouched for you, here, but that is all I can do. I am telling you, for your own sake, out of the respect I bear your parents, do not meddle further in this."

The finality of his tone told her that continuing to argue with him would be useless. They were halfway across the paved open area of iron benches and café tables that separated the last of the shops from the street in front of the station. Others were crossing the open area, too, heading for the station. She was glad of their presence to offset the occasional sweeping glances of the soldiers who were now loading sections of the barricade onto a truck. The incoming train had stopped at the station, and its disembarked passengers were beginning to stream out of the building and down the steps. An anxious glance at her watch told her that it was almost time for her to board her train. With the minutes ticking inexorably down, panic rose in her throat. Taking a deep breath, she beat it back.

Think. I must think.

She felt as if she were drowning and trying to save herself by grasping at the flimsiest of straws.

"Emmy — if Emmy comes. How can I get a message to her?"

"I can do that for you. If you will write it down."

What she picked up from his tone was that once he had done it, he felt he would have discharged any obligation to her.

"Yes. Yes, I will." Paper — a pencil or pen — did she have one? *Please . . .*

Stopping at one of the small circular tables, she set the shopping bag down on it, rummaged quickly through the contents, and came up with an envelope and a stubby pencil.

Tearing off a piece of the envelope, careful to make sure that it bore no identifying information, she started to write, then hesitated as it occurred to her that letting anyone, even such a longtime family loyalist as Vartan, know that she was staying at the Ritz might be dangerous. If her note should fall into the wrong hands, putting her address down in writing could prove utterly disastrous. With what had happened to her parents, the specter of betrayal had become terrifyingly real. Whether as Genevieve Dumont or Genevra de Rocheford, she could be arrested as quickly as anyone else if she was suspected of helping the Resistance.

"Be quick," Vartan said. Despite the day's breeziness, beads of sweat dotted his forehead and upper lip. He shot stealthy glances all around, down the length of the open area, over the queued-up shoppers, toward the train station, at the soldiers.

His fear fed her own. Gripping the pencil so hard her knuckles went white, she bent over the table and scribbled her message.

I need to see you. I'll be at the place where I dropped your birthday necklace, 9 in the morning for the next few days.

There. Only three people left in the world would know where that was, and she was one of them.

On her sister's never-to-be-forgotten fifteenth birthday, when they had been staying at the Ritz, their parents had presented Emmy with a pendant composed of five diamonds positioned around a large central pearl to form the shape of a star. "Because you are our shining star," Lillian had told Emmy with the tender, proud smile she always reserved for her elder daughter. It was the end of the evening in which they had seen Josephine Baker, the four of them were riding in the specially hired horse-drawn carriage taking them from an après-theater dinner back to the Ritz, the girls were in the filmy white *jeune fille*–appropriate evening dresses selected by their mother, the air was warm, the lights of Paris twinkled magically against a midnight velvet sky sprinkled with stars. After they stepped down onto the cobblestones of the place Vendôme, while the carriage clattered away, she had asked to see the necklace. Emmy had lifted it out of its presentation case and handed it to her, and she had held the lovely thing up by its chain to admire its sparkle by the flickering gaslight of the streetlamps — and promptly dropped it. To her horror, to everyone's horror, it had slithered through the grates of a storm drain and been lost forever.

"Finished?" Vartan's impatient mutter warned her time was up. On the impulse of a moment she dashed off a final word: *Bébé.* Using the once despised nickname as her signature would both conceal her identity from outsiders and leave no doubt in her sister's mind that the message was indeed from her. Then she folded the paper into a small square and handed it over.

"You will make sure she gets it?" Anxiety creased her brow as he shoved it into a pocket.

"Yes." The increased tempo of his breathing coupled with the restless movements of his eyes left her in no doubt of how eager he was to be gone.

"What if you don't see her?"

"I don't need to. I will leave it where she knows to look." Vartan straddled his bicycle and touched his forehead to hers. "Good luck to you, Mademoiselle Genevra. And to the baroness."

"And to you," she said, but he had shoved off and she wasn't sure he heard. A moment later he pedaled unchecked past the watching soldiers. Feeling equal parts bereft, vulnerable and frightened now that she was well and truly on her own, she turned and hurried toward her train.

It was huffing and puffing its way out of the station before something dawned on her: the slim hope she was clinging to that Emmy might show up and know what to do was not her last, best chance of saving their mother after all.

She had someone else she could turn to. She had Max.

Chapter Seventeen

Genevieve thrust a handful of francs at the driver of the bicycle taxi — she'd been lucky to get one — and rushed from the dark street past the startled guard through the Casino de Paris's stage door. A line of long black cars parked in front of the theater's main entrance on the rue de Clichy told her that tonight's performance came with a full contingent of Nazi VIPs in attendance. The show was always standing room only, with a few hopefuls usually plucked from the walk-ups to prop the wall at the back. That the people queued up in the standby line to the left of the box office were the only ones still waiting told her that the bulk of the audience was already inside.

At least they hadn't canceled yet. But the decision had to be close.

The panic of possibly missing her own show was just beginning to subside. Her train had been late, the metro had broken down and the line to use the pay telephone had been so long that she'd started walking instead. By the time she'd spotted the bicycle taxi, she was running.

If she was lucky, Max wasn't here and didn't know. He'd been especially busy since they'd been in Paris and often missed the opening numbers.

Her head pounded, her nerves had long since unraveled and terrible images of what might be happening to her mother ran on a continuous loop through her mind. The horror of what she had witnessed in Cherbourg was burned indelibly into her memory. Thinking about it did no good, but burying such a powerful impression of unjust tragedy and grief was proving almost impossible. The idea of performing after witnessing that made her sick to her stomach, but the consequences of missing her show were potentially dire. With an audience full of Nazis, news of a cancellation would be widely broadcast and would focus unwanted attention and even suspicion on her and Max and the others, endangering them all. That she could not risk. But she was only now, as she pushed through the door into the bright, noisy, overwarm, perfume-scented backstage area, finally able to force what she had seen from her mind and, in the process, exchange Genevra for Genevieve.

As she struggled into her star persona, the scene that greeted her was so ordinary, so unchanged by the barbarity of what was happening out there in the world beyond this make-believe one, that it felt surreal.

"Genevieve! Oh, Genevieve! We were so worried!" A dozen relieved voices called out to her at once.

"I know. I'm late. Oh, dear, let me through."

Focus. Keep putting one foot in front of the other.

She hopped over and stepped around and squeezed between knots of her girls, who crowded the narrow hallway outside the female *choristes'* too-small dressing room, getting their sparkly eyeliner painted on and their crimson lipstick touched up and their faces fluffed with powder. Those who already had their faces done were being helped into knee-length pale pink feathery capes. Along with itty-bitty brassieres and tiny sparkling panties that left most of their derrieres bare, glittery pink thigh-high boots and tall, face-framing pink bonnets, the capes constituted their costumes for the first song, which was about being young and happy and out and about in Paris. At the beginning of the song, the girls held the capes closed, presenting a picture of demure stylishness as they danced and sang among replicas of Paris's popular attractions. When they reached the chorus, they dropped their capes and twirled in their scanty remaining costumes across the stage, unfailingly to copious audience applause.

"Monsieur Lafont is about to expire of nerves," one of the girls said — a tall, slim blonde named Angelique, who was stretching out against the wall, one long, booted leg extended high above her head as she leaned into the movement. Her cape was puddled on the floor at her feet, and she was as casual in her near nudity as only theater people could be.

"We were afraid he would pop like a balloon! Pow!" Red-haired Honore, equally cape-less, looked up from the splits she'd just sunk into with enormous, rainbow-painted eyes as Genevieve stepped over her leg.

"He is so funny, that one," Cecile said as she finished adjusting her brassiere. "He is like a tomato. But with sweat."

"Quick, we must finish the toilettes." Therese Arnault clapped her hands sharply from the top of the hallway as she descended on the girls, who called her "Madame" to her face and "the Warden" behind her back. Bracket faced, gray haired and built on queenly lines, she was in charge of the chorus girls, and she ruled them with a rod of iron. "All of you, get dressed. And try to remember that you are supposed to be *ladies.*"

Rushing by with an acknowledging nod for Madame, who was making hurry-up gestures with her hands at the girls and looking harassed, Genevieve made it to her own private dressing room. Its wooden door bore a framed sheet of paper with her name printed on it in a semicircle above a large red star.

She burst through the door. Lacquered crimson walls, a green-and-blue patterned carpet, a corner fireplace, currently unlit: the room was large and cluttered.

"Thank the good God." Berthe stopped wringing her hands as Genevieve entered and sprang up from the green velvet sofa where she'd been sitting. "Even I was starting to worry. In these times, people can be gone in an instant, you know. Alive and then —" she snapped her fingers "— poof. Dead."

"Quick, help me get dressed." Genevieve dropped the shopping bag. Shrugging out of Berthe's coat, she let it fall to the floor, too, as Berthe whipped the scarf from her head. Her costume for the opening song hung from a hook nearby. The lights surrounding the large triple-sided makeup mirror were on, her cosmetics spread out in front of it. "I'm sorry I worried you. I stayed out longer than I intended."

"I knew you wouldn't miss your show. Didn't I tell everyone you would be here? Where did you go? And why did you wear my coat — never mind. You can tell me later. We must get you ready to go on."

Between the two of them, they had her stripped to the skin, bundled into her white satin dressing gown and seated in front of the triple mirror before Berthe finished talking.

Genevieve slapped cold cream onto her face and started wiping it off as Berthe snatched up the dangling jet earrings that were part of her costume and fitted them into her ears.

"Did you eat?" Berthe asked, and Genevieve's guilty expression must have given her the answer. "You didn't — I knew it. Even when there is food, you never eat. Fortunate for you that I set aside something from the mess just in case."

Ahead of each performance, a mess table with food for the chorus line was set up backstage, to be cleared away before the show began. Its fare wasn't particularly appetizing, but it was edible, and it had become a non-negotiable part of her contract with each venue. In this time of shortage, being able to provide for the people who worked for her was one of the things that made performing for the Nazis bearable. She tried to remind herself every day to be grateful for it, just like she reminded herself to be grateful that, even in the cities where food was becoming almost impossible to obtain, she and her people never starved.

She'd had nothing to eat since leaving the Ritz that morning. She wasn't consciously hungry — the day's upsets had taken care of that — but the headache and jittery feeling afflicting her would almost certainly be helped by food. And her show was grueling.

She knew she needed sustenance before she took the stage.

Berthe darted away from the dressing table while Genevieve finished wiping off the rest of the cream, then returned to smack a plate that held a small mound of reconstituted powdered egg on a slice of whole wheat toast down in front of her, along with a cup of coffee.

"Eat," Berthe ordered, grabbing the boots that went with her costume while Genevieve wolfed down the food. Berthe dropped to her knees in front of her, opening and positioning the boots, which were thigh high and sparkling but a deep fuchsia pink instead of the baby pink worn by the chorus girls.

Genevieve shoved her feet into them and extended each leg in turn so that Berthe could zip them up. She swallowed the last of the egg and toast, chased it with a gulp of the vinegary ersatz coffee, and started on her face while Berthe attacked her hair.

They were pros. Between them they made quick work of getting her hair and face stage ready. A final twist of a curl, a curve of deep red lipstick, and it was done. Genevieve jumped up, balancing on first one leg in its high-heeled boot and then the other as she stepped into the next piece of her costume, a deep pink waist-cinching strapless bodysuit, shimmering with sequins and strategically placed festoons of beads that moved with her every step.

"This thing has more bones than I do." Dropping the dressing gown, Genevieve leaned forward, shimmying as she tried to get herself positioned properly in the molded satin cups.

"You want the shape, you get the bones." Berthe stood behind her, grunting with the effort of trying to align the edges of the long zipper that closed the garment up the back so she could start zipping. She gave the two edges a yank. "Zip first, bosom *after.* You need to —"

The curtest of knocks interrupted. They had no time to do anything but look toward the door before Max thrust it open and strode into the room.

His eyes went straight to Genevieve, moved swiftly over her. The relief in his expression was impossible to miss.

"Max." She snapped upright. Momentarily forgetting that her costume remained unzipped, she took an impulsive step toward him, then stopped dead, clapping a hand to her chest to hold the bodysuit in place as the whole slithery pink garment threatened to drop. She was, she realized with surprise, fiercely glad to see him. Just when he had become her anchor in a turbulent world she couldn't have said, but there it apparently was.

"M'sieur Max!" Berthe planted her fists on

her hips and frowned at him. She might adore him, but everything from her scandalized tone to her stance made it clear she thought it was improper of him to barge into Genevieve's dressing room while she was getting dressed.

"Do you know what time it is?" His voice was perfectly even, but the real story was there in his eyes. They blazed with anger.

"I'm late. I know." News of her mother's fate, and what she hoped to have him do about it, trembled on the tip of her tongue, but Berthe's presence and the possibility of other listening ears close by made her swallow the words.

It would have to wait until she got him alone.

He closed the door with a backward shove and came toward her, lurching slightly on his stick as he dodged through the obstacle course that the bag and clothes she'd discarded had made of the floor.

"Where have you been?" He stopped in front of her.

So much for her hope that he wouldn't find out about her long absence.

"Out." For the moment it was the best she could do. Anyway, the idea that he thought she had to account to him for her whereabouts annoyed her. "Don't tell me you were worried about me."

"I stopped by the Ritz this morning to drop

off your coat and was told you'd gone for a walk. Must have been a hell of one."

"It was."

He caught her arm, his hand warm and strong, his long fingers curling around the supple flesh centimeters above her elbow.

"Ow." Wincing, she looked down in surprise to find that his fingers pressed into her skin almost on top of a set of bruises she hadn't even suspected were there: four perfect, and tender, print marks where Vartan had dug in his fingers earlier.

Max was looking at them, too, his face tightening.

He must have felt her eyes on him because his lids lifted and he met her gaze. As he recognized the bruises as proof of a man's — another man's — ungentle grip, the anger in his eyes transformed into something cold and hard that glinted at her.

He didn't ask, not with Berthe there. But he stood close enough that she could feel the tension emanating from him like an electrical charge.

To her vexation, her pulse quickened in response.

"Next time you plan to disappear for the day, do me a favor and let somebody know." He dropped her arm.

His tone, his expression, his whole attitude, aggravated her. She'd had a terrible day, had something hugely important to tell him, and he was acting like she'd run off on some kind of date.

"You're assuming I planned it." For the benefit of Berthe, who was watching the exchange round-eyed, she smiled at him. "I ran into some old friends."

Max shot Berthe a look that had her turning away to busy herself picking up Genevieve's discarded clothes.

"On your walk." His eyes were hard.

"That's right."

"Must have been a joyous reunion to have lasted all day."

"It was."

"Who are these friends?"

"No one you know."

"Women? Men? Schoolmates? Long-lost childhood companions?"

"A mix."

He studied her face. Then he leaned close, whispered into her ear, "You should probably know that whenever you tell a lie, your nose twitches. It's charming. Makes you look like a nervous little rabbit."

Her head jerked back. A hand automatically flew to her nose. "It does not."

He smiled at her, and she realized what she had just admitted. She should have remembered that Max was an expert in ferreting out information.

She lowered her hand. "Where did you imagine I was?" In the spirit of revenge, she batted her eyes at him and started walking teasing fingers up his immaculate shirt front. As always on nights when she had a show, he was dressed in a tux. Tonight, grim and cold-eyed, he looked far tougher than her artistically inclined piano playing manager should by rights look. He trapped her hand beneath his right before she reached his bow tie, imprisoning it against his chest. Beneath the smooth cotton of his shirt she could feel the firm muscles of his chest, the warmth of his skin.

Lowering her voice, she went up on tiptoe to whisper for his ears alone, "Surely not — with a man?"

His mouth thinned. His voice was as low as hers. "A girl didn't cause those bruises."

"Careful. You're going to make me think you're jealous."

His eyes flared at her. She had struck a nerve. "This isn't a game we're playing here."

"You're right, it's not. I —" Genevieve began, when a loud bang on the door made her jump.

"Five minutes, Mademoiselle Dumont."

That was her call. She needed to leave her dressing room now. Everything else was going to have to wait. Including Max.

"Your cape." Berthe, catapulted into action by the warning, darted toward where the deep pink cape waited on its hanger. Equally galvanized, Genevieve yanked her hand free of Max's hold and stepped back. Her bodysuit slipped once more. With a muttered curse she clapped her hand to her chest again, barely in time to keep her decent, and looked up to catch Max's eyes on the dangerous expanse of skin thus revealed. Seeing that near catastrophe, Berthe abruptly changed course, beelining toward her. "My God, you're not even zipped."

"I've got it." Tossing his stick onto the nearby sofa, Max dropped a hand onto Genevieve's shoulder and whipped her around. She might have argued, but outside the door the muffled thunder of a stampede of footsteps told her that the girls were rushing en masse toward the stage.

"Quick," Genevieve urged him over her shoulder instead, while Berthe flapped her hands in agitated acceptance and veered back toward the cape.

"Hold still," he commanded. She realized she'd rocked up onto her toes in her anxiety to get out the door. His hands were inside her zipper, inside her bodysuit, closing on either side of her waist to bring her down. The feel of them, big and warm and strong, gripping her bare skin sent a wholly unwanted shiver down her spine.

"Would you hurry up and zip me?" If her voice was a growl, it was because she was fighting not to sound breathless.

He fumbled as he tried to fit the ends of

the zipper together, his fingers brushing the small of her back. "Could they make this thing any smaller?" he muttered, and finally managed to get them connected, sliding the zipper upward. His knuckles grazed the indentation of her waist, slid up her spine . . .

She noted the quickening of her heartbeat with a combination of alarm and dismay.

Another bang on the door. "Three minutes, Mademoiselle Dumont."

"Ayeh!" Berthe turned back to the screen, where the glittering pink top hat with the wide black band that completed Genevieve's outfit hung from the top of a gilded knob.

Max stepped back. Grabbing her cape and gloves from Berthe, Genevieve pulled them on while bending her knees so Berthe could pin her hat in place at the correct jaunty angle.

"Go, go." Berthe shooed her away with a gesture.

Genevieve ran for the stage. Grabbing his stick, Max stayed right behind her. The hall was deserted. The girls were already in place in the wings. She could hear the master of ceremonies booming the introduction: "Ladies and gentlemen, the Casino de Paris is proud to present the Black Swan, the incomparable Mademoiselle Genevieve Dumont, in *Seasons of Love.*"

The orchestra started up. Pierre Lafont, red-faced and sweating, came around the corner just as she reached the backstage crossover. Upon seeing her, he lifted his hands and face skyward as if to express thanks to an almighty God and then hurried to join her.

"Mademoiselle, you will make of me an old man." He mopped his brow with a handkerchief as he rushed with her toward the stairs she had to ascend to reach the second tier of the stage set, from which she would make her grand entrance. The intro swirled around them. "If you could perhaps allow a little bit more time —"

"I'm sorry." She was genuinely contrite. "I will in future, I promise. I was out, and I couldn't find a taxi."

She reached the stairs and started to climb. Glancing down, she happened to get a glimpse of Max's face. He was looking up at her, frowning, his mouth tight, his eyes speculative.

She made a saucy little moue at him.

His eyes narrowed. Then, unexpectedly, his mouth twisted into a wry smile.

"Break a leg," he mouthed at her.

That won an answering smile from her.

For a moment, the merest sliver of a moment, it felt like old times.

Then there was no time to think about Max or anything at all except the performance she was about to give. The orchestra swung into the opening bars of the song. She could hear the girls' light-hearted call-and-response intro as they poured out onto the stage. Reaching the top of the steps, she got into position. Taking deep breaths to calm the butterflies that always afflicted her right before she went on, she waited for her cue.

There it was.

She squared her shoulders, lifted her chin and stepped through the curtain into the blazing spotlight like the star she was. Briefly she paused at the top of the wide ornamental staircase that led down to the stage to let the audience get its first look at her. On either side of the staircase, a line of chorus boys clad in tuxedos and top hats waited to help her descend.

Directing a brilliant smile at the rapturously applauding audience that the bright lights kept her from actually seeing, she took the gloved hands the boys on the top step extended to her and started to sing.

"Elle fréquentait la rue Pigalle . . ."

Chapter Eighteen

During the fourth song Genevieve had a scheduled break while the chorus performed without her. The number was the risqué "La java bleue," which they sang while dancing the java, a scandalous version of the waltz that began with the male *choristes* grabbing their female partners' derrieres and pulling them close. It was quite a spectacle, invariably engaging the audience's full attention. Even the stagehands watched agog from the wings.

This was the middle of seven songs that constituted the first act. She was on again for the next three. After that came intermission, followed by six songs. It was an exhausting program even under the best of conditions, which these were not. Already she was running on pure adrenaline. She had a headache in the form of a constant dull throb behind her eyes. The food she'd gulped had settled like a rock in her stomach. She was tired to the bone, and so tense she had to consciously remind herself to relax her diaphragm as she sang.

She was confident that no one in the audience could pick up on any of that. When she took the stage, she was totally focused on the performance she was there to give. But when she was offstage, like now, the headache and the unsettled stomach and the exhaustion came crashing down on her.

To say nothing of her burning fear for her mother.

What she should do was take this time to hydrate and rest. What she was doing was rushing to find Max.

Pierre, who with a couple of helpers was busy working on the scrim curtain needed in the next number and lately had exhibited problems rising and lowering, saw her from the wings.

"You're on again in ten minutes, Mademoiselle Dumont," he hissed in nervous warning as she went by.

"I know." She would have added a soothing *don't worry,* but that would have been useless: worry was part of the job, and apparently part of his nature, as well. Poor man, he was looking sweatier than ever. "I won't be late."

With the sultry music for a backdrop, she headed for the small office next to the prop room that Max had taken over for the duration of their run. Experience had taught her that she was likely to find him in there alone at this time, which meant that this would be her best opportunity to talk to him in private. Catching him on his own during intermission was always chancy: usually he was with people. After the show, he was often gone before she left the stage and Otto took her back to the Ritz.

Waiting until tomorrow felt impossible. Keeping her concentration and her energy up during her show was taking every bit of strength and determination she possessed. Once the show was done, she would be, too. Already she was anticipating collapsing in a throbbing mass of shredded nerves back in her hotel room.

But how could she sleep, how could she eat, how could she rehearse or go through another performance or do anything at all, knowing that her mother was possibly being tortured or killed while she did it?

The answer was she couldn't. She needed to tell Max.

Now that she was offstage, scenes from her childhood bombarded her: herself as a very little girl, seated beside Lillian at the piano in the green parlor as her mother taught her to play. She could see her own small fingers stretching to span the keys, see her mother's pale, elegant hands demonstrating, hear the hesitant notes of her first attempts at "Alouette"; herself a little older, maybe all of eight years, walking hand in hand with her father among the vines amid all the hustle and bustle of pruning and having him hunker down to show her the small buds that would turn into clusters of grapes; the four of them, Maman, Papa, Emmy and herself, running among the vines from smudge pot to smudge pot as darkness fell, setting the kerosene heaters alight when a hard frost threatened the crop.

In those days family had been a given, a fact of life that she took for granted, like air to breathe. The coming storms that would tear them apart, tear everything apart, were not yet even a cloud on the horizon.

Worry over Lillian's fate increased with every beat of her heart. It lurked beneath every note she sang, every practiced move in every number, every smile and gesture she gave the audience. It felt like a sharp-clawed animal had gotten lodged deep inside her body and was slowly, systematically tearing its way out.

The intensity of her fear for her mother and her grief for her father woke her to the fact that Vivi's death had left her emotionally numb. She saw now that she'd been drifting, not caring about anything or anyone, including herself. Nothing could reach her, not the fact that she'd committed murder, or Max's perfidy, or even the war, because the cold, hard shell that had encapsulated her heart on that day had prevented her from fully feeling.

Becoming Genevieve, singing, using the gift that was her voice to create a whole new life, was the only thing that had allowed her to survive. But surviving was all she'd been doing. Rescuing Anna had pierced the shell. Going to Rocheford — going home — had broken it wide-open by thrusting her back into Genevra's skin and making her feel again.

She'd already lost so much, and each loss had left her feeling like she was bleeding to death inside. She didn't think she could bear it if she lost her mother, too.

Telling Max what had befallen the missing baroness, that said baroness was in fact her mother and that she wanted, no, *required* him to arrange her rescue if he ever hoped to have her cooperation in any of his schemes again was not going to be easy. Filling in all the details to his satisfaction would probably take more time than this small break would give her, but any questions he had could be answered later. By presenting him now with the bare facts, she meant to at least get him started on contacting whomever he needed to contact or doing whatever he had to do to put a plan in motion to save Lillian. The most terrifying thing about this particular ticking clock was she had no idea when time would run out.

She wasn't even going to allow herself to think that the task might be impossible, even for Max. Over the years she had developed respect for his ability to get things done.

As she meant to make clear to him, she needed him to get this done.

The door to Max's office opened as she neared it. A man emerged, alone. She stopped, watched. As he closed the door behind him and came walking toward her through the shadowy backstage area, she recognized him: the bearded old man from La Fleur Rouge who'd brought Max word of her parents' fate: Hippolyte Touvier.

There was nothing outwardly suspicious about his appearance, or his movements, or even his presence backstage. Max often had backstage visitors. But her heart started tripping nonetheless. She knew why he had visited Max before. Easy to guess why he was visiting again.

She wore her costume for the next number, a body-hugging dress in the red, white and blue of the French flag that ended at the tops of her thighs in a froth of ruffles. Spangled with sequins, worn with sparkly red pumps and red net stockings held up by red satin suspenders, it had been designed to catch the eye, which in this instance was not a good thing. The relative lack of lighting in this part of the backstage area helped, as did the probability that Touvier had not, before, actually gotten a good enough look at her to recognize her. Her experience with Vartan and the others had opened her eyes to how wary these men were of strangers, and how suspicious a man in fear of betrayal could be.

She quickly ducked to one side of a prop Eiffel Tower and pretended to be studying the call-board on the wall behind it as he passed. As far as she could tell, he didn't notice her at all, and once he was gone, she breathed a small sigh of relief.

Then she hurried to Max's office. With a quick knock on the closed door — no reply — she let herself in.

Max wasn't there. No one was there. Her glance around the cramped, cluttered space touched on the old desk, the chair behind it, a file cabinet, a coatrack with Max's overcoat and hat hanging from it.

Either Max had slipped away before Touvier had left, before she'd gotten near enough to see him go, or Touvier had missed him entirely.

By now her heart felt like it was trying to beat its way out of her chest.

Touvier had promised to bring back the answer to Max's message as soon as he received it. Did he bring it?

A packet of cigarettes rested on Max's desk, beside the telephone, as innocuous as a notebook or a pencil. Except for the fact that the cigarettes were Gitanes. Max smoked Gauloises Bleues.

She crossed to the desk, picked up the

packet. It was open. A couple of cigarettes were missing. It looked like any ordinary smoker's ordinary pack.

Touvier had taken the message Max had given him and hidden it inside a cigarette. Was the answer Touvier had promised to bring hidden inside one of these?

Her pulse raced as she stared down at the packet. She should wait for Max.

But she already knew she wasn't going to. Perhaps he'd already received the message. Perhaps there was no message to receive. Perhaps these were simply cigarettes, anyone's cigarettes. But she had to check. She had to *know.*

Casting a nervous glance at the door — she didn't want to even imagine what Max's reaction would be if he caught her — she picked up the packet and tapped the cigarettes out one by one. Looking at them, feeling them, smelling them, quickly and nervously, she could detect no difference — wait, was this one slightly firmer in the middle? Even tightly packed tobacco tended to have some give to it.

Remembering how Touvier had done it, she pinched and pulled at the tobacco at the top. A plug came out in her hand. It was a solid stopper with a layer of tobacco cunningly affixed. Below it, a tightly rolled scrap of paper had been inserted into the empty cylinder that ended in an identical plug.

Her hands shook as she tipped the paper out. Unrolling it, she read the black, sloping handwriting with a glance.

Baroness a threat. Your orders are to rescue her if possible, otherwise execute her. Act quickly. You know what's at stake.

Genevieve had to read the message a second time before she could take it in. Cold sweat broke over her in a wave.

For a moment she stood frozen, staring at the scrap of paper. Her first impulse was to destroy it. That way Max would never receive it, would never know what it said.

Unless he'd already read it. Or Touvier let him know that he'd delivered the answer to his message, and Max checked with the source, who repeated it. Or there was a fail-safe, a backup way of transmitting such an order. Or — there were a thousand *ors*.

She couldn't destroy it. That wouldn't stop the message from ultimately getting through. And for it to turn up missing would arouse suspicion. Of everyone who had access to this office, probably, but also of her. Anyone could have spotted her entering Max's office.

One thing she had learned over the course of their association: falling afoul of the Resistance did not end well.

Her other option was to tell Max the whole story, *her* whole story, just as she'd meant to do, and beg him to go ahead with plans to rescue her mother while taking killing her off the table.

He would not deny her. Would he?

As Otto had said, Max was a soldier. If a speedy rescue proved difficult, would he flout a direct order? Even for her?

The truth was she couldn't be sure.

Hands shaking, she rolled the piece of paper up and put it back inside the cigarette. Careful to leave no trace, she replaced the plug, put the cigarette back into the packet and placed the packet back where she'd found it.

She was just stepping away from the desk when the door opened and Touvier walked in.

Chapter Nineteen

Touvier's arrival was so unexpected that Genevieve froze in place. The bearded, stooped old man stopped short, too.

His eyes were a blue so pale as to be almost colorless. In that brief time in which they were locked with hers, they turned as hard and cold as ice.

Finally, he flicked a look toward the desk. To the packet of cigarettes. His glance at it lasted for no more than a split second, but she saw. He was checking to make sure it was still there.

Could he tell it had been moved?

Fear clutched at her throat.

He stepped the rest of the way inside the room and closed the door. The soft click of the latch made her heart beat faster. The sounds of the theater, the music, everything now seemed far away. They were alone in that small space. She instantly felt claustrophobic. Her sixth sense screamed a warning.

"Mademoiselle Dumont." Like his eyes, his

voice made her think he was younger and stronger than she had at first supposed. He was part of the Resistance — he worked with Max — so the stooped-old-man persona was undoubtedly a pose. She realized, too, that just because he was a member of the Resistance rather than a Nazi did not mean she was safe in his company. In this time of heightened tension, even an inkling on his part that she might know too much, and tell what she knew, could get her killed.

She should have spoken as soon as he stepped into the room, she realized. Greeted his arrival with something innocuous, like *May I help you?* Or *Are you looking for Max?* Saying nothing made her seem guilty.

Her stomach knotted. She had to consciously work at keeping her breathing even, her expression bland. She couldn't tell if she succeeded.

He started toward her, his eyes intent on her face. It was all she could do not to take an involuntary step back.

Say something.

"Did you —" she began.

The door opened: *Max.*

She felt light-headed with relief.

His eyes went straight to her. Their expression was impossible to read. Before she got more than a glimpse, his gaze shifted to Touvier, who had turned to look at him. In those few seconds the atmosphere in the room changed drastically. The sense of menace dissipated like air escaping a deflating balloon.

The sultry strains of "La java bleue" once more filled the air. A portion of the dimly lit hallway and the darkened backstage area could be seen through the open door.

She felt like she could breathe again.

"Glad you could make it," Max said to Touvier, playing the affable host. He crossed to the desk, which brought him to her side. He picked up the cigarettes and pocketed them, oh so casually. She did her best not to let on that she noticed. His dark gaze slid over her face as, in a lowered voice, he asked, "Did you want me for something?"

"Yes, but . . ." She gave a slight shake of her head. "It can wait."

His answer was a nod. As he turned to Touvier, his arm slid around her waist. An easy move that brought her against his side — and under his protection. "I see you've met Genevieve. As I told you, she's something special."

The normalcy of his voice, which she had no doubt could be heard by anyone near the open door, practically shouted *nothing clandestine is happening here.* And that would be because, as he'd told her so often she'd grown sick of it, there were eyes and ears everywhere, and the best way to hide was in plain sight.

Touvier smiled at Genevieve. The smile didn't reach his eyes.

"She is indeed," he replied. "It is a pleasure, Mademoiselle Dumont."

Genevieve's answering smile might not have been the most genuine, but at least it was a smile. With Max beside her, she knew she no longer had any need to be afraid of him, but her body was slow to get the message. Every nerve ending she possessed screamed that, for a few moments there, she'd been in real peril.

Touvier continued, talking to Max now rather than her. "I've been enjoying the show immensely. I only wish I'd been fortunate enough to obtain a seat in the audience. But being backstage has its charms. Not the least of which is it has afforded me the opportunity to meet Mademoiselle Dumont." He made a small bow in her direction.

Genevieve felt like her cheeks might crack from the force it took to hold her smile.

"This is Hippolyte Touvier," Max said to her. The impulse to lean against him was strong, but she resisted it. She didn't want him to guess how truly alarmed she'd been, for fear that he'd wonder why. "He's producing a movie for Continental Films." It was the only authorized film production company in France. "He and I have been discussing the possibility of him casting you in a leading role."

Any flicker of excitement she might have felt was immediately extinguished by the realization that, whether there was truth to the statement or not, she was being used to cloak subsequent meetings between Max and Touvier. Hide in plain sight, indeed.

Max's hand rested atop her hip bone. He gave her a subtle squeeze.

"How exciting," she said. *Smile, smile, smile.* Beyond Touvier, she saw Pierre pop into view in the backstage area. He looked all around, his expression beleaguered. The music changed to the segue into the closing notes.

"I have to go." She pulled away from Max, gave Touvier one last artificial smile and left the office to hurry toward the stage. Spotting her, Pierre threw out both arms and made urgent beckoning gestures. That wrung some of the tension from her. With him clucking like a worried mother hen behind her, she took her place for the start of the next number.

The greenroom was already full by the time Genevieve left the stage after taking her final bow. As she walked toward her dressing room, she could hear the laughter and conversation emanating from it. The chorus routinely met with influential admirers in there after the show. Champagne would be flowing.

She only rarely dropped in on the après-show parties anymore, usually when Max needed information and thought she might be able to glean it from someone in attendance, or from the swirl of talk in general. Her standing excuse was that she was too tired after a strenuous performance. That was true, but the larger truth was, after so many years of socializing on demand, she had lost her taste for socializing. She also had no interest in forming the kind of liaison that often resulted from the gatherings. She might have gone out with certain men at Max's direction, but that was strictly business. Lately she'd had an additional incentive to avoid the parties: she was taking good care not to appear anywhere that would give Wagner a chance to press his attentions on her. After last night, that assumed even greater importance. Much easier to avoid the man entirely than to find herself in a position where she had to offend him by saying no.

Fortunately, tonight he wasn't in the audience. She knew that because, during her last curtain call, among many other floral tributes, she'd been presented with an enormous bouquet of flowers from him along with a note.

> I'm sorry I couldn't come tonight. May I take you to dinner tomorrow night after your show to make up for it? I'll be waiting for you at the stage door when you come out.
>
> ~ Claus von Wagner

Her strategy had been to fob him off with excuses until they left Paris. If he was going to wait for her by the stage door, that wasn't going to be possible. Of course, she could always exit another way, but he would probably see that as the ploy to escape him it would be, and be affronted. Better to once again plead after-show exhaustion. It was quite possible that he would counter with an invitation to a daytime outing, but she had only three days left in Paris, and over the past few years she'd practically turned gracefully wriggling out of unwanted dates into an art form. She could manage this.

In any case, there were far more urgent matters on her mind than how to deal with Wagner. She had to find Max and tell him about her mother, with no further loss of time. She'd already cranked up her courage and checked his office, only to find it empty and dark. Hopefully he would be waiting for her in her dressing room. With Touvier nowhere in the vicinity.

A pair of chorus girls came around the bend in the hallway. Still wearing the bright bird costumes from the final number, they were clearly in high spirits and just as clearly on their way to the greenroom.

"Genevieve!" They trilled a greeting almost in unison when they saw her.

"Wonderful job tonight," she told them.

"Are you coming to the party?" one of

them, Nadine, asked.

"Not tonight."

"You'll have fun," the other, Yvonne, urged.

"Especially if you stick with us," Nadine said, and the two of them burst into giggles.

"Some other time." She waved them off with a smile and tried not to breathe as she walked through the cloying patchouli-scented cloud of perfume that wafted in their wake.

Otto came around the corner next. He was wearing his chauffeur's uniform again. She knew what that meant. Max had gone.

"You blew the roof off the place," he said on a congratulatory note as she reached him. "I was on my feet clapping right along with everybody else."

"Thank you," she said. He turned to walk beside her as she continued on toward her dressing room. "Where's Max?"

"He asked me to take you back to the hotel."

"What's he doing?" Her voice was sharper than it should have been as her pulse started to race. By now he would have read the note. Would he already be on her mother's trail? *He won't have found her,* she told herself. *It's too soon.* Although the note had said *act quickly.*

Otto shrugged, and Genevieve stopped so suddenly that the long black feathers of her skirt swished forward around her legs. Ignoring the resultant tickling sensation, she turned and gestured at the three stagehands following her with their arms full of the flowers from her curtain calls.

"Take them to my dressing room, please," she said, and waited until they were out of earshot.

Then she looked at Otto. "I need to talk to Max. Is he at La Fleur Rouge?"

Otto shrugged again.

Impatience narrowed her eyes. "Wherever he is, I want you to take me to him."

Otto shook his head. "Can't do it."

"Why not? Where is he?"

"Who knows? Maybe he's got a date."

Genevieve's gaze skewered him. They both knew that wasn't the case. In the slightly more than three years that she'd known him, the number of times Max had gone out with a woman for other than business purposes had to be in the single digits. Oh, he gathered information as necessary, making himself charming to the Nazis' wives and daughters and sweethearts to find out what they knew, but a date?

At least, a date she knew about, she amended, as it occurred to her that she couldn't possibly know everything he did, and he had a lot of time when they weren't together. The thought was unsettling.

"When next I see him, I'll tell him you want to talk to him, shall I?" Otto's tone was soothing, as if he thought she was being irrationally fractious. Her mouth tightened, but before she could reply a group of chorus boys came around the corner. With a barely perceptible movement of his head, Otto suggested they get moving again.

Knowing he had a point, Genevieve swallowed what she'd been going to say and started to walk. He fell in beside her. The boys were shier than the girls, and she returned their more respectful greetings with a smile and a nod.

"I need to see him *tonight,*" she said when they were sufficiently far away. The edge in her voice was in no way blunted because she was whispering. She couldn't convey what she needed to convey to Max in a verbal message or note entrusted to Otto, she almost certainly wouldn't be able to reach Max by telephone and even if she did, communications by telephone were known to be unsecure, and she could hardly go searching for Max all over Paris. By herself. At night. After curfew.

She needed Otto.

"Take me to him," she said.

Otto looked at her. In her peep-toe shoes she was centimeters taller than he was, and the towering black plumes in her hair made her seem taller still. Still, despite his lack of size and his shock of white hair and the lines creasing his face, there was a sudden steeliness about him that reminded her that, like Max, he was something far different from what he appeared.

"He told me to take you straight back to the hotel after your show, and that's what I'll be doing." His voice was low, but the bulldog set of his jaw indicated that was his last word on the subject.

Her temper heated. "You know, I don't remember agreeing to the part where Max — or you — gets to dictate my every move."

"He's trying to keep you safe."

"I don't need to be kept safe. I need to talk to him. Tonight."

"Don't you think you've caused him enough problems for one day?"

Genevieve frowned, not understanding, and Otto went on, "He had people hunting all over Paris for you. He sent me out. He went out looking himself. He was frightened to death you'd gotten yourself in trouble somehow. He put off important business, for you." They reached her dressing room door and stopped. Otto's voice dropped even lower. "These are dangerous times, and the work he's doing is unforgiving. Let him do it."

"I'm not interfering with it."

"You're making him worry about you. That kind of distraction could get him killed."

At the thought of Max being killed, a shiver went through her. The reality of it was something she'd never really faced up to.

Now she did, and it was like an icy hand clutching at her heart. The harsh truth was that every day Max walked a tightrope. So did she, and so did Otto. So did they all, every single person who worked in secret to overthrow the Reich. One false move could send any of them — all of them — plunging to their deaths. All those years of being emotionally numb had in at least this one way been an advantage, she discovered. She'd never been truly afraid before.

Now that layer of insulation had been stripped away.

"Anyway, I couldn't take you to him if I wanted to. I don't know where he is," Otto said.

Genevieve found herself at a standstill. It was hard to accept, but the only thing left to do for the moment was pray that Max wouldn't find her mother before she could talk to him.

"You'll see him tonight?"

"Most likely."

"As soon as you see him, you'll tell him I need to talk to him?" she asked.

"I will."

"Tell him to come to me at the hotel."

"I'll do that."

She turned away. "I'm going to change."

"I'll pull the car around. Come out when you're ready."

She walked out the stage door into the brisk

night air a short time later, signed autographs for the small group of fans gathered there and slid into the back of the waiting Citroën. Berthe, who was with her, sat up front beside Otto. The two of them engaged in animated conversation, but Genevieve said little. She was so exhausted her brain felt fuzzy.

Traffic was minimal. Two military trucks, traveling together, came toward them, followed a few minutes later by a *Funkpeilwagen,* a direction-finding van that could ferret out the location of Resistance radio operators by tracking their wireless transmissions. Identifiable by its slow pace and visible antenna, it crept past, looking like a crawling yellow-eyed insect with its curved back and slotted headlights.

She wondered who it had in its sights tonight.

Worry lay heavy as a brick in her stomach, but as she listened to the Citroën's tires swish over the pavement, she found herself on the brink of nodding off.

She badly needed sleep. But she was afraid of it, too. Afraid of what might be waiting for her in the dark.

They were no more than a kilometer away from the Ritz when the air-raid sirens went off.

Chapter Twenty

The mournful wail of air-raid sirens was the first thing Lillian became aware of as she surfaced from the darkness she'd been lost in. They sounded close, far closer than they should have. Usually they were distant bleats borne on the wind from Cherbourg. But this — this nerve-racking screech seemed to originate directly overhead. Surely Paul had not had a warning system installed on their own roof?

Then she remembered: this was not Rocheford. And Paul was dead.

Everything came back to her in a rush. The grief, the horror. Jean-Claude. Andre. She had tried to swallow bleach but had been knocked to the ground before she could ingest more than a mouthful. Her head had smacked into the stone floor. The last thing she remembered was seeing stars — and the crushing pain of a German boot stomping her hands until she relinquished her desperate grip on the container of bleach. Mercifully, after that the world had gone black — until now.

She was alive.

Oh, God, why did you let me live?

As awareness returned, pain descended like a thunderclap. The physical was bad, but the psychic was worse. Her very soul bled.

She forced her eyes to open. They didn't work properly. The lids felt puffy, swollen, and she could only part them a crack. Her head swam as she tried to look around, her vision blurry. Every cell in her body cried out in protest as she moved, so she stopped. It didn't help.

The worst of the physical pain came from her mouth. Her lips, her tongue, the inside of her throat were all sheer burning agony. Her lips — she could just see them as she cast her gaze down — puffed out like inner tubes. Her tongue felt big as a cucumber. Misshapen and dry, its tip protruded grotesquely between her teeth. Her throat felt swollen and raw. The air she dragged in through her nostrils seared the inflamed tissue as her greedy lungs sucked it down.

Racked with thirst, she instinctively tried to swallow. She couldn't — she had no saliva. Simply making the attempt sent fiery needles shooting through her mouth and throat and left her drenched in sweat.

The all clear sounded. The sirens faded. The danger was over.

Her muscles relaxed. Her lids drooped.

Paul, are you here? She reached out for him, through time and space and death, and got no response. If he was out there, she couldn't find him.

She remembered the day they were married. A small wedding, in the church in Orconte. At eighteen years old, she'd been so in love with him, and so nervous at the idea of becoming his wife, that she'd trembled like a jelly. For the daughter of a village doctor to marry the future Baron de Rocheford was a big step up, socially. Even as she'd exchanged wedding vows with Paul, she'd made her own internal vow that he would never have cause to regret it, that she would be not only the best wife he could possibly ask for but, when the time came, the best baroness he could possibly ask for. After the wedding she'd set herself to mastering all the things she'd never had a reason to know: how to take her place in aristocratic society, how to run a stately home, how to raise her children to occupy a social position far different from the one she'd been born into. As the years passed, she thought she'd made Paul proud as well as happy.

She saw flashes of him with their daughters: his eyes bright with wonder and fear (and an excess of wine), a tender smile on his face as he'd held their silently blinking, blanket-wrapped first-born, Emmanuelle, a scant hour after her birth; a no less welcoming greeting for their squalling second born, Genevra, feisty from her first breath; in his bathing costume on the Côte d'Azur teaching them to swim: Emmanuelle with her fair hair tucked up under a cap, a frown of concentration on her face as she dutifully strove to follow his instructions to the letter, and Genevra, forgetting her cap, her black curls flying as she leaped into the water without listening to a thing he'd said; his eyes misty as he'd beheld Emmanuelle dressed for her first grown-up dance; his face flushed with pride as, settled into his favorite chair in the green parlor, he'd listened to Genevra play and sing.

Oh, Paul.

A rattle and a creak brought her back to the terrifying present with a start. She tensed, forcing her lids apart again as she sought the source of the sounds.

"You are awake, I see." A man's voice, speaking in French with an accent that was unmistakably German, was followed by the sound of a heavy door closing. She sensed rather than saw him, an impression of energy and movement outside the limited range of her vision. But there was no missing the vitality of his presence inside the room.

Unwilling to turn her head more than a few centimeters because of the dizziness that threatened to overwhelm her when she tried, she sought him out by carefully moving only her eyes. In the process she discovered that she was no longer in that hellhole of a cellar. She was, instead, in a tiny windowless room lit by a single small ceiling fixture. Four bare walls of what looked like smooth white plaster were interrupted by the closed door, a substantial-looking panel of dark wood. She lay on her back on a cot along one of the long walls with her left wrist chained to a ring in the wall. A light blanket covered her. What she could see of her manacled arm was hideously bruised, her hand discolored and swollen.

The room was cold, and from the sirens she assumed it was night: the aeroplanes almost always came at night. How long had it been since Paul had died? One day, two? Or more?

The German came toward her. He was large, a high-ranking officer according to his uniform, with short, dark blond hair. He reached the foot of her cot and stopped.

"Baroness Lillian de Rocheford, wife of the late Baron Paul de Rocheford." His tone was musing. It wasn't a question. He said it as if he had no doubt as to her identity. He seemed to expect no acknowledgment from her, which was wise because he got none. She watched him and breathed. "Allow me to introduce myself. I am Obergruppenführer Claus von Wagner." A pause while he studied her. "Do you know what you are facing, madame?"

She didn't answer, of course. She couldn't have answered even if she'd wanted to. Her mouth was so injured, so ulcerated and swollen, that she doubted she would ever be able to make normal use of it again. Certainly speech was beyond her. But her heart, her poor broken heart, started to thump.

Yes, I know. Although her mind slithered away from the knowledge.

"You were brought here to be interrogated, and eventually executed, as a traitor to the Reich. As you are no doubt aware, some of our interrogation techniques can be — unpleasant."

Death she welcomed. But dying, as she had already learned, was hard. Her insides shivered and shook at the prospect of more pain. She thought of the sufferings of Jean-Claude. She could not hold out against such brutality. She was not strong enough. Sooner or later she would scream to the skies every secret bottled up inside her.

Then she remembered her mouth — she couldn't talk. Her fingers were bent and puffed up to the size of sausages — she couldn't even write. He might torture her, but the silver lining that came with her injuries was that he would not be able to force her to reveal anything, because they'd already done so much harm to her that, physically, she could not.

The German picked up something from what to her slightly unfocused gaze appeared to be a pile of rags on the seat of a small wooden chair near the cot. He held it up, then turned it inside out, examining it. It was ripped and badly stained, but she recognized the deep green color: her sweater. The brown rag that still lay crumpled on the chair must be, then, her trousers. A quick inventory told her that she was not naked beneath the blanket. She wore a loose garment with sleeves that ended near her elbows and a hem that reached her knees. A dress? No, more likely a nightgown or hospital gown. Her lower legs and feet were bare.

While she was unconscious, someone had undressed her. The knowledge made her skin creep.

"Because you are a woman, and because I do not like to hurt women unless I must, I will tell you how you may escape such a terrible fate." He put her sweater down, picked up her trousers and proceeded to run the once fine wool between his hands before turning them inside out, searching them as if he suspected something might be sewn inside a hem or concealed in a seam, which, thank God, was not the case. "I have received information that you have knowledge of the Allies' plans to invade. I am particularly interested in the where and when. If you can tell me that — and do not think to lie to me, that would make me very angry indeed — there will be no need for the disagreeable consequences that your actions have brought upon you."

He had received information — it struck her that any number of people might be aware of Paul's habit of confiding in her. But they could not *know* she knew. She clung to that thought as he put her trousers down and picked up something else — her pendant. The small garnet heart dangled by its chain from his fingers as he held it up to look at it. Her own heart came unmoored, seeming to twirl through space right along with the dark red stone.

The girls had given it to her. A long time ago, for Mother's Day. Their entwined initials had been inlaid in gold in the stone's center. On the day they'd given it to her, her oldest watching her open the gift with her big eyes and solemn face, her youngest with her radiant smile, she'd been touched to her core, hugging and kissing them both and promising faithfully to wear it every single day.

She had, until the Nazis had stripped it from her.

Lost. All lost. The girls, Paul, everything.

"I see this means something to you." He watched her closely. She fought to lock down her memories, her heart. He would use them against her, she knew.

"*E* and *G.*" His tone was musing as he examined the stone. Hearing those cherished initials in his foul voice made her want to throw up. If she'd had anything inside her at all, she would have. "Whoever they are, they must be dear to you."

To close her eyes or look away would reveal too much. She stared back, her face as blank as she could keep it.

"So here is your choice." He pulled a wallet from his pocket, tucked the pendant inside. "You may tell me what I want to know, and thus avoid being tortured. As a reward, I might even let you live. Or you may be stubborn, which will merely be tedious for me, because it forces me to extract the information I require from you in ways you will, I am afraid, find most distressing. And then, having told all, you will be executed. A sad end, and so unnecessary. I urge you strongly to consider before you commit to such a course."

He started to turn away, stopped and turned back.

"One more thing. Your husband is dead, I am aware, but you have two daughters, do you not? Yes, my information is quite good. I am guessing — E and G." He smiled at her, a wide, good-humored smile that brought deep dimples to life in his cheeks. "I have given orders to have Mademoiselles E and G found, and brought here and subjected to the same fate you yourself select. So choose wisely, madame."

He walked to the door, opened it, then looked over his shoulder at her and said, "Someone will come in soon to take care of you. You must not think we neglect the health of our guests. We will restore yours to the point where you can answer, and then we will talk again, you and I."

Lillian felt cold to her bones as he left.

I've done wrong. Much wrong, and I will be judged for it. But I meant it for the best. All of it. Please, please, watch over the girls and keep them safe.

Closing her eyes, she prayed for death.

Chapter Twenty-One

Heart racing, Genevieve strode out of the Ritz the next morning toward where a group of soldiers gathered around a wheeled vendor's cart, one of several that had been set up in front of the Vendôme Column. Behind her, the hotel was hopping: the legendary bar was closed until afternoon, but the dining rooms were crowded with high-level German officers breakfasting with the rich and well connected. The smell of coffee and the clink of cutlery on fine china filled the air.

Outside, the day held the promise of warmth to come, but at the moment frost still sparkled on the potted topiaries on either side of the entrance and glimmered on the tops of the ornate black streetlights. Backlit by the morning sun, the towering blue-green obelisk cast a shadow across the cobblestones in the way of a pointer on a sundial. It ended almost at her feet as she moved quickly past the vehicles puffing out malodorous exhaust near the hotel's front door. Despite the bustle of activity in the square — the pedestrians, the bicycles, the flower and basket and toy vendors — all her attention centered on the woman behind that one particular cart.

Can it be . . . ?

It was not quite 9:00 a.m., not long before Otto would pick her up and take her to La Fleur Rouge, where she was scheduled to rehearse and also hopefully see Max. She'd been up for hours. The curfew lifted at 5:00 a.m. Shortly after that she'd flagged down a bicycle taxi and gone to La Fleur Rouge on her own to find him. He was not there, which left her both frustrated and speculating, not for the first time, about what exactly he did and where exactly he went after she retired to her hotel for the night. Leaving a note — *I need to see you NOW* — on the table where he couldn't miss it, she'd returned to the Ritz only to find Berthe up and worried about *her* whereabouts.

She was alone now as she followed the shadow's path. Berthe had gone down to the Ritz's cellar, site of what had to be the most opulent air-raid shelter in Paris, to retrieve some belongings left behind the previous night. They'd been escorted to the cellar by a bellhop bearing gas masks as soon as they'd arrived at the hotel. At the beginning of the war, the roar of bombers overhead and the subsequent explosions as the bombs rained down had sent them scuttling into shelters in whatever city they found themselves like mice hiding from a posse of starving cats. The specter of a deadly cloud of gas being released by the aeroplanes had been terrifying enough that they'd all carried gas masks with them everywhere they went. After years of such fears and attacks, the shrieking sirens and the descent into shelters had become old hat. Last night's bombers had been Mosquitoes — she could recognize most of the different aeroplanes by sound now — almost certainly targeting something *not* in Paris's center, like factories on the outskirts of the city or transportation hubs or railroad lines in the outlying areas. Champagne and caviar had been passed around the shelter by the Ritz's attentive staff, the gas masks had been used as pillows by the especially sleepy, or inebriated, and the atmosphere in the cellar as they waited for the all clear had been almost that of a party. By the time the sirens had stopped and they were allowed to go to their suite, they'd both been too exhausted (and too loaded on champagne) to account for such items as, say, Berthe's hat or her own shoes. Then she'd stayed awake as long as she could keep her eyes open hoping Max would show up, which he hadn't.

Upon her return to the hotel this morning, she'd been headachy and short with Berthe and cross with the absent Max and jittery with anxiety about her mother — until she'd carried her cup of coffee over to the window and looked out.

I think it is . . .

It was difficult to be certain of details at such a distance, of course, but there was something tantalizingly familiar about the deft movements of the woman behind the cart. Genevieve had spotted her from the window almost at once and felt her breath catch. Snatching up her coat and hat, she'd all but run from the hotel. Now, as she drew close enough to hear her speak, her last doubt vanished.

Emmy.

She hadn't heard her sister's voice in seven years, but she recognized it instantly. Though she'd been hoping to find Emmy here, praying to find Emmy here, still the reality of it shook her. Her heart beat faster. A pit yawned in her stomach. For a moment, listening, it felt as if she were being spun back through time.

Come on, bébé: Emmy always on time for dinner, for lessons, for everything, impatient when her junior caused them to be late. *Slow down, you:* Emmy yanking on her dress to pull her back when she bolted eagerly toward something exciting, like, say, company in the parlor or ice cream. Emmy elbowing her in the ribs when they played duets on the piano and she pounded the keys too fast. Emmy, cantering gracefully, yelling after her when she kicked her pony into a headlong gallop and took the lead as they rode down the precarious path toward the beach. *You're too little, Genny:* Emmy doing everything — learning to play the piano, going to dances, falling in love — first.

Although the joke in the family had always been that Emmy might do everything first, but Genny always did it with the most determination.

"— quite sure you won't regret it." Emmy spoke gaily to one of the soldiers as she handed over something wrapped in a bit of cloth and accepted some coins in exchange. "My grandmother's tarts are legendary."

Emmy had always resembled their father rather than their mother, with a square-jawed, high-cheekboned face that was serenely lovely in repose and blossomed into true beauty when she smiled. Her nose was narrow and straight, her mouth and chin determined, her skin tone tawny, her thick hair a soft caramel shade. She was the taller of the two of them, with larger bones and a fuller figure that had, once upon a time, incited a skinny little sister's envy.

"Fresh from Grand-mère's oven this morning," Emmy promised the next soldier in line, who asked when the tarts had been made.

Today, in a faded floral scarf and a loose brown coat that in no way resembled anything Genevieve had ever seen her always chic sister wear, Emmy looked entirely different from the vibrant girl of her memory. Her skin had lost its sun-kissed golden tone and was now on the waxy side of pale. She was thinner, a great deal thinner, bone thin as a matter of fact, which made her cheek and jaw bones seem more prominent and her nose sharper. She was still, as she had always been, more than merely pretty, but she looked — worn, somehow, underlining that the years since they'd last seen each other had not been good ones. Until she smiled.

That same incandescent smile.

Genevieve felt a twinge somewhere in the region of her heart.

"Molasses or squab?" Emmy asked the next soldier in line. Squab was a fancy word for pigeon. With food so scarce, there were hardly any of the homely birds left in the city. Vendôme Place itself, once home to hundreds of pigeons, was bereft of them. They'd all found their way into the cooking pots of the starving populace, usually to emerge under such noms de guerre as chicken, or duck, or squab.

"Molasses," the soldier replied. Of course, as a German, he would have access to plenty of meat.

Hovering behind the group of soldiers, Genevieve wasted a moment wondering where Emmy had gotten the tarts. It was almost a certainty that she hadn't made them. Unless she'd changed out of all recognition, her baking skills were nonexistent. In any case, the ingredients would have required either a sizable investment in black market goods or weeks of accumulated coupons. The scarcity of sweets made the molasses tarts in particular prizes worthy of their price. Only about one-third of Paris's bakeries were operating now, because there were simply not enough supplies of flour, oil and sugar, or fuel, to enable them to do so. With an unexpected flicker of wry amusement, she pondered the existence of a special SOE bakery turning out treats as props. Maybe baking tarts was what had occupied Max all night.

The soldier stepped back, bit into the tart and made noises indicative of his extreme approval while waving the soldier behind him forward.

"Mademoiselle Dumont!" One of the waiting soldiers became aware of her standing behind them, nudged his companions, murmured to them urgently, "It's the Black Swan!" Ogling, they all stepped back to clear a path. Discovered, she smiled and greeted them. If she'd thought about it, she would have at least grabbed Berthe's scarf to conceal her hair and partially hide her face, but upon spotting the woman behind the cart, she'd been so fixated on getting to her that it hadn't even occurred to her. She looked like Genevieve Dumont in the elegant trench coat she'd snatched out of the closet and thrown on over trousers and a blouse, with only the brim of a jaunty fedora to provide coverage for her face and hair.

Under the soldiers' close regard there was no more opportunity for clandestine observation. Stepping up to the cart, she found herself meeting her sister's narrowing eyes.

Like her own, like their mother's, they were a bright, clear aquamarine.

It instantly felt as if no time at all had gone by. A million scenes from their shared childhood passed between them in that single charged look. And then the final ones, the sequence of events that had led to the shattering of their family, rose up like a whole graveyard's worth of wraiths and the spontaneous surge of recognition and reunion arcing between them turned into something dark and cold and distant instead.

He's a terrible person! You can't go with him, Em! She could still hear the voice of her sixteen-year-old self in her head, shaking with urgency.

They were in a private parlor at the opulent Hôtel du Palais in Biarritz, on the Côte Basque. It was early in the morning, and the three of them, Lillian, Emmy, and her, were alone for the first time in days. Genevra had just burst through the closed French doors, desperate to find her mother and sister in a hotel crammed with guests. As they'd turned to look at her, frowning disapprovingly at her less than decorous entrance, at the clothes she'd hastily pulled on, at her tumbled hair, she'd blurted out what she'd hunted them down to say, afraid to wait even another minute in case she lost her nerve.

There was a moment of surprised silence.

"What are you talking about?" Lillian asked.

"Alain. He's — he's — Emmy shouldn't be with him."

"What on earth do you mean?"

"She can't — he —"

"Have you lost your mind?" Interrupting, Emmy fixed her sister with a glare. "Wasn't it just last week that you said he was perfect for me and I was so lucky to have found him? Or was that somebody else talking?"

"That was before. You don't know what he's done!" Genevra's voice shook. She was thin and coltish in loose trousers and a knit top, with an unkempt tangle of black curls and uncharacteristic dark smudges beneath her eyes from a nearly sleepless, life-changing, magic-filled and trauma-roiled night.

The previous evening Emmy had become a married woman, Madame Emmanuelle Giroud. The last few weeks had been hectic with all the excitement and drama of preparing for her wedding. While in better times the celebration of the marriage of the baron and baroness's elder daughter to Alain Giroud, the twenty-five-year-old only son of the wealthy and well-connected wine broker who sold Rocheford's award-winning vintages to the world, would have been held at Rocheford, the economic crash and its aftermath had left the house bereft of most of its furniture and all of its staff and the grounds neglected. Lillian had been beside herself as she had tried to contrive a wedding for her eldest daughter that would not shame them nor expose their penury to the bridegroom's family, their friends or what remained of the fashionable world. A solution had been found: the Hôtel du Palais was owned by an old friend of the family, who had agreed to a much reduced price and to accept future supplies of wine as payment. Everything had gone off beautifully. The guests the hotel was full of had stayed the night, and the celebration had stretched into the early morning hours. This morning even the indefatigable Lillian looked tired. Only Emmy didn't. Radiant with happiness, Emmy looked beautiful in her aqua traveling dress with her dark gold hair cropped short and curled so it framed her face in shining waves. She was moments away from leaving on her honeymoon with her new husband, who was outside supervising as their bags were loaded into the car. Genevra had seen him, tall and blond and extraordinarily handsome, through an upstairs window as she searched for her mother and sister, and had instantly become both furious on her sister's behalf and sick to her stomach upon catching sight of him.

"So, then, tell me! What has he done?" Emmy's question was sharp with challenge.

"Last night — after the wedding — he — he — screwed Madeline Fabron." Her voice dropped to a mindful-of-the-guests hush as she blurted it out. Madeline Fabron was the twenty-something second wife of the septuagenarian industrialist Georges Fabron, a contemporary and close friend of Alain's father.

"*Genevra.* That word! Do you even know what you're saying?" Regal in her cream lace sheath, Lillian shook her head at her, scandalized.

"He did not!" Emmy's furious denial came fast. She knew her sister knew exactly what the word meant — and what she was saying.

"He did too! He *did.*"

"Liar!"

"Girls!"

"I'm not the only one who saw them! Phillippe did, too. We were . . ." She broke off as a rush of emotions — joy, disbelief, embarrassment, shyness, along with so many others that she couldn't even put a name to them — threatened to tie her tongue. The thought that Phillippe Cheviot, their longtime friend and neighbor who'd been wild about Emmy for ages, was now, officially, as of last night, wild about *her* instead, brought a rush of warmth with it. Hugging the knowledge close, she tucked it out of the way for the present and plunged on. "We were walking up from the beach when we saw them. They were together in the gazebo. On your wedding night! You can't stay married to him, Em —"

"You're lying."

"Ask Phillippe if you don't believe me."

Emmy made a scornful sound. "Phillippe would say anything to break up Alain and me."

"He would not!" Although Emmy's words sent a shiver of disquiet through her. Hours after the wedding, when she'd come across Phillippe on the beach in front of the hotel, he'd been sitting all alone in the dark with his back against a rock, his thin face turned up to the moon, his finely chiseled features distorted as he wept. The tracks of his tears had silvered his cheeks. Heart aching for him, she'd dropped down beside him to comfort him, and . . . and . . .

"And *you'd* say anything to get in good with Phillippe. We all know you've been mooning after him for ages. What, did he pretend to see something and tell you so you'd come in here to make trouble? Well, it's not going to work."

"Phillippe did not send me. I saw with my own eyes —"

"Liar."

"Girls, *stop this.*" Lillian put an arm around

Emmy's shoulders. The two of them stood together, facing her. Emmy's eyes were bright with anger. Lillian's were dark with concern. "Genevra, you must be mistaken in what you thought you saw. Surely —"

"I'm not mistaken. He was on top of her, *screwing* her. I know what that looks like, believe me."

"Genevra!"

Emmy clenched her fists. "Alain never went downstairs again, never left me for the rest of the night after we went upstairs together. Not for one minute, do you hear? He was never anywhere near that gazebo, never anywhere near Madeline Fabron."

A car horn honked twice, the muffled bleat jarring. Emmy looked toward it and pulled away from Lillian.

"I'm going now." She started toward the door. "Goodbye, Maman." Then she stopped to fix her sister with the nastiest look Genevra had ever seen on her usually smiling face. "And as for you, you vicious little cat, if you ever repeat this to anyone, I'll make you wish you were never born, do you understand?"

A moment later Emmy was gone. The front door banged behind her. Genevra took a few impulsive steps to follow before stopping, stricken. What more could she do? Confront Alain, who would certainly deny everything and create a nasty scene that anyone might overhear? Through the leaded glass panel in the top of the door, she watched helplessly as Emmy, one hand holding her hat in place, her skirt flying, ran to join a grinning Alain as he waited for her behind the wheel of his car.

She felt sick.

Her mother came to stand beside her, put a hand on her shoulder. "Genevra."

She heard the trouble in Lillian's voice, saw the doubt in her face and gave up.

There's nothing more to be done.

Later, avoiding her mother who was busy seeing to the departing guests, she'd gone in search of Phillippe. He was nowhere to be found.

He'll come to me.

Even as she waited, she hugged the memory of the previous night close.

"You're so sweet. I'll marry you instead. Will you marry me, Genevra?" Phillippe's words, spoken as the moonlight poured over them, were what she'd dreamed of hearing for years.

Of course she'd thrown herself into his arms, smothered him with kisses, answered, "Yes, Phillippe. Yes, *yes,* I will."

Her parents would say she was too young. Her mother would say she could do better. But she would stand her ground; she would marry him.

If only he would come.

At first she hadn't been too worried. A niggle of doubt arose — had he really meant it? Was he having second thoughts? In the bright light of day, with all the emotion of Emmy's wedding behind them, had he looked deep into his heart only to discover that she was only Emmy's little sister after all?

He didn't come. They'd gone home, she and her parents, back to Rocheford, later that day, without her seeing him.

She was hurt. She was bewildered. She told herself that maybe an emergency had arisen, and he'd had to leave without finding her.

Deep inside, she was afraid, deeply afraid, that he was avoiding her, that he'd had a change of heart, that he regretted it.

It was only when she'd grown so desperate to see him that she'd gone to the farm he shared with his widowed father to seek him out that she discovered that he'd never returned from the wedding.

His father hadn't been too worried. A boy, his heart freshly broken — because Monsieur Cheviot, like everyone, knew how Phillippe felt, *had* felt, about Emmy — might not be in too big a hurry to return home.

It was several days before a search was launched. It was several more days before Phillippe was found. Dead, in one of the hotel's ornamental ponds. It was the judgment of the official who presided over such things that he had fallen in, perhaps hitting his head on one of the rocks with which the pond was edged, and drowned.

Genevra had been inconsolable. She'd attended the funeral, then locked herself away in her room until she'd cried all the tears she'd thought she was ever going to cry in her life.

And that had been the end of it. Her love, dead. Her great love story over almost as soon as it had begun.

Until not quite six months later, when Lillian had walked in on her daughter undressing in her bedroom. Taking one look at the rounded stomach Genevra had been so fervently ignoring, she'd asked, with shock, if she was pregnant.

That's when Genevra had faced the terrifying truth she'd been doing her best to deny, and, shaking, finally confided in her mother. That night, Emmy's wedding night, on the beach, she'd been so deep in love, so desperate to console the seemingly inconsolable Phillippe, that she'd succumbed to his embraces and his muttered words of love and given herself to him.

It was no comfort now to remember that he'd asked her to marry him and she'd accepted, that they'd been engaged, that she had considered them as good as wed.

Her mother had listened to her outpouring of words in growing horror.

"Phillippe's dead," Lillian said finally, flatly.

"Whatever you intended, whatever he promised, there's no making this right. The shame of it —" She broke off with a shudder. "My God, Paul mustn't learn of this. It will kill him."

The thought of her father knowing had done what nothing else could do: it stripped away every last bit of the bravado she'd been hiding behind. Fright and shame and grief for Phillippe and the sudden stark realization of the disgrace she was bringing down on the heads of her beleaguered family overwhelmed her. Crumbling to the floor, she burst into tears, shaking and sobbing as if her heart would break all over again.

Kneeling beside her, Lillian had swallowed her own distress in the face of her daughter's. Wrapping her arms around her, she'd held her as she cried and promised that she would take care of everything. That she would make everything all right.

Two weeks later Genevra had been sent away, supposedly to stay with friends in Switzerland for a few months so that she wouldn't be so lonely without Emmy, who had just returned from her extended honeymoon to her new home in Monaco. Actually, Lillian had taken her in great secrecy to Lourmarin, a beautiful small village in Provence, where she'd been hidden away in the house of Clotilde Arsenau, an old and trusted family retainer. The plan was that Genevra, living there under the guise of Madame Arsenau's widowed-far-too-young niece, would have her baby, put it up for adoption, and return to Rocheford and her old life with no one but herself, Lillian and Madame Arsenau the wiser.

Once in Lourmarin, she'd thought her life was over. Until Vivi was born.

When she held her daughter for the first time, Genevra had experienced such an overwhelming rush of love that she'd known it wasn't, known that instead she had a whole new life, and that new life was centered on the infant in her arms.

She'd refused to give Vivi up for adoption, begged to bring her home to Rocheford, clashed horribly with Lillian when her mother refused to even consider such a thing.

"*Absolutely not.* You'll be ruined," Lillian told her, in what was only their second meeting since Vivi's birth. The first had been immediately afterward, when Genevra, weak but furiously determined, had refused to allow her child to be handed over to the nice couple that had been found to take her. Instead of returning home with her mother, as had been the plan, she had stayed on in Lourmarin, defiantly taking a job in the village apothecary, determined to do whatever she had to do to keep her baby. She had continued to live with Madame Arsenau — Tante Clotilde — as her niece, and Lillian, although aghast at Genevra's unexpected intransigence, had continued to contribute to the household expenses. She had also continued, by phone call and letter, to beg her daughter to reconsider her position. This second meeting had included Emmy, who, although the sisters' relationship was far from what it had been before Emmy's marriage, had been recruited by their mother to help make Genevra see sense. In what Emmy and Lillian clearly considered this time of family crisis, past disagreements were set aside.

"I don't care," she'd replied.

"You should care. You will care, as you grow older and wish to go about in society again, or marry. You don't understand the consequences of an illegitimate child to your future. Or to the child's." Lillian reached for Genevra's hand. Genevra pulled it back out of reach. They — Lillian, Emmy and Genevra — stood together in the downstairs sitting room of Madame Arsenau's modest house. Lillian had been visiting Emmy at her new home in Monaco, and they had taken the train together, in great secrecy, to see Genevra.

"Her name is *Vivienne,* Maman," Genevra said. Vivi, all of eleven months old, lay asleep upstairs in her cot. Her mother and sister had looked at the sleeping child, looked at each other and then had asked Genevra to come with them downstairs so that they could talk.

Emmy said, "Genny, consider. Vivienne will be shunned. All her life, people will look down on her. They'll whisper behind her back. She won't be invited into people's homes, or to parties, or anywhere. No one will want to be friends with her. No one will want to marry her. Wouldn't it be better, for her sake, to let her be adopted, so that she can live a normal life?"

"I can arrange for a family close to Rochefford to take her," Lillian said, before she could reply. "You could still see her, make sure she's taken care of. For your sake, and for hers, it's the best solution, Genevra."

"I'm not going to give Vivi up for adoption. I *won't.*"

"What about the scandal to *us*?" Emmy said. "What about poor Papa? As hard as things are for him now, do you want to make them even worse? Do you want him to have to hang his head everywhere he goes?"

At the thought of Papa finding out, Genevra shivered inside. Not because she was afraid of what he would do, but because he would be so disappointed in her, and so ashamed.

"You care about the scandal," she told the two of them. "I don't."

"You don't care about anything except yourself," Emmy said. "You never did."

"That's not true. I care about you, both of

you. About the family. I want to be a part of it, but I can't give up Vivi. I won't."

"Then I'm afraid we're at an impasse," Lillian said.

They had parted with nothing resolved.

Then the unthinkable had happened: Vivi had died. And the world had stopped turning on its axis, and the foundations of her life had fallen away beneath her feet and her existence had turned into a long, cold, endless night. Haunted by bad dreams, riven by regret, self-condemned to what felt like eternal damnation, she'd descended into a state of shock from which she'd only just begun to emerge.

Everyone had said that what had happened wasn't anyone's fault.

She'd known it was hers.

If she could only go back, only change one thing about that afternoon — how often had she wished it? Only every second of every minute of every hour of every day since.

In the chaotic aftermath, as was made abundantly clear to her in the one frantic phone call in which her mother was able to get through to her, she could have gone home to Rocheford again. There was no longer the visible disgrace of an illegitimate child standing in her way, no longer any need to worry about scandal. She could rejoin the family. She could start her life anew.

But how could she go on with her life as it

was before, as if Vivi had never been? No, it was impossible. Genevra was forever changed, and she could never accept a future in which Vivi was forever forgotten.

"You didn't want Vivi, and now I don't want you. I never want to see you again." Her voice had been calm, her eyes dry. The worst agony she had ever experienced in her life had turned her insides to ice.

That same day she'd left Lourmarin, and shortly thereafter fled to America by ship, selling the cameo brooch left to her by her paternal grandmother to pay her passage. On board, she'd made the acquaintance of the ship's entertainers, Ruth and Frank Wilmore and their two sons, Bob and Gene. When Frank Wilmore heard her playing and singing to herself, late one night in the deserted piano lounge, he'd invited her to join their family band. This she'd done and spent the following two years touring America as part of what, as it turned out, had been the Frankie Wilmore Orchestra. Her voice was acclaimed everywhere they went, and she and the band grew increasingly famous. She might still have been in America if Frank hadn't died and the sons hadn't gone to war over who would assume their father's mantle, control of the band and, not incidentally, her. Their fight had ended up with her washing her hands of both of them and hiring a manager, who'd taken her to England. She'd been a minor sensation performing in London at venues ranging from the Monseigneur nightclub to the Palladium. That triumph had led to a European tour, which had taken her to Paris, where she'd been performing at the Moulin Rouge when the Nazis invaded.

During all that time she had lived as Genevieve Dumont. Genevra de Rocheford, having perished with Vivi, had ceased to exist.

Until her father's death and her mother's desperate plight had resurrected her.

Now here Genevra was, surfacing like a phoenix.

To find herself once again looking into Emmy's eyes.

Chapter Twenty-Two

The way in which they'd parted hung in the air between them.

They'd been angry with each other. Since then so much had happened. They were no longer the same people.

As it turned out, though, the differences didn't matter. Their entire history as sisters passed between them in that single look, along with a silent acknowledgment that whoever they were now, whatever life had done to them, they had come together with a mutual purpose: saving the life of their mother.

"It's such an honor to meet the famous Black Swan," Emmy said. It was imperative to give no sign to anyone who might be watching that they were anything other than chance-met strangers, and it was clear Emmy was conscious of that. Her face was bland. Her tone verged on gushing. But Genevieve could see that she wasn't astonished to learn of her other identity, and her sense that her sister had already been aware of her star persona was reinforced when Emmy continued, "I must tell you, I'm quite a fan."

All too conscious of the gawking, listening soldiers, Genevieve smiled. "Are you? That's very nice. May I have a tart?"

"Molasses or squab?"

"Molasses." Either would choke her, Genevieve was sure. She was having a hard time reconciling the knowledge that Emmy was an SOE agent with her memories of her always proper older sister, but so it apparently was. She cast about for a way to convey her vital message to her sister under the avid eyes and ears of their audience but could come up with nothing. From Emmy's presence, it was safe to assume Vartan had delivered the note she'd given him. She had no doubt he'd added his own bit to it, including the key facts of Lillian's arrest and removal to, presumably, Paris. With Emmy aware of their mother's desperate situation, finding a way to save Lillian no longer rested solely on her own woefully inadequate shoulders, thank God. She would have felt a profound sense of relief except for the dire necessity of acquainting Emmy with the order Max had been given, coupled with the difficulty of conveying such information there, with so many eyes on them.

"That will be forty francs," Emmy said.

Genevieve handed over the appropriate

coins. Dropping them, Emmy gave a frustrated exclamation and ducked behind the cart to retrieve what she could, while Genevieve swooped down on a coin that rolled across the cobblestones near her feet and the soldiers gave chase to a few more.

"How clumsy of me! Thank you," Emmy said to the soldiers as she straightened with a smile to receive the coins they returned to her. The soldiers, to a man, were dazzled and murmured incoherently. To Genevieve, who handed her the errant coin she'd captured, she said, "Thank you," as well.

"Here you are. I hope you enjoy it." A moment later Emmy passed over a cloth-wrapped tart accompanied by a quick but speaking look before turning to her next customer.

Clutching the tart, effectively dismissed, Genevieve did what she would have done if she had, indeed, just bought a random treat from a random vendor: she walked away with a smile and a wave for the soldiers whose eyes still followed her. Even after so much time had passed, she knew her sister well enough to know the look she'd been given meant something. And Emmy was never clumsy — the coin drop had been done on purpose.

She made sure to put the line of vehicles in front of the Ritz between herself and any onlookers — the hotel's outer wall was on her other side, with curtains drawn over the windows — then carefully unwrapped the tart. She saw the key at once. Emmy had stuck it in the tart so that the top part protruded through the crust. After a quick check of her surroundings to make doubly sure no one was watching, she pulled the key out. The caramelly scent of the molasses filling blended with the stench of exhaust from the cars as she used the cloth the tart came wrapped in to carefully wipe the key clean. From the look of it, it was a door key. Closer examination revealed that its shank had been engraved with an address: 2 rue Duphot.

She knew that street. It was nearby.

Pocketing the key, rewrapping the now slightly mutilated tart, she looked around to discover that Emmy, having apparently sold out of her inventory, was pushing the cart out of the square.

"Would you care for this?" she asked the young boy who was assiduously polishing the windshields of the parked cars in hopes of earning a few coins as payment, as she pulled an edge of the cloth back to show him the tart. With food now such a precious commodity, to throw such a thing away would have been nothing short of criminal, and her stomach was in such knots she wasn't even going to make the attempt. "I find I can't eat it after all."

"Would I? Thank you!" The boy — he couldn't have been more than eight — took the sweet with a look almost of reverence and devoured it in three bites.

Smiling at him, Genevieve walked back inside the Ritz. She penned a note for Otto — *Don't wait for me, I'll find my own way to rehearsal* — and left it with the receptionist with instructions that it be given to Otto upon his arrival. Then she headed on foot for 2 rue Duphot.

It was only a few blocks away.

The narrow, curving street was mixed residential and commercial. Buildings on either side abutted one another, forming canyon-like walls with just a narrow strip of blue sky visible above to keep her from feeling totally claustrophobic. Only a few people were about. A woman swept her steps. Another walked a dog along the street. A young girl on a bicycle pedaled toward her. A man, walking in the opposite direction, disappeared around a curve. Colorful awnings above doors and small signs hanging beside entrances denoted shops. The appearance of the houses was more varied.

Number 2 was a house, tall, narrow and dignified, with a stone facade that had been painted a soft, cheery yellow. Windows on either side of the front door had their curtains pulled tightly shut. On the stoop a blue ceramic pot held a colorful mix of poppies and lilies of the valley. The delicate white bells and bright red blossoms fluttered in the breeze that came whistling down the street as Genevieve mounted the steps. In the center of the flowers, a child's pinwheel whirred as it spun.

With one more quick look around to make certain she wasn't being observed, she used the key and let herself in.

Emmy was waiting for her.

They acknowledged each other with a quick exchange of glances as Genevieve stepped into a dark, wood-paneled center hallway, the most distinguishing feature of which was a steep staircase along one side that led to the floor above. The hall was cold and smelled musty.

Moving past her without a word, Emmy closed and locked the door, then turned back. "You're looking well."

"Thank you. As are you." The exchange was slightly stilted. Genevieve was conscious of the gulf between them: time, and much else.

"I'm not, but we're not here to discuss that." Emmy beckoned. "Come into the lounge."

She led the way into a chamber that was only slightly less gloomy than the hall, thanks to the tightly drawn drapes that covered the large front window. Genevieve got a quick impression of a high ceiling, a long-unused fireplace, a worn carpet, and a few pieces of torn and scarred furniture — and several darker rectangles on the pale green walls where it was obvious paintings had once hung.

"Whose house is this?" The question was involuntary, prompted because something about the atmosphere made her uncomfortable. As her gaze returned to her sister, Genevieve crossed her arms over her chest. She had no desire to sit, and Emmy didn't appear to want to, either.

"It belongs to the owner of an art gallery in Montmartre. He and his family were arrested last year. They're Jews." Emmy gestured at the walls. "As you can see, they had a number of valuable paintings. The Nazis took them. The house they simply left. It's been ransacked several times. Everything that wasn't stolen has been badly damaged. We've been using it as a safe house off and on for some months now."

Unspoken but implicit in her words was the near certainty that the owners would never be back.

It was a tragedy that had become commonplace. Houses and businesses abandoned when their Jewish owners were rounded up and deported could be found in multiples in every arrondissement in the city. They were like tombstones, bearing silent witness to the atrocities that had claimed their owners. Neighbors and those who knew what had happened tended to avert their eyes and walk a little faster when they passed by, as if fearful of bringing such a fate down upon their own heads.

Genevieve thought of Anna and Rachel. An icy shiver slid down her spine.

Closing her mind to what she couldn't help, Genevieve looked at her sister. "You're with the SOE?"

Even with the evidence in front of her, she still found it hard to believe, and her voice held a note of astonishment.

"Vartan should not have told you that. He has a big mouth."

"He thought we were working together."

"Nevertheless."

"How did that come about?"

Emmy took off her scarf. Her hair, always thick as a horse's tail, was long now and had been braided and twisted into a fat bun at her nape.

"You know Alain died?"

Genevieve gave a curt nod. As determinedly as she'd walked away from her family, she hadn't been able to keep herself from discreetly inquiring about them when the chance presented itself, as it did occasionally as she toured, when she might come across someone who had recently traveled through Cherbourg, or who might have connections with the wine business, or even the odd newspaper. That she had sought out such news was, she saw now, an indication of how much she had missed them, although at the time she hadn't been prepared to acknowledge that even to herself. Thinking about them had meant thinking about the past, and that carried such pain with it that she'd refused to do it.

Emmy said, "My husband — my second husband, David Granville — is British. He's the third son of Lord Granville, the vice admiral, and after we married and moved to England, he was given a job at the War Office. When the Nazis overran France, the SOE was in desperate need of women who were fluent in French to go in and gather intelligence. When they learned that I *am* French, they approached me. I said no at first, but then David . . . He couldn't be talked out of going off to fight. He was with the Eighth Army and got taken prisoner at El Alamein. When that happened, I told them I would go. I've been carrying out missions for Baker Street for almost a year and a half now. I got in touch with Papa —" Her voice faltered.

"I can't believe he's dead," Genevieve said. Her chest ached with the grief she'd been carefully keeping at bay.

She saw her own pain reflected in Emmy's eyes. "I know. He was already working with the SOE when I arrived in France. I warned him of the risk he was taking, but you know him. He insisted on carrying on. Remember how Maman was always saying, 'There's no doing anything with him once he gets an idea in his head, so the only thing to do is not let it get in there'?"

That last was said in a tone that mixed affection with sorrow. It was something Lillian had frequently told them as a kind of rule of thumb for how she planned to deal with their sometimes stubborn father. They'd always translated it to *tell Papa only what you want him to know.* Even as the ache in her chest intensified, Genevieve nodded, and they both smiled a little mistily at the memory.

"Well." As though to provide herself with a distraction, Emmy carefully folded her scarf and tucked it into her coat pocket before looking at Genevieve again. Her manner grew brisk. "You said you needed to see me. Here I am. I can't stay long. Keeping on the move is the best protection against capture."

"I wanted to be sure you knew about Maman. She must be rescued, but I have no idea how to go about it. Vartan thought you could do it. I'm available to help any way I can. Sometimes being the Black Swan is very useful for things like getting admitted to places. Or getting out of them." At the last moment, Genevieve had second thoughts about adding what she'd learned the previous night. It occurred to her that, just possibly, as an SOE agent herself, Emmy might feel compelled to honor the order Max had been given. Almost as soon as the notion occurred, though, she rejected it. Emmy and their mother had always been extremely close. Whatever else might have changed in the ensuing years, she was as sure as it was possible to be that that had not.

"I'll remember that." Emmy's tone was noncommittal.

Genevieve said, "There's one more thing you should know. I've learned that the SOE has given orders that Maman is to be killed if she cannot be immediately rescued."

Emmy frowned. "Where did you hear that?"

Loyalty to Max kept her from revealing the details. Protecting him and his operation was ingrained in her by now.

She shook her head. "I can't say. But it's true, I give you my word."

Emmy said, "I trusted you enough to come and meet you, and to bring you here. It's your turn to trust me."

Genevieve gave her a long look. Emmy's face was older, with shadows in her eyes that spoke of difficult experiences and hard lessons learned since they had last seen each other, but she knew it as well as she knew her own. She knew her sister's character as well as she knew her own, too. In the end it wasn't even a tough decision to make.

She said, "I've been working for the SOE, too. For — someone — who got a message from — I'm quite sure it was London. I happened to see it. It was an order, I believe from whoever is in charge there. It said the baroness was a threat, and this person should see that she was executed if she couldn't be rescued. Act quickly, he was told."

"I haven't heard of any such order." She paused and seemed to reflect. When she spoke again, it was almost as if she were talking to herself. "But then, I wouldn't. I'm based with the Maquis, and I work with a network of cells to coordinate airdrops and sabotage and intelligence gathering, things like that. Papa's cell was one of those in my network. Now that it's been destroyed and can be of no more use to us, I wouldn't ordinarily be involved. I would have been notified that the cell was gone, and that would have been that. It's only because Vartan contacted me — because of the personal connection — that I went to Cherbourg. That I'm here."

Genevieve felt a flutter of alarm. "You do mean to rescue Maman?"

This time Emmy's smile was small and grim. "It won't be easy. But of course I'm going to try. I have friends I hope can help. Papa knew something that I'm afraid he told her, which the *boche* must suspect. Which anybody must suspect who knew how they were together. That explains why they've kept her alive and brought her here to Paris. She must be being very brave, holding out, but they *will* succeed in torturing it out of her, and then they'll execute her." Her expression turned thoughtful. "I can see why your friend was given that order. If she was not my mother, I would agree with it."

Genevieve was horrified. "You would agree with murder? Of an innocent woman?"

"The fight is so desperate, and the consequences of losing are so enormous. If the Nazis prevail, it will be the end of the world as we know it. They will engage in mass slaughter on a scale that makes everything they've done up until now seem like nothing. Any of us who survive will wish we were dead, I promise you."

Genevieve shivered. "What does she know that's so dangerous?"

Emmy grimaced. "If I'm right, and I'm very much afraid I am, details of the planned Allied invasion of France. The Nazis have gotten wind of it, but everything possible is being done to mislead them as to when it will happen, and where. It's vital that they not learn the truth." Her gaze locked with Genevieve's. "There. I've told you a big secret. Now you must tell me one. Who is this man you're working for? He'll be trying to locate Maman, too. Perhaps I can use what he's turned up in his search. At the very least I must know who to watch out for."

Still Genevieve hesitated. "You would not — I don't want anything to happen to him."

"Oh, is he cute?"

That unexpected bit of teasing, the sudden sparkle in Emmy's eyes, was so like the Emmy of old that Genevieve was startled. It brought her sister back to her as nothing else had, in a way that was heartwarming and gut-wrenching at the same time.

"It isn't that," Genevieve said, and was only aware of how defensive she sounded when it was too late to do anything about it. Emmy's smile flashed. Genevieve frowned quellingly at her, and suddenly it was as if all those years they'd spent apart had vanished in the blink of an eye. "He's doing important and valuable work, and to interfere with it or cause harm to come to him would be a huge disservice to the partisans. Also, it would be wrong."

"I understand your concern for his work." Emmy's tone was grave, but that teasing sparkle still lurked in her eyes. "If we're lucky, we'll never come anywhere near him, and if we're not, you can be sure we'd never do anything to harm one of our own agents. I just prefer to approach this nearly impossible task with as much information as possible. So who is he? Come on, *je te tiens, tu me tiens,* I need to know."

Chapter Twenty-Three

Emmy's casual use of their catchphrase from the old days disarmed her. It was one more nearly irresistible reminder of the tie that had once bound them. That *did* bind them. For better or worse, they were sisters, and in it together, still.

As Genevieve came to that realization, the last bit of her reserve with her sister melted away.

Who could she trust in this matter if not Emmy?

"My manager," Genevieve said. "Max Bonet." She saw no need to add that Max was really Max Ryan, a Brit. A tiny sliver of caution on Max's behalf? Perhaps.

"He's based in Paris?" Emmy's tone was all business.

Genevieve shook her head. "I'm constantly on tour. He travels with me. Before Paris, we were in Brussels. Next we tour France, and then we go to Madrid. As an artist, I can move freely between countries. I can do a lot of things ordinary citizens can't. Max uses that."

"How did you get involved with him?"

"He helped me out of a jam in Morocco and started acting as my manager." She saw no reason to go into more detail. "I didn't know he was with the SOE until later."

"Must have come as quite a shock."

"It did."

"Ironic that we both took such different routes only to end up in the same place. Could you ever have imagined that we'd end up as spies?"

"Never." Genevieve's response was heartfelt.

"It's an insane world." Emmy grimaced. "My code name's Merlin. As in the hawk, not the wizard. What's yours?"

"I don't think I have one. Max keeps me out of it as much as he can. In case something should go wrong."

"Probably wise of your Max."

"Believe me, he's not my Max."

"If you say so. For our network, your code name will be Lark. Anyone who works with me will know you by your code name only, if I have to mention you at all. If I send someone to you, or any message comes from me, that's the name that will be used. If you get a communication that's supposedly from me that doesn't use Lark or Merlin, don't trust it. It's not from me."

"I'll remember."

"Congratulations, you just officially became a War Bird."

Genevieve looked a question.

"That's what they call us, back in London. Because we're women — birds, as the Brits say. They think it's funny. Men can be so juvenile." She made a face. "So I played right into it and picked bird names for my network. I don't think Baker Street's gotten the joke yet."

Genevieve smiled. "Maybe one day."

"Maybe. All right, let's get on with this. The first thing to do is find out where Maman is being held. See if you can discover from your — oh, sorry, *not* your Max where he is looking, and if he should find her, let me know at once. Or if you have any other sources of intelligence, particularly among the *boche,* this would be the time to tap into them. If someone as prominent as Baroness de Rocheford is being imprisoned and tortured in Paris, there will be whispers of it floating around. If you learn anything, you can leave a message here. Put it beneath the rug on the left side of the fireplace." She walked over and lifted the corner of the rug to demonstrate. "Right here. If you do leave a message, pull the pinwheel out of the flowerpot out front and lay it on its side among the flowers. That way I'll know to come in and look. The flowerpot is a signal, by the way. As long as it's out there, it's safe to come into the house. If it's ever missing, don't come anywhere near. Understand?"

Genevieve nodded. "Yes. I may not be able to find out anything," she cautioned. "A lot of German officers hang around backstage, but they don't usually have anything on their minds but the girls. And Max tends to be closemouthed."

"Well, do what you can. And take care not to let him or anyone else catch on to what you're doing. If the Nazis get an inkling, they could lay a trap for us with Maman as bait. As for Max, you mustn't tell him anything about me, or that I'm going to try to rescue her."

"Why not?"

"He might try to stop me from interfering, by, say, reporting me to headquarters. This is outside the scope of what I'm supposed to be doing, and if they find out, I'll almost certainly be ordered to stop and return to my assignment. Not that I'd obey, but it would complicate things. Or he might work faster to try to get to Maman before I do, so he can use his own judgment on how to deal with the problem she represents. The only people who care if she comes out of this alive are you and me, you know. Everybody else on our side just wants to silence her before she can tell what she knows."

Cold gripped the nape of Genevieve's neck

as she faced the truth of that. "I thought of telling Max who I really am — he only knows me as Genevieve Dumont — and that the baroness is my mother, and asking him to take killing her off the table and concentrate on rescuing her instead."

"Will he do that, do you think?"

Honesty forced her to say, "I don't know."

"Then it's best to say nothing, rather than alert him to the fact that you have an interest in this. If he's guarded in what he says to you, or if he lies outright, it might send us looking in the wrong direction. The time frame for saving Maman is so short we can't afford to make a mistake."

"Maybe you two could work together."

"I doubt he would agree. And even if he did, what would happen if we reached her and he decided that the better course would be to execute her?" She shook her head. "That would end badly for one of us. No, I'd rather work on my own, with people I trust."

"Do you think you'll be able to rescue her?"

"I'm going to do my best."

That wasn't the guarantee Genevieve had hoped for, but she suspected it was honest. "You'll keep me informed, won't you? When you find her, and about what happens?"

Emmy nodded. "If I have a message for you, I'll lay the pinwheel down in the flowers just as you're to do for me. The message will be in the same place, under the rug. If we should have to stop using this house, if you come by and the flowerpot is gone, I'll find a way to get a message to you. I saw you coming out of the Ritz. You're staying there?"

"Yes."

"Of course you are. You're the Black Swan. A *star.* That is so you. You were always one to land on your feet, no matter what." Emmy's tone was fond, rueful. "One day you'll have to tell me how that came about. We looked for you after you left, you know, and once we found you'd gone to America, I wrote, more than once. So did Maman." She looked inquiringly at Genevieve, who shook her head: she'd never received the letters. Not surprising, since she'd constantly been on the road with the band. "Once we figured out that the famous Genevieve Dumont was our very own Genevra, we kept track of you. Maman wanted to come see you in person, but the war began — and then we didn't want to pull you into this." The slightest of smiles. "We should have known that you would find a way to get yourself right in the thick of it anyway." She pulled her scarf out of her pocket and put it on again as she moved toward the hall. "Come, I must go. And so must you. It's much safer to keep meetings like this brief."

They were almost at the front door when Genevieve gave voice to something that had only just begun to trouble her. "Will I see you again?"

Emmy finished tying the scarf beneath her chin. "In Paris? I don't know. I'm going to have to work fast if I'm to get to Maman in time. If I succeed, I may have to leave the country with her right away. If something goes wrong — well. Nothing in life is certain, is it? But let's hope so. I hope so."

Genevieve stopped walking. Having just found her sister again, her heart was heavy at the thought of losing her.

"I've missed you," she said. "I'm sorry I stayed away so long."

Emmy stopped walking, too. The sisters stood facing each other.

"It hurt Maman badly." The look Emmy gave her was stern.

"And — Papa?" The catch in her voice when she spoke of him would, she suspected, be there for a long time to come.

"He thought you were safe in Switzerland, well into the war. He was happy you were safe. And then, when he knew you were the Black Swan, he was so proud."

"I should have come back," she said. "I should have written. I just — I couldn't. I —"

"Blamed us for your daughter's death. I know."

The pain stabbed through Genevieve, sharp as a knife. "I didn't blame you, I — I didn't want to pretend she never existed." She couldn't talk about Vivi still and so went mute as the familiar choking sensation strangled all utterance.

But Emmy had once known her well. And, it seemed, she still did.

"Oh, Genny, I'm so sorry about what happened." Emmy wrapped her arms around her just as she had done when they were girls, and the younger one was hurt or suffering in some way, and held her tightly. Hugging her back, Genevieve found a surprising amount of comfort in the warm embrace of the big sister she'd always turned to in times of trouble. "I'm so sorry for what you've gone through. I'm sorry for everything I did that contributed to it. And I did contribute to it, even though I had no idea at the time. I found out — much later — that what you said about Alain and Madeline Fabron was true."

Genevieve closed her eyes against the pain. "I told you," she said into Emmy's hair. Her voice was scratchy, but she was grateful to be able to speak at all.

"I know. I never should have brought him home, I never should have married him and I should have listened to you about him when you tried to warn me. My only excuse is I was so young. And so in love."

If there was ever a time to hold on to a grudge, now — in the height of war, where life and family were more precious than anything — wasn't it. "It's in the past," Genevieve said. Her voice was stronger, and she could breathe again.

Letting go, Emmy stepped back, only to catch Genevieve's hands and look at her earnestly. "It is, but — there's something I have to tell you. I was going to wait until after we deal with Maman, but who can say where any of us will be then? And you should know." She took a breath. "Phillippe's death . . . it wasn't an accident." She swallowed hard. "Alain killed him."

Genevieve felt as if, for a moment, the ground shook. "What?"

Emmy tightened her grip on her hands. "That morning, the morning after our wedding, long before you came to talk to Maman and me, Alain went out very early for a walk, to smoke a cigarette and to check on the car. To get to the garages, it was necessary to walk along the path through the ornamental ponds, so that's what he did. Phillippe saw Alain on the path, or was waiting for Alain by the car — I'm not sure about that part. Alain never said exactly. But he confronted Alain about betraying me, about being with Madeline Fabron. He didn't say anything about you being with him when he saw them together, and I never told Alain what you said to me. I didn't want Alain to hate you, and I suspect Phillippe wanted to keep you out of it, too. In any case, Alain never knew you knew. Which was well for you, for us all, because he attacked Phillippe over it, and killed him and threw him into the pond, and just . . . just walked away and went on our honeymoon with me, as if nothing had happened at all."

Genevieve felt disoriented, dizzy. "My God, Emmy." The crushing weight of what might have been settled like a vise around her heart until it seemed to struggle to beat. Her love for Phillippe rose up from where she had so long ago tucked it away to make every cell in her body quiver with pain. The difference that having him alive and with them would have made in her and Vivi's life — the ramifications were so enormous that she could barely take them in. The one absolute certainty that cut through the rest was that if Phillippe had been alive, he would have married her, and she would never have been whisked away to Lourmarin in disgrace to have her baby — and Vivi would not have died. "How have you lived with this? How could you possibly have lived with this?"

"I didn't know." Emmy's grip on her hands was all that was keeping Genevieve from sinking to the floor. Her own hands were icy. Her nails dug into Emmy's palms. Far from noticing, Emmy held on tight and looked at Genevieve with sorrow and compassion and guilt all combined in her eyes. "Not for a long time. I was blind to what he was. Deliberately so, I think. He was handsome and charming, on the surface, at least, and rich — rich was important then. You know how things were with us, so bad Papa even feared losing Rocheford. So I saw what I wanted to see. I was a fool, I know. Underneath it all he was beastly, horrible, as I eventually found out to my sorrow."

"Was it bad? The marriage?" Genevieve could scarcely get the words out. But it was obvious to her that Emmy was hurting, too.

Emmy grimaced. "After only a few months, he started to hit me. By the time we'd been married a year, everything I did made him angry and it kept getting worse. When I came with Maman to see you in Lourmarin that time? I was already worried about being gone too long, about what he would accuse me of doing while I was away and how angry he would be when I got home. If I even spoke to a man, he thought I had taken a lover. He was . . . cruel. He said if I told anybody what he did to me or left him, he would kill me. God forgive me, as bad as it was with him, I was sure those were just idle threats. Then one night he told me what he had done to Phillippe. He taunted me with it. That was too much — too terrible. I knew I couldn't stay. I ran away the next day despite his threats and went home to Rocheford. But Papa wasn't there, and Alain came after me. By then I was frightened to death of what he'd do, to Maman as well as me. I was going to go to the police, tell them about Phillippe, but I had no proof, and if Alain found out I told and they didn't arrest him . . ." Emmy shivered. "As he kept telling me, his family was so rich and had so much power that by then I was convinced he could get away with anything. But he was actually almost nice, that day, and so polite to Maman, acting as if nothing were wrong. Trying to fool her. Trying to get me to come back to him. I had told Maman about all of it, about what he had done to Phillippe, about everything. She was so brave, so calm, playing along with him, letting on that she thought nothing of me arriving at Rocheford as I had and that I would go back with him as a matter of course. And I was thinking *never, never, never,* but I was so scared. And then . . . Alain died. That night, before Papa ever even got home. Just went into some kind of fit and dropped down dead. It was so unexpected — and such a blessing! The whole time afterward, up until we buried him, I kept saying *thank you* to God in my prayers."

"Oh, Em." Now it was Genevieve's turn to hold on to and steady her sister, who was looking as pale and emotional as she still felt.

"It's over," Emmy said. "After he died, I just wanted to forget about him. I could have gone to the police about Phillippe then, but what would have been the point? And there was still no proof. So I did nothing, just stayed home with Maman and Papa and tried to forget it all, everything Alain had done, all the bad things that had happened. I thought my life was over, that I would live hidden away at Rocheford forever, and I was fine with that. Then I met David, who is the kindest bear of a man. So big and gentle. And he took me away, and the war came and . . . Now he's in a POW camp at the mercy of the Germans, who have none." Her lips quivered, and Genevieve could see the worry and fear for her husband in Emmy's eyes. But before she could say anything, Emmy's lips firmed and her eyes took on a determined glint. "Anyway, here we are."

"Here we are," Genevieve agreed. The sisters looked deep into each other's eyes. Genevieve drew strength from what she found for her in Emmy's gaze, and she thought Emmy did the same.

"But you — what I suffered doesn't compare to what you suffered, and are still suffering. I can see it in your face. To lose your little girl as you did — it must have been hell. It must *be* hell."

More pain squeezed Genevieve's heart.

"I can't . . ." Shaking her head, she tried to explain that she couldn't talk about it, but the words wouldn't come. She saw in Emmy's face that her sister understood.

"One more thing you should know," Emmy

said, and Genevieve almost winced in anticipation of something else that would cause pain. "The last time we spoke, Papa said one reason he was fighting so hard to drive out the Nazis was so that France would be safe and life would go back to the way it was and you could come home and we could all be together again."

Genevieve's heart felt as if it were cracking in two. *Papa,* she thought, as all the love they'd shared rose up inside her like a dawning sun, filling her with its brightness and warmth. She pictured its rays expanding beyond her body through the universe to hopefully find and touch him, too.

He's with Vivi now. A crystal-clear image of her tall, handsome father holding hands with her beautiful little girl appeared like a sunburst in her mind's eye, comforting her with its promise of eternity, strengthening her with its assurance of the immortality of the bond they shared. Phillippe appeared in the picture, too, on Vivi's other side, so young, so stalwart and handsome and just as she remembered him, and the thought that Vivi was with them, that the three of them had found one another, allowed her poor broken heart to finally begin to heal.

"The past is the past," Emmy said with brisk resolve. "All we can do is think of Maman now."

Taking a deep breath, Genevieve tucked

that moment of precious communion away deep inside her heart and turned her focus to the present. "Yes."

Emmy gave her hands one last squeeze before releasing them. "We should go. We don't want to leave together. You go first. I'll follow in a few minutes and head in a different direction."

"All right."

Reaching the door, Emmy stopped with one hand on the knob to give her a long look, as if to memorize a dear face she might not see again. Even as Genevieve recognized that look for what it was, Emmy opened the door. A gust of cool air swept in, disturbing the dust, making Genevieve clutch the brim of her hat to keep it from blowing off. Emmy swept a pseudocasual look up and down the street, then turned back, gesturing for her to exit.

"Be careful, *bébé,*" she said as Genevieve walked past her.

Genevieve's chest felt tight at hearing the once despised nickname in her sister's dearly familiar voice. Shades of their shared childhood twirled through her head. She ached for the innocence of those halcyon days.

She ached for her sister, her family. For what might have been.

"You, too." The smile she threw over her shoulder at Emmy was tremulous. Then she stepped out into the bright spring sunlight.

An unexpected whirring sound caused her to glance down, to find the pinwheel spinning merrily in the midst of the swaying flowers at her feet.

The door closed behind her with a whoosh and a click, and any chance for one last parting word with her sister was lost. There was nothing for it but to walk on down the stairs and head back toward the hotel.

More people were out and about now, patronizing the shops, occupying several small tables of an outdoor café, going on about the business of their daily lives. A car sputtered past her, its roof laden with the round tanks containing the natural gas that fueled it in this time of strict gasoline rationing.

As she neared the end of the street, she glanced back because she simply couldn't help herself.

Her sister hurried in the opposite direction, a nondescript brown figure with her head lowered and her shoulders hunched against the wind. With a shopping bag hanging from her arm and a seam drawn up the backs of her bare legs to simulate the stockings she couldn't obtain, she looked like one more anxious housewife whose primary preoccupation was finding enough food to feed her family, on her way to queue up for whatever her coupons might allow her to purchase for the day.

It took an effort to look away. But Genevieve did, and walked on. The next time she glanced back, Emmy was nowhere in sight.

Chapter Twenty-Four

The note she'd left for Max loomed large in her mind. As she made her way to La Fleur Rouge, Genevieve fervently hoped he hadn't yet seen it and she could tear it up without him ever knowing anything about it. The excuse she'd come up with in case he had found it after all felt flimsy, and she really didn't want to have to trot it out.

All the hallmarks of a rehearsal in progress — a blast of music, the thump of dancing feet, the smell of sweat — greeted her as the lift doors opened.

She'd left the note propped against the lamp where he couldn't miss it. It was gone. Her stomach sank even as her appearance garnered a clamorous response.

"Hello, Genevieve!"

"Look, Genevieve, I learned the steps!"

"Genevieve, Madame says we must turn to the left, but I thought —"

A single look around confirmed Max wasn't there. Anxiety quickened her breathing.

Rehearsal didn't pause just because she'd arrived. The space was crowded with pirouetting, bell-kicking *choristes,* the girls bare legged and barefoot in leotards and the boys bare chested and barefoot in tights. They continued belting out "La chanson du maçon," a new addition to the second act, even as she waved and answered back in response to the greetings, took off her hat and coat, grabbed a leotard from the costume rack and went into the bathroom to change.

She was drained both physically and emotionally, and sick with worry over her mother. But the hard truth of the matter was she had a show that night, and the next night, and the next, with only a few days off here and there. That was her future ad infinitum. Rehearsing was a necessary component of what she did. Having skipped the previous day's rehearsal, she could not miss this one. *The show must go on* was a fact of theatrical life.

In addition, she had to keep up the regular rhythm of her life as Genevieve Dumont in order to do the work Max needed her to do. The survival of her mother was uppermost in importance, but at the moment there was nothing more she could do to ensure that. She could only trust that Emmy had Lillian's rescue in hand.

When the number started at the top again, she was dressed and ready and plunged right in. With Madame Arnault at the piano pounding away, and the chorus coming in and out on cue, she sang and danced her way through first the numbers that were deemed to need extra work, then the others. Finally, she ran through the opening song of the second act, a plaintive "Parlez-moi d'amour" in which she, alone onstage, accompanied herself on the piano.

Rehearsal ended in the early afternoon. On tenterhooks about where Max was and what he was doing, she went into the bathroom to wash and change before heading downstairs, where a car and driver, presumably Otto, would be waiting to take her back to the Ritz. She was prepared to grill Otto about Max's whereabouts, but as it happened she didn't have to.

Max sat at the piano, a cigarette dangling from his lips, his dark head bent, his broad shoulders partially blocking out the light from one of the windows. The familiar smell of his Gauloise drew her like a beckoning finger. As she walked toward him, she realized that he was idly picking out the notes of "Parlez-moi d'amour."

Have you found her? Have you — please, God, no — killed her?

His face was untroubled. His hands, those tan, long-fingered hands, moved over the keys with the sensitivity of an artist.

He didn't look like a man who'd just come

from murdering or ordering the murder of a helpless woman.

On the other hand, he also didn't look like a British spy.

She was so wound up with fear for her mother that she no longer trusted her instincts where he was concerned.

He stopped playing when he saw her, took the cigarette out of his mouth and stubbed it out.

"You wanted to see me?" he asked as she stopped beside the piano.

The note. Of course, he was referring to the note. She trotted out the excuse she'd come up with for it.

"Wagner is going to be waiting for me outside the stage door tonight. He expects to take me to dinner after the show." Her tone was abrupt, as if she blamed him.

"Is that so?" Max stood up and reached for his stick, which rested against the piano. There were no dark circles beneath his eyes, no lines of dissipation around his mouth. He wore a gray suit and tie, his hair was combed smoothly back from his face and he was clean-shaven. She wished she didn't know how deceiving those saturnine good looks of his could be. "That's a pretty big fish you've caught."

"I haven't *caught* him. And I'm not going."

"Why not?" He came around the piano and took her arm, urging her toward the lift.

"Sounds like it should be a pleasant evening. The note you left made me anticipate something more alarming. To say nothing of the urgent message you sent by way of Otto."

"I'm glad you hurried right to my side to find out what was going on. I only left the note for you —" she glanced at her watch; it was half past two "— at about half past five this morning. That was, oh, some nine hours ago. And Otto was last night. Where have you been?"

"Here and there. You badgered the life out of Otto, then got up at the crack of dawn, came over here and left me a note saying you needed to see me *now* to tell me you're going to dinner with Herr Obergruppenführer?" His brows lifted at her.

She'd known it was a flimsy excuse. Wagner's invitation was nothing she couldn't have dealt with on her own, and he knew it as well as she did. She scowled. "I'm *not* going to dinner with him. And it's your fault I'm in this fix. You can damn well get me out of it."

"I gladly would, but I doubt he'd be willing to take me to dinner in your place." They were across the room by then. He hit the button for the lift. "We have an appointment, by the way. In an hour. At Radio Paris."

"So that's why you turned up."

"I turned up because you sent for me. The radio show just happened to coincide with that."

"Uh-huh."

"Don't sound so skeptical. You know I always turn up for you."

"Sooner or later. And I hate Radio Paris."

"I'm not asking you to marry it. Just sing for it." He took her hat and coat from the pegs she'd hung them on, plopped her hat onto her head, helped her on with her coat and put on his own hat.

"Do you ever *listen* to their broadcasts?"

"Frequently."

"They're nothing but propaganda. They even change the lyrics to songs. Did you hear what they did to 'With My Girlfriend'?" Indignantly, she sang: "In the garden of England, deception has flourished . . ."

"We work with what we have."

"I'm tired. I'm hungry. I want to go back to the hotel."

"After you sing 'Seule ce soir' over Radio Paris, I'll take you back to the hotel immediately."

"Why 'Seule ce soir'?"

"It's one of my favorites." His voice was bland.

"You're going to get me arrested one of these days." She straightened her hat, tied the belt of her coat and frowned at him.

"For what? Singing 'Seule ce soir' over the radio? There's nothing in that to get you arrested. It's a beautiful song, and hearing you sing it so beautifully will brighten the hearts of your countrymen. You're doing a public service."

She snorted.

He shook his head. "There's that skepticism of yours again. Where's your trust in your fellow man?"

"If you mean *you,* I left it somewhere back in Brussels."

"You do have a fixation with that, don't you?"

"You *lied* to me, you *manipulated* me —"

"On the other hand, I could have left you to rot in jail in Casablanca. Or worse. The way I look at it, you're coming out way ahead."

"Since I'm liable to get arrested and shot at any time, I'd say it's pretty much a draw."

"I told you, you do what I tell you, I'll keep you alive."

They stepped inside the lift when it arrived, and Max hit the button that started them down.

She said, "Kind of short notice, isn't it? I'm surprised the radio station was willing to accommodate you."

"They're not accommodating me. They're accommodating you, and at the same time they're doing themselves a favor. They don't often get the chance to put a star of your magnitude on the air, and they know we're only in Paris for these last three days."

Genevieve's chest tightened as she realized

that he must be confident of solving the problem that was her mother within that time frame. He would hardly leave Paris until the situation was taken care of. Would he?

Speculating was useless. She didn't know enough about that side of him, about how he operated, about what he did when he wasn't with her, to make anything but the wildest of guesses. For the first time she realized how thoroughly he had insulated her from the work they did. Otto had said he protected her, and she was just beginning to realize how true that was.

The lift stopped and they stepped out. Even at this time of day she could see customers in the parlor, but the hall was deserted and they encountered no one as they walked outside. The Citroën was parked by the side entrance. Max opened her door for her, then got behind the wheel.

She caught herself chewing her lower lip as the car pulled away from the curb, but she immediately stopped, hoping he hadn't noticed.

"Where were you this morning?" Max asked. His tone was casual, but she knew him. Otto must have told him about coming to pick her up at the Ritz and instead getting a message saying she'd make her own way to rehearsal, which was unprecedented. Of course he homed in on it. She was a fool not to have been expecting it. Her only excuse was she'd been so busy coming up with that other lie that she'd forgotten about the need for this one.

"Here and there." She threw his words back at him while she did mental gymnastics trying to come up with a reasonable explanation.

"Seems to be a lot of that going around."

"Seems to be."

"You want to be a little more specific?"

Ordinarily she would have simply said no and left him to stew, but under the circumstances she didn't want to ratchet up his curiosity any more than it already was. "Remember those friends I told you about? I met them for breakfast."

"The friends with the steely grip?"

He was referring to the bruises on her arm, she knew. She didn't want to have to come up with another lie to explain those away, so she reverted to flippancy. "That's them."

"Ah. A last-minute engagement, I take it?"

"Yes. And you?"

"Mine was a last-minute engagement, too."

"At five in the morning?" She could only presume that wherever he'd been had something to do with Lillian. Time to do a little digging as to his whereabouts. "Where does somebody go at five in the morning, anyway?"

One corner of his mouth quirked up. "If you mean me, who says I went there at five in the morning?"

As the implication that he'd been out all night sank in, her knee-jerk reaction — that he'd been with a woman — was immediately replaced by the more obvious one, that he'd been out hunting Lillian. The thought made her stomach twist.

"There's a curfew, in case you've forgotten. If you were to be caught out on the streets . . ."

"Worried about me, Genevieve?"

"Worried about what will happen to me if something happens to you." Her voice was tart. "You have all the important documents. And if you're arrested, you might talk."

He laughed. "Ouch. That's putting me in my place."

They turned onto the Champs-Élysées, joining the steady stream of traffic. Cars, trucks, bicycles in various iterations and a horse-drawn carriage shared the wide boulevard. Pedestrians crowded the sidewalks, dodging around the queues that were barely shorter than they had been that morning. The horse chestnuts lining the street were abloom with pink-and-white flowers, and sunlight sparkled over all. The scene was almost idyllic — except for the gaunt faces and worn clothes of the people they passed, the ubiquitous swastika banners, and the soldiers and military vehicles that were everywhere.

Radio Paris was headquartered in the Poste Parisien building. It was differentiated from its next-door neighbor, the gaudy Lido, the famous cabaret that, along with the Moulin Rouge, was the Casino de Paris's biggest competitor, by lines of triangular balconies marching across its front and the huge bronze disc with a pair of back-to-back *P*s that crowned its roof.

Inside the building, Genevieve was greeted effusively by the manager and taken up to the broadcast studio, where Jean Hérold-Paquis, whose daily news reports regularly called for the total annihilation of Britain, was just signing off with his signature ringing pronouncement, "England, like Carthage, shall be destroyed!"

The irony of using this, the official Nazi radio station, to broadcast a signal to the Resistance was not lost on her, but she had only a moment to appreciate it.

"You want to dedicate this song to Elise, from Gervais," Max murmured.

Genevieve nodded, then the sound engineer came for her and she was stepping up onto the platform in front of the tall, square-framed microphone. A moment after that, she was flashed the green light that meant *you're on.*

"This song is dedicated to Elise, from Gervais," she said into the mic, and sang "Seule ce soir."

The bowing manager kissed her hand, and his assistant presented her with a bouquet of roses on behalf of the station on her way out.

"I felt like a Christian in the Colosseum with the lions in there," she said when she and Max were back in the car again. The Citroën's engine purred as Max accelerated to get in front of a pair of bicycle taxis. Nestled on the seat between them, the roses perfumed the air. "And if you recall, that ended rather badly for the Christians."

"The key difference here is that these lions don't know you're a Christian. They think you're another lion."

"For now." They were on their way to the hotel, and she decided to take the opportunity to probe a little while she could. "So have you learned anything new about your missing baroness?"

He glanced at her. "Remember that, do you? Why all the interest?"

"I find the idea of a baroness on the run from the Nazis mildly fascinating."

"The twists and turns your mind takes are unfailingly intriguing. And as far as I know, she's still on the run."

"No word as to where she might be?"

"None."

"Where do the Nazis take people like that? When they're caught? If she were arrested in Paris, for example, where would she be held?" She tried to sound like the questions were prompted by nothing more than idle curiosity.

"Cherche-Midi is where they generally take women. Although it's hard to say."

That small tidbit was hardly news, and certainly not worth passing on to Emmy, who almost certainly would be already aware of it. Max was looking thoughtful now. A trifle nervously, she wondered what he was thinking. Impossible to imagine that he could be somehow linking her recent absences to her curiosity about the baroness, but still his expression made her uneasy.

"You know," he said. "It might be a good idea for you to go to dinner with Herr Obergruppenführer tonight after all."

She looked at him in surprise. "What? No."

"It's a chance to pump him for information we won't get any other way."

"What information?"

"The mindset of the top brass. There are rumors that some of them are ready to turn on Hitler. Feel him out about the SS's attitude toward der Führer. We also hear that Wagner is a friend of Rommel's. You could try to find out what he knows about what the Generalfeldmarschall is up to. You could pretend to be afraid, say you've heard rumors the Allies are getting ready to invade, ask him where he thinks the invasion will happen. If he says something generic like *on the coast,* ask him what the Desert Fox could possibly do to prepare for an attack by sea. Try to find out where, precisely, Rommel is concentrating his defenses. You know, bat your eyelashes, tear up if you have to, hang on his every word. I'm betting with a little effort you can get him to tell you everything he knows. Just be sure to remember what he tells you."

"Max —"

"You might even be able to find out something about the missing baroness." He threw that out there so casually that, if she hadn't known he was involved in his own desperate search for said baroness, she would have thought it was nothing more than a lure designed to tantalize her into more readily agreeing to do what he wanted. "If she's been arrested, Herr Obergruppenführer will almost certainly know of it. Tell him you've heard rumors that some members of the aristocracy have been working with the Resistance, and you personally are outraged by that and find it hard to believe. Get him talking, see what he says."

Up until then, she'd been appalled at the idea of going to dinner with Wagner. It felt rather like getting into the water with a shark and encouraging it to swim after her. Max had just opened her eyes to the opportunity it presented. Besides pumping Wagner for information for Max, there was a chance she could use him to locate her mother. As one of the hated SS's top interrogators, he might very well know where a prisoner brought to Paris for interrogation was being held. Where her mother was being held.

She would have to be careful, question him artfully. If he were to suspect her motives, she would be in terrible danger. Hitler had recently ordered that anyone caught aiding the Resistance was to be immediately executed. The only exceptions were for those slated for interrogation, and then the order was that they were to be executed as soon as the interrogation was complete. No exceptions.

Her heart slammed at the thought.

Reaching the place Vendôme, they pulled up to the Ritz. At this time of day, the hotel was bustling. Third in line, the Citroën crawled toward the entrance.

"All right, I'll do it," she said, picking up the roses as they reached the front of the queue and a doorman came forward to open her door for her.

"Good girl. And leave the roses. They're for me."

She looked at him, realized that the roses must contain a message, and remembered the low-voiced exchange he'd had with the assistant when the man had handed the roses over. She laid them back down with a grimace.

"Of course they are. Whatever was I thinking?"

The doorman opened the door and she got out.

"You're not the only one with admirers, you know," Max called after her.

She didn't have to look around to know that he was smiling.

Chapter Twenty-Five

"I was first a soldier, then a police officer, and then I became a soldier again." Wagner spoke over the forkful of pressed duck that was on its way to his mouth.

He had, as promised, been waiting for Genevieve outside the stage door after her show, and she had now spent the better part of two nerve-racking hours in his company. They were almost at the end of their meal, and he was waxing expansive under her outwardly admiring gaze. Having employed the age-old feminine stratagem of encouraging him to talk about himself, she was listening with every appearance of wide-eyed attention as he did so. She'd already learned that he was, indeed, good friends with Rommel, and that the general Wagner described as "invincible" was frustrated by the failure of those closest to the Führer to heed his suggestions for further fortifying certain areas of the coast that were deemed less likely to be targets for invasion. Nonetheless, according to Wagner, Rommel remained confident in his ability to beat back the Allies anywhere they might attempt a landing. Beyond a massive troop buildup in the Pas-de-Calais area, considered to be the most likely spot because of certain intelligence they'd received as well as its proximity to Britain, he'd ordered a slew of nasty surprises to be prepared for the potential invaders up and down the coast that would prevent them from progressing beyond the beaches, where, when the time came, he planned to cut them down in droves. She was, Wagner told her, not to harbor the slightest worry about such an invasion succeeding, because it would not.

Genevieve made an encouraging sound when he paused, and he continued with the far less interesting subject he'd been pursuing for the last quarter hour: how he'd come to occupy the position he was in. "When the police came under the control of the SS, I saw how efficient the organization was, how meticulous they were in carrying out their duties, how forward thinking they were in their policies. I have been with the SS ever since. We are the ones who are most loyal to the Führer. We were formed to serve as his bodyguards, you know. In the SS, our motto is My Honor Is Loyalty. And we live up to that motto every day."

He took another bite of duck.

She made big eyes at him. Mentally she was

busy trying to compile everything he'd told her into a list so that she could recount it to Max without forgetting anything. "That is so impressive. Yet there's a rumor going around that some of those closest to the Führer feel that Germany would be better served by a new leader."

His gaze sharpened. "Where did you hear that?" There was a snap to his voice.

The lightning change in his demeanor jolted her. *Careful,* she cautioned herself, and covered the jump in her pulse with a smile.

"The party circuit." She shrugged, kept her voice light. "You know what that's like. Lots of gossip, no way to know what's true."

"I do indeed." The sudden harshness in his face faded as he looked at her. "There is nothing to it. Der Führer is lionized by those of us who serve under him. What he is working to build now is a thousand-year empire, and we, all of us, are proud to be a part of it. Next time you hear any such talk, you may tell those who spread that kind of nonsense, from me, that our leader will remain in place for life, and in our hearts for eternity."

"You may be sure I will, if I should hear such a thing again."

"There will always be those who are disgruntled, or jealous." His tone conceded that not everyone felt as he did. "But the vast majority of Germans revere Herr Hitler, I assure you. Those of us in the SS would lay down our lives for him to a man."

The fanatical intensity with which he said that made her heart beat faster. This was a man who would not only die for what he believed in but kill for it, she had no doubt.

If he were to suspect . . .

The thought brought with it an inward shudder.

"Tell me more about the work you do." She did *not* bat her eyes at him. Well, maybe she did, a little. Damn Max for making her self-conscious about it. But she had to use what worked, and encouraging Wagner to think she was interested in him did. He had already told her a few generalities, using euphemisms like *examine* for interrogate and *enemies of the people* for those who fell into his hands, but nothing that led her to believe he had any knowledge of her mother or her whereabouts.

"I do what must be done for the good of the Reich. Having said that, everyone does not achieve the same results. There is an art to it." He speared another bite of duck, mopping it in the bloody sauce, and chased it with a swallow of wine. A very good wine, brought to the table by the proprietor personally, who uncorked and served it with bowing assurances that it had been kept back especially for Herr Obergruppenführer Wagner, whose favorite Parisian restaurant this was. "I have the reputation of being somewhat harsh in my methods, I am aware. Perhaps you have heard such?" Genevieve essayed a small, noncommittal smile for him to interpret as he would. "But you must not think I am harsh with those in my personal life. At heart, I am a gentle man, I assure you."

Genevieve felt her skin creep as she looked into his smiling blue eyes. He had always reminded her of someone, and it finally hit her who: Charles Lamartine. Wagner's eyes held the same predatory gleam as Lamartine's had when he looked at her, and as she recognized it, she promised herself that this night was the last opportunity she would ever give him to be alone with her. His cheeks were flushed with wine and the enjoyment of her company. He was once again sitting relaxed in his chair, and his expression was good-humored. None of that made a bit of difference. She'd already seen behind the mask into his true nature. The horrors of the torture inflicted on prisoners undergoing interrogation by the SS were legendary. Wagner's reputation in that regard was particularly damning. She could not think about it and maintain her admiring posture, so, not for the first time since meeting him, she forced all such thoughts from her head.

She'd gotten really good at that.

"I don't doubt it, Herr Obergruppenführer." She smiled at him. He smiled back, then startled her by leaning forward and taking her hand, which rested on the table beside her plate. His hand was warm, with thick palms and sausage fingers.

Once again she was reminded of Charles Lamartine.

Do not shrink away.

His eyes were intent on her face as he looked at her across the table. Set with flowers, a small flickering candle in a glass globe and the finest china, crystal and cutlery atop a starched white tablecloth, the round table was tucked into a discreet corner. Nevertheless, Genevieve had been aware that she was the object of continual covert observation from the other diners from the moment she'd entered the restaurant. Several of the women — and there were far more *chère-amie* types in slinky dresses than matrons in pearls — watched even now in a side-eyed manner they no doubt thought was discreet.

"Please, you must call me Claus."

Look pleased. Flattered. Smile. "Claus. And you must call me Genevieve."

"It will be my great pleasure to do so. Genevieve."

The dimples that gave him such an incongruously boyish look appeared. He was not an unhandsome man, but the physical sensation of his hand holding hers made her stomach churn. The thought of what those hands had done . . .

He slid his thumb over the back of her hand

in a subtle caress, setting her teeth on edge. It took every ounce of willpower she possessed not to yank it from his hold.

Instead she smiled, endured his stroking thumb for a moment, and gently withdrew her hand. Then, breaking eye contact for fear of what he might be able to read in her eyes, she glanced toward the waiter as if she required his services. To Wagner she said, "I wonder if I could possibly get another napkin? I've dropped mine."

Because she had pushed it off her lap.

"Certainly." He snapped his fingers, and the waiter glided over. "Mademoiselle Dumont requires another napkin."

The waiter draped the fresh linen over her lap with a flourish. For just a moment, as he straightened, their eyes met. She saw a flash of what she thought was real hatred in his eyes, mixed with cold contempt. The look was there for no longer than it took to blink, and then he dropped his lids and turned away. But she was shaken by what she had seen: he, a Frenchman, despised her, because he thought she was a collaborator.

It was the role she was supposed to play, the role in which she could best serve her country. But seeing the reflection of herself in that guise in someone else's eyes made her sick.

"Everything is to your satisfaction?" he asked Wagner, all obsequiousness now. She did not think he realized what his eyes had just revealed. He could not have meant for her to see it. Certainly if she had called Wagner's attention to it, or even intimated that his service was lacking or he made her uncomfortable, he would have been fired at the very least.

"Excellent as usual." Waving the waiter away, Wagner said, "One of the reasons I truly enjoy my visits to Paris is because of its fine restaurants."

"They're quite an enticement," she agreed.

The truth of the matter was most restaurants that remained in the city were of the storefront or sidewalk café variety, and of questionable quality. They were almost without exception plagued with the same scarcity of food that afflicted Paris's citizens and, as a result, were able to open only two or three days a week. The restaurants had been separated into categories, with the types of food they could offer, the prices they could charge and the clientele they were allowed to serve strictly controlled. A, B and E categories obtained food supplies on the black market and were able to offer simple meals to a wide variety of customers. Categories C and D were at a lower price level. They served families and the working class, and their dishes were prepared with the same ingredients the average household could obtain for themselves, which was not much.

But a handful of restaurants had been designated as *catégorie exceptionnelle,* and La Tour d'Argent was one of these. Its sixth-floor location on the Left Bank featured an unrivaled view of Notre-Dame cathedral during the day (at night, like now, the heavy curtains were drawn to satisfy the conditions of the blackout). Even in these difficult times, the atmosphere was elegant, the service superb and the clientele exclusively rich, famous or German, or some combination of the three.

It was late — half past eleven — and yet the tables were full of high-ranking officers and their families or companions, and rich collaborators. Ordinary people, whether French or German, could not afford the prices and would not be permitted to pass through the hallowed doors in any case. Seating was limited, as was access. At up to a thousand francs per meal, the food was the best that Occupied Paris had to offer.

Each time she took a bite, the emaciated faces and hungry eyes of her fellow citizens rose up to haunt her. She had to keep reminding herself that to eat with the appearance of enjoyment was both her job and the best thing she could do for them.

Wagner said, "I hope you are enjoying the sole."

I'm choking on every bite. "It's as delicious as you promised it would be. One of the best meals I've had in Paris, in fact. Thank you for inviting me."

"It is my pleasure. La Tour d'Argent is my favorite restaurant. I dine here several times a week."

"I can certainly see why you would. Everything about this place is spectacular."

She let her gaze wander appreciatively around the large candlelit room with its gilded arches and baroque details. The scent of wine and rich food, the glittering jewelry and fine gowns on the women, the well-dressed, well-fed-looking men seemed to belong to a place far removed from war-weary Paris. To be surrounded by so much opulence felt obscene.

"No more spectacular than you." Wagner's gaze slid over her. She was dressed with deliberate modesty in a long-sleeved, high-necked green silk dress accented only by a narrow black belt and a black silk rose pinned to her shoulder, but there was enough carnality in his eyes as they met hers to make her uncomfortable. "Allow me to tell you how beautiful you look tonight. I am the envy of every man present."

She smiled. "Thank you."

"It is my objective to surround myself with the spectacular, and the beautiful and the one of a kind. You are all three." He tipped his glass to her in a salute, then swallowed the last of his wine.

The waiter appeared beside their table, saving her from having to reply. His eyes blank now, his face etched in lines of polite concern, he cast an experienced look at Wagner's empty glass and plate and her nearly empty ones. "May I bring our dessert selections?"

Wagner looked at her. "Genevieve?"

There was a proprietary note to his voice, and she could tell how much he enjoyed addressing her in that familiar way in front of the waiter. The discomfort of being despised made her want to squirm in her seat, but she maintained her composure and replied with a nod.

The waiter removed their plates and brought a cheese board along with a selection of desserts. She settled on a demitasse only, pleading the richness of the meal. Wagner had cheese, and more wine.

"You must know everything that goes on in Paris," she said in a last desperate attempt to learn what she wanted to know as, finally, the remaining plates were taken away and the waiter presented Wagner with the bill. So far, she had gleaned a great deal of information that might be of interest to Max, but nothing that would help in finding her mother. The problem was she couldn't ask anything too direct. If he were to get the slightest inkling of what her true purpose was . . . She shuddered inwardly. The thought of finding herself in his power made her go cold with fear.

He smiled as he pulled out his wallet. "Not quite everything."

"I bet you know —" But she broke off. As he extracted the necessary banknotes from his wallet, a delicate gold chain with a small red heart dangling from it was dislodged.

For a moment, as it hung there against the smooth brown leather, she gaped at it.

Fortunately, he was occupied with counting out francs and didn't notice the sudden, stunned riveting of her attention.

"— everything that goes on in Paris," she finished lamely, as he handed the payment to the hovering waiter, spotted the errant piece of jewelry hanging from his wallet and restored it to the inner compartment where it had been tucked away.

"Not quite as much as that." Smiling at her, he pocketed the wallet, then walked around to pull her chair out for her. "But I confess to knowing a great deal." His tone was light.

Managing a smile for him, she rose as though nothing had changed. But she was shaken to the core.

She knew that pendant. There was no mistaking it: a thumbnail-sized garnet heart on a finely wrought gold chain, complete with tiny gold letters *E* and *G* carved into the center of the heart.

She and Emmy had given it to Maman one long ago Mother's Day.

Chapter Twenty-Six

Wagner has seen Maman . . . or has seen someone who has seen Maman.

That Genevieve knew for sure.

Is he the one interrogating her? Torturing her? Maman of the delicate skin and fragile bones . . .

The horror of it shook her, but there was no way to ascertain the answer.

My God, will he go to her after leaving me?

Her breath caught, even though there was no way to know that, either.

Perhaps someone gave him the necklace. Whoever is interrogating her. But why? Why does he have it? Could he know I'm her daughter? Could this all be a setup, part of an elaborate trap?

The thought sent terror shooting through her veins. Her gut said no. A lightning review of their interactions convinced her that his interest in her was just what it seemed.

But again, there was no way to be sure.

Her eyes fixed on his face, and she tried to look interested in what he was saying. She'd lost the thread: she had no idea what he was talking about.

Can we find her by following him?

That was the urgent question. A flutter of hope stirred inside her as the possibility occurred. It was certainly worth a try. Only . . . she couldn't do it. The actual doing of it had to be left to Emmy.

I can't get a message to Emmy until the curfew lifts.

The desperation she felt was almost unbearable.

Remaining in Wagner's company, behaving as if nothing had changed, was one of the hardest things she'd ever done.

But she did it.

Smiling. Acting as if she liked him. Pretending nothing was wrong.

He took her back to the Ritz, sitting beside her in the back seat of his official Daimler-Benz, with his driver, a peach-faced boy he curtly addressed as Lutz, behind the wheel. It was a short ride through dark and deserted streets, but it seemed to go on forever. He didn't try to squeeze her knee or paw or kiss her, which was a good thing, because at that point she was so racked with nerves she probably would have jumped out of the car. But he did sit so close to her that their bodies brushed, and even that was enough to require extreme self-discipline on her part to endure. She supposed she could thank the rigid code of behavior demanded of a German officer for his restraint. Her standard line of defense against such an attempt, which was always a possibility when carrying out these close-and-personal missions at Max's behest, involved outrage, a "what kind of girl do you think I am" diatribe and the power of her stardom, which provided a certain amount of protection. If that didn't work, she had no objection to slapping an offending face.

They talked for the duration of the ride. Or, rather, he talked and she listened, although her mind was in such turmoil that she barely registered a word. But her nods and smiles kept him going until they reached the hotel.

The burning question she wanted to ask him was *Where are you going after you drop me off?* But she didn't ask it, afraid to alert him to her interest. Besides, if he was going to wherever her mother was being held, he almost certainly wouldn't tell her. So she bit her tongue and stayed silent.

To her dismay, he came in with her, accepting the salutes of the sentries on duty at the door with a quick one of his own. The lobby was full of a mix of German officers and affluent civilians in stylish evening wear, many of whom flashed curious looks in their direction as, with his hand on the back of her waist, ostensibly to guide her while in reality seeking to claim public ownership, he escorted her across the room. She glimpsed familiar faces — Edward, the waiter from room service, carrying drinks on a tray; Georges, from the Little Bar talking on the telephone as he looked out at the ebb and flow of people; Charles Ritz, the owner's son, glad-handing his guests; Coco Chanel with her German lover making her way up the *grand escalier.* The Ritz's restaurants and bars were crowded, and the walls echoed with music and laughter. Though it was hours after curfew, the hotel, while observing blackout protocol, was in full swing. In those of the city's establishments that catered to the occupiers and their sycophants, Paris's nightlife flourished as if there were no such a thing as a war.

As they reached the lift, she was on pins and needles for fear that he expected to come up with her. To turn him down might make him angry, which she didn't want to do unless there was no other course open to her. Angering a man like Wagner came with a price — danger. To avoid having to say no, she'd learned, the best thing to do was keep the question from being asked in the first place.

With that in mind, Genevieve hit the lift button and immediately turned to Wagner. In case he was harboring any misapprehensions about how this evening was going to end, she meant to make it clear that she was going upstairs alone.

"I had a lovely time tonight. Thank you." Smiling, she thrust out her hand.

To her relief, he showed no disposition to argue.

"The pleasure was entirely mine." Taking her hand, he lifted it to his mouth and kissed it. She felt the moist heat of his mouth against her skin and barely repressed a shudder. "Dare I say I hope this is only the beginning of our friendship?"

God forbid. "I hope so, too."

The lift doors slid open.

"Good night." Withdrawing her hand, she stepped into it.

"Good night, Genevieve." It was only when the lift door was closing, and he added, "I'll be there tomorrow night after your show. Just walk out the stage door and I'll be waiting," that she realized that, at some point — probably during the course of their one-sided conversation in the car, when she was too shocked from seeing her mother's necklace to know what she was saying — she must have agreed to meet him again.

For another dinner? Almost certainly.

Every cell in her body recoiled at the thought.

There was nothing to do about it at the moment, though, other than hope her wide-eyed surprise hadn't been noticed. As soon as the doors closed, she wiped the back of her hand against her skirt in an attempt to rid herself of any trace of his mouth. At the same time, she consoled herself with the reminder that she could always come up with an excuse to put him off. Then it occurred to her that, now that she knew he'd had contact with her mother, spending more time with him might be a good idea.

She could learn things. Even, perhaps, find out where her mother was being held. In case Emmy failed.

On the other hand, Wagner would take her continuing availability as encouragement, and the thought of encouraging him made her light-headed with fear. His intentions went far beyond kissing her hand. From the beginning, what he wanted from her had been there in his eyes.

She didn't know if she could go through with meeting him for dinner again.

You don't have to decide right now, she told herself. *Tomorrow is plenty of time.*

Meanwhile, she needed to talk to Emmy. She was desperate to talk to Emmy.

Although perhaps Emmy already knew where Lillian was. Perhaps a rescue was already underway, or being planned.

Please, God.

Her stomach tied itself in knots at the thought of what might be happening even now, and how helpless she was to do anything about it.

Once in her suite, she found Berthe waiting. Assuring her devoted henchwoman that she was fine and didn't need her, Genevieve sent her off to bed. She went into the bedroom, scrubbed her hands until the one Wagner had kissed was red, undressed, took a quick bath, pulled on her slip-like nightgown and wrapped herself in her robe. She meant to go directly to bed but found she was too agitated to sleep and instead ended up back out in the sitting room pacing restlessly while her thoughts raced. She stopped, abruptly, only when a soft knock sounded on the door to the suite.

It was well after midnight. She took a step toward the white-painted panel, then paused to frown at it.

Who could it be? Hotel staff? Not at this hour. Surely — *surely* — not Wagner. Or — a raid?

She went cold with fear.

The door opened.

The resultant leap of her heart subsided almost instantly when she saw that it was Max.

Tension left her body in a rush. Her shoulders sagged. She was so glad to see him she instinctively reached out with both hands and took a quick couple of steps toward him. Her instant impulse — to grab onto him and tell him about the garnet heart and Wagner and her mother and thus put the whole nightmare situation into his capable hands — she just as swiftly quashed. It only took remembering Touvier and the order Max had been given.

She stopped short, let her hands drop. "Max." Her voice was flat.

He had his back to her as he softly closed the door and hadn't seen. Looking around now, he spotted her standing there in the middle of the sitting room. Lit only by a pair of small lamps, with the curtains well drawn against the night, the room was full of shadows.

"You're up," he said. "I thought I was going to have to go drag you out of bed."

She didn't know what she looked like — or, she did: nothing like her usual glamorous self with her face scrubbed clean and her hair pushed back behind her ears and all wrapped up in her blue chenille bathrobe, with fuzzy mules on her feet — but, having slid over her once, his eyes fastened on her face.

"Is something wrong?" he asked.

She couldn't tell him. Not the truth.

"You just broke into my room." She folded her arms over her chest.

"It's not breaking in if you have a key." Handsome in his tux, a little louche looking with a five-o'clock shadow darkening his jaw and his bow tie loose so that the ends hung down past his open shirt collar, he walked toward her, holding the key up, letting it dangle between his thumb and forefinger, to illustrate.

"Who gave you a key?" She frowned in an effort to hide whatever he had obviously seen in her face.

"I always have a key." He pocketed it. "I just don't often use it."

"By often, I hope you mean never."

"Aside from now? Absolutely."

"You're lying. I can tell."

The lazy smile he gave her made her wonder how many times he'd been in her rooms without her knowing it. For what purpose? To check up on her? To search it? The thought was aggravating rather than alarming.

"Since you're up, can I assume you were expecting me? Or were you waiting for someone else?"

"Oh, someone else, of course. I always look like this when I'm expecting company in my hotel room after midnight. Only, silly me, I'm never expecting company in my hotel room after midnight. So maybe I just couldn't sleep."

"You look beautiful, as you know you always do." A teasing glint came into his eyes. "A little *jeune fille* for some tastes, but me, I like the look, so don't worry."

"I wasn't worried, believe me."

"So why couldn't you sleep?"

"Because I just had dinner with a Nazi who tortures people for a living?"

"Ah."

She narrowed her eyes at him. "What do you want, anyway?"

"What do you think? Information. I saw you getting cozy with Wagner in the lobby, by the way. I take it from that the evening went well. So what did he have to say?"

She wasn't sure how she felt about the idea that he'd been watching without her knowing it. "Where were you?"

"In the bar. I wanted to make sure you got back to the hotel safely."

"What would you have done if I hadn't?"

"We'll never know, will we?" Setting his stick aside, he made himself comfortable on the sofa and looked up at her. "Well?"

She told him everything she thought he might be interested in. The only bits she held back were the parts pertaining to her mother. By the time she'd finished, they were both sitting, he on the sofa and she in a chair flanking it, so close their knees brushed. Leaning toward him, talking softly but animatedly, she racked her brain for every last detail.

"That was good work," Max said when she finished at last. Despite how late it now was, he seemed wide-awake and full of energy. While she . . . she felt drained. Limp even, as if she had just survived an ordeal, which she supposed reliving her dinner with Wagner was. "A shame he knew nothing about the baroness you're so interested in."

There was no change in his expression — Max was a master at never revealing what he was thinking — but she knew perfectly well that the topic was more important to him than his casual tone implied. He never missed a thing — had he somehow picked up on the real magnitude of *her* interest in the topic?

The thought was unsettling. The only thing to do was to brazen it out.

She shrugged. "If he did, my questioning was too subtle to elicit any details."

"Better too subtle than the opposite."

"That's what I thought, too."

"So the whereabouts of the missing baroness remains a mystery?" The sudden gleam in his eyes was, she thought, searching, and she vowed not to bring up the subject of the baroness around him again.

"It seems so, yes."

"Probably for the best." His tone dismissed the subject, and she was able to relax again. "You have any trouble with him?"

Despite the offhand way he dropped the question, she knew what he was asking: if Wagner had gotten out of line with her.

She shook her head. "No. He asked me to call him Claus, and kissed my hand before I came upstairs."

"I saw that."

"He asked me to have dinner with him again tomorrow night." The words were abrupt. Until she said it, she hadn't even been sure she was going to tell him. She wanted to find an excuse to refuse. At the same time, she was afraid to break the connection, because of her mother. So far Wagner was the only link she was aware of. With an unhappy flicker of self-knowledge, she realized that she'd told Max because she knew him well enough to know that he wouldn't turn down an opportunity to continue using her to get to Wagner. She wouldn't be able to get out of it now: Max would make her go.

Max's mouth tightened. Just fractionally, but she saw it. His hand, in the act of reaching into his pocket for what she assumed were his cigarettes, hesitated. "Did he?"

She said nothing.

"You should go."

She'd known it. Max was ever one to seize opportunities, no matter the cost. Even if the cost was to her.

"Should I?"

"Everything you find out helps us. Wagner is a valuable resource. One you have the unique ability to access." Pulling the cigarettes from his pocket, he tightened his fingers around the pack to the point where she wondered if he was going to crush it.

"Then I'll go."

"You want to be careful. Herr Obergruppenführer doesn't strike me as the kind of man to be satisfied with kissing a woman's hand for long."

"I'm aware of that. I can handle it."

He nodded. What else was he going to do? Obtaining information from terrifying men was part of her job.

"What time are you meeting him, and where?" His voice was strictly business now.

"At the theater after the show, like tonight."

"We'll go over some of the things you want to try to get him to talk about before you go." He returned the pack of cigarettes to his pocket without ever having so much as tapped out a smoke.

"All right."

With the air of one who'd finished talking, he reached for his stick and rose to leave. She stood up, too, and their bodies brushed. As their eyes met in instinctive reaction, she was conscious of an almost overwhelming urge to lean against him, to let him take her weight, just for a minute or two. Not only the weight of her body, but the weight of her abhorrence for Wagner and her aversion to going out with him again, and the weight of all the troubles that crowded in on her, and the weight of the war and her mother and Emmy and all the losses that had been and might still be to come.

She was just so tired of it all and so *frightened,* and if she could only get some relief from all the weight, just for a little bit, she would recover sufficiently to start feeling brave again. Then she realized that it wasn't so much that she had been brave before as that she had been numb, and that frightened her, too, because she no longer knew what the world felt like without the numb.

The one thing she was pretty sure of was that leaning on Max was not the answer. He was a spymaster and she was his tool. He would protect her, but she could not be sure that it would be for any longer than it suited his purposes to do so.

She took a step back. The heel of her slipper caught in the carpet. She stumbled and almost went down hard.

"Careful." He caught her with an arm around her waist and pulled her upright so that she fell against him.

Her cheek came to rest on his chest and her hands splayed out on either side of his waist to get her balance, and there she was, exactly where she both did and did not want to be. The faint, familiar scent of his cigarettes smelled like home to her now, she realized, and she realized, too, that he had dropped his stick to catch her and seemed to have no trouble standing straight and tall without it. Leaning against him, absorbing his solid strength and warmth and the comfort of his arms around her, she wanted to stay. She could feel the rise and fall of his chest as he breathed. Her hands were between his jacket and his shirt, and she could feel the firm muscles of his waist. She liked how tall he was, and how much bigger and stronger he was than she.

She could have closed her eyes. She could have clung.

She didn't. She pushed away, took a couple of steps back. To survive, she told herself, she needed to be able to stand on her own two feet.

She needed to *not* depend on Max.

"All right?" he asked as his hands dropped to his sides. She nodded. There was something in his eyes as he looked down at her. She frowned as she tried to identify what it was. A kind of wry acceptance? Resignation, even? As if he was coming to terms with a fact he didn't much like but could no longer avoid.

It made no sense. Or if it did, she was just too tired to make sense of it.

He turned away, bent to pick up his stick. Then he started toward the door.

"Max —" She said his name without having anything to follow it with. The truth was, and she hated facing it, she wasn't ready for him to go.

He looked back at her, his expression a question.

"Good night," she finished lamely, because she couldn't think of anything else.

He nodded, opened the door and walked out without another word.

Chapter Twenty-Seven

Slipping out a side door of the hotel shortly after 5:00 a.m., Genevieve kept her head down as she hurried away from the place Vendôme. No soldiers were on duty at this entrance, and she was able to get away without being noticed. It was still dark out, the kind of purple-tinged darkness that presages the rising of the sun. She stayed close to the buildings as she walked quickly toward 2 rue Duphot. The rumble of traffic from the nearby rue de Rivoli, a foghorn tooting on the slightly more distant Seine, even the slam of a window closing somewhere above her, served as mere background noise to the thudding of her heart. The note, folded, was no larger than her thumbnail, and it was concealed inside the hem of her sleeve — she'd snipped a stitch to make room — but if she was caught with it, it was enough to get her killed.

A surprising number of people were up and about. Like her, they all seemed to be slinking through the gloom as if they didn't want to be seen.

The flowerpot on the stoop came into view as she turned the corner onto the street. The house was dark, but one or two buildings nearby showed light through their windows. It would not be long, she knew, before the sidewalk cafés were open and people started queuing up at the shops.

To be safe, she approached on the opposite side of the street. A boy was out sweeping the cobblestones in front of a shop with long, slow strokes of a handmade broom. The rhythmic swishing sound was the opposite of soothing, which would be, she realized, because her nerves were so on edge. She passed him, keeping her face averted, and dodged another boy who careened past on a bicycle. This one had a cloth bag full of newspapers to sell strapped across his body.

Her heart clearly intended to pound its way out of her chest. Her fingers tightened around the key in her pocket.

The house loomed like a crouched, sleeping beast.

Go on. Get it over with.

Casting a wary look up and down the street — as far as she could tell the only person near enough to see her was the street sweeper, and he had his back turned — she crossed to number 2, climbed the steps and used the key to let herself in.

Once she closed the door behind her, the inside of the house was black as pitch. It was cold as well, far colder than outside, and she guessed that there'd been no heat on in it for a long time, since its owners were arrested, probably. She stayed where she was for a minute as her eyes struggled to adjust. Her senses were on high alert, extending way beyond their usual radius in an attempt to probe the depths of the house. Emmy had said they used it as a safe house — was someone there? Was *Emmy* there? She'd gotten the impression that Emmy was staying elsewhere, but that might have been wrong.

Barely breathing, standing still as a post, she listened for sounds beyond the usual creaks and whispers endemic to an old building, absorbed faint smells of dust and damp and something vaguely floral that might have been a lingering trace of cologne, and tried to sense whether she might not be alone.

She heard a distinct thud, and the tiny hairs on the back of her neck catapulted upright.

What was that? A small dull sound, as if something heavy but padded had dropped. It had come — she thought it had come — from the stairs, where they turned and rose again just beyond the landing.

Blindly she stared in the direction of the sound.

It could have been anything, but . . . She was getting a terrible kind of electric feeling that someone was there, lurking unseen in the dark.

Her pulse skittered. Her mouth went dry.

"Is anyone here?" She couldn't help it. She had to know.

No answer. She didn't know whether to be glad or sorry. She did know that she couldn't simply stand there forever, holding her breath while she listened for something more.

Do what you came to do and get out.

Her eyes had adjusted as much as they were going to. There was just enough gray light filtering in through the window at the stair landing to enable her to see the doorway to the lounge. Whether or not someone was holed up in the nether regions of the house, she had to move. As quietly as she could, afraid with every breath she drew of bringing someone who wasn't Emmy down upon herself, she stole into the sitting room, which was even darker than the hall. Groping her way along, she found the corner of the carpet mainly by touch. Lifting it, she tucked the scrap of paper, with its tiny, precise handwriting that detailed what she had seen, beneath it and lowered it back into place.

Then she left with the swiftness of precipitous flight.

It was only as she emerged out into what now seemed like the brightness of the predawn gloom that she realized how loudly her pulse thundered in her ears and how fast and hard she was breathing. Carefully, quietly closing the door, she turned the key in the lock with a feeling of intense relief and turned to go.

Paying not the smallest amount of attention to her, the boy still swept the street. Now she found the slow swish of his broom steadying.

During the approximately five minutes she'd been inside the house, nothing out here had changed. That was reassuring.

She was halfway down the steps before she remembered the pinwheel. Difficult to see in the shadow enfolding the stoop, she heard its faint hum as it spun in the wind. Letting out her breath in a frustrated hiss, she went back up, pulled the pinwheel out of the dirt and laid it down among the flowers. The faintest whiff of lily of the valley followed her as she turned and fled.

At the end of the street, as a result of a random glance in a darkened shop window, she became aware of two men in tan trench coats crossing the street maybe half a block behind her.

Their hats were pulled low over their eyes, but their faces were turned in her direction.

There was something about them — warning bells went off in her head.

The gestapo were everywhere these days, spying on everyone, arresting indiscriminately, killing on no more than a suspicion of complicity with the Resistance. Desperate to stomp out the French underground in the face of the Allied invasion that everyone knew was coming, although no one could say for sure where or when, they'd turned particularly savage. In the last weeks their numbers had multiplied until they swarmed through Paris like an invasion of cockroaches. Many favored tan trench coats.

Her heart jackhammered.

Were they watching the house? Do they know what it is? Did they see me leave?

The frantic questions chased one another through her head.

They had to have seen her leave. They were *right there.* If they were looking, that is. Maybe they hadn't been.

Maybe two men in the kind of coats the gestapo favored just happened to be walking down this particular street at this particular time, and just happened to be looking steadily in her direction.

And maybe not.

She did not speed up. She did not look back. She kept on walking, same pace, same rhythm, through the lavender-tinted light toward the rue de Rivoli, while her breathing turned ragged and goose bumps raced over her skin.

Picturing herself being hauled before a firing squad like those poor souls in Cherbourg made her go all light-headed. Balling her suddenly cold-as-ice hands into fists, she thrust them into her pockets.

Hard as it was, she forced herself to maintain a steady pace.

Her mouth went dry. Her pulse drummed in her ears.

The glimpses she got in the shop windows she passed told her the men were behind her now, walking casually along, more easily tracked as the sun rose and the shop windows grew shiny with it, reflecting like mirrors.

Even if she were to lose them now, they could come for her anytime they liked. At the hotel, at the theater, onstage . . .

Panic churned her stomach.

The men walked faster, not quite fast enough to spook their prey should she happen to spot them, but fast enough to eventually catch up.

Maybe they didn't know who she was. If they were watching the house, maybe what they saw was just some random girl coming out. Maybe they only wanted to ask her a few questions, and if she played dumb, they'd let her go.

Maybe was a weak and pitiful word on which to stake her life.

That it took so long to dawn on her was a sign of how frightened she was. She'd dressed to escape notice in Berthe's box coat, with Berthe's scarf tied over her head. Given the uncertainty of the early morning light, with them behind her and at the distance they were, they couldn't possibly have gotten a look at her face. If they didn't know who she was, if they hadn't seen her leave the hotel and followed her from there — *I would have spotted them, I'm almost sure* — then they could not know she was Genevieve Dumont.

A tiny flame of hope flared inside her.

If I can get away from them, I have a chance. Run.

It was her only shot.

Abandoning all attempts at subterfuge, she rounded the corner and dashed up the dark, deserted street toward the relative busyness that was the rue de Rivoli. Her shoes clattering on the cobblestones sounded loud as gunfire to her terrified ears. Her breathing came in lung-wrenching pants. This side street was a canyon, narrow and walled in by buildings. A wild look around told her that there was no exit, nowhere to go but straight ahead. Dashing up stoops, banging on closed doors, pleading for help, could, if she happened to choose a residence with someone who would actually answer the door and then take her in with a minimal explanation and in the face of putting themselves in danger, get her off the street faster. More likely, such an attempt would just slow her down and lead to her getting caught. Her best hope was to keep running and reach the rue de Rivoli in time to disappear.

It's no good, there's too far to go, they'll turn

the corner and — will they shoot me?

The gestapo was notorious for shooting fleeing suspects.

A nerve-shattering creak overhead proved to be an old woman who threw open an upstairs window, stuck her head out, peered up and down the street without seeming to notice Genevieve looking up at her wide-eyed as she tore along the pavement below, and withdrew. A pair of schoolchildren in uniforms exited a house at the end of the street, walked the few meters to the rue de Rivoli, turned left and walked out of sight.

An odd whispering sound behind her sent an icy tremor shooting down her spine. She snapped a frightened look back: a bicycle was coming on fast. Head down, feet pumping the pedals, the man riding it — the *civilian* riding it — was clearly in a hurry.

A quick, compulsive snap of her eyes beyond him told her that the trench coats had not yet appeared.

The bicyclist passed her. Even as her head swiveled to follow his progress, he braked with a squeal of tires, fishtailing so that the bicycle skidded directly into her path.

Gasping with fright, she jumped back. He leaped off, grabbed her arm.

"Here." He yanked her toward the bicycle, gave a jerk of his head up the street. "Jean's Café, across from the Grand Palais. Go."

Who he was or where he'd come from

didn't matter. He was old and shrunken and bundled up in a threadbare coat and . . . she didn't care.

Grabbing the bicycle with a breathless "Thank you," she hopped on and pedaled as if her life depended on it. Which she was very much afraid it did.

Behind her a muffled shout — the trench coats? — caused her to tense in terrified anticipation. *Is it them? Will they shoot me?* But she was flying now, bent low over the handlebars. *Almost there.*

She burst out onto the rue de Rivoli, into the stream of automobiles and trucks and bicycles and horse-drawn carriages and assorted other conveyances that was heavy enough even at this early hour to provide cover, and she allowed herself a single glance back. The man who'd given her the bicycle was nowhere in sight. The trench coats, shouting, raced up the narrow side street in pursuit.

Go, go, go.

Darting into the middle of traffic, legs working like pistons, tires bumping over the uneven pavement, she dodged around a crowded, lumbering bus, then raced toward the place de la Concorde.

Once there, difficult as it was, she forced herself to slow down and blend in. Riding full tilt while weaving in and out of the diverse traffic around Paris's largest public square would attract attention when what she needed to do was disappear. A trio of bicycles — women on their way to work, from the neat hair and modest skirts of the riders — rolled placidly along not too far in front of her. Easing in behind, she tried to look like she was one of them.

Her heart kept on hammering. Her hands gripped the handlebars so tightly her knuckles ached. She was tense, breathing hard, not daring to look around lest she should call attention to herself by doing so.

Jean's Café — should she follow the man's direction and go there? He'd saved her by giving her the bicycle, when if he'd wanted to he could have held her for the trench coats. She had to assume that he was part of the Resistance, but how had he known that she was, too, and needed help? Had he simply seen her running and figured it out?

Or had he, perhaps, been watching the house? Or even been inside the house?

Was he connected to Emmy?

For the first time, Genevieve was in the thick of the spy game, alone, with no protection and no one to call the shots.

The additional difficulty she faced was that she was famous. The more people who saw her, the more people she spoke to and interacted with, the more likely it was that someone would recognize her as Genevieve Dumont.

For anyone to know that Genevieve Dumont was on the run from the gestapo endangered not only herself but Max and his network, as well.

If she went to that café, the secret was likely to be found out by at least the people who presumably would be waiting there.

Once it was known that Genevieve Dumont was working for the Resistance, she had to expect the word to get out.

At the very least, her usefulness would be at an end. She almost certainly would be arrested and might well wind up dead. The same might befall Max.

The scream of sirens behind her made the hair rise on the back of her neck. She wobbled and almost fell off the bicycle before regaining control. From the sound of them, they were still some distance away, but approaching fast. A quick, impossible-to-resist glance over her shoulder found no sign of police cars barreling toward her, but the shrieking sirens grew louder by the second. There was so much activity on the place de la Concorde that she guessed she might not see them until they were almost upon her.

An icy conviction that those sirens were coming for her gripped her.

Peeling away from the group finally as she reached the Champs-Élysées, she was drenched in sweat despite the cold air that nipped at her cheeks. Her breathing was as ragged as if she'd been running for days. The sirens were all she could hear.

I have to get off the street.

More people were out and about now that the sun was up. The murky lavender of dawn gave way to an increasingly bright morning. As cars passed her and other bicyclists and people on the sidewalk glanced her way, she felt hideously exposed.

Jean's Café was up there on her left, across from the swastika-draped Grand Palais, with its enormous banners announcing its latest exhibition of Nazi propaganda. Titled *Commerce and Industry* in big white letters against a red background, it touted "the excellent French economic results during collaboration." She spotted the café's sign, took in the striped awnings, the two large front windows, the small tables out on the sidewalk, empty at this very early hour, the small dark man in the apron — Jean? — stepping out through the glass front door.

And rode on past.

Without knowing who the man who'd given her the bicycle was or who he worked for, it felt too dangerous to follow his directions. She could not risk it. She needed to get back to the hotel.

On the other side of the wide boulevard came a Nazi patrol: two soldiers striding along with an eager bulldog pulling at a short leash. Given a wide berth by the civilians crowding the sidewalk, they walked with purpose, looking to the left and right, staring hard at everyone they passed.

They seemed to be searching for someone. Her chest clutched. She had to tear her eyes away from them, put her head down, pedal. *Not too fast.*

A bicycle rack nestled between two of the horse chestnuts lining the street caught her eye. If they were looking for her, they were looking for a girl on a bicycle. Coasting in, she jumped off and shoved the bicycle into place between the bars. Then she walked quickly away. The lines outside the shops were already long and growing longer. She tried to look like one more worried housewife anxious about what her coupons would allow her to purchase for the day.

Pulling the scarf off, she crammed it into her pocket. That left her hair and face exposed, but she feared the plaid scarf might be memorable. Berthe's plain black coat was ordinary enough that with one glance around she saw three nearly identical ones. Turning up the collar to partially hide her face, she almost jumped out of her skin as first one screaming police car and then another raced past down the wide boulevard, dodging traffic as they went.

A few minutes earlier and she still would have been on the bicycle. Her knees went weak at the thought.

Head turned away as if she were looking in the shop windows, terrified of encountering another patrol on her side of the street, she kept walking. Not hurrying, but steady.

By the time she saw an empty bicycle taxi, her nerves were flayed raw. Flagging it down, she said, "To the Ritz, please," then huddled in the cart's depths until she was safely back at the hotel.

Head down, dodging anyone she feared might recognize her, she managed to retain a veneer of composure until she was in her suite. Then she tottered to the sofa and collapsed.

It was still so early that Berthe was not yet up. If she was lucky, very, very lucky, no one would ever know she'd gone out.

Otto showed up at nine to take her to rehearsal. She was, outwardly at least, her usual self as she walked out the front door of the Ritz and slid into the back seat of the car. In fact, she'd taken pains to look extra glamorous in a sleek black suit with her hair brushed into shining waves that framed her face, and vivid scarlet lipstick. It had occurred to her that the best thing she could do, just in case the Nazis were out there looking for a mysterious girl in an oversize coat and shabby scarf who'd left a Resistance safe house, then managed to elude them on a bicycle that morning, was to be Genevieve Dumont, the star, and simply go about her day.

Genevieve Dumont knew nothing about that frantic girl on the bicycle.

"You see Max last night?" Otto asked on the way to La Fleur Rouge.

"He came by the hotel," she said. Then she frowned. "Why? Haven't you seen him?"

"Not since he left the theater after last night's show. I just like to check to make sure he's alive."

"He is. Or at least he was, last I saw of him." Curiosity got the better of her. "He seems to be spending a lot of nights away from the studio lately. What's he doing, anyway?"

"Don't know."

"And you wouldn't say if you did," Genevieve concluded.

His shrug confirmed it.

"He'd better be careful, or he'll get arrested for violating curfew. And won't that leave us holding a fine kettle of fish."

Otto grinned, but they arrived at La Fleur Rouge just then and that was her only reply.

Between wondering if Emmy had gotten her message and if the gestapo had discovered her identity and was going to storm the studio and haul her off at any minute, a knot of dread took up permanent residence under Genevieve's breastbone. She was so distracted during rehearsal that she twice missed her cue. That was so unlike her that Madame Arnault suggested she take a break, and Cecile, concerned, asked if she had a headache.

Genevieve took the break, and agreed she did.

Afterward, freshening up, she was still such a seething bundle of nerves that her hand was unsteady as she applied her lipstick, creating a crooked line, and she had to wipe it off and apply it again.

When she emerged from the bathroom, it was to discover that the studio was empty except for Max. He leaned against the wall right outside the door.

She took one look at him in his gray suit and narrow tie — shoulders propping the wall, arms crossed over his chest, a grim set to his jaw, clearly waiting for her — and knew she had trouble.

Chapter Twenty-Eight

"The answer's no," she said as his eyes slashed to her, because as everybody knew the best defense was a good offense, and she walked by him like she didn't have a worry in the world. She wore a silky white blouse with her slim black skirt — her suit jacket hung from a peg near the lift — and she could feel him looking at her as she passed. She held her head high, putting a little extra oomph in her walk because she knew he was watching, and distracting him was, she felt, her best hope for warding off whatever this was. Her pumps clicked on the hardwood floor. Her heart started a drumbeat in her chest. "To whatever hideous thing you're here to try to get me to do."

He made a sound that was a cross between a grunt and a growl, shoved away from the wall — he dropped his stick, which hit the floor with a clatter — and came after her. Grabbing her elbow, he pulled her around to face him.

"Hey!" She tried to yank her arm free without success.

"Nice try, but it's not going to work." He was holding both elbows now as his eyes raked her face. The wall was right behind her, maybe a step away, and he was right in front of her, boxing her in. The curtains were open; dust motes danced in slanting rectangles of sunlight that lay in patches on the floor, but the windows were on the opposite side of the room, leaving his back to them and his face in shadow. Hers, she knew, was well lit. He could undoubtedly see every nuance of her expression, which had probably been his goal when he'd pulled her around like that. "Feeling guilty, angel?"

"I've told you before, don't call me *angel.*"

"I'll call you anything I want. And I notice you're not answering the question."

Her chin came up. Her pulse drummed, but she would be damned before she'd let him see.

"Of course I don't feel guilty. Guilty about what?" She tried yanking her arms free, but his grip was too strong. The abortive movement ended up with her having backed herself up against the wall, and him still holding on to her arms, not quite pinning her there with his body but close. She could feel the cool, smooth plaster against her back, through the thin nylon of her blouse. She could feel the heat and solid strength of him scant centimeters away.

"You tell me."

If he hadn't been holding on to her arms, she would have pushed him away. As it was, she had to content herself with a glare. "Let go of me. What is wrong with you?"

He shifted his grip to her wrists, holding them against his chest. The man from last night, the man whose strong arms she'd wanted to rest in and whose broad shoulders she'd wanted to shift her burdens onto, was long gone. Whatever had brought about the change — and she had a sinking feeling she knew what it was — the look in his eyes gave her pause. She wasn't afraid of Max, but if she hadn't known him so well, if she'd been anyone other than herself and her relationship with Max had been anything other than what it was, right in that moment she could have been.

"Suppose you tell me what you were doing this morning on the rue Duphot."

Bullets of panic shot through her bloodstream.

He knows. He knows. *What does he know?* How *does he know?*

Her spine stiffened with not entirely feigned indignation. "Do you have someone *following* me?"

He bared his teeth. *"Tell me."*

"If you must know, I went there to give someone something." She was purposely vague. Her response was less of an answer than a way of buying time while she decided just how much to reveal. Damn it. *Damn it!* Why hadn't she foreseen *this,* and had a story ready to deal with it? "Remember those old friends I told you I ran into the other day? One of them."

He inhaled. Drawn through those bared teeth, the air made a whistling sound that, coming from anyone other than Max, would have been chilling. "Don't lie to me."

"Are you having my room watched? Or the hotel? How low can you get?"

"How low can I get?" His fingers tightened on her wrists. "Not as low as a double agent, believe me."

"What?" Her eyes widened in shock.

"That's what Touvier suspects you are. He's the one who's been having you followed, not me. You have any idea how close you came to being killed this morning?"

That rattled her. "The gestapo —"

"The gestapo would've had to queue up. By Touvier and his crew. The only thing that's keeping them from coming after you at the hotel or here or the theater is that they're afraid of me. That nice chap with the bicycle? He was one of Touvier's. If you'd gone to Jean's Café — it *was* Jean's Café, wasn't it? — as he'd told you, you would have found yourself with a bag over your head being whisked off somewhere to be interrogated by members of Touvier's cell. And then shot, if your answers didn't satisfy them. As they probably wouldn't, if you lied to them the way you're lying to me."

"You can't really think I'm a double agent!"

"Can't I? Because you've been so honest with me up until now?"

"You don't trust me?" Her voice quivered with outrage.

"I don't trust anybody. It's how I've managed to stay alive. And you've been coming apart at the seams lately. Behaving erratically. Asking questions about things you'd normally have no interest in."

"So you just assume I'm guilty? What are you going to do? Torture me into confessing? Kill me? I got away from Touvier, and so you're here to finish the job?"

"Don't play games with me. There's too much at stake."

They were practically nose to nose now, snarling at each other.

"What makes you think I'm playing games? You've caught me! If I'm a double agent, your duty is clear. Turn me over as a traitor. Kill me yourself."

He gave her wrists a shake. "You bloody fool, if it was anybody but me standing here, you wouldn't even get a chance to explain. *Tell me what the hell you were doing at five in the morning on the rue Duphot.*"

His eyes — she'd never seen that particular

glint in them before. It was ugly, even deadly.

She was going to have to tell him. Not the whole truth — not the part about her mother, at least — but some of it.

"I went to a safe house, all right? Number two rue Duphot. It's used by the Resistance. Hardly a place a double agent would visit."

"Unless she was reading messages left there by our agents and reporting on their contents to the Germans." From his reaction, he'd known about the safe house, known what that address was.

"You know that isn't true!"

"That's what Touvier thinks you're doing."

"He's insane."

"Then what were you doing?"

Her lids drooped as she frantically calculated how much to reveal. It was no more than a fraction of a second before she caught the involuntary action and snapped her gaze back up to his again, but it was enough: he'd seen. His face had hardened. He watched her with a fierce intensity. Waiting to catch her in a lie? Thank goodness she'd told the truth about rue Duphot being a safe house! She had to fight the urge not to wet her lips. For her mother's sake, for Emmy's, she was going to have to lie very carefully, while staying as close to the truth as possible.

"If you must know, I dropped off a note. It contained some of the same information I gave you last night, and I was passing it on to the friend I was telling you about," she said. His eyes flared, his breath hissed, his lips parted. Before he could let fly, she quickly added, "It's not what you think, so don't go exploding all over me before I can explain."

"Please do explain." His voice was ominously even. Dark color stained his cheekbones. His eyes — they were no better. She still didn't like the look in them.

"The other day, when I told you I'd run into some old friends . . ." Her hands rested in two tight fists against his chest. His hands, big and tan, looked brutally strong wrapped around the pale skin and fragile bones of her wrists.

He wasn't hurting her. Max had never hurt her, and she was as sure as it was possible to be that he never would. Still, the accusation Touvier had made against her was as serious as they came. The penalty for getting caught betraying the Resistance was death.

"One of them —" she paused as his face changed, subtly, but she caught it, and she thought he must be remembering the bruises on her arms, and assigning her "one of them" to the man he'd assumed was responsible "— was someone I was once very close to. I hadn't seen *her* in a long time, since before you and I met, but there she was. She knew I was singing at the Casino de Paris, and that I had access to a lot of high-level German officers. She told me she was with the Resistance, and she asked me to get some information for her — about which trains leaving Paris were least likely to be searched. So I did. I wrote it down, and, as she had asked me to, I left the note at the house on rue Duphot this morning. And then I left."

For a moment he simply looked at her. Then he swore, softly and violently. "So what you're telling me is that now this friend of yours knows that Genevieve Dumont, the Black Swan, is amenable to working for the Resistance. *Do you really think that was a good idea?*"

"It was a onetime thing. A favor. I don't expect to hear from her again."

"After all the trouble I've gone to to shield you, to keep you the hell out of it as much as possible, you — *told a friend.*"

At the look on his face, she fumbled for something that would make her story more palatable to him. "I didn't want her to think I was a . . . a collaborator."

"Yes, you did. That's what you want everyone to think." He said the words very slowly and distinctly, as if she might have trouble understanding them. "That's your cover. That's what allows you to do what you do. That's what allows me to do what I do." His eyes blazed at her. "Bloody *hell,* Genevieve. You have to know how bloody stupid that was."

"You're hurting my wrists." Even though

he wasn't. But a distraction was definitely needed.

"Am I, now?" He released her wrists only to put his hands on either side of her waist and crowd her back against the wall. His body was solid muscle, and she could feel every well-honed centimeter of it. She was instantly, reluctantly aware of him as a man in a way she hadn't been for a long time. Her breath caught. Her first, knee-jerk impulse was to shove him away. That would be a waste of time, she realized almost instantly. He was far too big to be dislocated by a push from her, and also, possibly, the action might reveal too much about the way he was making her feel. Instead she stood fast, holding her ground, head tilted back, hands splayed over his chest because they had nowhere else to go, glaring up at him.

She said, "You give information to people not in our network. Touvier, for example."

"What I do and what you may do are two entirely different things. Touvier runs his own cell, but it's part of my network. I've worked with him for years. This friend of yours —"

"She won't tell anyone. I'm sure of it."

The sound he made could have been mistaken for laughter if it had held even the slightest trace of humor. It didn't. "You're sure of it. Do you realize you've put your life in her hands? What's her name?"

Too late, Genevieve saw the danger. "Why

do you want to know?" she parried.

"Out with it. You've made a mistake. I'll go and fix it."

Suspicious, she searched his face. "You won't — hurt her?"

"Is that what you think of me, Genevieve? Really?"

"What I think —" Genevieve said slowly as the truth of what she was saying hit her like a brick "— is that you're very good at answering questions with questions when you don't want to actually answer them."

"I'm going to have her checked out." His tone was impatient. "Give me her name."

She considered making one up but had an instant horrible vision of some poor innocent woman with whatever name she gave being snatched off the street and tortured, or worse. That was not an outlandish thought. After all, he'd accepted the order to kill her mother if she couldn't be rescued without an apparent qualm. He had a ruthless side; she'd encountered it before. Would he kill this poor fictional woman if it was necessary to protect what he had built? She had no doubt at all that, if he thought it prudent, the answer was yes.

"No," she said. "I don't think I will."

His eyes narrowed. His hands hardened on her waist.

He said, "If she is what you say she is, we'll soon find out, and none of us will have to worry anymore about it. If she's not — did it ever occur to you that she might have been setting you up? That she might be an agent for the Germans? That she might be a collaborator herself?"

"She's not." Her tone was positive. "I know she's not."

"Give me her name."

She took a deep breath. "No."

"Genevieve —"

"No. I'm not going to, so you're just going to have to take my word about her."

"Do you have no concept whatsoever of the danger you've put us all in? I want her name."

"No."

"You work for me, remember? In a case like this, telling me no is not an option."

She narrowed her eyes at him. "I want you to listen closely to what I'm about to say. *No.* No. No. No. And if you keep pushing me, I'll quit being your caged songbird, and then what will you do?"

"Is that a threat?" His head dipped so that, with her head thrown back, their faces were mere centimeters apart. She could feel the warmth and weight of his body — everywhere. Small details — fine lines radiated from the corners of his eyes; his irises had black rings around them; he was clean-shaven, but she could see the faintest shadow of dark stubble on his cheeks and jaw — imprinted themselves on her consciousness.

He smelled, very faintly, of his favorite Gauloises and spicy shaving lotion. Of their own volition, her eyes dropped to his mouth — beautifully carved, curling with impatience — before shooting back up to clash with his.

"Yes," she said.

His mouth tightened. He leaned closer, whispering into her ear. "Do you know why pretty little songbirds are kept in cages? To keep them safe from beasts."

His breath feathered her skin. She felt the moist heat of it all the way down to her toes.

Useless or not, revealing or not, she shoved him hard. Without releasing her, he obligingly fell back a step, and she glared at him.

"I need a name, Genevieve." His voice was brusque.

"So you can torture her? Kill her?"

"I don't torture. And I only kill when I have to, and only what needs killing."

"Do you realize how cold-blooded you sound?"

"Sometimes killing what's a threat to you is the only thing you can do. As you should agree."

She knew what he was alluding to: Charles Lamartine. Even the thought of that night, what she'd done, how it had ended, made her shudder.

"You know I had no choice."

"I do know it. What happened that night came down to you or him, and you did what you had to do to survive. I don't blame you for it. I applaud you. I was bowled over by your courage even then. What you don't seem to understand is that this may be another one of those only-one-can-walk-away situations."

"You *can* be persuasive when you want to be, can't you?" The smile she gave him was small and tight. "But the answer's still no. And you can't bully me into changing my mind, or sweettalk me into it, so you might as well quit trying."

Their eyes clashed.

It was galling to know that the hammering of her heart wasn't only because she was fuming and on edge and nervous about the lies she was telling and the secrets she was keeping. Some of it — a lot of it — was about him.

"If I wanted to bully you, I would have done it long since. As for sweet-talking you, there was a time I could've asked anything of you, and you would have done it."

Now it was *his* eyes dropping to *her* mouth. Just for a second — no time at all — but that quick, glinting look was suggestive enough to send heat rolling through her in a thick, slow tide. Her breathing quickened. Butterflies — dozens of unexpected, oblivious butterflies — fluttered to life in her stomach.

Her eyes blazed at him. "That's not true."

"We both know it is."

"Are you *proud* of having deceived me?"

"What is it they say about love and war? Just remember, when this all started, it was *you* who came running to *me.*"

"I didn't know what you were. What you *are.*"

"You knew I'd see you safe. And afterward, when you could have gotten out, you chose to stay. All this time I've kept you safe, just like I'm trying to keep you safe now. From this woman, from Touvier, from your own bloody stupid, ungrateful self." His eyes raked her face. "If your friend is what you say, why are you worried?"

"Because I don't trust you."

"Is that so?" One long-fingered hand moved to cup her jaw, trapping it. He held her face still as his eyes bored into hers. "If we're going to talk about trust, you know what I thought to myself when I was listening to you tell me all about leaving a note for your friend just now? *Hello, little rabbit.*" And he dropped a mocking kiss onto the very tip of her nose.

His words shook her, but that was nothing compared to what that brief touch of his mouth on her skin did: jolted her with a lightning bolt of electricity that had her nails digging into his shirt and her toes curling in her shoes.

She sucked in air. Then she slapped him.

The crack of her hand on his face still echoed through the studio when a ding announced the arrival of the lift.

Chapter Twenty-Nine

Max's fingers on her jaw hardened to iron. His body went rigid. His eyes blazed down at her.

Genevieve blazed right back at him, furious.

For the space of maybe a couple of heartbeats, the air around them sizzled with — something. Then he leaned close so that only she could hear: "Just so you know, I told Touvier that the reason you were at that safe house this morning is because I sent you there."

Then he pushed away from her. At the same time Otto walked out of the lift, spotted the two of them and stopped dead in obvious surprise.

The atmosphere in the studio was so tense it practically crackled.

Even as Max turned toward Otto, the imprint of her hand was darkening on his cheek.

Otto wouldn't miss that. Indeed, she

watched his eyes narrow on Max's face as Max, scooping up his stick and running a hand through his hair to restore its order, walked toward him.

"Take Genevieve back to the hotel, would you?" he said to Otto in a perfectly normal tone.

"Um, but what about . . ." Otto's eyes flicked from Max to her and back.

"I have other things to do this afternoon." He glanced back at her. His eyes glinted at her like black glass, but other than that there was nothing to be read in his expression. Still she had no doubt at all about what those "other things" entailed — trying to find out the identity of her "friend." She only hoped Emmy's connection to the safe house was well hidden. "As for you, once Otto gets you back to the hotel, stay there until he picks you up to go to the theater. From now until we leave Paris, unless you clear it with me first, you don't go anywhere without Otto. Understand?"

Earlier she might have blown up at him, but learning that he'd told Touvier that he'd sent her to the house on rue Duphot, and had thus taken the onus onto himself if it turned out that she was the double agent Touvier suspected her of being, had blunted the worst of her anger at him. Other things still rankled: that he'd even for a moment harbored a suspicion that she might be a double agent, that he'd so cavalierly dismissed his early deception, that he was still using what had happened in Casablanca as a way to persuade her.

And also that, despite everything, he'd made her feel things for him that she'd never wanted nor expected to feel again.

She responded with a curt nod.

He walked past Otto, stepped into the lift and was gone.

Otto stared after him, then fixed accusing eyes on Genevieve. "God in heaven, what did you do to him?"

As instructed, Otto took her back to the hotel. Genevieve got the impression that he watched from behind the wheel of the Citroën until she was safely inside. However unsettling she found being placed on what amounted to house arrest by Max, it dimmed to nothingness in the face of the shock of learning that Touvier suspected her of being a double agent and had set people on to watch her. There was real danger in that, and she was glad that her stay in Paris was almost at an end. Under the circumstances, restricting her movements seemed wise.

The lobby was busy, but not as busy as it tended to be in the early morning or evening. Genevieve made it to the lift with no more than a quick wave for the receptionist and wasn't surprised to find herself alone in it.

Hitting the button for her floor, she stepped back and was idly watching the door close when, at the last possible second, a woman slipped through the opening to join her in the lift.

Genevieve's first impression, from the black uniform with its starched white apron and cap, was that she was one of the hotel's legion of maids.

"We only have a minute." It was Emmy's voice, Emmy's face beneath the neat white cap. Even as Genevieve recognized her with a quiver of surprise, Emmy grabbed her hand and continued speaking rapidly. "We've found Maman. At least, we think we know where she is. We followed Wagner and watched him go into a house that's been converted into a secret prison across from the Parc des Buttes-Chaumont. He used a key to let himself in. We saw what pocket he keeps the key in. We've devised a plan to get her out, but it requires us getting our hands on Wagner's key, which is why I've come to you. When do you see him again?"

Genevieve found herself infected with Emmy's urgency. "Tonight. He's taking me to dinner."

"Is there someplace I can get to him, get to the two of you, some public place where we can interact without making him suspicious?"

As Genevieve did a lightning review of the possibilities in her head, the lift jolted a little as it reached the third floor, then continued its rise toward the fourth.

"He meets me at the stage door and escorts me into his car. Sometimes there are fans. If you pretended to be a fan, he wouldn't think it suspicious that you're there."

"Immediately after your show ends?"

Genevieve nodded.

"I'll be there. When you see me, make a distraction. Something to keep his attention on you and off me while I get that key. Can you do that?"

"I — yes." She'd been going to say she would try, but the time for merely trying was long gone. This she would *do.* "But if you steal his key, he'll notice. Maybe not immediately, but soon. He's intelligent. He'll remember any distraction I make. He'll remember you. And he might blame me."

"I'm not going to steal his key. I'm going to borrow it, for a moment only, to make an impression in wax. We'll put it back into his pocket without him ever knowing it was gone and make our own key from the impression."

"You can do that?"

"You'd be surprised what I can do." Emmy smiled. "We're going to get this done, *bébé.*"

The lift reached the fourth floor and stopped. The door began to open. With a quick squeeze, Emmy dropped her hand, stepped out into the hall, and was gone.

■ ■ ■ ■

The next time Genevieve saw Max was that night at intermission, when he beckoned her into his office for just long enough to go over some topics he wanted her to press Wagner on. As uneasy as she had been about seeing Wagner again, Emmy's directive had cranked her anxiety level up until she was practically jumping out of her skin while doing her best to act as if nothing was wrong. As she entered and he closed the door behind her, his eyes were remote, his mouth was hard and his attitude told her that their quarrel had not been forgotten. Well, she hadn't forgotten it, either, and with Max, she wasn't in the mood to pretend.

"Aren't you afraid I'll betray you to him? I mean, if I'm a double agent and all." She smiled a faux-sweet smile as he stepped behind his desk.

"If I thought you were a double agent, you wouldn't be standing there."

"Oh, does that mean you already would have had me killed? Lucky me that you believe me, then. How's the search for my friend coming? She really is a partisan, and she really won't betray me. I promise you."

"Would you stop talking and listen? We don't have much time."

The look he gave her was grim. Hostility

arced through the air between them.

He started briefing her on the topics he wanted her to touch on during dinner. His tone, his whole attitude, was completely businesslike. If she hadn't *known* what had transpired between them in the studio earlier, she would have had no inkling of it.

Even her hand mark on his tanned cheek was gone.

That was Max, able to separate the personal from the professional to a remarkable degree. Except for when it was time for her to go on-stage, she was not that disciplined. In fact, after the last few days, she feared she teetered on the brink of turning into an emotional wreck.

Dressed in the strapless scarlet ball gown that was her costume for the opening number of the second act, her solo rendition of "Parlez-moi d'amour," she stood with one hand on Max's desk and listened in stony silence as he instructed her to try to find out the German High Command's reaction to the recent Allied air raid on Calais. Also, she was to mention that she'd heard a rumor that the First US Army Group under General Patton was amassing an army in Kent, England, and ask him if he thought it could be true.

From scraps of conversation she'd overheard between Max, Otto, and the motley collection of partisans with whom they'd interacted over the past few months, she knew that the First US Army Group was actually entirely fictitious, an assemblage of inflatable tanks, shell airplanes and phony fuel depots designed to trick Luftwaffe reconnaissance pilots into thinking it was a real army being positioned for an attack on Pas-de-Calais. She knew, too, that when she was talking to Wagner, she must not seem to know too much about those or any other troop movements, fake or real, or anything else military related. She must appear to be merely seeking reassurance that the idle chatter she'd heard didn't mean an Allied invasion was imminent, and that Paris was a safe place for her to be. It was a fine line to walk, a tightrope where one misstep could end in disaster.

Usually she was able to carry out such assignments with cool detachment. That had been, she realized, because since Vivi's death her emotions had been anesthetized against any deep feelings, bad or good. Now that the numb had gone, the peril inherent in the mission was enough to make her cold with dread. Add in the fact that she was going to have to stage a distraction for Emmy, and then, if she didn't get caught doing that, once again feign interest in Wagner for some hours afterward, and she was jittery with nerves. Wagner was a predator if she'd ever seen one, a man whose touch made her sick, and knowing that on this their second date in as many days he would almost certainly feel that their relationship was progressing to the point where he might expect to do more than simply kiss her hand, her stomach tied itself in knots.

"You have no idea what it's like to have to sit across from a man like that, pretend to admire him, let him kiss your hand or worse," she flashed as Max finished by suggesting that she ask Wagner if he'd heard the latest rumors, which maintained that the Allied invasion wouldn't be launched against France at all, but rather against Norway. "What if he leaps on me in the car?"

"Cough a few times during dinner. Pretend to be coming down with a cold, or, better yet, influenza." Max's response was actually helpful, if callously delivered. "Tell him you're feeling chilly, and that all day long you've been alternating between feeling cold and hot. That should do it. Wagner is known to be paranoid about contracting an illness."

A knock on the door, followed by an anxious "Mademoiselle Dumont, are you in there?" kept her from answering him. The voice belonged to one of the stagehands, sent by Pierre, she had no doubt, to hunt her down.

"Yes, I'm coming."

"You're needed onstage" was the reply.

"I'll stop by your hotel room later." Max followed her as she turned to head for the door, and she knew he meant so that she could report back to him on what she'd learned. She could feel him behind her — it was unsettling to realize how aware of him she'd become — but she didn't look around. Instead she responded with a curt nod. He opened the door for her without another word. She passed through it with a swish of her full skirts to be greeted by the stagehand and then, a few steps later, swept up by a visibly relieved Pierre.

"Why do you do this to me?" Pierre scolded as he hurried her along. "One day you will miss your cue and it will be me who is forced to take your place onstage. And I, I assure you, sing like a frog. We will be ruined, all of us, ruined."

By the time the show ended, and Genevieve, having changed out of her finale costume and dressed now for dinner, walked out the stage door into the crisp night air, she was having to grit her teeth to ward off an attack of the shivers that had nothing whatsoever to do with the weather.

She paused on the stoop. A glance found Wagner's car, parked near the foot of the shallow flight of stairs that led down to the street. His driver, Lutz, stood beside the open rear passenger door from which Wagner was emerging.

Coming toward her from the direction of the busy rue de Clichy, a group of women, five maybe, or six, in what looked like theater-going finery, were just meters away.

Even in the darkness, Genevieve had no trouble recognizing Emmy as one of the women.

Their eyes met through the shadows. A silent message passed between them. Almost immediately Genevieve looked away, to find Wagner approaching the foot of the steps.

He was smiling up at her. She smiled back and started down toward him.

"There she is! The Black Swan!"

"Mademoiselle Dumont! Mademoiselle Dumont!"

"You're my favorite singer!"

"Will you sign my program?"

The shrieks, from the women as they rushed toward her, were loud enough to drown out even the sound of traffic on the nearby busy street. As she looked toward them in feigned surprise, she lost her footing, tumbling with a cry down the remaining stairs. It was a short distance, but the fall itself — the sensation of falling — rocked her to the core. As a result, her stunned immobility as she lay where she had fallen was not one bit feigned.

"Genevieve!" Wagner was down on one knee beside her seconds after she hit the pavement.

"Mademoiselle Dumont!" Lutz, on his feet, hovered behind Wagner.

"Oh, no, is she hurt?"

"She's lying so still!"

"I'm a nurse! Let me through!"

The women gathered around, too, crowding in close, exclaiming. One dropped to her knees beside Wagner and ran a hand along Genevieve's arms. Lying on her side, Genevieve blinked up at the sea of faces above her. The fall had been deliberate, intended to provide the distraction Emmy had requested. Physically she was unhurt, apart from what might be a few bruises. Emotionally she was shaken. Focusing her vision was difficult, and the look she turned on Wagner, she surmised from his reaction, must have been dazed enough to alarm him.

"Genevieve! *Mein Gott,* are you hurt?" Wagner loomed over her, touched her cheek. She took a deep breath, fought to pull herself together. Behind him she saw Emmy, who'd been crouched on his other side from the woman who claimed to be a nurse, stand up. Again their eyes met.

Emmy gave her the slightest of nods.

"Nothing appears to be broken," said the woman who claimed to be a nurse, having just finished running her hand down Genevieve's legs. She stood up, too.

Emmy was already turning away.

"I — I think I'm all right," Genevieve said to Wagner. "If you could just help me up."

Taking her arm, Wagner spoke angrily over his shoulder. "You! You women! Get back!

This is your fault. Lutz, get them away."

"We never meant to hurt her!"

"We just wanted an autograph."

"Lutz!" Wagner slid an arm around her back. Genevieve forced herself to rest limply against it.

"You're lucky not to be placed under arrest. Go quickly. Go!" As Wagner helped her to her feet, Lutz shooed the women away.

Chapter Thirty

The light from the ceiling fixture was dim and gray, but it shone so rarely that when it did, it felt as blindingly bright as the noonday sun. It came on only when someone entered the small windowless room and was switched off again as they left. Otherwise, the darkness was absolute. The Germans were sticklers for a schedule, and by now Lillian knew that the light came on like clockwork every three hours, when someone checked on her. It gave her a rudimentary way of gauging the passage of time.

Physically she was better, a little. Her tongue, while still hugely swollen, no longer protruded through her lips, and with some effort she could actually press her lips together, even if she couldn't yet completely close her mouth, which was still burnt and raw and so hideously painful and damaged that she had to take liquids and nourishment through the needle they'd inserted in her arm. Her other injuries were better, too, although when she'd thought to pull out the needle — far better to die from a lack of fluids than in any way the Germans might devise for her — she'd found that both arms were restrained, the left one chained to the wall and the right one tied to the frame of the cot. In any case, her hands still didn't work well enough even to allow her to flex her fingers. The damage done to them terrified her until she realized that she wasn't going to live much longer, so she wasn't going to need them ever again. The nurse who cared for her with brutal efficiency assured her that all of her, her hands, her arms, her ribs and even her mouth, would eventually heal. Ordinarily that would have been good news. Here, it was not. The moment she could speak, the moment they thought she was capable of giving them the information they sought, they would torture her until they were convinced they could get nothing more from her. Then she would be killed.

The thought of the former made her nauseated with fear. The latter she welcomed.

Please let me die before they find the girls.

Her worst fear was that at any moment the door would fly open and one of her daughters would be shoved into the room.

Emmanuelle and Genevra, the light and the dark. They'd all been so happy together once. Images came to her in waves. The girls would sing, and put on shows, while she played the piano. The two of them would play dress-up, rummaging through her jewelry, traipsing around in her nicest clothes, while she scolded at the mess they made, then laughed at how absurdly grown-up they looked.

How, how, had they been brought to this, her family? Never in her wildest dreams could she have imagined so many blows from fate.

With death looming so close she could almost feel its icy breath on her cheek, she was racked with regret. The worst was that she had allowed society's strictures — the importance she had placed on society's strictures — to estrange her from her little one, her Genevra. That she could have allowed such inanities to come between them now seemed impossible. If she could only go back, only have it to do over again, she would have kept her pregnant daughter at home where she belonged, embraced her illegitimate child with open arms, defied the gossip and shaming and condemnation with her head held high.

She regretted her estrangement from her daughter with her whole heart. But there would now be no chance to make amends.

Soon she might be forced to make a choice between her country and her children. Which, in the end, would be no choice at all. What mother would not do anything she could to save her child?

They would be the stick that broke her.

You should not have told me so much, she reproached Paul.

Because Paul was with her, in this dark cold cell of a room. All she had to do was close her eyes and there he was. He paced the floor while the nurse tended her, lay down beside her when she was alone, held her when the fear became overwhelming or the pain was especially bad. With all her heart she longed to shed her broken and vulnerable body and leave with him — but she couldn't. She was trapped in the prison of her own frail flesh.

The sound of gunfire roused her at what she judged was somewhere around 11:00 p.m. At first she wasn't sure what she was hearing. The first two loud bangs could have been anything from dropped cooking pots to a backfiring car. But the sharp rat-a-tat that followed was unmistakable: an automatic pistol.

Just outside her door.

Her eyes opened wide. She would have sat up, but even without the restraints, that much movement was impossible for her now. Straining to listen, trying to make sense of what was happening, she stared sightlessly into the dark.

Running footsteps, near at hand.

"Stop them! They're imposters!"

Boots on hardwood, in the hall outside her door. A lot of commotion, shouting. In German, which convinced her that the voices belonged to the guards.

"Over there, by the window! Dieter, look sharp."

"Halt!"

A bang. *Rat-a-tat. Rat-a-tat.*

A cry: someone was hit.

"Got him!"

The thunder of more jackboots racing past.

"There's someone else on the stairs! *Halt!*"

Rat-a-tat. Rat-a-tat. The sound of glass shattering.

"He's gone out the window! Go, go!"

"Look out! In the vestibule!"

Rat-a-tat. Rat-a-tat. Rat-a-tat. Rat-a-tat.

A man's scream, from somewhere below.

"Do you see any more?"

It sounded like — an escape attempt? A raid by outsiders on this place, this prison? Lillian's heart pounded as she struggled to make sense of it, strained to hear more. Just noise now. No more gunfire, loud voices rather than shouts, stomping rather than running feet. In the distance, a siren.

Her door flew open so hard it banged against the plaster wall. She started violently, her heart leaping into her throat. The light came on. As she blinked against its brightness, a German soldier stepped inside, sidearm out and ready. He looked at her cringing in her cot, warily scanned the room. In the background, growing louder by the second, multiple sirens now wailed, which she thought must mean they were racing toward the building. She could see blue smoke from the gunfire in the hallway outside the door.

"This one's here," the soldier called to someone she couldn't see.

"Check the others. Do a count." It was an order.

"How many got away?" The question was shouted from somewhere farther away.

"One, maybe two" came the reply, from just outside her room, as the soldier turned on his heel and switched off the light.

"Find them," she heard, and then the soldier, striding into the hall, slammed her door shut behind him.

She was once again left alone in the dark, while the chaos outside the room was reduced to muffled sounds that she tried her best to make sense of with little success. Her mind raced, her breathing came fast and ragged.

Cold tentacles of fear clutched at her soul.

Paul sat down beside her on the cot and held her poor ruined hand.

Chapter Thirty-One

By the next night, Genevieve was a bundle of nerves. She sang, she danced, she sparkled during her numbers with the energy she was always, without fail, able to summon when she went onstage, but inside she was so tense that it took every ounce of professionalism she possessed to put on the show the audience had paid to see.

To begin with, she was terrified every time she allowed her thoughts to drift to what might be happening to her mother. With every hour that passed, she feared that Lillian's chances of surviving shrank.

Then Max hadn't shown up in her hotel room the previous night. She'd sat up for hours waiting for him, and he hadn't come. Not that she'd wanted to see him — quite the opposite — but she'd had news: Wagner had assured her that she had no need to fear a successful Allied invasion because the entire German Fifteenth Army had been relocated to Pas-de-Calais to overwhelm the Allies with sheer force of numbers if they should be so foolish as to try to invade there; and dinner had been interrupted by a soldier arriving tableside to whisper apparently urgent tidings into Wagner's ear. Turning red with what she'd thought was anger, although it could have been alarm, Wagner had stood up abruptly, apologized and left the restaurant with the soldier, leaving Lutz to take her back to the hotel.

On one hand, Wagner's premature departure had been a huge relief: after her fall, he'd been solicitous of her to the point where he was practically hovering over her as they ate, stroking her arm, patting her cheek, and in general giving every indication that he had amorous hopes for the balance of the evening. On the other hand, she was terrified that whatever had caused him to leave might have had something to do with Emmy and the attempted rescue of their mother. Knowing no details, she could do nothing but wait and worry. And of course she'd heard nothing from Emmy all day.

Still, only something of major importance would have drawn Wagner away, and *that,* plus the news about the Fifteenth Army, was what she'd wanted to tell Max. What she was *still* wanting to tell Max, who was apparently occupied with urgent matters of his own.

In related news, a huge bouquet of flowers had been waiting for her at the hotel when she'd returned from rehearsal that afternoon. Wagner had sent them, along with a note:

> My dearest Genevieve,
> Please accept my most profound apology for abandoning you at dinner last night. It was unforgivably rude, I know, but unavoidable as I had to respond to an emergency. That same emergency has required me to travel to Stuttgart, where I am resigned to staying for the next few weeks. I am desolate to be obliged to part from you so abruptly, and to miss the last of your Paris shows. Once I am settled, I will ring you up if I may to discuss when and where we can see each other again, which I hope to do at our mutual earliest convenience.
>
> Ardently,
> Claus

"Where is Max?" she'd demanded of Otto when he'd driven her to rehearsal, but Otto had professed not to know. Angry, but feeling that what she'd learned from Wagner was too important not to be passed on as soon as possible, she'd told Otto, who'd promised to convey it to Max without delay.

Max hadn't shown up for her show.

Instead, sometime during the last number of the first half, the Nazis did.

Flushed and overwarm from the stage lights

despite the flimsiness of the short gold flapper dress she wore for the first half finale, she came offstage to find at least a dozen soldiers storming through the backstage area. Checking at the sight, she caught her breath at the drawn sidearms, the gray-green uniforms, the young German soldiers striding along the halls, their faces set and pale under the dim lights.

A raid. She heard the terrified whisper being passed around among the crew, and had an instant, horrible flashback to Anna and Rachel, and Rachel's fate.

They're here for Max was her first petrified thought, and she thanked God that he wasn't at the theater. Then it occurred to her that, coming so close on the heels of her by-the-skin-of-her-teeth escape from the gestapo yesterday, or even maybe from something to do with Emmy and their mother, they might very well be there for her.

Her stomach dropped clear to her toes.

"You girls, go to your dressing room and get your papers ready. You boys, do the same," an officer barked at the chorus as they came flooding offstage in her wake. The lively closing music of the final song of the first half still filled the air along with the unseen audience's thunderous applause, providing a surreal backdrop to the frightening scenario backstage. The *choristes* stuttered and stumbled, wide-eyed and visibly nervous as they realized what was happening and were corralled by soldiers who divided them up and herded them along like livestock. There was massive confusion as stagehands, makeup artists, costumers, *choristes,* performers who hadn't been onstage for the last number and anyone else unlucky enough to find themselves behind the scenes at the time were rounded up by the soldiers.

Heart pounding, Genevieve looked desperately around for Pierre, for Otto, for somebody to find out what was happening and *handle it.* The closest she came was Madame Arnault, whose face was white and fearful as she was hurried along with the rest. The fact that there were no protests from anyone, that everyone was compliant, that Madame was as meek as the youngest of the *choristes,* told Genevieve as eloquently as anything could have how bad this was.

It was abundantly clear: there was no one to question what was happening except her. If the soldiers were there to arrest her, there would be no escaping them anyway. She was too well-known, and the only possible route of escape without going right through them would be to turn around, go back onstage, jump off and make her way out through the audience. Getting caught trying that would be tantamount to screaming, *I'm guilty.* Better to face down whatever this was and try to bluff it out.

Gathering up her courage, squaring her shoulders, she approached the officer who seemed to be in charge, the one who'd been barking orders, the one who was now directing his subordinates to separate out the stagehands and take them to the prop room.

"Good evening," she began as she reached him, careful to be polite. The Germans were a touchy lot: if their egos were offended, more often than not heads would roll. Her heart was beating so hard now that she feared he would hear it. Her only protection from the soldiers' all-encompassing power was her star persona, and as the officer swung around in response to her greeting, she deployed it like a peacock spreading its tail feathers. He met her gaze, his expression disagreeable. She saw that he was about forty, dark haired and hollow cheeked, with sharp features and penetrating eyes. "We are in the middle of a sold-out performance. I am hoping you can tell me the purpose of this extremely ill-timed . . . visit?"

His eyes swept her, and his expression changed, becoming almost pleasant.

"Mademoiselle Dumont." He bowed stiffly. "It is a pleasure. I am Captain Hahn. Forgive this intrusion, but we have received information that one or more members of the Resistance may be operating among the theater company here. We must search, and verify identities, but we don't wish to disrupt your show any more than we have to. Please, continue as you normally would. This is intermission, is it not? I see no reason why the second half should not go on as usual."

They were searching for members of the Resistance operating among the theater company? The enormity of it slammed into her like a freight train. She felt her blood turn to ice in her veins. Her heart continued to beat, but in thick, sluggish strokes.

She was terrified of what he might read in her face. She couldn't let him see that she was afraid.

"The second act can't go on without my chorus," she said. "Or the crew. Or, in fact, anyone backstage. They all have a role to play."

"Your first song after intermission is a solo in which you accompany yourself on the piano, is it not?" He smiled at her, a superior smirk that would have annoyed her if she had not been so frightened. "I have had the pleasure of attending your show, you see. My wife is quite a fan. By the time you have finished with that, all your people should be free to continue on as usual. Minus any who are found to be working against the Reich, of course."

"Of course. That goes without saying." She returned his smile with one of her own, hopefully not as wooden as it felt. "Excuse me. If I am to perform as usual, I must go change."

He inclined his head. Walking away from him, she was careful to keep her head high and her movements unhurried. Honore and Cecile rushed past, holding hands, their faces chalky with fear. The girls flashed frightened looks at her, and she put a comforting hand on Honore's arm in passing, but with the soldiers all around, they didn't speak. Hahn did not seem to harbor any suspicion about her, unless he was very good at concealing his true thoughts and was just waiting to spring some sort of trap. The thought made her insides twist, but, once again, there was nothing to be done. As far as she could see, her best course of action was to cooperate and hope that they found nothing. There were, she saw as she walked toward her dressing room, guards at both backstage exits, preventing anyone from leaving.

If they found whoever they were looking for, there would be no escape.

A soldier, young and pink cheeked, waited inside her dressing room with Berthe.

"I told him I had to be here to help you change." Berthe's voice sounded strained. The soldiers' mere presence was an excruciating ordeal for her, Genevieve knew.

"Yes, that's true," Genevieve said to the soldier. "If I am to perform, I must change, and I can't change without her help."

"Very well," the soldier said. "I'll wait outside the door. When you're done here, I'll escort you to join the others. Not you, Mademoiselle Dumont — we all know who you are — but her."

"I vouch for her," Genevieve said. "She has nothing to do with anyone you're looking for."

"Nevertheless, I must take her to be examined. Orders, you understand. I'm sure nothing will be found to be amiss, and if so, she will return to you shortly." He looked at Berthe. "I'll be right outside when you're ready. Please, don't be too long."

He left the room, closing the door behind him.

She and Berthe exchanged frightened looks. Of course, Berthe knew nothing of what she and Max and Otto had been doing for years now. She had no idea of Max's true identity, or that he was an SOE agent, or that Genevieve and Otto worked for him. But Berthe had lived through the bloodbath that was the German invasion of her homeland and all the terror and brutality that had followed. Her husband's death and her own near death at the hands of the invaders had left her with an abiding fear of them along with a permanent scar upon her soul.

More to the point under the present harrowing circumstances, to get her out of Poland, Max had provided her with forged papers. It was those papers that she was going to have to present to the soldiers now.

Genevieve flew to the other woman's side.

"It will be all right," she whispered. "You'll show them your papers, and they'll glance at them and be done."

"Who are they looking for?" Berthe's answering whisper shook.

"I don't know. Pray they don't find whoever it is."

"Tak." Only in moments of extreme agitation did Berthe lapse into Polish. *Tak,* Genevieve knew, meant yes.

"Help me change. We must behave normally, as if we have nothing to fear. For the benefit of the soldier outside."

Berthe nodded.

"It was very hot under the spotlights in the last number. See how flushed my cheeks are," Genevieve said clearly, although in reality any flush she might have experienced had vanished with the raid.

"Let me powder them. That will tone them down," Berthe replied, going along.

With dismay Genevieve saw that she was pale as milk and her hands were shaking. Catching Berthe's hands between her own, she rubbed them briskly to warm them. The other woman submitted with mute misery.

"When next you go out, try to get more of this carmine lipstick," Genevieve said. "It doesn't melt under the lights. And the liquid rouge is very good. You should get that, too."

She gave Berthe a look of encouragement.

"I will, but as you know, stage cosmetics are almost impossible to find now."

Despite the nerves afflicting them both, they continued with what they hoped would pass for a normal conversation, although Genevieve was sure neither would remember later a single word that was exchanged. In the meantime, while going through the familiar motions of getting Genevieve ready for the second act, Berthe regained some of her color and her hands ceased to shake.

Berthe had just finished doing up the back of her scarlet ball gown and was shaking out the full skirt when there was a knock on the dressing room door.

"Fräulein, I've been asked to bring you along now."

Both women froze and exchanged a look. Berthe reached out an icy hand, and Genevieve squeezed it.

"One minute," Genevieve called, and whispered, "Remember, you've done nothing wrong."

Berthe nodded. Then she gathered up her ID cards, went to the door and stepped out into the hall where Genevieve could see the soldier waiting for her.

"Don't forget to powder your nose," Berthe called back to her. Her voice was strong and steady.

"I won't," Genevieve answered, and smiled at her as the soldier closed the door.

Alone in her dressing room, she barely made it to her dressing table before her knees gave out and she had to sit down on the bench. A glance at the clock told her that she had a little less than ten minutes before she needed to head for the stage. She looked in the mirror to find that her face was paper white. With her black hair swept up into a chignon to expose her neck, and the strapless ball gown leaving her shoulders bare, she looked almost as vulnerable as she felt.

She closed her eyes, fought for calm.

Please don't let them find anything wrong with Berthe's papers. Please don't let them find anything wrong with anything. And please keep Max away from the theater until this is over, and don't let them be looking for him.

"You dirty little slut, did you really think there would be no payback for what you've done?"

Those words, spoken in a low, guttural voice, caused her eyes to pop open and her head to whip around toward the source.

Touvier emerged from behind the dressing screen in the corner, a long-barreled black pistol in his hand.

It was aimed at her.

Chapter Thirty-Two

Genevieve barely managed to swallow the cry that threatened to burst from her lips.

She couldn't scream: it would bring the soldiers. And they might seize Touvier, but because he knew about her and Max and Otto, that would in all likelihood end with them all being arrested, tortured and killed. A scream might also result in him shooting her before the soldiers ever reached her.

"What are you doing?" Her voice was hoarse. "Don't you know there are soldiers here? If you shoot, you'll bring them down on us all."

"You'd like that, wouldn't you?" Touvier wore a shirt and trousers. The shirt was gray, the trousers black. Both were dirty and ripped in places. The shirt had a dark stain the size of a dinner plate just above his waist on the left side. She thought it might be dried blood. "I am not so stupid." He made a gesture indicating the pistol. "This is a High Standard. Suppressed."

Genevieve's eyes widened on the pistol. Its long barrel made it distinctive. She'd seen it before, or at least one like it, in Max's possession. It was issued by the SOE, and its salient feature was that it was silenced.

"You're injured . . ."

"Whose fault is that? Did you gloat, last night? You told them we were coming, didn't you? *Didn't you?*"

"I don't know what you're talking about." She felt as if a giant hand were squeezing her chest. Frantically trying to put the pieces together, she realized that he'd been hiding behind the screen the whole time she'd been in the dressing room with Berthe and even before. He must have been in the theater when the soldiers arrived. Had he ducked into her dressing room then? Or had he already been hiding behind the screen, waiting for her? Had he come on purpose to kill her? Her heart pounded as he walked toward her, moving with apparent difficulty, although the pistol in his hand never wavered. It was pointed at her head. Every nerve ending she possessed screamed that she was in mortal danger. She had to try to reach him, get through to him. "You're bleeding. Let me help you."

"You can't pull the wool over *my* eyes." His pale blue eyes burned with hate as he looked at her. His face was contorted with emotion. His beard looked as though he'd been clawing at it. "I'm not Bonet, to be dazzled by a pretty face. Did you think I wouldn't notice that you'd moved my cigarettes? *Don't move.*" He snarled that last as she shifted on the stool.

She stopped moving and sat very still as he drew close enough to touch her. Keeping his left arm tucked against his side as if to protect whatever injury he'd incurred, he circled around behind her, the mouth of the pistol just inches from her head. He smelled faintly of old meat and damp. That would be the blood, she realized. Glued to him through the mirror, her eyes followed his every move. Her heart galloped like a runaway horse.

"Whatever it is you think I did, I didn't do it," she said. It took every bit of self-control she possessed to keep her voice calm, matter-of-fact. Her mind was a whirling dervish. She had no doubt at all that he would shoot her instantly if she gave him reason. She suspected that his intention was to shoot her no matter what she did.

What could she do? The question formed a desperate beat in her head. If she didn't show up onstage when she was supposed to, presumably someone would come to find out why. But that brought with it the problem of Touvier, captured, telling all he knew to the Germans. And she might very well not live that long. His face bore the expression of a man bent on a terrible vengeance.

He said, "You were at the house on Duphot Street. How did you know about it? Who told you?"

Breathe. In, out. She would not, could not give Emmy up. In case she did not survive, this madman might turn on her sister next. The mouth of the pistol brushed the back of her neck. It was cold, hard, terrifying. She shrank from it before she caught herself and went still. Cold sweat broke out on her forehead. Her chest felt so tight she could hardly breathe.

"Max sent me there." She latched onto the excuse Max had whispered into her ear like a lifeline. "Monsieur Touvier, you're wrong about me. I have never told the *boche* anything that was not meant to deceive them. I've acted, always, on behalf of the Resistance. My heart is purely French."

"Stand up. *Now.*" Disregarding her words as completely as if she'd never spoken them, he nudged the back of her neck with the pistol. Looking at him through the mirror, Genevieve despaired even as she rose, slowly and unsteadily. *I have to do something . . .* Her eyes fell on the crystal jar of loose face powder on her dressing table. It was near her hand, which lay flat on the dressing table's glass top to support her unsteady knees as she got to her feet. The jar was heavy. It was open. The lid and fluffy pink puff she'd whisked over her face not many minutes before lay beside it.

The powder was white and fine, like flour. She could fling it at him, hoping that the powder would blind him or at least make him shut his eyes, and hit him with the jar —

Then what? Grab his gun and shoot him with it? Run for the door?

Her stomach nose-dived as possible outcomes chased each other lightning fast through her mind. None of them were good.

The dressing room door opened before she could make a move, or decide to make a move, causing both of them to jerk around to face it. Her heart jumped. She caught just a glimpse of the hallway as the opening door blocked her view of whoever was entering. Touvier grabbed her arm, holding her fast beside him. She stood slightly in front of him now, his hand tight on her arm, her skirt spreading out like a rose in bloom around both their legs. The gun was behind her. She could feel it nudging her spine.

The sight of Max as he closed the door, then took a few limping steps into the room with the aid of his stick, was the best gift she could have hoped for.

"Thank God." Relief turned her bones to water. All thought of their quarrel was forgotten. Touvier's grip on her arm prevented her from rushing toward him. Instead she took a deep breath and embraced him with her eyes. It hit her, then, that no matter what private disagreements they might have, she trusted Max absolutely.

He stopped short, the water droplets beading on his black hair and broad shoulders providing silent evidence that he'd just come in from outside and it was raining. His expression instantly turned to one of surprise.

"What the hell?" Max looked from her to Touvier. She didn't think he could see the gun from where he was standing, but a heartbeat later something changed in his expression that told her he knew it was there. Of course: he could see it through the mirror.

She almost stuttered in her haste to get the words out. "He thinks I —"

"Shut up." Touvier's voice was hoarse. He jammed the pistol into her spine, hard enough to wring a soft *ooph* from her. "I warned you about her." Addressing Max, whose mouth had thinned slightly but whose expression was otherwise unreadable, he leaned a hip against her dressing table. She got the impression that his injury had left him weakened. She hoped, devoutly, that that would make a difference. "She betrayed us."

"I didn't. You know I didn't." Her eyes stayed fastened on Max's face.

"I heard you were involved in an operation that went wrong." The look Max gave Touvier was grim. Genevieve felt a fresh spurt of terror: Did the operation he was talking about have anything to do with Emmy, with her mother? The timing was right, and Touvier and his men were involved somehow with the house on rue Duphot, as was Emmy. "What happened?"

"The bastards knew we were coming. They were lying in wait. Three good men killed at the scene. Cantor, Dardenne, Yount." With each name, Touvier shoved the gun into her spine again, making her jerk and wince. She expected — something — a glance at her, a frown, but Max didn't react. "Me, I escaped by the skin of my teeth. Helian, too, got away, as far as I am aware. Jobert was badly wounded. They found him lying in the street, made him talk before he died. He gave up every name he knew. You are fortunate he knew nothing of you. The Nazis are rounding up the rest of my cell now, as is evidenced by their presence here. I came with a warning, but arrived too late. They know about me, of course, which means the only thing left for me to do after I finish here is run. The blood of everyone lost is on *her.* And on you, for not listening."

"I already told you I don't know what you're talking about," Genevieve said. To Max, she added, "There are soldiers here. Their captain told me that they're searching for Resistance members operating among the theater company." Her voice cracked with urgency.

"I saw them when I came in. They checked my papers, let me pass."

"And how would the Germans know there are Resistance members operating among the theater company if you didn't tell them, *salope*?" Touvier jabbed her spine with the gun again, savagely enough to make her gasp. "Jobert knew nothing of that."

"How would I know? Would I tell on myself?" she hissed.

"If you are one of them, there is no danger in that to you. To Bonet, though, and to —"

"Quiet." Max held up a silencing hand.

The sound of several sets of heavy boots striding past the door caused Touvier to break off midsentence and Genevieve to go still as a post. Her pulse roared in her ears as she focused on the hallway beyond the dressing room. What was happening out there? Were the soldiers in the process of conducting an actual physical search of the building? At any second one of them could throw open the door. Or knock, to summon her to the stage.

She might be no worse off if the soldiers stormed in now, but there was Max.

A glance at the clock told her that she had five minutes left until she was supposed to be onstage. Someone would be coming to get her soon — she opened her mouth to warn Max, then decided she dare not mention it lest it spur Touvier to act immediately.

"Who else knew about your plans?" Max asked.

"No one I would not trust with my life. A message was left confirming the mission at the rue Duphot. *She* was there shortly afterward." Touvier jabbed her with the gun once more. She was so terrified by now that she barely even flinched. "You were unfortunate that I was having you watched." He switched his attention to Max. "Your operation is still intact, Bonet? Then you should welcome me killing her to keep it so."

At this confirmation that Touvier meant to kill her, Genevieve's knees shook.

"You make a good case for it, my friend, but I want to ask her a few questions first," Max said. He switched his attention to her. "If you've been playing a double game, this is your chance to tell the truth. Confess, and perhaps we'll be merciful. Who is your contact with the Germans?" He came toward them, lurching slightly on his stick. His voice was low but harsh. His eyes were hard on her face. His jaw was tight.

Her eyes never left his. "There's no one. You know there's not."

"*Stay where you are, Bonet.* This is not your decision to make. You are too closely involved."

Max stopped. Frowning, leaning heavily on his stick, he was still more than two meters away.

"Your only hope is to tell the truth," Max warned her in that same harsh voice. She thought, hoped, prayed he was acting, playing for time. But if his intention was to leap on Touvier, she feared he was too far away. Touvier would pull the trigger and she would be shot before Max ever reached him.

His face told her nothing.

"Enough talk," Touvier snapped. Genevieve heard a metallic snick, which she thought might be a precursor to the trigger being pulled. Her blood ran cold. To her he said, "You're a traitor, and you deserve a traitor's death."

"Max —" She couldn't help it. Panic curled through her voice. The feel of the pistol lodged against her back made her dizzy. The bullet would blow through her spine . . .

"Let her answer. It's important that we know." Max looked at Touvier first, then switched his attention to her. "Who is your contact?"

"I don't have one!"

"Stop lying, you." Touvier's fingers squeezed her arm so hard that she made a small pained sound. He was growing more agitated.

"Are you feeding information to Wagner?" Max's tone as he addressed her was rough with anger.

"No!"

"There is no more time for your questions," Touvier growled at Max, while frantic scenarios aimed at saving herself chased each other through Genevieve's head. *Should I try slamming my elbow into his injured side? Throwing myself to the floor?* Her stomach lodged in her throat. Her knees went weak. She sagged and had to catch herself with a hand on the dressing table. "She must be dealt with before she can —"

Max's arm jerked up. Something whizzed past Genevieve's cheek to hit behind her with the sound of a fist smacking flesh. Touvier's hand fell from her arm. He dropped like a marionette with its strings cut.

She leaped away as he landed with a thud at her feet, clapping a hand over her mouth to stifle any sound.

Touvier lay sprawled flat on his back, his pistol inches away from his outflung hand. A small black hole now punctuated the space between his open, staring eyes. Even as she looked at it, blood began to trickle from the hole. His eyes glazed over as she watched.

She felt her knees start to give way as she watched him die.

"Are you all right?" Max's arm came around her from behind. She turned into him, letting her head drop to rest against his chest, clinging to him as she took a series of deep, shaking breaths.

"Genevieve?" His tone was urgent. His arms wrapped around her, warm and strong, hugging her against him, and she was thankful to let him take her weight. His shirt felt smooth against her cheek. His chest was unyielding beneath. He smelled of the outdoors, and rain, and Max. The combination was insanely comforting. "Did he hurt you?"

"No," she managed. "I'm all right." Then, on a note of disbelief as she made sense of what she'd seen, she said, "You shot him. With your stick."

"It's also a gun. If certain adjustments are made. I would have done it sooner, but you were in the way."

She tucked away the knowledge that all this time his stick had had the ability to be transformed into a gun — a gun with a silencer — and she hadn't known it to mull over later. "He was going to kill me."

"Yes."

She shuddered. "Thank God you came."

"Yes." His arms tightened around her. "I know you've had a shock, but I have to get rid of him before anyone comes. Can you sit down on the —"

A knock on the door made her jump.

"Mademoiselle, I was asked by Captain Hahn to say please come to the stage now." It was the voice of the soldier who had taken Berthe away, calling through the door.

Max's arms around her had gone iron hard.

"One minute," she called back, and was proud and relieved when her voice didn't squeak.

She pushed away from Max. He let her go, moved fast. He grabbed Touvier's pistol, shoved it into his pocket and snatched her dressing gown from where it lay discarded nearby. Wrapping the garment roughly around Touvier's head, to avoid leaving a trail of blood, she realized, he gathered the corpse up in his arms like a baby and stepped behind the screen and out of sight.

It was enough to save them if someone did no more than cast a cursory glance into the room. But if there was any kind of a search . . .

Her stomach tied itself in a knot.

Where Touvier's head had lain, a scarlet puddle of blood soaked into the carpet. Horror shivered through her, followed by fear. It could be seen from the door. With a panicked glance around, she yanked the sparkly skirt of the costume she had recently changed out of from the top of the dressing screen and dropped it on top of the blood. At the same time she realized with alarm that the air smelled, just faintly, of gunfire. And Max's stick lay in the middle of the floor.

She shoved the stick beneath the dressing table skirt, grabbed a perfume bottle and spritzed the air.

With relief she discovered that the gunpowder smell was no match for the deep floral bouquet of Chanel No. 5. And the sequined tulle of the sparkly skirt revealed no hint of the dark secret it hid.

Grabbing her courage with both hands, she crossed to the door, opened it and smiled at the soldier waiting for her.

"I am to escort you," he said, and she replied, "How very thoughtful."

Heart pounding so loudly she feared he could hear it, she closed the door behind her and walked with him down the hall.

CHAPTER THIRTY-THREE

The master of ceremonies bawled, "Ladies and gentlemen, Mademoiselle Genevieve Dumont!" to open the second half of the show.

Genevieve's palms were sweating. She stood center stage, front, as the curtains parted and the trio of spotlights hit her. Their warmth was welcome — she was freezing cold — but the sense of exposure that came with them was not. Dazzled by their brightness, unable to see beyond the first few rows, she did her best to block from her consciousness the soldiers standing guard in the wings. A few stagehands — enough to work the curtains and lights — apparently had been cleared by the Nazis and allowed to go about their business, because that's what they were doing, but they seemed to be under constant watch. There'd been no sign of Berthe or any of the chorus on her way to the stage. She could only pray that they would be released soon. A search of the theater was being conducted, just as she had feared. Knowing how methodical the Germans were, she had no doubt it would be thorough. That thought, coupled with the ticking time bomb that was Max trapped in her dressing room with Touvier's corpse, was part of what was making her palms sweat. And her heart race. And her knees quiver like jelly.

The other part, which was just starting to set in, was reaction to having almost been killed. And to having a man killed right in front of her. Having *Max* kill a man right in front of her.

For her.

I can't think about that now. I have to think about the music, the song.

"Parlez-moi d'amour" was staged with her alone at the piano. She played; she sang. No other accompaniment, no backing vocals, no chorus or dancers or spectacle of any kind to take the focus off her performance.

The audience was on its feet, welcoming her back. The deep red horseshoe that was the auditorium sounded like it was full to bursting.

I am Genevieve Dumont. She summoned the protective armor of her star persona and felt it settle around her like a cloak.

For the first time ever, she wasn't sure it was going to be enough.

Lifting her chin, she smiled gaily at the audience, then as more waves of applause hit, she curtsied and threw kisses to them in acknowledgment.

While she'd been greeting them, the grand piano had been carried out to occupy center stage behind her. Turning toward it with a theatrical swish of her skirt, she reached out desperately to grasp the talent that was the one thing in her life that had never failed her.

Max was in the wings. She spotted him with a sense of shock. There was no mistaking his tall, lean form. Deep in shadows, his eyes fixed on her, he was flanked by a pair of soldiers.

Was he under arrest? Did they find him with Touvier's body? Did they know what he was?

The gloom surrounding him coupled with the dazzle of the spotlights in her eyes made it impossible for her to read anything in his face, his stance.

Hahn stood near him: she recognized his vulture-like profile as he turned his head to track her progress.

My God, my God.

The spotlights following her felt bright as a thousand suns. There would be no concealing her slightest expression, her smallest move from such a close observer as Hahn.

I must act as if nothing's wrong.

Smoothing her voluminous skirt beneath her, she took her seat on the bench. Chills coursed through her body. She had to set her teeth against the bone-deep cold that threatened to set them to chattering. Seated now, too, the audience was silent. She could feel their anticipation reaching out to her.

She adjusted the microphone, took a breath, positioned her feet on the pedals and her hands on the keys.

To her horror, she realized her hands were unsteady. Fine tremors shook her fingers.

She couldn't play like this.

Panic formed a hard knot in her chest, tightened her throat.

She wasn't sure she could sing.

Her stomach turned inside out.

You can do this. You have *to do this.*

Hahn was watching. The soldiers were watching. Every single Nazi in an audience full of them was watching.

Swallowing in an attempt to loosen up her throat, she flexed her fingers, wet her lips.

The choking sensation didn't abate.

The expectant silence of the audience increased in intensity until she could feel it beating at her like a battering ram.

She could feel the weight of Hahn's gaze.

Someone slid onto the bench beside her, startling her. She threw a quick, questioning glance sideways.

Max.

A warm wash of relief did battle with the chills attacking her as she watched him settle his stick — he'd found it; what did that mean? — on the floor near his feet.

If he was in custody, desperate, afraid for his life, afraid for hers, it didn't show.

His eyes were steady on hers. He was so close their bodies brushed. The spotlights picked up blue highlights in his black hair, threw shadows that emphasized the chiseled bone structure beneath his hard, handsome face.

"Duet?" he murmured.

As all the conversations they urgently needed to have — *Are you under arrest? What did you do with Touvier's body?* — were clearly impossible under the circumstances, she whispered back, "Yes, please."

Whatever happened after, right now she had Max, solid and capable, beside her. Already she could feel the worst of the choking sensation receding.

He started to play. She closed her eyes, folded her hands in her lap and willed the music to fill her.

The first vocal cue came, and she wasn't ready. Her throat still felt a little stiff, her diaphragm tight.

She didn't worry. She'd performed with Max many times. Not on a stage like this, but in bars and nightclubs and rehearsal halls and a host of other places. He could carry the song until she could take it.

"Parlez-moi d'amour . . ." Max sang. He possessed a nice baritone with good timbre and shading, a little husky, decent range, not quite

professional quality, but certainly adequate for this song. She listened to his familiar voice and felt the fear that had wound itself around her throat and diaphragm fade, felt the tension in her muscles ease, felt the music flowing inside her again with all the life-giving force of the blood in her veins.

"Parlez-moi d'amour . . ." The words came trilling out of her throat, blending with his. He stayed in the lower register, the harmony, as her voice soared above his, taking the vocals to the haunting, arena-filling levels that had made her famous. They shared the microphone, their faces so close she could feel the warm prickle of his cheek brushing hers. She was searingly conscious of how close her mouth was to his, of the latent power in his body, of the quicksilver grace of his hands on the keys. As the song reached its crescendo, she could feel a magical kind of chemistry flowing between them, feel the audience's rapt reaction, feel the electricity in the air. At last, almost reluctant, she brought it down, entwining her voice with his, ending on a softly poignant note that she held as he played beneath it. At the end, as they looked deeply into each other's eyes and the music faded away, the intensity of their connection was such that she was startled when the audience broke into rapturous applause.

Wrapping an arm around her waist, Max slid his lips across her cheek. She felt the heat of it clear down to her toes. Entirely of its own volition, her body softened and leaned into him. She felt almost intoxicated and was not entirely sure if it was from the music — or the man.

"Carry on as usual. They don't know about us," he whispered into her ear.

For maybe half a heartbeat, she was transfixed by the feel of his lips brushing the delicate whorls.

Then she registered the message. Just as quickly as that, the magic of the music and the performance evaporated.

She came back to earth with a thud. Touvier, Hahn, the search. The audience, applauding wildly.

The terrible danger they were in.

Fear settled like a rock in her stomach. With thousands of eyes on her, most of which were Nazi eyes, she did the only thing she could: pretend like everything was fine.

Head clear now, she looked at Max, to find that his eyes were fixed on her face.

"All right?" he asked quietly.

"Yes." Her voice was equally low. Her eyes held his. "Max — thank you."

He gave her a small, wry smile. "Anytime, angel."

She didn't find the endearment so provoking now.

They were still seated on the piano bench. His arm was still around her. She was still snuggled into his side. To anyone watching, she realized, it must look like they were sharing a private, intimate moment. In keeping with the atmosphere they'd created with the song. Which was over.

Time to survive the rest of the night. At least she felt better. Stronger.

"Come take a bow," she said, and pulled Max up with her. He grabbed his stick and they walked to the front of the stage and stood together, hand in hand, as the audience rose to its feet.

He took a bow, kissed her hand, then released it and left her, center stage front, to acknowledge the accolades alone.

Then the curtain rang down, and she had to hurry away to change for the next number. Hahn was still in the wings. He was talking to Max and ostentatiously applauded her as she passed him. She smiled and waved in response and tried not to let herself be overcome with anxiety by the sight of the two of them together. Max had told her that the Germans knew nothing of them and to carry on as usual. The only thing she could do was assume he was right.

The *choristes* whose papers and persons had already passed inspection were changing in the utility room for the next number. More trickled out of their dressing rooms one at a time as they were apparently cleared.

At the moment, the search seemed to be

concentrated on the trap room storage area beneath the stage and the crossover behind it. Soldiers filled both areas. From what she could see through the open door of the trap room as she passed it, they were opening trunks and boxes, examining equipment large and small, looking in closets, looking everywhere and at everything.

Cold shivers chased each other down her spine.

What are they looking for? Who are they looking for?

She thought of Max's office — did he have anything incriminating in there? She thought of her dressing room, of Touvier, and felt nauseated.

Berthe, pale and perspiring but free, was in her dressing room when she reached it. A desperate glance around found nothing incriminating. Touvier's corpse was not there. At least, nowhere that she could see.

What had Max done with it? Apprehension turned the rock in her stomach into a boulder.

Her spangled skirt was gone, too. A hardly noticeable damp spot on the carpet was the only hint that remained of what had happened.

"I only have a few minutes, so we must be quick," Genevieve warned for the benefit of the soldiers in the hall as she closed her dressing room door.

The minute it was shut, the two women flew together.

"What happened?"

"They checked my papers."

"There was no problem?"

"They are pigs." Berthe's broad face relaxed into a grim smile. "Stupid German pigs. Thank God."

As this feverish, whispered exchange took place, they were getting Genevieve ready for the next number, something they'd done so often together that they did it like clockwork.

Genevieve had to know. "Was Max here in the dressing room when you got back?"

"No one was here. A soldier was outside the door."

How had Max managed it? Her nerves tightened to perilously near the breaking point.

A knock. "Mademoiselle Dumont, it is time for you to return to the stage."

The same soldier. Where the stagehand who usually delivered the message was, where Pierre was, she could only guess: probably still being detained for inspection.

"Sing fast," Berthe said. "The sooner we can leave here, the better."

Berthe's joking — or not joking — order underlined what Genevieve already knew: as long as the soldiers remained in the theater, none of them were safe.

The show went on. Genevieve doubted that

the audience noticed any difference, but backstage, the nervous dread of the performers and crew, the heavy atmosphere created by the soldiers' presence, the awful anticipation that accompanied the search combined to create a cloud of fear that lay over everything. Her show almost never had mistakes, but tonight notes were flat, dancers tripped, musicians missed their cues.

She herself had to work hard with every song to keep the grinding tension from corroding her performance.

When, finally, blessedly, she was climbing the ladderlike stairs up to the catwalk for the finale, she was so drained that each step was an effort. The last notes of the penultimate number, the cancan, blasted riotously through the theater. Below, the dancers had just taken their final bow and were running offstage. A pair of soldiers stood in the prompt corner, which was usually where Pierre could be found during performances. She didn't know where Pierre himself was. She caught a glimpse of Madame Arnault herding the girls toward the greenroom, where they were now changing while the utility room was turned inside out. As she reached the catwalk, she scanned as much of the backstage area as she could see for Max. If he was down there, she couldn't find him. The soldiers had already searched his office and had evidently found nothing to interest them.

Maybe they'd get through this.

"Mademoiselle." Yves the stagehand was there to usher her to her swing. She followed him, the long black feathers of her skirt rustling as they trailed over the narrow metal walkway, holding her head carefully so as not to snag the plumes of her tall headdress on anything. It was dark up there so high above the lights, and cool and quiet as the few workers allowed on the grid of metal beams and catwalks took care to make as little noise as possible.

She settled herself on the gilded swing, and held on as Yves signaled the stagehands working the crank that she was ready. Then she was away, arcing six stories above the audience before being slowly lowered into place. The final song, "J'attendrai," was a beautiful one, and she closed her eyes and focused on it to the exclusion of everything else, letting the heartbreak of it fill her as the opening violins started to play.

"Halt! Stop where you are!" The roar was followed by the pounding echo of running footsteps high above her head. Her eyes flew open, and she looked up, aghast, to see a quartet of soldiers near the ceiling, pursuing a man bolting away from them. A collective gasp below her told her that the audience, too, had seen. Cloaked by the shadows at the top of the house, the fugitive fled along the very catwalk from which her swing was launched. That particular narrow pathway didn't run all the way across the top of the theater. To escape the soldiers, he would have to dodge along a connecting catwalk and clamber down a ladder to the crossover and from there try to exit the theater.

"Halt!" Two of the soldiers, having apparently spotted the potential escape route, branched off onto an intersecting catwalk, clearly hoping to intercept their target. They were brandishing guns in one hand, holding on to the railing with the other. The clatter of their jackboots on metal rang through the theater. "Halt or I'll shoot!"

The man, seeing that he was in danger of being cut off, daringly vaulted the railing and landed on a catwalk that didn't connect to the ones the soldiers were on. He scrambled up, darted away. Genevieve's mouth fell open as he burst out of the deepest of the shadows into an area of reflected light and she recognized him.

Pierre.

Impossible . . .

A loud bang sounded. Pierre screamed, toppled over the rail and fell, plummeting past her with his arms flailing and his coat flapping like a bird shot out of the sky.

The wet, explosive sound as he hit the stage apron was hideously familiar. Looking down in horror, Genevieve knew instantly that he was dead. She went dizzy as the sight of the still figure sprawled on the ground catapulted her back to the worst moment of her life.

CHAPTER THIRTY-FOUR

"Lower the damn swing! *Now!*" It was the one clear thing Genevieve heard, she didn't know how many minutes later. An eternity.

Max roared it from the floor of the auditorium as she hung there, some thirty feet above the ground. She was doing her best to stay conscious so as not to let go of the flower-bedecked chains and fall to her death herself while the theater revolved around her like a carousel and a terrible, rising darkness threatened to whirl her away.

He was there to gather her up when someone responded to his shouts, when the swing was close enough to the floor so that he could grab her. She practically fell off it into his arms, thankful for his strength, glad she no longer had to fight the ringing in her ears or the dizziness that made her feel like she was spinning away or the crushing horror that descended on her in waves, because Max was there and he would take care of everything.

"Let's get this off you." He was talking

about her headdress, the towering plumes that bobbed and swayed and had taken on all the weight of millstones pulling at her neck as she'd grown dizzy and weak. Between the two of them they got it off. What he did with it she didn't know, because she melted against him, burying her face in his shoulder, breathing in the safe, familiar scent of him as she fought with every bit of self-preservation remaining within her to shut out everything else.

"I'm taking her out of here," he told Hahn, as with a snapped order at someone the German joined the contingent of soldiers surrounding Pierre's body. Max mitigated the fierceness of his statement with a stiff "With your permission, of course." That nod to the officer's supreme authority galled him, she knew, but it was necessary because Hahn could snap his fingers and have them both shot, for no more reason than he wanted to.

"A thousand apologies! I would not have had this happen for the world. Our objective was to make an arrest, not endanger our friends and create a spectacle."

Hahn must have cast a baleful look at his men as he spoke, because one of the soldiers piped up with a timid-sounding, "Sir, we caught him with a radio. He is the one we were searching for — the radio operator. He was trying to escape."

Smiling, sweating, tomato-faced Pierre a

radio operator for the Resistance? It was the most dangerous work of all, with an average survival time that was measured in weeks, not months.

Her heart contracted. *A hero.*

"We will discuss this later." The ice in Hahn's tone disappeared as he said to Max, "She is not hurt?"

"Physically? I don't think so, no. But look at her. She's sensitive, an artist, and this is too much for her. It's a miracle she didn't fall! She needs to get out of the theater, be someplace quiet where she can grow calm."

Genevieve was aware enough to realize that he had only one arm wrapped around her, because, of course, in the presence of the enemy, he could not be seen to not need his stick.

"Certainly you may take her away. When she's feeling better, please tell her how much I enjoyed her show, and that I hope we may meet again under better circumstances."

A soldier said something, and Hahn must have turned to answer him because Max, with a muttered, "We're going to walk now," started off, slowly, taking her with him.

She would have thought he was being overcareful of her, but she discovered as she moved that her legs were unsteady and her head still swam and the heavy rushing sound she could hear was actually only in her ears. Her vision was fine, except she felt at a distance from things. As if she were standing on the outside of a building watching what was taking place within through a window.

"My God, did you see that?"

"Look, it's her! The Black Swan!"

"Genevieve, hello! Over here!"

"At first I thought it was part of the entertainment. Then —"

"Mademoiselle Dumont, loved the show!"

Snatches of conversation reached her ears through the noise and commotion swirling around them as the audience was ushered from the auditorium. She didn't respond to the voices calling out specifically to her because she couldn't. It took all her strength to keep moving. Without Max's support, she would have collapsed in a heap. A few of her girls in their bright bird costumes huddled together near the stage. Someone somewhere finally thought to kill the stage lights. An unwary glance back found one of the soldiers around Pierre's body kneeling to close the dead man's eyes. The moment when death was truly acknowledged, when all hope was relinquished.

She got a flashing image of another, infinitely loved pair of eyes being oh-so-tenderly closed and went ice-cold and lightheaded all over again.

After that she saw nothing at all, because she kept her eyes tightly shut and her face buried in Max's shoulder. If she allowed herself to look, or think about it, or remember . . .

She couldn't let herself remember. She would shatter into a thousand tiny shards if she did.

"Here, put this on." Max slid out of his jacket and wrapped it around her. He had a brief exchange with a soldier. Then they were through the door, stepping outside, and the combination of the cold night air and light rain that blew into her face revived her enough so that she felt able to lift her head from his shoulder and look around.

Rue de Clichy in front of the theater was crowded with vehicles. After a niggle of initial surprise, Genevieve realized that the show had been cut short by only about ten minutes and the previously arranged rides were arriving as scheduled to pick up the audience. In that same vein, she saw that Otto was in place with the Citroën.

Max bundled her into the back, got in beside her.

"What happened?" Otto's tone made it clear that all it took was one look at them to know something had. Not a surprise: if she was half as pale as she felt, she must look like a ghost, and Max had his arm around her in the car, which he never did. Huddled in Max's jacket, pressed against his side, she still shivered from head to toe. Her heartbeat felt erratic. She had to work to keep her breathing even.

Max said, "I'll fill you in later. Take us to the studio."

"Why not the hotel?" Genevieve asked him as the car moved off. She might be leaning against Max, but her head was up and she was once again functional. She was doing her level best to regain her composure, to close her mind to the terrible events of the night, to fight off any link to the past.

"Because the place is going to be packed. Because you don't want anyone to see you like this."

"In my costume, you mean?" Because she had just realized that under his jacket she was still wearing her black swan costume from the last number. Coupled with the fact she was reasonably sure no one could tell, just from looking at her, now that her head was up and her eyes were open and she was talking and walking, that she was shaking to pieces inside, her attire seemed to her to be the most logical explanation.

Max leaned close, whispered, "I mean this," so only she could hear, and touched a forefinger to her cheek. It wasn't until he held it up and she saw the moisture glistening on the tip of his bronzed finger that she realized tears were rolling unchecked down her face.

She looked at him in mute dismay, then dashed her knuckles across her cheeks to wipe away the tears.

They kept falling. Now that she was aware, she could feel the hot wet slide of them against her skin.

"Here we are," Otto said as the Citroën rolled to a stop in front of the side entrance to La Fleur Rouge, which from the outside was as dark as the rest of the city now that curfew was upon them.

Max got out and came around to open her door, then leaned in to say to Otto, "Go back and get Berthe and take her to the hotel." He helped her out of the car, supporting her weight and doing his best to shield her from the rain by tucking her against his side, then leaned back inside the car to say, "There's a body shoved up the chimney in Genevieve's dressing room. Later, when everybody's gone, go back and dispose of it." She guessed from his lowered voice that she wasn't supposed to hear that, and she really didn't hear what Otto said in response. But Max's reply was a terse "Touvier," so she assumed Otto had asked who the corpse was.

The thought of Touvier, coupled with this new information about what Max had done with his body, made her dizzy all over again. It was too much. And Pierre . . .

Don't think about it, she ordered herself fiercely. *Any of it.*

She concentrated on pulling herself together as Max shut the door and the Citroën pulled away.

Inside, the brothel was in full swing. Music, laughter and a cacophony of sound bombarded Genevieve from the moment she stepped through the door. Max's arm was around her still, but she walked steadily toward the lift. Her throat was tight with grief, her stomach was knotted with it and she had to keep dashing away the tears that stubbornly continued to fall. But she walked without needing to lean on him for support, and that was something.

Until the music that was coming at her from the lounge changed to her own voice singing "J'attendrai" from the recording she'd made for Odeon Records the year before.

The images of herself on the swing, of Pierre falling, of his body lying still and broken in front of her spun in a kaleidoscope of horror through her mind. She would have collapsed in a shivering heap right there if Max hadn't had his arm around her.

"Genevieve?" He looked at her in consternation as she sagged against him.

She didn't answer. She couldn't. Her throat was choked with sobs that she refused to let escape. But she could do nothing about the tears that rolled down her cheeks.

"It's all right. I've got you." He scooped her up in his arms as easily as if she were a child. Sliding her arms around his neck, she buried her face in the warm hollow between his neck and shoulder as he carried her to the lift.

Chapter Thirty-Five

When they reached the studio, Max took a moment to lock the lift door so no one else could get into the studio, something he rarely did. He didn't put her down but instead put down his stick and juggled her around a little while he used the key, and so she noticed what he was doing. And, noticing, Genevieve immediately wondered what he was locking the lift against. Was he afraid there were more vengeance-minded partisans out there who thought she was secretly working for the Nazis? The idea that operatives from her own side might be seeking her out to kill her made her blood run cold.

Or did he fear that the Nazis, realizing their mistake in letting them go, might come storming after them?

She would've asked him, but she couldn't get the words out around the lump in her throat. Her head had come up as she tried to see what he was doing with the lift. Now it dropped back to rest limply on his shoulder.

The tears still rolled down her cheeks, nothing she could do about them, but she refused to bawl like a baby in his arms. And if she tried to speak, she was afraid that that was exactly what she would do.

"It's just a precaution." He knew her so well: he guessed what was worrying her anyway. He was walking with her now, carrying her across the studio as if she weighed nothing at all, holding her close against his chest, his voice a soothing murmur in the silence of that vast open space. The music didn't reach up here, for which she was thankful. He hadn't turned on the light, and she knew that was because the curtains were open. Tall rectangles of changeable grayish light from the moon, which, tonight, was playing hide-and-seek among the rain clouds, slanted across the floor. "Only a handful of people know about this place. Even fewer know that you're working for the Resistance. Otto and me, a couple of blokes at Baker Street, one or two others. Problem is, it's possible one of them told someone else, and word gets around. Then, of course, there's your friend."

The slight hint of acid in his tone reminded her of their quarrel. She didn't care. He might still be angry at her over that, but he was *there;* now that she thought about it, he was always there, and that's what mattered. Touvier flitted through her mind again; with an icy stab of fear, she wondered if he'd told anyone else of his suspicions about her, but she forced him out. Unfortunately, thoughts of him led to thoughts of Pierre, which led to . . .

No. She took a deep, ragged breath that sounded suspiciously like a sob as she tried to close the door on her memories.

Tonight the door wasn't working properly: images kept spilling through. It was because, she thought, now that the numb was gone, her emotions were like a raw nerve freshly exposed.

"Cold?" he asked, and that's when she realized how badly she was shaking. The studio was dark, but not so dark she couldn't see. Solid leaden shapes of furniture in the gray; the glint of his eyes; the hard planes and angles of his face. They were in front of the sofa, she saw at about the same time as he said, "Here, hold on a minute," and set her on her feet. Her legs immediately threatened to give way, and would have done so if he hadn't kept a precautionary arm around her. She grabbed onto his shoulders as he caught up the blanket that had stayed folded on the back of the sofa since he'd covered her with it before, and wrapped it around her. "How does this bloody enormous skirt come off? Ah, yes." Having seen her put it on many times, he found the hook-and-eye closures that fastened at her waist with no trouble and released them with the deft movements of a man to whom such things were not a mystery.

Her skirt dropped to the floor with a rustle of feathers. She was left in her bodysuit and suspenders and net stockings beneath his jacket, which covered her almost to her knees, and the blanket, which was warm and enveloping.

Didn't matter: she still shook like a jelly.

Tucking the blanket closer around her, he tilted her chin up and peered at her face through the gloom. Since the day of Vivi's funeral until the night she had rescued Anna, she hadn't cried, not once. Since then, since the numb had gone, the tears had reappeared along with the feelings that prompted them. And now this: the deluge. Jerking her chin free, she scrubbed the blanket across her eyes and tried to say something, but her throat wouldn't cooperate. What emerged instead was exactly what she'd feared: a deep, rasping sob. Followed by another. And another.

"All right, then. Here we go." He picked her up again and sank down on the sofa with her on his lap. As if that one sob had opened the floodgates, she wept noisily now. The shame of it burned in her, but there was nothing she could do. She curled against him, buried her face against his shoulder in a vain attempt to muffle the pathetic sounds she was making, and shivered and sobbed and clung. His body heat, the solid strength of his arms around her, the familiar cadence of his voice were the anchors to which she held fast as she did her best to stop, to turn off the tears, to no avail. "There's no shame in crying, you know. You've been so strong, my brave girl, but you don't have to be strong now. There's nobody here but you and me, and you've had a hell of a night. Actually, a hell of a few years. Cry all you want." She sniveled and whimpered — had he really called her *his* brave girl? She was shocked to realize how much she liked it. She fought for control as one hand emerged from the blanket to clutch his shirt front: another anchor, firmly grasped.

"You were every inch the star tonight. Not only onstage, where you dazzled as you always do, but offstage, as well. I've worked with seasoned commandos who, when faced with the same terrible circumstances, wouldn't have kept their heads as well as you. You should be proud of yourself. I'm proud of you."

His words ignited a warm glow inside her. Her shivering eased. The whimpering and sniveling subsided until the sounds she was making were more on the order of occasional gasping breaths.

"Genevieve." His tone changed, became almost conversational as he asked, "Do you remember the first time we met?"

She managed a nod. Her face was so close

to the warm column of his throat that she could feel the rasp of stubble on it and the underside of his jaw when he moved his head. She could smell his shaving lotion, just faintly, along with cigarettes and a lingering hint of rain. Her tears still fell, dampening his shirt, but they were lessening. His arms held her comfortingly close. His shoulder made a broad, sturdy cushion for her head. His chest felt solid as a wall.

He makes me feel safe, she thought, and then realized that he always had.

She let go of his shirt to slide her hand around his neck as the iron bands squeezing her heart started to loosen.

"I was playing the piano," he said. " 'We'll Meet Again' — I even remember the song." She remembered, too, all of it, including the song; she could hear the piano playing still, the tinkling music was what had drawn her into the bar; she could picture him, a dark, handsome stranger, bent over the keys. "And keeping an eye on the bar owner, who didn't only work for the Nazis but two-timed them with everybody, including us, when this girl walked in. She was wearing a white dress and a black hat and she knocked my socks off. And that was before she walked right up to my piano and started to sing."

Her lips curved. She'd needed to pay for her supper that night, and her lodging soon after, and she'd been hoping to garner some tips, or even a semipermanent gig, by horning in on his.

"Up until then, I'd thought of Casablanca as a hellhole. Hot as an oven, dry as the Sahara and everybody out to get everybody. Any night I didn't end up with a knife in my back I counted as a good night. I'd banged up my leg pretty thoroughly a couple of years before when my plane crashed. Broke the femur in three places, broke my knee, burned the hell out of the whole thing, so bad I couldn't fly anymore. So I was out of the RAF, and my mother — did I ever tell you about my mother? French, like yourself, concert-caliber pianist, married my father and moved to London at eighteen. She'd made sure I spoke French like a native, so I got shuffled over into the SOE. I wasn't too happy about it, to say the least, but God and country, you know. You do what you must."

She listened with growing attention. In the beginning, he never would talk about himself, even when she'd tried to get him to. Of course, once she'd discovered what he was, she'd understood his reluctance and even been glad of it, because whatever he might have told her would have been a lie. Then, having found out he was SOE and that whole bit, she'd been too angry at him to ask again.

He kept talking. "Then you started coming around, singing with me, and I started taking you places, and, yes, it did occur to me that you'd be a hell of an asset for us, but what I remember most from those days was thinking that Casablanca was starting to grow on me. It took me a while to figure out that the only thing that had changed about Casablanca was you."

She drew in a breath, flicked a glance up at him. He was looking down at her, and she realized that even there, on the sofa, the dark was leavened with enough moonlight to allow him to actually see her. Probably, because of the angles, better even than she could see him: the strong line of his jaw and the straight nose and the dark glint of his eyes.

And his mouth. With a slant to it now that looked almost . . . tender.

Her heart started to beat a little faster. The hand that was settled behind his neck slid up over his collar, touched the thick, crisp strands of his hair.

"My orders were to set up a spy network, and that's what I did. A bar musician was a good cover. You meet a lot of interesting people and hear a lot of interesting things that way, but it didn't give me the ability to travel easily between countries or provide access to the kind of high-level people or information I needed. You, your voice, your growing popularity as a singer — I saw how I could use you."

At that she narrowed her eyes at him. But she was not, she realized, as angry and hurt and bitter about how he'd manipulated her as she had once been. She'd been involved in the work for long enough now to recognize that, sometimes, hard choices had to be made.

"I wasn't sure how to make the approach. I wasn't sure if I was going to make the approach. You were so young, and there was something — fragile — about you. You were just what I needed, but I didn't really want to get you involved." He brushed a few errant strands of her hair out of her face and tucked them behind her ear. The slide of his fingers over her skin left a trail of heat that lingered. "Then after that night, after what happened with Lamartine, you *were* involved, *we* were involved and I didn't feel like I could just let you walk away. My first allegiance had to be to my country, and this was, and is, a fight for her life. For the life of civilization as we know it. You were the perfect vehicle to take the network I was building where it needed to go. So I did what I felt I had to do." His mouth twisted into a wry smile. "I knew you were going to hold it against me. I just didn't realize you were going to hold it against me for years."

She took a deep breath and realized that the lump in her throat was gone.

"You're lucky. I've decided to let it go." Her voice was low and scratchy, but at least she was able to talk. The tears had stopped, somewhere in the course of listening to him, and she was no longer shaking. Instead she felt at home in his arms. The fear and pain and grief were still there, but they'd receded to the point that she was able to shove them away where they belonged, deep in the recesses of her mind.

And that, she realized, had been his intention all along: to distract her, to give her thoughts another direction. To talk her down. He knew her well enough to know just how to do it.

He said, "Have you now?"

"You shouldn't have tried romancing me is all. That was dirty pool."

"Angel, to be clear, I wasn't romancing you to get you to help me. Well, not entirely."

She let that pass in favor of giving him a searching look.

"You used to call me *angel* a lot. When you were romancing me. But when you stopped romancing me once I found out what you were really up to, you stopped calling me angel, too."

"If I stopped, it was because I didn't want to take any further advantage of a girl I'd jockeyed into working for me. And because in this line of work any kind of close, personal relationship just makes everything more complicated. And dangerous."

"You started calling me *angel* again a few days ago." As the reason became appallingly obvious, her eyes widened on his face. "That's because you think it's almost over, don't you?"

"Think what's almost over?"

"There you go again, answering a question you don't want to answer with another question. You know what I'm talking about — the war. The Resistance. The work we're doing together. Everything."

"What I know is a big push is coming. If it doesn't go our way, God help us all."

"What about —" she almost said *us,* but that sounded far too personal, like a relationship rather than the professional association they'd maintained "— our work?"

His face tightened. "I've known for a while now that we'd have to close up shop soon. If it comes down to the kind of all-out fighting that I think's getting ready to happen, there won't be any place left on this continent for girl singers or big traveling shows, nothing like that. I just wasn't sure of the timing, when to pull the plug. Now I am. With what happened tonight with Touvier, with the Germans knowing an invasion's coming and desperate to stamp out any trace of the Resistance before it happens, it just got too dangerous. After this show tomorrow, it's over for you. I'm going to scrap the rest of our tour and set up a special performance in Spain for next week. From there you're going to the States. It's the only safe place to sit out what's coming. Unless I very much miss my guess, Europe's going to be a bloodbath soon."

His tone, the set of his jaw, the perceptible hardening of the muscles cradling her told her how serious he was.

"We're all going? The whole troupe?"

"The troupe's going to Spain, where they should be safe enough. No one will come looking for a bunch of backup singers. Who the Nazis and anyone else with an ax to grind will be looking for is you. You're the one who has to get far enough away where they can't reach you."

"You're coming with me, right?"

"I'll see you onto the plane for the States. Then I'm coming back to France."

She sat straight up in his lap. "What? No!"

His mouth quirked. "You're a civilian. You go. I'm a soldier. I stay. That's the way it works."

"You expect me to just run away?"

"I expect you to do as you're told."

"You can't force me to go."

"You've done your job. It's over. You keep on with it, you'll get caught and die. I'm not going to let that happen. I want you out of harm's way. Now, while you can still get out."

"I'm not leaving you."

She realized what she'd said, what she'd revealed, that she'd just ripped the lid off their professional association and made it personal even as his eyes darkened on her face.

"We've had a good run. The trick is to know when it's over."

"Do you think you're the only one who wants to win this war? I do, too. I need to stay. I can help."

"I'm done letting you risk your neck."

"It's my neck. If I want to risk it, what do you care?"

He didn't reply for a moment. His eyes looked black in the uncertain light as they met hers.

"I care," he said. His voice was low, gravelly.

Her heart started to thump. "Do you?"

His mouth twisted. He replied with a single curt nod. Then he slid a hand around the back of her neck, pulled her close and kissed her.

Chapter Thirty-Six

The kiss was soft and slow, hot and demanding, earthshaking, heartbreaking. Somewhere in the middle of it, Genevieve figured out that she was in love, and had been, probably, for a long time. She also figured out, from the fact that Max had let his guard down enough to be kissing her at all, that he'd made up his mind that they would be saying goodbye soon, whether she liked it or not.

She didn't like it. But much as she hated to face it, she knew he was right. Touvier had almost killed her tonight. The Nazis had searched the theater. Two bullets dodged. But sooner or later, her luck would run out.

Her mother — panic twisted through her at the thought of abandoning her. *I can't.* Anything could have happened, or be happening, to her. If Max had found Lillian, done something about Lillian, she was as sure as it was possible to be that she'd know, so she didn't think he had. Anyway, there'd been no time. But there was Emmy. Had the raid that had caught up Touvier's cell and killed Pierre also ensnared Emmy? The possibility made her stomach knot with fear, and the worst thing about it was there was no way to *know.* If that — the worst — hadn't happened, Emmy was still out there doing her utmost to save Lillian, and maybe by now she'd succeeded. The fact that she'd heard nothing might as easily mean something good as something bad. Emmy knew that tomorrow night was her last night in Paris. She would be in touch. If Genevieve hadn't heard from her by the time she took her final bow tomorrow night, *then* she could panic.

But for now there was this amazing development that was her and Max.

"I care, too," she said, quite loudly, just so there was no mistake, when at last she came up for air.

His eyes were heavy lidded with passion as he looked down at her. "You sound very certain."

"I am."

Their faces were inches apart. Her arms hugged his neck. The blanket and his jacket had fallen away, and his arms were around her. One hand, big and warm, caressed her bare shoulder. The other had stopped moving a moment before, centimeters into the act of pulling down the zipper that did her bodysuit up the back, as if he'd had second thoughts about the wisdom of what he was doing. It was now splayed flat against her rib cage. She could feel the size and shape of it through the skintight satin.

Just the feel of those big hands touching her was enough to make her shiver.

He said flatly, "You're leaving."

"I don't want to go."

"If something happened to you, if I let you stay and you were killed, I'd put a bullet through my own brain. You being caught would end up getting us both killed."

Disregarding the horror of it, that was far and away the most romantic thing she'd ever heard. He must have been able to see the softening in her eyes because he said, "Like the idea of that, do you?"

She batted her eyes at him. "It's just like Romeo and Juliet."

He looked revolted. "I take it back. If you get killed, I'll get smashing drunk and go on with my life."

"That's not better."

He relented. "It's not true."

"I would want you to, though."

"We're going to circumvent the whole problem by getting you out of here before it happens. No more arguments."

"No more arguments," she agreed.

At the slight smile he gave her, her heart throbbed like a sore tooth. The numb was definitely gone, and emotions, she was rediscovering, were a mixed bag. She loved him so much it hurt, and the thought of losing him hurt even more.

She'd just found him. Or, at least, just found that she loved him. She wasn't ready to leave him.

"Max." She tightened her hold on him.

"Hmm?"

"What if they catch you? What if you get —"

"They won't," he said. "I won't." Then he kissed her again and she kissed him back and somewhere in the process they lost the thread of the discussion.

By the time he called a halt by putting firm hands on either side of her waist and lifting her off his lap, her mouth was swollen from his kisses and the top of her bodysuit was down around her waist.

"Max," she protested as he set her down on the sofa and stood up, breathing hard, running a hand through his black hair. His shirt was partly unbuttoned, and his bow tie hung loose on either side of his collar. She was flushed and trembling, melting inside like butter in the sun, and she would have stood up, too, and molded herself against him, except she didn't think she could stand up. His eyes dropped from her face to her breasts, small pale globes now plumped and dazzlingly sensitized by his hands and mouth. She could almost feel the heat coming off him as he looked at her, and her lips parted and her breathing quickened in response.

"Come back," she said, and patted the sofa beside her invitingly.

His eyes blazed at her. Then his fists clenched at his sides, his jaw hardened and he glanced away.

"I want you to take a moment and think." His voice was hoarse, and he was talking to the window or the wall or whatever was over there instead of her. A little shy now that he'd whisked himself away, she struggled to pull her top back into place. "We've been thrown together under the most adverse conditions imaginable, surrounded by danger, our lives on the line every day. You may think you care about me, but when this is over, when the world is sane again, you may feel differently. The smart thing to do would be wait, make a date to get together after the war, see how we feel then."

"I don't want to wait until after the war. One or the other of us might not make it until after the war."

He was looking at her again, watching with a grim expression as she made necessary adjustments to her top so that she was at least minimally decent, but he didn't say anything. His silence told her what she already knew: her words were true.

He said, "I don't feel right about . . . carrying on with this, and then sending you away and not seeing you again for months or years or maybe forever. You should wait for someone you can . . . be with long-term. Build a life with."

Her clothes were more or less back in place, and her legs were more or less recovered. She stood up, took the two steps necessary to reach him, slid her hands up his shirt front to rest on his shoulders and swayed toward him.

"I want to be with you."

He caught her by the waist before she could plaster herself against him. In the dark glass of the nearest window, a blurry reflection of them both caught her eye: her in nothing but her shiny black bodysuit, still only partly zipped up, with suspenders striping pale thighs above shapely legs in net stockings and pumps, her black hair cascading in waves around narrow shoulders; him far taller and broader of shoulder, his black hair disordered, his jaw dark with stubble, his white shirt and black trousers the perfect foil for his lean, powerful build. Her heart skipped a beat: louche, decadent, slightly scandalous, the people in the reflection looked like they belonged together, a matched set.

His tone was skeptical. "For less than a week."

"It's better than nothing."

"It might not be."

"I care —" a pale and puny word, but she was being cautious with her feelings and his, and wasn't ready yet to go beyond what he had admitted to "— about you. Is this you saying you got it wrong before and you don't care about me?"

He hesitated, and his face tightened. His reply, when it came, was almost reluctant. "I'm not saying that."

"Well, then."

"Well, then, what?"

"I'm not a virgin, if that's what's worrying you."

His eyes flickered. "I didn't expect you to be. And for the record, I'm not, either."

She had to smile a little at that. "I didn't expect you to be."

"Genevieve —"

She said, "I'm going to think of however long we have left together as a gift. If we don't make the most of it, I know that I, at least, am going to regret it for the rest of my life."

His hands tightened on her waist. For a moment he seemed to study her face.

She smiled at him.

"To no regrets, then." His voice was very quiet. Then he bent his head and kissed her.

After that, what happened, happened.

Her previous experience consisted of the single fumbling act of love that had given her the blessing that was Vivi. Which, except for the type, if not the depth, of the emotion involved, bore absolutely no resemblance to what she shared now with Max. Their coming together was torrid and primitive and hungry and electric, and, in a word, a revelation.

When exhaustion finally sent her off to sleep in the small hours of the morning, they were in his bed, she was naked in his arms, and he had just reached down and retrieved a blanket that had fallen to the floor and pulled it over them both. When she woke up, the first pale fingers of dawn were starting to creep in through the windows. After a surprised moment in which she blinked through the lightening gloom at the open curtains, the plain white walls and the unfamiliar bed because they made no sense, she realized that the tensile warmth beneath her head was, in fact, a man's muscled chest. Max's muscled chest.

He was naked, she was naked, and they were wrapped around each other and all tangled up in a single blanket.

Remembering what they'd done, she went rosy all over. Then, to her consternation, she glanced up to find that he was awake and looking at her.

What did one say to a man after a night like that?

"Good morning," she tried, not flustered at all. She raised herself up on an elbow and, in the process, without really meaning to, took in every detail of his wide shoulders, muscular arms, tapered chest. A wedge of black hair thinned as it trailed down past his navel to disappear beneath the modesty-saving blanket. Flat on his back, he tucked an arm beneath his head, the better to watch her as she clamped a careful hand against the top of the blanket to hold it in place and started to rather self-consciously disentangle her legs from his prior to getting up.

"Good morning." His tone was grave. His mouth was unsmiling. His eyes — she met them, almost unwillingly, and, beneath the lurking twinkle he couldn't quite hide, what she saw in them for her made her lips part and her heart start to thump. "Sleep well?"

"Yes, I — yes. You?"

"Like a rock."

It was an inane conversation she knew. But she was wrestling with the problem of how on earth she was going to get out of bed, because she couldn't just stand up naked, and if she took the blanket, then *he'd* be naked and — she was quite sure, from his responses, from his expression, that he was aware of her predicament and enjoying it.

Of course he was. That was Max. She narrowed her eyes at him.

He smiled at her. Then he said, "Genevieve, who's Vivi?"

Chapter Thirty-Seven

The question hit her like a blow to her heart. Her eyes flew to his face. Her expression must have reflected her shock because he said, "You called for her in your sleep."

The room tilted sideways. *Oh, no,* she thought. *Oh no, oh no, oh no.*

"Genevieve?" Max frowned at her. Her eyes fastened on him, her anchor, as all around her the world started to spin. "What is it?"

She couldn't talk. She physically could not make her lips move. It was all she could do to breathe.

As if his speaking her name had conjured them, the images crowded into her head. She could *see* Vivi, hear her voice, feel the warmth of her little body in her arms. She felt the blood leach from her face.

"Are you ill?"

At the alarm in Max's voice, she managed to shake her head. Her heart felt like it was caught in a vise that was slowly tightening. The pain was excruciating. She was propped up on her elbow, staring at Max without really seeing him. Her vision was focused inward, on snippets of Vivi's life playing out on the screen of her mind's eye, and she was helpless to do anything about it. She was dizzy, aching with loss, terrified that the movie in her head wouldn't stop until it reached its shattering end.

Max sat up even as she sank bonelessly back against the pillows. Her hand, strictly of its own volition, still clutched the blanket, holding it in place on her chest. She closed her eyes. It was a mistake. The images came faster. The dizziness got worse instead of better. Grimly she concentrated on battling it back.

Max said, "Is this about what happened last night? Touvier? Lafont?"

Of course. Pierre's death must have brought on the dream. She should have foreseen . . .

A long shudder racked her.

"Genevieve, talk to me." He was leaning over her. She knew he was there. She could sense him, feel that tingle akin to an electric charge that, lately, had alerted her to his proximity. She took a deep breath and opened her eyes to find him frowning down at her. Broad shoulders, solid as a rock, blocked out her view of the room still spinning around him. Sturdy and unmoving, the hard-muscled arm propped beside her head served as a bulwark against the encroaching shock waves.

She focused on his face, concentrating fiercely on each familiar feature, on the here and now as opposed to the past. His hair was disheveled, his jaw was dark with stubble, and the lines around his eyes and mouth were deep with worry. He looked slightly dangerous, totally disreputable and wholly dependable.

She made a tremendous effort. "I can't —" She broke off, shook her head.

"Can't what? Talk to me?" He stroked her cheek. "Whatever it is, you know you can. You can tell me anything."

Not this, she wanted to say, because even thinking about it hurt too much. To resurrect the memories, to have the images rise up in her head, was to relive them all over again. To put what had happened into words . . .

She sucked in air, the sound more sob than breath.

"You're scaring me," he said. His hand felt warm and strong against her cheek. His thumb feathered the corner of her mouth.

She looked up into his lean, dark face and drew strength. Her chest ached, her throat was tight and the vertigo afflicting her was making her feel sick. But the past was over, was behind her, was composed of ghosts and memories and dreams, and he was real and alive and *there.* His eyes held hers, encouraged her, willed her, compelled her. She'd given him her loyalty. She'd trusted him with her life.

"Who's Vivi, angel?" His voice was almost unbearably tender.

She loved him.

Genevieve reached down deep and dragged the words up from what felt like the depths of her soul.

"She was my daughter," she said, and closed her eyes.

He said something that sounded profane, but she didn't hear it, not really, because she was battling the fresh upsurge of pain, fighting the sting of tears, resisting them with everything she had.

"God Almighty." He gathered her up, holding her tightly against him as he rolled onto his back. Draped skin to skin across the width of his chest, she wrapped an arm around his neck and buried her face in the warm curve of his shoulder and reminded herself, fiercely, to breathe. "Tell me what happened, Genevieve."

Her eyes were hot with tears. Her throat burned with them. But last night she had cried an ocean's worth to no avail. The dream had come back. The pain once again twisted through her like a knife. The wound still festered. The images lived inside her.

She wanted Max to know. She needed Max to know. This was such a vital part of her, her center, her core. Without knowing the part of her that belonged to her daughter still, he could never really know her. And without knowing her, how could he love her?

Breathe.

"She . . ." She paused, gritted it out. "*Vivi* died."

Her tongue and lips formed the once familiar sounds as if they'd last done so just moments before. The syllables, emerging in her voice for the first time in seven years, were as poignant and as powerful as a nearly forgotten prayer. As her precious little girl's name hung in the air, waves of emotion crashed into her, threatening to tear her from her moorings and tumble her beneath the surface of grief's stormy sea. But she held on to Max, held on to the present and, this time, managed to stay above the waves.

She was, she realized, trembling in his arms.

"Can you tell me the rest? You couldn't have been much more than a child yourself."

"Eighteen. It was my eighteenth birthday." She felt him go perfectly still and guessed that he was making the connection between what she was telling him and her too-heavy imbibing on her most recent birthday, as well as on the other birthdays she had spent in his company. But the memory surged forward, assaulting her, ripping at her heart. She almost flinched, almost turned away, almost pushed the past back behind the wall she had so laboriously built over the ensuing years to contain it. Clinging to Max, breathing deeply of his familiar scent, she managed to keep going by shying away from the worst of it and concentrating on the easier, less painful details.

Tilting her head, she slanted a look up at him and adopted a faintly jeering tone. "You didn't know I was a slut, did you? Pregnant at sixteen."

His arms tightened around her. His face bent toward hers. His dark eyes took on a fierce gleam. "You were never a slut. You think I don't know you well enough after all this time to know that? And if anyone else had said that about you, I'd be punching them in the face about now."

That wrung the smallest of smiles from her. He didn't smile back. Instead he stroked her hair, kissed her forehead and said, "Go on. Pregnant at sixteen."

She told him about Phillippe, that she'd loved him, that he'd died. She told him about discovering she was pregnant, about her own and her family's shock and shame, about being sent away in secret to have her baby.

She told him about the fourteen months of her daughter's life. About how beautiful her child was, how quick to learn, how funny, how beloved.

As she talked, the other, darker images gathered strength, crowded closer, forced their way toward the forefront of her mind. Vividly colored, sharply real, and devastating.

Until finally she reached that day, her

eighteenth birthday, and the handful of moments that divided the *before* of her existence from the *after.* Her voice faltered, but he murmured encouragement. Wrapped in the solid strength of his arms, her head resting on his chest so that she could hear the steady beat of his heart beneath her ear, she found the courage to go on. Husky and hesitant at first, the words tumbled out as that last, terrible memory unfolded like a movie reel in her head.

Chapter Thirty-Eight

"Maman! Happy birthday!"

The sun was sinking behind the mountains of the Luberon Massif, bathing the tiny provincial village of Lourmarin in a warm golden glow. Hurrying along the narrow street, walled in by whitewashed houses rising up three stories to end in clay tile roofs, Genevieve — no, not Genevieve, she'd still been Genevra de Rocheford then, although she didn't tell Max that — looked up smiling at the sound of her small daughter's voice calling to her, parroting the phrase she'd learned only that morning in all the excitement of waking up to her mother's birthday, complete with a tableful of wrapped presents, a number of which were for Vivi, because Genevra hadn't been able to resist and had promised treats.

The basket over her arm was heavy with fat Toulouse sausages, a loaf of crusty bread and two jars of fourteen-month-old Vivi's favorite fig jam. Sent to the market by Clotilde, the former housekeeper at Rocheford whom Lillian had paid to take her in but was almost like a real aunt to her now, Genevra had left Vivi behind because there was flu in the village and she didn't want Vivi exposed. She was looking forward to the birthday feast Clotilde was preparing featuring, among other delicacies, a casserole of Basque chicken and a chocolate cake. Having hurried, she should reach home again right on time for the meal. In fact, she could already smell its savory aroma —

Because the window was open.

The second-story window, some twenty feet above the cobblestones, had its sash thrown up. Its simple white curtains fluttered in the breeze.

On the heels of a harsh winter and a cold, wet spring, the day's relatively balmy temperature had prompted someone — Clotilde, or perhaps Lydie from the village, who came in daily to help care for Clotilde's elderly mother — to open the front bedroom window, presumably to allow fresh air into the winter-stuffy house.

"Maman!" Vivi waved enthusiastically, her mop of black curls bobbing, her small cherubic face wreathed in smiles. Genevra could see only her head and raised arm; her dimpled chin barely topped the sill. Then the little girl turned sideways and climbed onto something — probably the cushioned footstool from in front of the nearby chair, which she liked to push around the floor. In a moment she was standing, hanging on to one of the curtains for balance. Framed by the faded blue shutters bracketing the window, her small sturdy body was visible to her knees, or rather to the ruffled hem of her pink-sashed white silk party dress that reached just below them. Vivi hadn't been wearing it earlier. Clearly someone had changed her dress in honor of the festive dinner to come.

Genevra realized that she could see her child in such vivid detail because there was nothing between the two of them but a distance of maybe forty meters — and air.

Ice-cold fear grabbed her by the throat.

"Vivi! Get down from there! Get away from the window!" Spurred by a dreadful premonition, she started to run. Her eyes stayed fastened on her child. "Vivi, do you hear me — get down!"

"Happy birthday, Maman!" Waving, hanging on to the curtain, Vivi bounced up and down with glee.

Genevra dropped the basket, paid no heed to the contents as they rolled clattering away down the street.

"Vivienne! Stop! Get down!" Shrieking the words, she ran as fast as she could, though her legs felt as if they were plowing through wet cement. The blood roared in her ears. Her heart pounded like it would beat its way out of her chest.

The curtain ripped.

Still clutching it, Vivi lost her balance, toppled out of the window —

"No!"

— and plummeted to the ground like a plump white bird shot out of the sky.

Panting, shaking, Genevieve broke off her hesitant recital there and wrenched herself out of the memory, because she couldn't bear to revisit that heart-destroying scene for another second.

"Genevieve —" Max's arms tightened around her.

"She was dead. Dead when I reached her." Her voice was hoarse. Try as she might, the images lingered, fading but there, smoky wisps of the past that wouldn't leave her alone. *A flutter of white silk; a splash of crimson on the gray ground.*

She'd thrown herself screaming to her knees beside the small still body lying crumpled on the cobblestones.

"It's all right. I've got you." Max's voice pulled her the rest of the way out, brought her back to the present, made the images, finally, retreat.

Safe in the sanctuary of his arms, she shivered and gasped and wept hot tears into his chest. He rocked and petted her, crooning wordless murmurs of comfort until all her tears were spent, until she lay limp and exhausted against him.

"I'm so sorry, angel. So bloody sorry." He stroked her hair, her arm, her back.

She nodded. Her eyes were closed, and the tremors that had racked her were receding. The vise that always crushed her chest when she thought of Vivi had loosened its grip. The pain was still there, but it was a softer, more manageable pain.

As if, by sharing it with him, she'd weakened its power over her.

He said, "You should have told me. Long ago."

"I can't . . . talk about it." Taking a breath, she realized something. Her eyes opened. Her head lay on his chest, and she tilted it so that she could see his face. Like the bed, like the room, like the entire studio, he was painted in shades of purple and lavender as dawn claimed the sky. His lean, dark face was so much a part of the landscape of her existence now, so familiar, so *dear,* that her heart flooded with warmth as she looked at him, and that helped ease the pain, too. "I *couldn't* talk about it. I've never been able to. You're the first person I've ever told."

"I'm honored." His voice was low and grave.

"I couldn't feel anything, after. It was like — I was alive, but not really present in my life, if you can understand that."

"I can. Soldiers who experience terrible

things in battle sometimes report a similar reaction." His hand came up, and he wiped the last lingering traces of tears from her face with gentle fingers. "To lose a child, and that when you weren't much more than a baby yourself — it would have broken a great many people. You didn't break."

"I came close."

"Not that I ever saw." He smiled at her, a quick wry twist of his lips that did funny things to her insides. "Did I say you were brave, last night? I didn't know the half of it." Then his eyes darkened. "Last night — my God, Genevieve, if I had known, I would have been gentler."

She knew he was thinking about the fierceness with which they'd come together and the brevity of her one previous physical experience, that single encounter with Phillippe. The love she'd had for Phillippe had been real, but it belonged to the girl she had been then, not the woman she was now, and had long been eclipsed by the joy and the agony that was Vivi's life and death. What she had once felt for Phillippe was a tiny candle compared to the blazing sun of love and connection that she now felt for Max.

Pulling herself together, she let the past go. "You were perfect," she said, and smiled at him. Then she kissed him and crawled on top of him to prove it.

Later they had to hurry to dress and leave

the studio for fear that Madame Arnault or some of the chorus would arrive for rehearsal. Faced with the choice of wearing her black swan costume from the previous night or borrowing something slightly less eye-catching from the rack of costumes, she opted for an outfit designed for a song from *Girl Crazy.* The neat blue dress with its white collar, cinched waist and full skirt looked enough like an ordinary day dress that she could wear it without attracting attention. The swan costume got added to the rack of costumes, where she hoped its presence would pass unnoticed until she could discreetly retrieve it.

Still too shy to dress in front of him, Genevieve made use of the bathroom, doing her best to eradicate all traces of the night they'd spent, doing a creditable job of eliminating signs of tears and lack of sleep but able to do nothing about her slightly swollen lips or the stars in her eyes. She felt lighter emotionally than she had in years, but discovering her feelings for Max had left her feeling vulnerable, too.

Emerging fully clad, not quite sure what to expect or how to behave, she found him in his boxers in the act of shaving in a mirror above the kitchen sink. She was entranced by the process — and by the sight of him in his underwear, which showed off all manner of manly muscles, while he scraped bristles and soap lather from his face. She also got her first good look at his leg: from midthigh to just above his ankle, it was crisscrossed with ugly raised white scars that, he assured her when he saw her looking at it, made the damage appear far worse than it was, as much of the mobility had been restored to the injured tissues over time. Its appearance had proved useful the few times he'd had to drop his trousers to prove his injury, he told her, but other than that he was rarely aware of it anymore.

In the absence of Otto and the Citroën, they took a bicycle taxi back to the hotel. The morning light was soft and hazy with the promise of a sunny day to come. The air smelled of blossoms and green growing things with an undercurrent of the Seine. By mutual if unspoken agreement, they'd chosen to keep the unexpected turn in their relationship to themselves, so once out of the studio there was no hand-holding, no hugs or kisses, none of that. But there was something in his eyes when he looked at her that made her heart beat faster every time she encountered it. And she — every time she looked at him, she could feel butterflies taking flight in her stomach.

The solution, of course, was for them not to look at each other. But that was hard to do. She wanted to look at him, to touch him, to spend every available moment with him. Despite the newfound happiness bubbling inside her, she was supremely conscious of the darkness and danger all around them, and that they had so little time.

She couldn't think about it. If she did, it would spoil the few days they had.

With Max, relying heavily on his stick again now that they were back in public, a few steps behind, she was walking through the Ritz's lobby toward the lift when she spotted Emmy.

Her sister was seated alone at a table in the outdoor patio, sipping from a delicate china cup. To all outward appearances, she was a guest idly watching the comings and goings in the lobby. Clad in a fashionable fur-trimmed coat and a cloche hat, her hair freshly bobbed, Emmy looked completely at home in her surroundings — and totally different from the Emmy whom Genevieve had encountered in the elevator, or out front on the place Vendôme.

She knew the moment her sister saw her. Emmy paused for the merest fraction of a second in the act of lowering her cup back to its saucer. Across the busy lobby, their eyes met. Then Max caught up to her, said, "Something wrong?" into her ear, and Genevieve realized that her step had faltered at the same time that Emmy had hesitated with the cup.

Shaking her head, she smiled up at him and walked on. Together they took the lift up to her suite.

But everything had changed. Anxiety fizzed like soda pop beneath her skin. Emmy's presence in the lobby almost certainly meant one thing — she had news. Genevieve didn't think it could be good. Despite all the years in which they hadn't seen each other, some things hadn't changed, and what she'd read in Emmy's posture was fear.

Max went up with her. His plan was to use the telephone in her suite to start laying the groundwork for her "special performance" in Spain. The hotel telephone system wasn't secure, but then the calls he would be making were perfectly legitimate. And if the Germans *were* listening in, the calls would reinforce the reason behind her sudden decampment with her troupe to Spain.

She hadn't told Max who her mother was, or that her sister was the friend she'd been meeting and was, not coincidentally, with the SOE, none of that. Her family had remained suitably anonymous — *Maman, my sister* — as she'd told him about Vivi.

Now she was faced with a dilemma: Emmy was there, in the hotel, clearly needing to meet. Should she tell Max? The radical alteration in their relationship since she'd last talked with Emmy dictated that she should. Even if she hadn't been entirely certain that he would do his utmost to rescue rather than execute her mother for her sake before, she was now.

Then she remembered the ruthless efficiency with which he'd dealt with Touvier. And him saying, *I'm a soldier.*

She loved him. She had, and would, trust him with her life. But with her mother's — suddenly she wasn't so sure.

What she urgently needed to do was nip down and talk to Emmy. While Max was safely on the telephone. Depending on what her sister had to say, that might help her decide.

Berthe, pale and looking as though she hadn't slept well, hurried out from the vicinity of her bedroom to greet them as they walked into the suite.

"You're safe." Berthe beamed with relief. "Of course, I knew you were with M'sieur Max, so I wasn't worried . . . much."

Reminded of Pierre's fate, and Touvier and the raid, Genevieve felt unwelcome weight settle back onto her shoulders.

"Was there any more trouble after we left?" she asked.

"With the *boche,* there is always trouble. At least we were allowed to go." As she spoke, Berthe bustled around, opening the curtains so that the morning light poured in, twitching cushions on the sofa into greater plumpness. "Are you hungry?" Her glance encompassed Max, who'd walked on into the room while Genevieve still stood near the door. "Do you want me to call down for breakfast?"

"Genevieve left her finale costume at the studio," Max said before Genevieve could reply. "Otto should be downstairs with the car by now. Do you think you could go to the studio and retrieve it, then drop it off by the theater so it will be ready for tonight?"

It was all Genevieve could do not to blink at him in surprise. Max interested himself in many things about her performances, but not her costumes. Having Berthe do what he'd suggested would have ordinarily never occurred to him. He wanted to get Berthe out of the way.

She didn't think this sudden wish to be private with her was because he wanted to whisper more sweet nothings into her ear.

It didn't require genius to conclude that he'd noticed her moment of recognition in the lobby when she'd spotted Emmy and meant to demand an explanation.

Her heart stuttered as she shot a veiled glance at him. He stood in the center of the room now, all handsome, affable elegance as he smiled at Berthe. But she knew him.

Behind the outward appearance of good humor lay suspicion.

She wasn't going to get away from him before he got his explanation. The question was, should she lie?

Panic dried her mouth.

"Yes, of course," Berthe said.

That wasn't a surprise. Genevieve couldn't

remember a time when Berthe hadn't agreed to do whatever Max wanted. But from the look Berthe shot her as she grabbed her coat, Berthe, too, suspected Max's motives for wanting to get rid of her. That look commiserated with her, said something like *Uh-oh, what did you do?*

As Berthe left, Genevieve walked to the window and looked unseeingly out at the bustling square.

The door clicked shut. The silence that followed grew so unnerving that Genevieve finally had to turn around.

Max leaned a shoulder against a nearby wall, arms crossed over his chest, stick leaning against the wall beside him, looking at her. The smile was gone.

"Who was the woman on the patio?" he asked without preamble. She took a breath, still unsure about what to do. He added sharply, "And don't lie to me."

A knock sounded on the door before she could answer.

His face tightened. He cast the door an impatient look, then, when the knock was repeated, said something under his breath that she guessed was a curse and went to answer it.

From where she stood in front of the window, Genevieve couldn't see the door, which was located in its own small alcove. She heard Max open it — and then nothing.

Max didn't say anything. No one said anything.

A moment later the click of footsteps was followed by the sound of the closing door.

Emmy walked into view, with Max looming not far behind her.

Chapter Thirty-Nine

"There's been a problem," Emmy said as their eyes met across the room. She looked beautiful and composed in her eau de Nil coat, with its brown fur trim and matching hat that had her newly short curls rioting beneath it, but Genevieve read anxiety in the faint line between her eyes. Her pulse quickened. To have her sister, who'd been so adamant about the need for secrecy and concealment, walk into her hotel suite with Max present and say such a thing, the situation must be dire.

"Genevieve," Max said. She'd been focusing all her horrified attention on Emmy. Now her gaze switched to him. He was looking beyond grim. No trace of the charming, compassionate lover who'd coaxed her secrets from her and wooed her into losing her heart to him was to be seen in the hard gaze he turned on her. "Care to introduce us?"

Genevieve's stomach twisted. Their love was so new. It was like a nestling that had barely tested its wings. After last night, after everything that had passed between them, for him to find out that she'd been working behind his back while keeping vital information from him might, she feared, do it serious damage. She could only pray it wouldn't deal it a blow from which it couldn't recover.

Her lips parted, and then she hesitated and glanced at Emmy. The time for lying was clearly past, but . . .

"I wouldn't have come," Emmy said to her, "but I had no choice. The situation's changed drastically. To have any chance of saving Maman, we're going to have to move fast. And we're going to need his help."

"Maman?" Max looked from Emmy to Genevieve. *"Maman?"*

Her pulse quickened and her chest went tight as she sought a way to ease into it, to soften the truth, but there wasn't one.

"This is my sister," Genevieve said. "That friend I've been meeting whose name I wouldn't give you? It was actually her."

"Emmy Granville," Emmy said. "I'm with the SOE, too. Code name Merlin. You can check with Tommy Bowden at Baker Street if you have doubts."

Max shot a blistering look at Genevieve. She knew what it meant: *You told her about me?*

"I had to." Feeling increasingly wretched, Genevieve answered his silent accusation.

"There was a situation . . ." She broke off and looked at Emmy. The time to worry about her and Max would come later. For now the focus had to be on Lillian. "What's happened?"

"The rescue attempt failed. They've taken her somewhere else."

"Oh, no —"

"Stop right there. I want to know what you're talking about. Everything." Max's voice was sharp.

"We need him," Emmy repeated to Genevieve, and, even as Genevieve succumbed to an inner wince, looked at Max. "Our mother is part of the Resistance. She's been arrested by the Nazis. She knows the truth about where the upcoming Allied invasion is to be launched, and they suspect she knows, and if she isn't rescued immediately, they *will* succeed in torturing it out of her."

Max looked thunderstruck. "She knows the truth about where the invasion is to be launched?" He turned to Genevieve. *"What's your mother's name?"*

There was no help for it. And he knew now, or soon would, anyway: she could see the dawning realization in his eyes. After all, he was looking for her mother himself, for just that reason. How many women could the Nazis be holding with that information?

Genevieve put up her chin. "Baroness Lillian de Rochefnord."

Max's face was a study in growing, angry comprehension. "Lillian de Rocheford is your mother?" His voice sounded like it was being dredged up from somewhere deep in his gut.

"I was born Genevra de Rocheford." Genevieve's voice was flat. She'd known from the moment Emmy had walked into the suite that there was no way this was going to go well, and the reality was even worse than expected.

For a moment he simply looked at her. Then he said, "And you didn't tell me?" His voice was expressionless now. Like his face. He glanced at Emmy. "Now that I'm looking for it, I can see the resemblance. It's in the eyes."

Genevieve drew in a breath. She knew that face, that voice. "Max —"

"We'll talk later," he said. There was an undercurrent to it that sent ice down her spine. She would have said more, crossed to him, grabbed him by the lapels, shaken him, *something,* until the cold distance had vanished from his eyes, except Emmy was there and he was already shutting her out to focus on her sister. "Am I right in assuming you were part of Touvier's attempt to rescue the baroness two nights ago?"

"Yes," Emmy said.

"What happened?"

"We suspected that Wagner was in charge of her interrogation and followed him until our suspicions were confirmed, and we found the secret prison where she was being held. We watched him let himself in with a key, then identify himself to the guards stationed inside. The plan was that, at a time when Wagner was occupied elsewhere, some of our men wearing SS uniforms would let themselves in with a key, which we hoped would allay the suspicions of the guards, and remove my mother from the premises. If they were challenged, they were to present forged papers ordering that she be given over to them for transport to another location. Unfortunately, in the middle of the operation something went wrong. They were found out. They're all dead, I think. Everyone in Touvier's cell."

Genevieve knew from the sudden flicker of Max's eyes that he had no intention of telling Emmy what had actually happened to Touvier. She knew she, herself, would never tell anyone, not even Emmy. An act of revenge from a partisan who'd been close to Touvier wasn't likely, but it was possible, and the thought of bringing such danger down on Max made her shudder.

"Not everyone," Max said. "I understand that Jacques Helian escaped with his life."

"*Did* he?" Emmy's face tightened. When she spoke, her words were slow and thoughtful. "He was Touvier's second in command. He knew about Papa's cell — I remember Papa once spoke of meeting with him instead of

Touvier. If he got away —"

"He could be the traitor."

"My God, the one who betrayed Papa?" Genevieve's heart thumped.

"And the operation to rescue Maman," Emmy said. She looked at Max. "He needs to be found. And questioned, at the very least."

Max gave a curt nod. "I'll put the word out. He knows nothing of me. Does he know about you?"

Emmy shook her head. "I don't think so."

"Let's hope not," Max said. "You were there at the rescue attempt?"

Emmy shook her head. "I helped with the planning, and I made the key, but I was waiting elsewhere for them to bring my mother to me. I've been on the move since I found out they were discovered. The gestapo are sweeping the city for anyone connected with that network, and you can never be sure where is safe, or who to trust. Helian being a case in point. I never would have thought . . ." She narrowed her eyes at Max. "How did you hear of it?"

"There are people who talk to me." Max's answer was evasive, and he was frowning as he asked, "What made you suspect Wagner could lead you to the baroness?"

Emmy didn't say anything. From her silence, and the way she didn't glance her way, Genevieve knew that she guessed that Max wasn't going to like the answer, and she didn't want to cause what she obviously deduced would be additional difficulties for her sister.

"I told her." At this point there was nothing left to do but tell the truth. Max might be angry, but there was more at stake here than their relationship. "Wagner had our mother's locket. I saw it when he took me to dinner that first time, and I recognized it. That was the message I took to rue Duphot. To Emmy."

Max's lips thinned, but before he could say anything else, she added, "And just to make a clean breast of it, I also helped her get hold of Wagner's key."

"How?" His voice held an ominous note.

"By staging a distraction that last night I went to dinner with him so she could grab it and make a copy of it."

"What kind of distraction?"

"I fell down the stairs outside the theater. Emmy was there, pretending to be a fan."

Max said nothing, but the stony glint in his eyes told her how much he objected to that. She was relieved when he turned his attention to Emmy.

"The baroness has been moved, did you say? To where?"

Emmy frowned. "I don't know."

"If Wagner has her still," Genevieve said, "I may know where she is. He sent me a message, apologizing for having to cancel dinner.

He said that an emergency had called him away to Stuttgart."

"Stuttgart," Emmy said, in the same tone she might have used for *hell.*

"That makes sense," Max said. Although something about it made his face go sour.

"What?" Genevieve looked from one to the other of them.

"When female prisoners are taken there," Emmy said, her voice sounding hollow, "it's usually because they intend to execute them immediately. Executing French women in France tends to make the Germans unpopular with the locals. They can execute them without repercussions in Stuttgart. They even have a guillotine in the prison courtyard for that very purpose."

Genevieve's stomach dropped. "As soon as she talks —"

"Yes." Emmy looked at Max. "The bastards will make her talk, and then they'll cut off her head. Traveling into Germany is difficult just now, but we have to find a way to get to her. Right away, because I'm guessing we don't have much time."

"What if we don't have any time? How long can she possibly hold out against the things they do to people? If she's with Wagner, she's already in Stuttgart. What if they've . . ." Genevieve couldn't bring herself to finish. She shied away from even thinking about it.

Max said, "I've been told the baroness is

injured to the point where she can't communicate. They're waiting until she's better to start actively interrogating her. Which was why I was taking the time to plan an operation to reach her that wouldn't have failed."

"Touvier's timing, not mine." Emmy's reply was in response to the censure in his voice. Her tone turned urgent as she added, "In Wagner, our mother is in the hands of one of the most brutal torturers in the SS. He *will* make her talk. You know how vital it is that she doesn't reveal what she knows to the Germans. We *must* find her and get her out of there. I know your reputation. The Huntsman is practically a legend. Will you help us?"

Max looked from one to the other of them. Finally, in a tone gritty with resignation, he replied, "Yes."

Relief and a rush of gratitude toward Max washed through Genevieve. "I can ring him up. Wagner. Tell him I have a few days free and see if I can get him to invite me to visit him. He will, I'm sure of it."

"No," Max said. "Tensions are running too high, and too much could go wrong. You'd be going into the belly of the beast, and at the worst possible time. You're keeping to the plan we agreed on earlier. I'll find a way to get myself and enough people to do the job into Stuttgart without you."

"They're scrutinizing everyone coming into Germany," Emmy warned. "They're going mad with fear of spies, and of dissidents from within rising up and conspiring with the Allies. Genny's idea is a good one. It will take us right to where we need to go without creating any suspicion. She should definitely ring the bastard up."

"No," Max said again. "First of all, if *she's* calling *him,* that'll immediately raise a red flag in his head. Then, when his prize prisoner is snatched away while she's there, I think he's going to guess she might have had something to do with it."

"Then what do you suggest?" Emmy sounded impatient.

"Like I said, leave me to deal with it."

"No," both girls said in unison.

"If you thought you could get the job done on your own, you wouldn't be here," Max said to Emmy. He switched his attention to Genevieve. "You're going to Spain."

"I'm not going to Spain. I'm going to Stuttgart, if I can wrangle an invitation," Genevieve said. "I'm your best chance of getting close to Wagner."

"He wants to leave us behind because killing Maman will be far easier than rescuing her, and he thinks we'll interfere with that," Emmy said.

Max's eyes rested on Emmy's face. From their non-expression, Genevieve knew Emmy was exactly right.

"Touvier was right about one thing. I read

the message you got from London. The one concealed in the cigarettes he left in your office. You were ordered to kill my mother if you couldn't rescue her." Genevieve gave him a level look. "Tell me you won't kill her."

Their eyes met. "I won't," he said.

Emmy scoffed. "And we're just supposed to take your word for it?"

"I don't see that you have any choice." Max's voice hardened as he looked at her. "If we're going to work together, you need to get one thing clear — this is my operation. I'm in charge."

"Just because you're a man —" Emmy began, but Max cut her off.

"Not because I'm a man. Because Baker Street gave me the assignment. And because I'm your superior officer. *Major* Max Ryan."

The look on Emmy's face told Genevieve that Max had scored a point. Then Emmy gave a stiff nod, and she was sure.

"Max." Genevieve gave him a troubled look. "You really won't kill Maman, will you?"

Max hesitated for just long enough for her to know the answer. He must have seen the recognition of the truth in her eyes, because his jaw tightened. "I'll do my best to rescue her, I promise. If we reach her and she can't be saved, the unpleasant fact is I may have to kill her. If I were to find myself forced to do such a thing, it will only be because there is absolutely no other way, and she'll still be far better off than if she's left to the tender mercies of Wagner and the Germans." He paused. "Will you trust me to do my best to save her, Genevieve?"

Their eyes held for a minute. Then Genevieve nodded.

Emmy rolled her eyes. "Oh my God, I thought you said you two didn't have a personal relationship."

"Does it matter? I trust him, and you can, too."

The sisters exchanged measuring glances.

"Fine," Emmy said. She looked at Max. "Although I want to go on record as saying I *will* do anything possible to rescue her."

"I have no objection to that," Max said. "I'll do everything possible to rescue her, too."

After that, they debated possible courses of action until Max ordered the discussion tabled until later. It was agreed that Emmy would go to a safe house Max knew of in the Bois de Boulogne and stay there until 4:00 p.m., when the three of them would meet up again in the nearby public gardens and make further plans. After that, Genevieve had to head to the theater for her final show, which, given the events of the previous night, she dreaded.

"You will make sure to be there as agreed, won't you?" Emmy whispered into her ear as they embraced before she left. "Your Max seems to like to do things independently, and I don't want him leaving me behind."

"I'll make sure," Genevieve promised. She didn't even object to Emmy's calling him "your Max" now. Because he was, even if he was clearly still not happy with her.

When Emmy had gone, he came to stand over her. She was sitting in the chair by the sofa and had to look up at him.

"Genevra de Rocheford," he said. "That's quite a web of deceit you've spun. Is there anything else you'd care to tell me?"

Genevieve sighed. "I'm Genevieve Dumont now. I haven't been Genevra since I first left France. Everything I told you last night is true. I just held back the names. When I heard Touvier talking about Baron and Baroness de Rocheford — my parents — it shocked me. I thought I was done with them forever, but . . . it turns out I wasn't. That day I was gone all day? I went to Rocheford, our old home near Cherbourg, to see if my mother might have taken refuge in a secret place she liked to go to that I knew of there. That's where I learned that Emmy was with the SOE. We've been in contact since then, about finding our mother."

"You couldn't have told me any of this?"

"I couldn't talk about it. After —" She broke off, pressed her lips together, swallowed. After not being able to speak her daughter's name for so many years, she was still getting used to saying it out loud.

"After Vivi died," she went on, carefully enunciating each syllable of her child's name. The painful constriction in her chest that was there every time she thought of her little girl hadn't disappeared, but it was better. She could still talk; she could still breathe. And she could speak Vivi's name. "I needed to put everything about my past behind me. My family was part of that."

She didn't know what her face revealed, but his mouth twisted with wry acceptance and his eyes softened.

"All right, I understand. Still, no more secrets."

"No more secrets," she agreed.

He bent, slid a hand behind her neck, dropped a brief, hard kiss on her mouth. She kissed him back, then when he broke it off and straightened, she stood up, too, wrapping her arms around his neck, going up on tiptoe to press against him, kissing him like she would never stop, kissing him until her knees went wobbly and the butterflies that apparently now lived in her stomach whenever he was around took loopy flight.

When he lifted his head at last, the smile he gave her was enough to make her heart take flight, too. The problem with having the numb gone, she was discovering, was that her emotions, all of them, were so new and intense that it was like someone who had been blind suddenly gaining the ability to see the world and being dazzled by all its rainbow colors.

"You are the most beautiful thing I've ever seen in my life, and you're distracting me. I have things I must do." Lifting her arms from around his neck, he stepped back, chucked her under the chin, grinned at the indignant look she shot him and then at the sound of the door opening moved away from her entirely.

It was Berthe. They greeted her, then Max said, "I have to go." As Genevieve automatically, reflexively followed him to the door, he added for her ears alone, "Don't leave the hotel until I come for you, understand? No rehearsal, no anything."

She nodded. "We *are* going to meet Emmy as agreed, right?"

"Of course."

The telephone in the suite rang as he spoke. He paused with his hand on the knob, and they both listened as Berthe answered. They heard the murmur of her voice, and then she popped into view. They were standing in the small alcove, and she looked at them wide-eyed.

"Obergruppenführer Wagner is calling," she said in a hushed voice. "From Germany."

CHAPTER FORTY

The train ride from Paris to Stuttgart took more than ten hours. That was longer than usual, because the engineer was constantly having to stop as debris from a series of recent Allied bombings was cleared from the tracks before they could go on. There was, in addition, the wait at the border when every passenger was questioned and their papers were exhaustively examined. By the time they were once again chugging through the tall mountains and breathtaking forests of Germany, the atmosphere on the train was oppressive. Heavily armed soldiers patrolled the cars throughout the journey, checking papers, searching rucksacks and suitcases, calling out unfortunate passengers to answer a series of questions about their reason for traveling and for more thorough searches of their persons.

They were a group of five: Genevieve, Max, Emmy, Berthe and Otto. Berthe was the one Genevieve was most worried about, but she'd refused point-blank to be parted from Genevieve, and Max had allowed her to come. The rest of the troupe had been sent on to Spain, where, officially, they would all meet up in four days. Unofficially, after this upcoming performance in Stuttgart, the plan was for a couple of Lysanders to land and whisk them all, including the hopefully newly rescued Lillian, out of Germany. Max and Otto would be dropped off in France, and Genevieve and the others would fly on to England and safety.

That meant she and Max had even less time than she'd thought: two days. Every time she looked at him, her heart shivered at the thought of parting. What made it more difficult was that, in front of the others at least, they had to do their best to behave as if nothing in their relationship had changed. As Max said, the mission was too important to allow for distractions.

In his telephone call, Wagner had asked Genevieve to come to Stuttgart to give a private concert for an unspecified "special event" three days hence. Without being more specific than that, he couched it as being much like the private concert she'd given at the Spanish embassy where they'd first met, although if it was at all possible (he'd said with a chuckle), he'd like her to sing more than two songs. He would, he concluded, consider her acceptance a personal favor.

Even if she had not badly needed to go to Stuttgart for reasons of her own, refusing such a request would have been nearly impossible. With Germany in cruel ascendancy, Wagner was a dangerous man to offend, or to make an enemy of.

"I'm very much looking forward to seeing you again, Genevieve" was how Wagner had ended the phone call, his voice warmly caressing. "I'll be counting the hours."

"I'm looking forward to seeing you, too, Claus," Genevieve had replied, sweet as honey. She hadn't missed the troubled look on Max's face as he'd stood beside her, listening. In every moment of repose since — backstage at her last Paris show, at the studio later where they'd spent the (unforgettable) night together, at the Ritz the following morning (where Berthe had said nothing at all about Genevieve's absence the previous two nights, thus earning her undying gratitude), and then later on the train — he'd been looking positively grim.

By traveling to Stuttgart, they were, as he'd said, going into the belly of the beast. But the mission was so vital that there was no turning away from it.

She learned from Emmy, because of course Max remained as tight-lipped as ever, that Helian had been picked up by the Resistance, identified as the traitor, and executed. She couldn't rejoice in the killing of anyone, but she did feel a rush of cold satisfaction at the knowledge that justice had been administered.

Before leaving Paris, Genevieve had managed to get away for a private errand of her own. She'd sneaked off to the place de la Bastille to check on Anna. The same nameless woman had answered the door. She frowned at Genevieve, clearly remembering her from before, but did not invite her in.

"I've come to see Anna," Genevieve said, but got no further before the woman shook her head.

"She is not here any longer. She is with the Sisters in Vère." The woman started to close the door.

"Wait. Here." Having gathered up all the cash she could scrape together without alerting Max or anyone else to what she meant to do, Genevieve had put it in an envelope with the intention of giving it to Anna's caretakers. Pulling it out of Berthe's shopping bag, she thrust the envelope at the woman, who paused in the act of closing the door to take it.

"It's money. For the children," Genevieve said.

The woman took the envelope and looked at it, then at her with the first flicker of vulnerability Genevieve had seen from her.

"Thank you," the woman said, then, "Bless you," and closed the door. Sending prayers winging skyward for Anna's safety and well-being, and indeed for the safety and well-being of all the children, Genevieve made it back to the hotel with no one the wiser and in time to change and leave to meet Emmy.

It was after 9:00 p.m. when they reached Stuttgart. To Genevieve's relief, Wagner wasn't there to greet them. They were met and whisked through the station by Lutz, Wagner's cherub-faced driver. She and Max were ushered into the back seat of the Daimler that Lutz was driving, while Emmy, Berthe and Otto followed in a second car with another driver. Herr Obergruppenführer Wagner, was, Lutz explained as the Daimler rolled through the darkened streets of the heavily industrialized city, unavoidably detained by business that evening. He would, however, meet Mademoiselle Dumont the next day upon her arrival at Eber Schloss.

"Eber Schloss?" Genevieve asked as she looked out the window at the wide streets and classical architecture of the city, dark now because of the danger of Allied air raids. Even by uncertain moonlight she was able to see gaps like missing teeth in the neat rows of buildings, and the ragged skyline where bombs had left behind broken steeples and partly destroyed chimneys and roofs.

"Up there." Lutz pointed.

Peering out through the glass, Genevieve looked up in the direction he indicated. In the distance, visible only because it was, at that moment, silhouetted by the moon that had just come out from behind a blanket of heavy clouds, the slender turrets and crenellated ramparts of a Gothic castle were visible, perched high atop a snowcapped mountain that towered above the town.

"How beautiful," Genevieve said, while Max looked silently out at the mountain. "Will we be staying there?"

"I regret, not tonight, no." Lutz turned a corner and the schloss was lost from sight. "The visitors at Eber Schloss are very important and security is extremely tight. While they are with us, no one is permitted to go up or down the mountain after dark. Even I must stay in town tonight. Herr Obergruppenführer Wagner has arranged that you will stay tomorrow night at the schloss, after you sing for him and his guests."

"The schloss is where I'll be singing?"

"Yes."

"If I'm not mistaken, Eber Schloss is Herr Obergruppenführer's family home, is it not?" Max asked. As Lutz agreed that it was, Genevieve glanced at Max in surprise: she hadn't known that.

"I look forward to seeing it tomorrow night," Genevieve said.

"You will find it most impressive," Lutz promised.

The Daimler pulled in to the forecourt of a building identified by a sign above its massive front doors as Der Rote Fuchs. A *Gasthaus,* it was a large, sprawling half-timbered structure that, from the outside, was as dark and deserted as the rest of the city.

"Herr Obergruppenführer Wagner apologizes for the accommodations, but the Palast Hotel, where he would have had you stay, was damaged in a raid last month. This place is less conspicuous, and thus less likely to attract bombs. We hope." Lutz said that with a slight smile and a kind of gallows humor that reminded Genevieve of how young he actually was. "If it should prove less than satisfactory, you have only to let me know."

He went in with them to make certain all was as it should be, but he needn't have worried: the hospitality of the staff and the quality of the accommodations were more than satisfactory — as was the fact that, due to the absence of suites, they each were given their own rooms.

The final plans for the rescue of her mother were still not fixed, because much depended on the exact circumstances in which she was being held, but it was understood that it would happen tomorrow night. Genevieve prayed for success and longed to see her mother safe, but what that also meant was that tonight would be her last night with Max.

"I'll be back as soon as I can" was the last thing he whispered into her ear as they reached the top of the central stairs, where the *Gasthaus* divided into separate wings and the men were escorted in one direction, the women in another. After exchanging a few words with Emmy and assuring Berthe that she didn't need her, Genevieve went into her own room, a large chamber with heavy dark furniture, a fur spread on the bed and numerous tapestries depicting bloody hunting scenes on the walls. She bathed in the en suite, changed into her nightgown and robe, and settled down to wait with growing anxiety for what seemed like a very long time until the knock on her door that she'd been expecting came.

Flinging herself out of bed, where she'd finally taken refuge from the drafts, she opened the door to Max, who was dressed in an overcoat and hat. He was sprinkled with snow and smelled of it and the outdoors. They came together like magnets as soon as the door was closed behind him. He felt cold and damp and big, and his unshaven jaw was rough against her skin as she wrapped her arms around him and kissed him. He kissed her back so thoroughly that she found herself trying not to look as swooningly besotted as she felt, when at last he let her go to take off his coat and hat. Climbing back into bed, she sat with her back against the headboard, pulled the fur spread up around her shoulders — the room was cold, and her nightgown was thin — and regarded him anxiously.

"Did you find her?" she asked. She knew what he'd been doing: getting the lay of the land, as he put it, with Otto.

"Baroness de Rocheford is not on the list of prisoners currently held in Stuttgart." As he imparted that bombshell, Max pulled the dark sweater he was wearing over his head, folded it and laid it on a chair near the bed. That he had changed the suit, white shirt and tie in which he'd arrived for the sweater and a pair of dark trousers before going out told her that wherever he'd been, he hadn't wanted to be seen.

"She's not here?" Genevieve's heart stood still. "Or — are we too late?"

"If you're asking whether she's been executed, the answer's no. That would have been noted. The Germans keep meticulous records, thank God." Relieved of her worst worry, she watched as Max pulled off his undershirt, reflexively admiring the heavy muscles of his shoulders, his dark-furred chest and taut abdomen. "The prison was bombed a few weeks ago. Several of the most important prisoners were transferred. And they stopped accepting new arrivals until it can be repaired. She's never been held there."

"So where is she?"

"I'm not sure yet." He sat down on the edge of the bed to take off his shoes and socks. "I'm meeting with someone later who I'm hoping can tell me."

"What if we got it wrong? What if she's not in Stuttgart at all?"

"Given the timing, and the fact that Wagner's here, I think she is. There are lots of places around the city where she could be being held. It's even possible that she's up there at the family homestead."

"Eber Schloss?" Genevieve thought of the mountaintop castle and felt her stomach twist. Then the too-casual tone in which he'd said that last registered, and she gave Max a sharp look. "My God, you think she's there, don't you? You've thought it all along. You knew that was Wagner's home, knew the prison had been damaged and guessed that if he was in Stuttgart, that's where he'd take her. *That's* why you didn't put up more of a fuss about me coming with you to Stuttgart. I'm your ticket in."

"Something like that." His tone was brisk as, now barefoot as well as shirtless, he stood up.

"You couldn't have told me?"

"At this point, it's pure speculation. You're here because I believe in covering all the bases."

"Uh-huh." Genevieve eyed him skeptically, then had another thought. "If she's up there, I can get us in, so that's not the problem. The problem's going to be getting back out, isn't it?"

"That's usually the problem. We won't go

in without a way out, I promise."

"I thought you had to meet someone." She said that as he shucked his trousers, folded them and placed them on the chair alongside his sweater. She'd already learned that he was neat with his belongings, washing out his shaving cup each time he used it, hanging up his towel to dry between uses, folding his clothes when he took them off, and she found it endearing. She'd also discovered how gentle he could be, that he was meticulous about using protection, that he didn't like the scars on his leg touched, and that lightly scoring her nails up and down his lean sides made him squirm like a fish on a hook, because he was fatally ticklish. Little things, all, but what they added up to was that she was getting to know Max, whom she'd already thought she knew through and through, in a whole new way.

"I do," he said.

I'm so in love with you it's crazy, she thought, as, wearing nothing but his boxers, he crawled into bed with her. But she didn't tell him. Either he would say it back or he wouldn't, but either way, knowing would only make things worse, because right now was the only time they were going to have, maybe for a few weeks or months or even years, however long it took for the war to be over, or maybe — please God, no — forever.

I won't think about it now.

She gave him a severe look — with the sigh of a man at last finding comfort, he was stretching his long length out on the mattress while tugging at her enveloping fur — and said, "Well, then?"

His arm snaked around her and he pulled her down into his arms. "Not till 3:00 a.m.," he said, and kissed her.

Chapter Forty-One

Max left her at about two thirty and was gone until just after five. By the time he returned, Genevieve was about to jump out of her skin with anxiety. Unable to sleep after he left — not that she'd gotten a lot of sleep before — she'd washed, dressed, examined the heavily carved furniture, worked at deciphering the story the tapestries told, then gave up trying to occupy her mind and simply worried and paced.

When she heard his soft tap at the door, she threw it open and all but dragged him inside.

One look at his face as he closed the door behind him and parked his stick beside it and she knew something was wrong.

"She's not here." She voiced her worst fear, grabbing onto the front of his overcoat even as he was unbuttoning it.

"Shh." It was a reminder that it was not yet dawn, and outside and inside the *Gasthaus* most everyone was still asleep. "She's here."

His words were reassuring; the gravity of his tone was not.

A light scratching at the door interrupted. Genevieve shot an alarmed glance toward it, but Max turned away with a quick "It's all right" and opened it.

Otto, Emmy and Berthe filed in. They were all fully dressed. Genevieve was slightly surprised at the inclusion of Berthe, but on the other hand, Berthe had been briefed on why they were here, had chosen to come and was therefore putting her life on the line just like the rest of them. She deserved to know what was going to happen, and Max evidently thought so, too, as was evidenced by her inclusion in this, a clearly prearranged meeting.

"Sit down," Max said to them all as he closed the door. He'd taken off his coat as the others had entered and now walked into the center of the room.

Otto and Berthe took the two chairs. Emmy sat on the edge of the bed, and Genevieve sat beside her. Whatever happened, knowing her sister was in this with her provided at least a small degree of comfort.

They looked at Max expectantly.

He said, "We all know why we're here. Our mission is to get Baroness de Rocheford out of the hands of the Nazis before she's tortured into telling what she knows, which is the truth behind Operation Overlord, and which if revealed will be disastrous for the course of the war. Earlier tonight I was able to confirm what I suspected. The baroness *is* being held at Eber Schloss. Genevieve will be singing there tonight, and we'll all accompany her as her entourage. That will get us in, and provide us with the opportunity to do the job we came here to do."

The other three nodded as if this was something they knew. Genevieve frowned. There was something odd . . .

Max glanced around. "Anybody have any difficulty out there?"

He was talking to the others, not her. They — all three — shook their heads. Genevieve got the distinct impression that they'd been carrying out assignments from Max while she'd been safe in her room waiting for him to return.

Max looked at Otto, who said, "I was able to get what I need."

Max looked at Emmy. She said, "There are two ways to reach the castle. A road and a cable car. Both are heavily guarded, and both are shut down completely at night. The guards stay on duty all night, however. Getting out is going to be as difficult as we thought."

Max nodded, and *looked at Berthe.*

Genevieve's eyes riveted on Berthe as she started to speak, saying, "There's a flat field about two kilometers north of town that will work for a landing field."

"Wait. What?" Genevieve exclaimed. "Berthe —"

Berthe, who, with her round cheeks, braided coronet of hair and loose black dress, looked exactly the same as she always did, smiled at her.

Suspicion crystallized into certainty. Genevieve asked, "Are you an *agent*?"

"I am, yes."

Genevieve stared at her for a moment, then shot a fulminating look at Max. "Could I talk to you for just a minute?"

Hopping off the bed, she headed for the bathroom. He followed and closed the door.

"Berthe's an agent?" Her voice was no less outraged because she was careful to keep it down.

He sighed. "She and her husband were part of the Armia Krajowa, the Polish Resistance. After his execution, and her failed execution, the Nazis were looking for her, and she needed to get out of Warsaw. She's been working for me since I took her on board."

"All this time, and you didn't tell me?"

"What you don't know, you can't reveal."

She practically gnashed her teeth at him. "I can't believe you didn't — what about *no more secrets*? Oh, I see, that's strictly a one-way street."

"It was, because you have a role to play." He took her hands. She jerked them away.

"You're the face of the operation, the Trojan horse that gets us to places and through doors we'd never be able to access without you. Be fair — if you'd known what Berthe was, would you have been able to treat her simply as your dresser and maid?"

Would she have behaved differently toward Berthe if she'd known? Honesty compelled her to admit the truth: probably, at least in subtle but perhaps telltale ways.

Max, clearly able as always to read her face, continued without waiting for her to reply. "Everything we did, all of our safety, depended on the Germans accepting you for what you appeared to be and nothing else. Your knowing the truth about Berthe could have done us no good and might have ruined everything."

"All right, I see what you're saying," she conceded reluctantly.

"So we're good?"

"Yes."

He smiled at her. She frowned at him. His smile widened. Opening the door, he gestured to her to precede him and followed her out.

Genevieve found herself the cynosure of three pairs of interested eyes.

Even as she returned to her spot on the bed beside Emmy, she looked back at them — Berthe, the quintessential maid with her round cheeks and placid gaze; Otto, the old man, wrinkled and wizened; Emmy, the lovely showgirl with her head of blond curls and willowy form — and realized with a sense of amazement that this unlikely assortment of individuals was a crack team of seasoned spies. Then she glanced back at Max, who'd just reclaimed his place in the center of the room. Tall and lean in the same dark sweater and trousers he'd been wearing earlier, his black hair pushed carelessly back from his face and still damp from the rain, his jaw rough with early morning stubble, he looked every bit their commanding officer. Which, in fact, was what he was.

"Gave him what for, did you?" Emmy whispered as Genevieve sank down beside her.

Genevieve could do no more than give her sister a quelling look as Max resumed speaking as if there'd been no interruption.

"Ordinarily we'd get down to working out the details now, but something unexpected has come up. The reason why the baroness was brought here, the reason why Genevieve was invited here to sing, is that there is at this very moment a gathering of some of the most important government officials, SS leaders, and military officers in Nazi Germany at Eber Schloss. They're here to map out possible responses to the potentially imminent Allied invasion. I've been on the radio to Baker Street, they've been in touch with the blokes in the War Rooms, and as a result we have new orders in addition to the old orders. We are to rub them all out. Oh, and we're on our own. Tommy Bowden very apologetically explained that he would send a crack team of paratroopers in to help, but the weather here over the next twenty-four hours is supposed to be bad. That also means we can't count on our ride home." He looked at Otto. "You have the schloss's floor plans with you?"

Otto nodded.

Max said, "Right, then, let's get to work coming up with a way to get the job done. We don't have much time."

It was very nearly over for her. Lillian knew it even before the sound of heavy boots approaching along the stone floor of the corridor made every shivering cell in her body tense, even before the metallic clank of a key in the lock followed by a long creak announced the opening of her cell door, even before the sensation of light hit her closed lids and she opened them a wary crack to find Claus von Wagner standing over her cot, shining a torch down at her face.

"It is time, madame," he said. At a signal, two soldiers stepped around him, pulled her from the cot and, with each grasping an arm, partly carried and partly dragged her from the cold dankness of the unheated cell.

And this time it *was* a cell. Hewn of rough

stone, the windowless walls were fronted by floor-to-ceiling iron bars. The cot was rickety metal with a thin smelly mattress and rag of a blanket. The corridor was narrow, with more rough-hewn stone walls and an uneven stone floor. Light from dim electric bulbs set into the wall was augmented by the merest hint of daylight that spilled around a corner — a window must be out there somewhere, although she couldn't see it.

But she could smell the damp and mold, the pine notes in Wagner's aftershave, her own stench. That last shamed her, although it was through no fault of her own — she'd had no opportunity to bathe since they'd captured her.

Beyond the shame, the odor — all the odors — carried an even weightier significance. During the time that had elapsed since her middle-of-the-night removal from her previous prison, during her nightmarish journey by rail and car to this mountain fortress — she'd gotten a glimpse of it as the vehicle in which she'd been transported had driven up a nearly vertical road and then been processed through heavily guarded iron gates — she'd healed sufficiently so that her sense of smell had returned. And last night she'd awakened herself by crying out in her sleep.

The guards — there were three on this corridor alone — must have heard. Someone must have told Wagner.

"Chain her up," he directed as they passed into a larger room. Frantic darting glances found a metal table against one wall, its surface covered with an ominous selection of tools; beside it, a metal desk with an office chair pulled up to it, a ledger on its top; on the opposite wall, what looked like a doctor's examining table. Manacles hung from the back wall. Turning her to face the front, the soldiers snapped the manacles around her wrists, yanked her legs roughly apart and clamped more manacles around her ankles so that she was spread-eagle against the wall. The manacles were heavy and cold but loose enough not to be painful, for which she supposed she could thank her emaciated frame. She could feel the shape of the individual stones through the thin brown dress they'd given her to wear, without underclothes, for travel. Her feet were protected from the floor by her own sturdy shoes, returned to her for the same purpose.

On the table with the tools was a Bunsen burner. Her eyes locked on it as Wagner turned it on and ignited the resultant rush of gas. The whoosh of the flame taking hold sent ripples of fear over her. Terror flooded her mouth with acid.

Wagner looked at her. "Now then, Baroness, you will tell me where this invasion by the Allies will happen." His tone was mild.

The hoarse, strangled sound she made in

response was dredged up from somewhere deep in her diaphragm.

"That is not quite *Paul,* which is what I'm told you cried out in your sleep, but it's a start. I might even say a promising start." He picked up a knife from the table. It was long and thin, with a flat blade and a wickedly curved edge. The hilt, incongruously, was painted a cheerful yellow. He turned it over in his hands as if to examine it, then held it out so that the blade was in the flame.

Her stomach cramped.

"First I must apologize," he said, rotating the knife. "I would start with a small torture, maybe break a finger or two, give you time to consider what keeping your secrets might mean. But I am busy with guests today, so I haven't much time. Here is what I regret to tell you is going to happen — I am going to destroy your lovely face. You know how ugly and disfiguring burns can be, do you not? Yes, I am sure you do. I am going to place this red-hot blade against your face as many times as it takes until you tell me what I want to know."

He withdrew the knife from the flame.

Lillian stared at it in horror.

Without another word, he turned and laid the flat of the knife against the side of her jaw.

The sizzling sound made by red-hot metal

connecting with cool soft skin was instantaneous.

She screamed, jerked her face away. The pain made her dizzy, made her sick.

The new, charred smell in the air came from her own burnt flesh. She retched and gagged, but her stomach was empty and nothing came out.

"Your voice is regaining its volume," he said approvingly as he returned the knife to the flame. "We must congratulate ourselves. We're making progress. Now, I'm going to ask you again — where will the Allies launch their invasion?"

Shaking with fear, eyes on the knife, Lillian made sounds, babbled, tried to turn her face away — and then he grabbed her hair and pressed the knife to the smooth curve of her cheek. She screamed again, fighting his fist in her hair, fighting the chains that held her tight against the wall to no avail as she tried to escape the searing agony.

"Did I mention I have little time?" His tone was genial as he let go of her hair and lifted the blade away, returning it to the flame. Her legs had collapsed. She hung from the chains now, her nostrils filled with the scent of her own burnt flesh, shaking so badly the iron links shackling her to the wall clattered. "I propose to speed things up. If you don't tell me what I want to know, right now, instead of ruining your face, I'm going to put out your eye."

Lillian's heart seized up with horror. *Please, God — please, no.*

He turned back toward her with the newly reheated blade. Holding it up, he let her see it: the metal glowed red.

"You do have such pretty eyes," he said, peering into her face as he drew closer. "What a pity."

A wave of cold sweat drenched her. Tears sprang forth to roll down her cheeks. Blinking, swallowing, she turned her face away, straining her neck in an effort to escape.

He grabbed her hair.

"Where will the Allies launch their invasion?" His voice was gentle. He leaned close.

She closed her eyes, squinched them tight. Shook, gasped, strained.

"Last chance," he said, and held the knife over her closed left eyelid, so close she could feel the heat.

Her throat convulsed. Her tongue moved. It worked, she could —

"Pas-de-Calais," she croaked.

He laid the red-hot blade of the knife against her eye anyway.

Chapter Forty-Two

"Mademoiselle Dumont, I am sorry, but only your name and an accompanying maid are on my list." The sentry at the big iron gate at the top of the mountain looked at her unhappily through the Daimler's rear window, which Genevieve had rolled down at the first hint of trouble. In the driver's seat, Lutz, already frazzled at being dragooned into transporting five passengers when he had expected two, had been making apologetic sounds at the guard leaning into the car. They'd already had to pass through an armed checkpoint at the base of the mountain, and military vehicles packed with soldiers had lined the road. But this sergeant in his heavy greatcoat and fur-lined hat that was buckled tight beneath his chin to protect him against the cold came armed with something else: a list fastened to a clipboard.

And Max, Otto and Emmy weren't on it.

"If I'm to put on a show for Herr Obergruppenführer Wagner and his guests, I must have what I need," Genevieve said. Her breath created small puffs of vapor in the pine-scented air. The temperature in the town below had been chilly. Up on this snowy mountainside high in the clouds, it felt as if winter had no intention of going away. "Monsieur Bonet is my accompanist, Monsieur Cordier is my piano tuner and sound engineer, and Madame Chastain —" the name on Emmy's forged travel documents "— is my duet partner. I would not have paid for their travel from Paris to Stuttgart if I did not need them." She paused and did her best to look affronted. "Indeed, if I cannot have them, I cannot perform. Corporal Lutz, please turn around and take me back to town."

"Mademoiselle Dumont —" Eyes wide with alarm, Lutz skewed around in his seat to look at her. Berthe, beside him, all bundled up in her black coat and scarf with her hands folded on her lap, stared stolidly straight ahead. Beside her, Otto in his scruffy Russian hat looked old and shrunken and anxious. "I cannot! Herr Obergruppenführer Wagner will be most upset. He —"

"Turn around," Genevieve interrupted firmly. "I will not do a show that is not up to my standards. I will go back to Paris."

"No, no, that won't be necessary," the sentry said. Having taken the measure of the two in the front seat, he looked at Max and

Emmy, who sat with Genevieve in the back, then withdrew from the window. "Go ahead," he said to Lutz, and waved to whoever was in charge of opening the gates.

As the Daimler passed through to the final sweep of road leading up to Eber Schloss, Genevieve glanced back to find him busily jotting down a note on his list.

Big dirty drifts of snow lay on either side of the narrow road, and more snow, deep and pristine, covered the steep slopes leading up to the castle. When the car went around the last in a series of hairpin turns, Genevieve had a breathtaking view of the valley below. Spread out over a succession of rolling hills and deep valleys, tucked around the curling blue ribbon that was the Neckar River, it was covered in a light dusting of snow that made it look like it had been sprinkled with powdered sugar. The town itself boasted a beautiful Flemish Gothic town hall and a baroque palace that had once belonged to the House of Württemberg. In addition, it featured a variety of seventeenth-, eighteenth- and nineteenth-century architecture as well as many parks and churches. On the outskirts of the city, the ugliness of what looked like an army barracks spread out over a flat plain. It was actually a labor camp for the conscripts brought in to work the factories for which Stuttgart was known. Those same factories had caused the city to become a target for numerous Allied bombing raids. Seen from her vantage point high on the mountain, Stuttgart looked like a giant had stomped through, wantonly breaking buildings and trees, leaving craterous footprints in the streets and on the ground.

On what was almost the opposite side of the mountain, she caught the briefest of glimpses of a pair of steel cables, appearing spider-silk thin at this distance, glinting silver against the leaden sky. Suspended high above vertical cliffs and deep ravines, those cables and the cable cars they ordinarily carried represented the only other means of accessing Eber Schloss. Rising from the valley below up an even steeper section of mountain than the one the Daimler was climbing, the cable cars had been stopped as a security measure while the VIPs were visiting the schloss.

Genevieve thought she probably wouldn't even have spotted the cables if she hadn't been looking for them. But she *was* looking for them because the cable cars had been tapped as their only way out.

Assuming they survived long enough to attempt escaping by them.

Just thinking about it made her heart pound, so she tried not to.

They turned a final corner. Sweeping vistas of pine trees and snowdrifts and low-floating wisps of gray clouds blocked the cables from her sight. Instead she was treated to the full glory of Eber Schloss as the Daimler arrived with a swish of tires at its front door.

Rising from a plateau that had been blasted out of the top of the mountain, Eber Schloss was a fairy-tale castle à la the Brothers Grimm. Built of dark gray limestone that sparkled faintly even on this overcast day, its turrets were tall enough to disappear into the clouds. Crenellated battlements, narrow mullioned windows and an enormous oaken front door blackened by time added to the impression it gave of an ancient and impregnable fortress.

Genevieve's attention was distracted as one of the soldiers on guard hurried up to open her door for her — and Wagner came running down the castle's wide front steps.

Her heart slammed into double time even as she allowed the soldier to hand her out of the car. Shivering a little at the cold despite her trim wool coat, she assumed her best smile and held out both hands to him.

"Claus!"

He beamed, dimples forming deep creases on either side of his mouth, his eyes sparkling blue as he came toward her.

"Genevieve." He caught her hands, carried them to his mouth one at a time and kissed them. Then he leaned in to press a warm and possessive kiss to her cheek. "Welcome to Eber Schloss. I am honored to have you here at my poor home."

"Your 'poor home,' as you call it, is breathtakingly beautiful," Genevieve said as he continued to hold her hands. "I am surprised you can ever bring yourself to leave."

"Sometimes it is a wrench, I will admit, but I must go where duty calls." He glanced past her, and his smile faltered. A barely perceptible tightening of the skin around his eyes announced his awareness of Max's presence even before he continued with "Ah, Monsieur Bonet. I am of course honored to have you, too."

"It is I who am honored to be here," Max said. A glance told Genevieve that he was looking doubtfully at the long flight of stairs while leaning heavily on his stick. He was, she reflected, very, very good at what he did. While she hoped, no, prayed, that her performance would be good enough, certainly he was a better actor than she was. Her nerves were already frayed.

"Max will be playing the piano for me." Genevieve's tone was gay as she freed her hands, only to tuck one into Wagner's arm. She waved a vague hand at the others. "Emmy and I are to duet, Otto is to tune what I am sure is your dreadfully out-of-tune instrument, and Berthe, as always, takes care of me. I have such a show prepared for you! You will be pleased, I promise."

"I am looking forward to it more than I can

say. Please, come inside where it's warm." He was already starting up the steps with her when his attention was caught by — something. Genevieve followed the direction of his gaze to find that he was looking at the admittedly truly impressive amount of luggage Lutz was lifting from the trunk.

Her heart started thumping so loudly she was afraid he might hear it. If he were to order a search of her bags . . .

"You will be thinking that I've come to stay a month!" Squeezing his arm, she laughed. "Most everything in there is for the show, of course. I have costumes, and cosmetics and props — just you wait. Because I wanted this performance to be special. Is there someplace where they can be taken? A bedroom, perhaps . . . somewhere quiet where I can also rest between the rehearsal and the performance?"

"Of course. I've already ordered that overnight rooms be prepared for you and your maid, although of course more can be found to accommodate the rest of your party. Anything else you need, you have only to ask." He looked at Lutz, raised his voice. "Have Mademoiselle Dumont's things brought in. Schneider — he is my butler," he added in an aside to Genevieve before raising his voice to call to Lutz again, "will tell you where to put them. Tell him to find rooms for the other guests, as well."

As they continued on up the stairs, Wagner's entire focus was on her, just as she'd intended for it to be.

Her luggage did indeed contain costumes, cosmetics and props. They were packed in alongside enough sticks of C-4 explosive to, as Otto put it, bring the whole bloody mountain down.

Chapter Forty-Three

"Remember, you end 'Embrasse-moi' with a glissando — make sure it's loud so Otto can hear it — then stand up, take a bow and leave the room during the blackout between songs. Do not dawdle. Go into the anteroom, out the side door, down the stairs. The bomb will blow exactly four minutes after the last note of the glissando. By then you want to be well away." Max's voice was low. His hands were warm on her bare upper arms. They were in the bedroom that had been allotted to her. He stood behind her, handsome in his tux, looking at her through the dressing table mirror. She was ready for the opening number, wearing her gold-fringed flapper dress that showed a lot of leg. A headband studded with glittering gold butterflies was in her hair. "If anything goes wrong, if for some reason you're prevented from leaving the room, go right into the next number. Sing those first notes loud, for God's sake."

Genevieve was so nervous she felt cold all over.

"Understand?" he said.

"Yes." Her voice was surprisingly strong given how shaky she felt inside. Their eyes met through the mirror. He smiled at her.

The concert was scheduled to start precisely at 9:00 p.m. It was almost that now. Wagner and his guests would have finished dinner. She had declined his invitation to join them on the grounds that she needed to rehearse and get ready for her show, and had instead, along with Max and the rest, consumed a light meal as they worked. At that moment the guests should be settling into chairs that had been placed in what Wagner called the Knight's Hall high up in the east turret.

Max squeezed her arms, then turned back to the others. For these last few minutes before they went into action, they'd all gathered in her bedroom. Besides the dressing table, it was furnished with a large ornately carved bed, a washstand complete with basin and pitcher (the bathroom was down the hall), a large wardrobe in lieu of a closet, and a fainting couch. The color scheme was deep green and maroon. Her suitcases were neatly arranged beside the wardrobe, which held only a few things. The costumes needed (and not needed) for the various numbers were already hung in the small anteroom adjacent to the Knight's Hall.

The bedrooms were lower down in the schloss and too far from the Knight's Hall to make any of them practical as changing rooms. They were, however, a good place to shelter from the coming explosion.

"You all know the plan." Max looked from one to the other: Otto, Berthe, Emmy. Dressed for their roles, they waited near the door. "Except for Otto, who'll be in the room beneath the Knight's Hall waiting to press the detonator, we all stay with Genevieve until our parts in the show are played. Berthe, you go in first and pass out programs." Forty copies of the list of songs for the night's entertainment had been prepared, typed by Berthe on a machine in a small office off the schloss's kitchen; "Embrasse-moi" was the third of a supposed ten numbers. By then, they felt that the program's staging, which included blackouts between songs, should have become familiar enough to the audience that they would think nothing of one more blackout. With their program in front of them to let them know how much more was to come, there was no reason they all should not remain happily seated in anticipation of the next song. "Then you leave and start making your way down toward the kitchen. If anyone challenges you, tell them that you're fetching a drink for Mademoiselle Dumont, and no, they can't fetch it for you because only you can prepare it in the way she likes."

Berthe nodded. They'd been over the plan before. Multiple times. "Emmy, you sing the first number with Genevieve, then you, too, leave and start making your way down to join Berthe. Same excuse if challenged. I'll accompany you and Genevieve on the piano, then accompany Genevieve alone as she sings the next number. Then I leave and get into position. Genevieve, you accompany yourself to 'Embrasse-moi,' end on a *loud* glissando, take a bow and leave. Otto, you wait four minutes from the time she ends the glissando and hit the detonator. We know the baroness is being held directly below the kitchen, in a cell off the west corridor of the dungeon. We three want to be in place to extract her at the exact moment when the bomb goes off. There should be enough noise and confusion then to allow us to get in, get the baroness and get out with a minimum of trouble. We rendezvous in this room, pick up Genevieve and head for the cable car staging area, where Otto, having by that time gotten the cable cars up and running, will be waiting. Then we get the hell off this mountain." He looked around. "Any questions?"

"Just one. Why do I have to wear lederhosen?" Otto asked plaintively. It was, Genevieve knew, his attempt to lighten the atmosphere, which hummed with tension.

"Because it was the only outfit that could be found to fit you. Because it makes you look dopey." Berthe's response was tart. She'd been in charge of scrounging up something for Otto to wear — no one had thought to bring a costume for him. Looking at Otto, Genevieve had to smile. He looked like a wizened German elf.

"Any other questions?" Max asked. No one had any. "Then let's go."

As the others headed out, he caught Genevieve by the elbow, waited until they were alone, pulled her into his arms and kissed her.

She kissed him back as if she were afraid she might never again get the chance — which, indeed, she was.

"You get the hell out of that room right after the glissando," he said in a low, fierce voice as he let her go. Not the most loverly goodbye, maybe, but the sentiment was there.

Her heart skipped a beat. If this went wrong, and it could very easily go wrong, he could die, she could die, they all could die.

"Max —"

"Tell me later."

With a hand in the small of her back, he pushed her out into the hallway in front of him, then stopped to close the door. Farther down the hall, Emmy, in a fringed silver dress that was a close twin to the one she wore, had stopped and was looking back in search of her. Genevieve caught up. Her sister grabbed her hand.

"You look white as a ghost," Emmy said. "You always did get nervous when you had something important to do."

"I can't help it. I still do."

Emmy squeezed her hand. "Don't worry, *bébé.* We'll pull this off."

The pounding of her heart and the knot in her stomach might be telling her otherwise, but Genevieve said, "I know we will," and walked toward the waiting hall full of Nazis, holding her sister's hand.

The Knight's Hall was a large, round stone-walled chamber cut straight across at the front like an egg with its top sliced off. The gorgeous Bösendorfer Imperial grand piano was located on a small platform in front of that straight wall. Two doors allowing access to the room were also located on the straight wall, one on either side a few meters behind the piano. Two soldiers each stood formal guard in front of the doors. In the quarter-round lobby area outside the doors, more soldiers provided security for the high-level personnel in the room. Medieval in appearance, the Knight's Hall had a high vaulted ceiling and six narrow uncurtained windows through which Genevieve, as she awaited her introduction, could see nothing but black, which told her how dark the night outside must be.

Lutz had been given the honors. He stood

now at the front of the stage, his back to her as he looked out at the room that had grown quiet for him. His face was pale under the lights, and she realized that having the attention of so many superior officers and high-level officials on him was causing him stress.

Still, his voice was loud and commanding as he made the introduction. "As you know, Obergruppenführer Wagner has arranged a very special treat for tonight. Coming to us straight from her smashingly successful show in the most famous city in the world, the city that is renowned for offering the very best in entertainment, please allow me to introduce for your pleasure the incomparable Mademoiselle Genevieve Dumont, the Black Swan of Paris!"

Gesturing to where she waited in the shadows, Lutz retired from the stage while the audience clapped wildly.

Taking a deep breath, Genevieve walked out into the light, waving as she crossed to one of the two standing microphones set up in front of the piano.

The room was cold, but she was sweating bullets. Behind her, Max was already seated at the piano pounding out the intro. Entering from the other side of the room, Emmy arrived at a second microphone at the same time she did.

They'd rehearsed this. Genevieve knew how it was supposed to go. But she hadn't counted on how standing in front of this particular audience would make her feel.

Looking at the rows of very important men in their Nazi uniforms smiling as they applauded, she knew she should have felt strong, determined, justified. But her stomach was a pit, her heart pounded like a drum and her pulse was going haywire.

The mood in the room was already celebratory. The audience had been jubilant about something — she'd heard several satisfied mentions of Pas-de-Calais and witnessed a number of the guests clapping each other on the back — even before she'd entered, and her appearance had incited them into a roar of appreciation.

Not important enough to rate a seat, Lutz stood along the wall with a cadre of what she assumed must be other similarly situated aides-de-camp. A few more rank-and-file soldiers than were supposed to be there lurked just inside the doors, sneaking in, she guessed, to watch the show. In front of her, the high-level audience cheering from the seats seemed to stretch out forever. What she and Max and the others were doing was important, necessary, even good: she needed no convincing of that. But the knowledge that in less than an hour nearly all the people in this room would be dead, and she was going to play a part in killing them, chilled her to her soul.

Max hit her cue.

"Paris sera toujours Paris . . ." she sang jauntily, with Emmy chiming in just as they had rehearsed. The two of them shimmied and high-stepped and in general put on quite a show, and when they finished, the loudly appreciative audience was on its feet.

Then came the blackout. The soldier Otto had put in charge of the light switch timed it perfectly (the Germans were nothing if not punctual). When the lights came back on, Emmy was gone. Genevieve, in a different costume, was seated beside Max at the piano. Together they played and sang.

Finally, with Max gone, accompanying herself on the piano, she started "Embrasse-moi." Alone for this final number, she shivered a little as her fingers hit the keys. If her playing was gingerly at first, it quickly grew in confidence. *Get through it,* she told herself grimly, and that's what she did. There'd been no outcry, no questions raised, nothing at all said or apparently thought as first Emmy and then Max had left the room and not returned. All was going as planned, and she knew she should have been feeling heartened. Looking out at the audience, she saw Wagner watching proudly from the front row. The high-ranking officers surrounding him, their medals and various insignia glittering in the light of the overhead chandeliers, smiled and drank and in general appeared to be having a marvelous time. She reminded herself once again that what she and Max and the others were doing would strike a terrible blow into the very heart of the Nazi leadership.

It could shorten the war, and that could save thousands upon thousands of lives.

Her heart still knocked. Sweat still trickled down her spine. She said a quick prayer for God to have mercy on their souls. Then she hit the glissando. Played the final notes with extra oomph.

Stood up, took a bow. The audience jumped to its feet. She blew kisses to them.

On his feet, clapping with loud enthusiasm, Wagner caught her eyes, held them, smiled broadly at her.

The blackout fell. Quaking, she hurried out, past the sentries that stood guard at the doors, into the anteroom, where she kept on going out the side door and down the narrow, curving stone stairs.

Holy Mary, Mother of God, pray for us sinners now and at the hour of our deaths . . .

She was three flights down, rushing along the labyrinth of corridors that led to her bedroom, when the beautiful Bösendorfer piano, which Otto had earlier stuffed full of C-4, blew.

Chapter Forty-Four

The force of the blast knocked Genevieve to her knees. The schloss shuddered like a dog shaking off water. The sound was apocalyptic. Her ears rang as she staggered to her feet and ran, closing her mind to what the blast meant — all the men in that room instantly dead. Screams, shouts, a terrible rushing roar — fire, that sound was fire — followed her.

The explosion roused Lillian, shook the stone wall from which she hung, filled the cold dank air with grit and smoke and a hideous burning smell that, in the aftermath of what she had endured, terrified her to her bone marrow. Limp, disfigured, despairing in mind and soul, she was in so much pain from what the Nazi torturer had done to her eye — her poor blinded, destroyed eye! — that the other pain, the searing agony of the burns to her face, her swollen, damaged mouth, her bruises and broken bones, was pushed into the background.

"We're not finished, you and I," Wagner had said when they'd brought her around from the faint she'd fallen into after he'd pressed that red-hot blade against her closed lid. It had burned through her flesh with the smell of scorching meat, while she screamed and did her best to fight the restraints that held her and then fainted. Restored to consciousness, she was aware enough to know that she was still manacled to the wall, aware enough to feel it when he grabbed her hair and tilted her face up so that he could examine his handiwork, aware enough to hear him. "I am interested to know what else you can tell me. And you still have one good eye."

He'd released her hair then; her head had dropped to loll limply forward. Inwardly she'd seethed with hate even as, outwardly, fear wrung a shudder from her.

"I must go now," Wagner told her. "But later I'll return and we'll continue. Enjoy what's left of your sight while you can, Baroness."

He'd gone. Still manacled to the wall, she'd succumbed to the terror and the pain and shivered and sobbed and sunk into the nightmare-filled semiconsciousness from which the blast roused her.

Now she lifted her head to the sounds of shouts and pounding feet. The watery, blurred vision in her one remaining eye allowed her glimpses of her captors running past the closed door of the room she was imprisoned in. The door had a glass window in the top, and though the figures beyond it were little more than shapes, she could tell they were gray male shapes — German soldiers.

At the sound of gunfire, Lillian tensed.

More shouts, screams, all against the backdrop of a series of muffled booms, a distant roaring. The swirling cloud of gray dust had settled, covering everything. The smell of burning, so terrifying to her now, was strong and growing stronger. The distant roar she could hear — what could that be but a huge and growing fire?

My God, will they leave me to burn alive?

Shaking to the point that the chains holding her rattled, she could feel the fear, corrosive as acid, surging in her throat.

"She's not here!" The cry — a woman's voice — cut through her growing panic. Her head lifted. She knew that voice. "Maman! Maman, where are you?"

Emmanuelle. A burst of adrenaline rocketed through her veins. She didn't know how, but that was her daughter.

A terrible possibility assailed her. Had Wagner done as he'd threatened and found her child?

Her blood ran cold at the thought.

"Maman, if you can hear me, answer me!"

She knew the nuances of her daughter's

voice. That wasn't how she would sound if she'd been captured or was being threatened. It was how she would sound if she was desperately seeking her mother.

"Here," Lillian screamed, or tried to scream. Harsh and painful, her voice was no louder than a croak. She tried again, willing her body to rally, willing herself to find the strength to shout. "Here!"

It emerged no louder than a hoarse bark, no proof against stone walls and doors and all the outside noise of fire and chaos.

"Search the other cells. Hurry." A man's voice, unknown. He and Emmanuelle were farther down the hall, where the cells were, where she had been. They were looking for her. Emmanuelle worked for the SOE. Was it possible — had they come to rescue her? Her heart pounded with fear even as a tiny bud of hope began to blossom inside her.

"Here!" No louder than before. Would they think to look in this, which from the outside looked like a doctor's examining room?

"Maman! Maman, can you hear me?"

"Here!" She dragged in lungfuls of air, never mind how much it hurt rasping past the still raw tissue of her mouth and throat. *"Here!"* There it was, a squawk more than a yell, but loud. *"Here!"*

A shape at the door. A woman.

The door burst open.

"Emmanuelle!" It emerged as a thankful

sob as her heart soared and shook with love and gratitude and fear for her child and all manner of wild emotions. Her daughter came flying to her, Emmanuelle in a dark sweater and trousers with a pistol in one hand and a leather pouch in the other.

"Maman! Oh, Maman!"

Her daughter's hand, a gentle, hesitant touch on the uninjured side of her face. Her expression, horrified, aghast.

Lillian's heart stuttered with fear for her child. If she should be captured, if Wagner should get his hands on her as he had threatened . . . "You have to go. Leave me."

"I'm not leaving you. We're going to get you out of here." Emmanuelle was already looking down, fumbling in her pouch. It was her stubborn voice. Lillian knew that one, too: there was no moving her when she sounded like that.

The worst news, the most important news, had to be told while she could tell it. "Your papa — they killed him."

"I know. Maman, don't talk." She pulled something from her pouch — a skeleton key? "Save your strength."

"You have found her?" Another woman rushed in after Emmanuelle. This one, middle-aged, plain faced, with braids pinned around her head, she didn't know. She, too, carried a pistol and a different bag, a military rucksack. "I have a medical kit — what does she need?"

Lillian said, "Something for the pain."

"I see." The woman stopped in front of her, dragging the last word out as she took in her injuries with a single comprehensive look. Instead of registering horror or shock, she shook her head, muttered "Filthy Nazi pigs" and immediately delved into her rucksack. Emmanuelle, on her left, fit the key into the lock on that manacle. It opened with a creak. Her left hand suddenly free, her arm dropped like a felled tree and she sagged helplessly toward the floor. But that tiny bud of hope in her heart grew. My God, could they really save her?

To her surprise she found herself craving life with a feral fierceness.

"Berthe, catch her." Emmanuelle pushed past the other woman to get to the second manacle. Berthe shoved a solid shoulder beneath Lillian's armpit, holding her up. Lillian felt a prick and looked around to discover the needle of a syrette, a single-dose syringe of the type used to treat soldiers in the field, being plunged into her arm.

"Morphine," Berthe told her in response to Lillian's surprised look as she withdrew the syrette. "Just enough to treat the pain. You'll stay awake."

"Thank you."

"Be quick!" A man — tall, lean, black haired — appeared in the doorway, his tone urgent. He held a rifle.

The second manacle fell away. Lillian would have fallen if Berthe hadn't been holding on to her. Emmanuelle dropped to her knees, made quick work of the irons around her ankles.

A German voice: "Drop your weapon! Or I shoot!"

The man in the doorway whirled in response to the shouted command and fired.

"Let's go." He threw that at them as he disappeared from the doorway. She could hear him running — could hear gunfire in his wake.

Her daughter and Berthe already each had an arm around her.

"Wait. I need —" Desperate for a weapon of her own, prepared for a fight to the death and promising herself that she would not allow her daughter to be taken or herself to be captured again, Lillian lunged for and snatched up the yellow-handled knife from the table where Wagner had left it. Then she found herself being lifted almost off her feet as the other two grabbed her and took her with them toward the door. They emerged into the hall as a number of German soldiers, sidearms drawn, burst into view around a bend in the hallway.

Lillian's heart lurched. The sound she made was a moan of horror.

The man jumped out of a doorway, mowing down the soldiers in front with a burst of gunfire. Screaming, the casualties fell. The survivors jumped back out of sight.

"Get out of here," he yelled at the women. "Quick! That way!" With the other two all but carrying her between them, they ran in the opposite direction.

The man was firing his weapon again as the soldiers tried another rush around the bend. Badly outnumbered, he still managed to hold them off.

The three of them reached the end of the hallway and ran across a large empty room into another hallway. With the help of terror or morphine, Lillian managed to provide at least minimal help. But she was slowing them down.

Berthe missed a step, looked back. "Can you manage her? I must go back and help M'sieur Max."

"Yes. Yes, I've got her." Emmanuelle's arm clamped tighter around her waist as Berthe withdrew her support, whirled and, weapon at the ready, raced back toward the gunfire.

"Come on, Maman." Lillian could feel her daughter's tension, feel the tremendous effort she was putting forth.

Leave me, she almost said again as Emmanuelle dragged her on, but she knew her daughter wouldn't.

Her legs felt wobbly. Her heart pounded so that she was afraid it would burst from her chest. Knowing that Emmanuelle's fate was entwined with hers, Lillian summoned every last bit of strength she possessed. She was weak, but she couldn't falter or Emmanuelle would be lost along with her. She reached down deep inside herself, praying for the will to keep going.

"You can do this." The desperation in her daughter's voice filled Lillian with fear. "Maman, did I tell you Genny is with me? She came with me to rescue you. She's waiting for us. You have to run with me now, so we can get to Genny."

"Genevra?" The rush of excitement that accompanied the instant image of her younger daughter, so lively and sweet with her black curls and dazzling smile, the heart-shaking news that she was here and waiting sent a burst of energy through her. There it was: the strength she needed. "She is here?"

"Yes," Emmanuelle said.

"My God," Lillian breathed, as it occurred to her that Wagner had them both, her two daughters, within his reach. If he caught them . . .

Terrified of the consequences if they didn't get away, she ran on with her older daughter toward her long-lost youngest, knowing all their lives depended on her ability to find the strength.

CHAPTER FORTY-FIVE

Spurred on by the sounds of the fire and shrieks and shouts and a distant popping that was almost certainly gunfire, Genevieve made it to her room and shut the door. Shaky with fear and reaction, knowing she needed to hurry, she followed the plan and did what she was supposed to do. Whipping off the frothy red skirt she'd been wearing over a black bodysuit, she jerked on trousers, pulled on socks and thrust her feet into sturdy shoes: they would be escaping in the open air, and the night was cold. She grabbed her sweater as well as the coats for herself, Emmy, Lillian and Berthe that had been tucked into her luggage. Arms loaded, she was just straightening when the door to her room, which she'd discovered upon arrival didn't lock, raising questions in her mind about Wagner's intentions upon assigning her the room, burst open.

Whirling, she found Emmy lurching through the door with her arm around a wilting figure that bore no resemblance to the mother she remembered. She was staggered by the visible injuries, by the frail and ragged form. But even as Emmy nudged the door shut behind them, an unerring recognition sent some primal piece of Genevieve's soul flying toward her mother as unerringly as a homing pigeon. It was as if the seven years they'd been apart vanished just that fast. The connection was still there, unbroken, she discovered, and she was reminded of the revelation she'd had after her abortive visit to Anna: the tie that bound mothers and daughters was like no other. It was eternal, stronger than any separation, stronger even than death.

So it was with her own mother. She felt a wave of such shattering love and connection that her heart shook.

"Maman." Dropping the coats, she instantly ran across the room. "Thank God!"

"Genevra." Lillian wrapped her in a fierce embrace. "I'm so *glad* to see you." Lillian's voice throbbed with emotion. Genevieve could feel her mother trembling. "I'm so sorry I sent you away. I'm so sorry I never got to know my grandchild. I was wrong to care what people thought, wrong to care about anything except you and your daughter. I regret it so much. I beg you, please forgive me."

As she registered the emotion in Lillian's voice, the part of her that had blamed Lillian for Vivi's death, the hard, cold knot that had lived inside her for seven years, seemed to melt. Now she saw that it had formed because in her deepest heart of hearts she really blamed herself — if she hadn't gone out that afternoon, if she'd taken Vivi with her — and the burden of that had been too great to bear. She had shifted it onto her mother in order to survive.

"I forgive you," she said, and at the same time she found the distance and perspective to forgive herself, too. "None of that matters now. Maman, you're hurt." Wrapped in her arms, Lillian felt fragile enough to break. Genevieve found herself wishing with all her heart that she could heal the injuries and take the pain away and make her mother whole again. She felt so fiercely protective that it was almost as if their roles were reversed, and she was the mother and Lillian the daughter.

"It's not that bad."

At Lillian's answer, Genevieve's mind spun back through the years — that was her mother, always trying to reassure her. But now, as an adult, she knew better. Lillian's voice was a croak, hardly recognizable. Her face — her beautiful, fine-boned face — was hideously damaged, with one eye swollen shut and her skin marred by livid stripes. She was bone thin, unsteady on her feet and filthy. What Genevieve could see of her body in the ragged brown dress that was all she wore was black and blue with bruises and marked with other injuries.

"It looks bad." Even as she bled inside for Lillian's suffering, Genevieve was overwhelmed with love and regret. "I'm so sorry this happened to you. I'm so sorry I stayed away so long. I should have come home sooner. I love you, Maman."

"I love you, too, Genevra, my dear one. How I have missed you." She pressed a kiss to Genevieve's cheek.

"I've missed you, too." She'd just now realized how much. The first time she'd performed in Paris, she'd almost gone down to Rocheford to see her parents, but the thought of Vivi and then the Nazi invasion had kept her from following through. Now her heart ached with remorse. Tears stung her eyes. "Papa —"

"He loved you. You loved him. That's all that's important." Lillian's voice was firm.

There was more, much more that needed to be said on that and other subjects, but now was not the moment, Genevieve knew. There was no time.

"Maman, sit for a minute. We have to get ready to go. And you need warm clothes."

"How are we going to get out of here?" Lillian's voice shook, and Genevieve felt her heart turn over at the fear in it.

"Don't worry, Maman," Genevieve said.

"We have a plan," Emmy added.

"You shouldn't have come for me, you girls. You're in terrible danger here. I've put you in terrible danger."

"Of course we came for you." Genevieve kept her arm around her mother's waist as she led her toward the fainting couch. Emmy, she saw, had crossed the room and was leaning against the wardrobe. By now she should at least be putting on her coat. "And you don't have to worry about Emmy and me."

"I always worry about the two of you," Lillian said with conviction. "I always will."

"Get the knife away from her," Emmy warned as Genevieve helped Lillian sit down.

Genevieve realized that her mother was indeed clutching a wicked-looking knife in her fist. The cheerful yellow hilt belied the businesslike length of the blade. Gingerly she took it and laid it down on the small table next to the fainting couch.

Then she grabbed up the sweater she'd been planning to wear with the intention of putting it on her mother.

"Genny, do you have something I can tie this up with?" The strain in Emmy's voice caused both Genevieve and Lillian to look at her.

Still leaning against the wardrobe, Emmy was holding up the hem of her dark sweater — she'd changed into it and trousers in the anteroom before going after Lillian — and looking ruefully down at a long gash just above her waist on the right side. Blood poured from it in a steady stream.

"Emmanuelle, my God, what happened?"

"Emmy! Maman, don't move." Genevieve snatched up the skirt, a cascade of multicolor silk ruffles, she'd so recently discarded and rushed to her sister. "Are you *shot*?"

"A little bit, it seems." Grimacing, Emmy rested against the wardrobe as Genevieve pressed the wadded-up skirt to her side.

"How bad is it?" Lillian sounded terrified.

"Not bad." Emmy's tone was reassuring, which, Genevieve knew, was largely for their mother's benefit. Like Lillian, Emmy was making light of her injuries so as not to alarm someone she loved. "Not much more than a scratch. The bullet just gouged out some flesh as it passed right through. But it's bleeding like the devil."

"Hold this." Genevieve caught her sister's hand, placed it over the makeshift bandage, then grabbed a long woolen scarf out of the pocket of her coat. "What happened?"

"The soldiers all left the dungeon when the bomb went off, but then some of them came back. There was gunfire. I got hit. Right when I thought we'd gotten away clean, too." Emmy's shrug tried to dismiss it.

"You didn't say anything," Lillian said.

"Because it's nothing," Emmy replied.

"Where's Max?" Trying not to think terrifying thoughts, wanting to distract their mother, Genevieve asked what she suddenly badly wanted to know while she wrapped the scarf around her sister's waist and knotted it in such a way as to apply pressure to the wound. "And Berthe?"

"Max stayed to hold off the soldiers while Berthe and I got Maman away, and then Berthe went back to help him." She took one look at Genevieve's face and added, "Don't worry. Last time I saw him, your Max was fine. I know he said to wait for him here. But I'm starting to feel a little weak and — I think we should go on to Otto."

"I do, too." Knowing that both her mother and sister were injured with only her to help them was terrifying. What would happen if . . .

"The blood! It leads this way!"

The shout in a harsh male voice was muffled, but the fact that they could hear it galvanized all of them: it almost certainly belonged to a soldier, and it wasn't far away.

"God in heaven, I've left a trail." Emmy stared in horror at the floor. Genevieve followed suit. Drops of blood, gleaming crimson, led from the door to where Emmy stood. Undoubtedly there was more outside.

Lillian tried to rise from the couch. "You girls —" her voice shook "— stay here. I will go out there, give myself up."

"Maman, *stop. No.* You and Emmy have to

hide. In the wardrobe, quick." Genevieve grabbed Lillian, hustled her toward the wardrobe where Emmy was already squeezing inside. She practically shoved Lillian in, too, as more shouts punctuated the sound of numerous boots on stone pounding toward them.

Emmy said urgently, "Genny, the blood —"

"Shh. I'll deal with it. Just stay in there and stay quiet." She shut the door, then turned wide-eyed toward the hall. She looked at the blood on the floor: there was a lot, with no time to wipe it all up. But if she didn't, and the soldiers saw, they would be caught, the three of them. They would be arrested. They would be killed. Unless —

Quick as the thought, she snatched up the knife her mother had carried in and sliced her own arm. Blood welled up, flowed. The sting of the cut made her eyes water. She dropped the knife as dizziness assailed her. Staring down at the blood running down her arm, then dripping to the floor, she had to sit abruptly on the fainting couch.

She'd no sooner done so than the door was thrown open with such force that it bounced back on its hinges.

Wagner stood in the doorway at the head of what seemed to be a gaggle of soldiers, staring at her as she sat there looking back at him while she clutched her bleeding arm.

Her heart almost stopped. The hair stood

up on the back of her neck. It was all she could do to keep the shock, horror, fear out of her face.

She wasn't sure she succeeded.

"Genevieve," he said. She could read nothing, nothing at all, in his tone.

He looked just as he had before the bomb went off. Not so much as a hair was out of place. He'd been inside the Knight's Hall; she'd seen him as she left.

How had he escaped? Had something gone wrong? Were they all alive? Had the mission failed?

Whatever the answers, she had to work now to save herself and her mother and sister.

Act, she told herself. *Act like you've never acted before.*

"Claus." Her voice quavered pathetically. She looked — she hoped — thankful to see him. "Oh, Claus. I'm hurt, can you help me?"

His eyes ran over her. The rapid progression of expressions on his face — concern for her, surprise, doubt — had her stomach twisting in fear.

"The blood's a false scent," he said over his shoulder to his men. "Go back to the east turret and help them battle the fire. Save what you can."

"Jawohl." The smartly snapped-off rejoinder was followed by the disappearance of the soldiers and the sound of multiple sets of boots retreating.

Wagner came in and closed the door. "Let me bind up your arm," he said almost tenderly, pulling a handkerchief from his pocket as he came toward her. "How did you hurt it?"

"The explosion." She took care not to call it a bomb — because how could she know it was a bomb? — as he dropped to one knee in front of her, took hold of her bleeding arm and started to wrap the handkerchief around it. "I was knocked to the ground. I — cut it on something."

"This happened while you were changing your costume?" He tied a knot to secure the makeshift bandage, then applied pressure with his hand on top of the handkerchief. The force of it made the cut throb rather than sting, which was worse.

"Yes." She would be relieved he wasn't hurt, wouldn't she? "I'm so happy you weren't injured. What happened?"

"A bomb was set off in the Knight's Hall. By traitors who will, when we catch them, pay a terrible price. I regret to inform you that everyone who was in the hall at the time — your audience — is dead. My schloss is burning as we speak. Fortunately it is stone, and the fire can be contained."

"Oh!" He pressed on her cut with such force that she cried out and reflexively tried to jerk her arm away. He held her fast. His fingers dug into her flesh. Her eyes flew to his face. He suspected: there was no mistaking the import of that grip. Or the look in his eyes.

He smiled at her. The dimples that made his smile so outwardly charming appeared.

Cold fear twisted her stomach, dried her mouth. Her heart pounded so loudly she feared he would hear it.

She was looking into the face of evil.

"It might interest you to know that I thought you appeared pale during your last song." His voice was silky. "When you took your bow and left, I followed you to see if you were all right. I went into that small room where you change your clothes. You weren't there, but the door at the other end of the room was just closing. I thought you must have gone out through it, so I followed again. That's when the bomb went off."

His free hand caught her chin, held it while he examined her face.

"Who do you work for?" He hurled the question at her.

Terror swirled in an icy tide inside her. She had to fight to keep it at bay.

"What? No one! What are you talking about?" She looked pleadingly at him. "Claus —"

"It's you and Bonet, and that man of his — it's all of you, isn't it? Even the pretty blonde." He came up off his knee, releasing her cut arm, looming over her, pushing his face so close to hers that she could feel his hot breath. "Who sent you to —" He broke off, staring at her. "*Mein Gott,* the eyes."

"Claus, you're wrong, I've done nothing —"

"What a fool I've been. How could I have been so blind? You've been tricking me all along, haven't you? You're a dirty bitch of a *spy. Those are Lillian de Rocheford's eyes.*"

That last was a howl of pure rage. He throttled her before she could react, wrapping both hands around her neck, pushing her down on the fainting couch, looming above her, squeezing, squeezing . . .

Wildly she kicked and fought and clawed at his hands and gasped for air.

There was none. No air to be had. He was too strong. She wheezed, bucked, struggled, beat at him with her fists. His face, the room, everything started to blur.

He wouldn't let go. She couldn't make him let go. He was crushing her windpipe, choking the life out of her.

"You will tell me — *ah!*"

He gave a short, pained cry. His face contorted as he released her neck at last. Even as she sucked in a great, shuddering, life-saving breath he tried to straighten and reached a clawing hand behind his back.

Then he pitched forward to lie motionless beside her. A knife — *the* knife — stuck out of his back. She stared in shock at the bright yellow handle quivering between his shoulder blades.

Lillian stood over him, her poor injured face alight with hatred.

"Bastard," she said, and spat on the corpse.

Chapter Forty-Six

"He would have killed me," Genevieve concluded her account of what had happened to Max as they descended the last flight of narrow, curving stone stairs that led to the cable car staging area. "My mother saved my life."

Having reached her room only a minute or so after Wagner's death, Max, his cane long gone, was carrying Emmy, who'd fainted in the wardrobe from, presumably, blood loss. Emmy was conscious again, but the urgent need to escape meant that they couldn't wait around for her to recover enough to walk reliably. According to Max, Berthe had gone directly from the dungeons to assist Otto in case he should need it, so it was just the four of them. Genevieve had her arm around Lillian, who could walk only a short distance without support and was having trouble negotiating the stairs. The smell of burning was strong now even on the lower floors, and gray wisps of smoke were starting to float along even the most remote hallways and stairwells. The sounds of the fire formed a galvanizing backdrop for all the commotion associated with the aftermath of the explosion: shouts, running feet, crashes and bangs from inside the schloss itself, and, outside, the wail of multiple sirens.

Fire trucks, certainly. Police? Ambulances? Would security even let them up the mountain?

What was there to secure now that all the principals were dead?

"Thank God you were there, Baroness," Max said. "I was delayed. I would have been too late."

"It's not the first time I've killed an evil bastard." Lillian's voice was grim. "Or the first time I've killed for my daughters, for that matter."

Genevieve's eyes widened at that, but there was no time for questions. They were at the bottom of the stairs.

Max said, "Through that door. Quickly."

The door he indicated led outside onto a narrow walkway protected by a parapet. As Genevieve shoved through the door and emerged out into the night, the cold wind whipped at her. They were, she saw, at the very base of the schloss. Looking down was a mistake: the drop was staggering. In front of her, at the end of the vertigo-inducing stone path, the slate roof and open sides of the staging area waited. A cable car was already —

With a sense of shock she realized that the reason she was seeing everything so clearly was because the night was lit up with a pulsating orange glow. And the reason for that was the fire raging in the castle above them. The east turret blazed like a torch against the night-black sky. Hot ashes and glowing red sparks swirled downward on the wind. A rising column of dense smoke bisected the pale face of the moon.

"The moon's out," she said to Max, who was right behind her, stepping as carefully as she was along the walkway. The parapet protecting them from falling hundreds of feet was only knee-high. One wrong step, one too-strong gust of wind and it would be easy to topple over.

"Here's hoping we've got our ride home." Max's reply confirmed what she'd thought. If they could get off the mountain, now that the moon was out, there was at least a chance that a Lysander might be down there somewhere, waiting.

"Hurry, hurry." Berthe rushed out of the staging area toward them. Emmy, who'd been carrying Berthe's coat, tossed it to her. Berthe shoved into it — everyone else wore theirs, and in addition they'd taken the time to bundle Lillian into a pair of Genevieve's trousers and a sweater; the cable cars were open on the sides and the ride down the mountain would be freezing, with no guarantee about what would be waiting for them at the end — and grabbed Lillian on her other side. Together they were able to hustle her into the staging area at a near run, with Max right behind them.

Above them, the battle to save the schloss raged. The hungry stretch of the flames, the roar and crackle of the fire, the shouts of those fighting it, the whirlwind of heat, the burning smell, and what looked and sounded like a battalion's worth of soldiers rushing around made for a terrifying and terrifyingly beautiful tableau.

It would take just one sharp-eyed soldier to look around and see a cable car descending the mountain.

"There it is," Lillian breathed as the end of the platform came into view. Otto, his white hair blowing in the wind that blew through the open-sided structure, bundled to his teeth in a coat and scarf, stood there beckoning them on.

A cable car waited, its sides and top bright blue, attached to the cable by a long metal pincer known as a grip. It held six people, standing room only. There were four cars on this circuit, and whether setting this one in motion would get all of them going Genevieve didn't know. This close, she could hear the rumbling motor. Only the sounds of the fire had kept it from being heard beyond the staging area.

"Get in." Otto's voice was urgent. He stood by a giant lever, ready, she assumed, to throw it as soon as they were on board.

Two bodies sprawled on the floor near one wall. Soldiers: they must have been guarding the cable cars. Otto must have had to kill them. So inured to death was she now that she felt barely a twinge.

Between them, she and Berthe got Lillian into the car, their feet clattering on the metal floor. It felt flimsy, with a series of struts holding up the curved roof and a lot of open air in between. Max, with Emmy's arm wrapped around his neck, was right behind them.

Genevieve looked back in time to see Otto shove the lever forward. The car lurched and lifted, floating above the platform as it headed toward the edge, its side-located door still open. A small, bright explosion in the general vicinity of the lever — "He blew the mechanism so no one can stop us," Max explained in response to her alarmed look — was instantly followed by Otto bolting after the now rapidly moving car. His intention was clearly to leap on board before it cleared the platform and launched itself out into the night.

A group of soldiers burst out of the schloss, through the door they'd just exited onto the walkway that led to the staging area, weapons in hand.

Loud shots rent the air as they fired at Otto, the cable car and everyone in it.

"Stop! Stop the car!" they yelled, rushing toward the staging area.

Otto dropped, rolled and came up firing a weapon of his own at the soldiers. Two were cut down immediately, toppling over the parapet with hoarse cries. The others — four — dropped to the ground, sheltering behind the low stone wall.

"Otto! Come on," Max shouted, depositing Emmy on the floor beside Lillian with more haste than care. They'd all hunkered down below the car's metal wall when the gunfire had started. Looking back, she saw Otto glance toward them at Max's shout, then race after the car, snapping off shots behind him as he ran.

Pulling a pistol out of his pocket, using the car's wall as a shield, Max provided cover fire.

"Stop him! Stop him!" Firing back, the soldiers did a hunched-over run toward the staging area. Like the others, Genevieve was nearly knocked off her feet as the car reached the end of the platform and swung out into space, rising toward the first of the pylons. Otto ran toward the edge of the platform, but it was too late, the cable car was away, he would be left behind —

The soldiers fired relentlessly.

"Jump!" Max bellowed, snapping off more

shots before thrusting the gun into his pocket. Otto did, pocketing his own weapon as he hurled himself after the car.

He caught the edge, grabbing on with both hands, his weight tilting the car as his body hung unsupported over the terrifying emptiness below.

Max leaped toward him.

As the gunfire continued, Otto cried out, let go.

Max snatched at him, caught his wrist, held on. The cable car climbed, lurching terrifyingly as it reached the pylon and progressed past it, then started its downward slide.

"Give me your other hand." Reaching down, Max tried to catch Otto's flailing hand. When he didn't succeed, he locked both hands around the one wrist he already held.

Genevieve and Berthe both rushed to help. The cable car was descending now, moving fast, closely following the snow-covered terrain. A last jut of land remained before it would launch out over what looked, to Genevieve's frightened eyes, like a thousand-meter-deep abyss. Terrified that Otto's weight would pull Max over the side, Genevieve locked her arms around his hips and held on, hoping that adding her weight to his would make a difference. Berthe leaned over the side, trying to grab hold of any part of Otto that she could.

The sound of shots being fired made Genevieve flinch and Berthe pull back.

"They can't hit us. We're too far away now," Max yelled.

Looking back toward the staging area, Genevieve saw that two soldiers had somehow made it onto the structure's tile roof. Clearly visible in the orange glow, they were pointing their weapons down. From the direction of the white flashes leaving their muzzles, they weren't firing at the car but at — she gasped as she realized — the heart-stoppingly slender cable supporting the car.

"They're trying to shoot through the cable," she cried.

A steady stream of curses fell from Max's lips. She could feel his muscles bunch as he strained to haul Otto up and into the car. In only a few meters, they would be launched out over the abyss.

A thud, accompanied by the sudden rocking of the car, made Genevieve glance around. Her heart leaped with fear as she saw a soldier clinging to the other side of the car. He must have slid down to the spit of land, leaped up and grabbed hold as the car passed over him.

She'd no more than registered his presence than she heard a metallic clink and he let go, disappearing from view.

Blinking in incomprehension, she looked down at the floor of the car where the small metal object he'd dropped rolled.

"Grenade!" Berthe shrieked. Genevieve had no time to even register what was happening before Berthe cast herself face-down onto the floor — and a tremendous boom lifted the car and her body.

"Berthe!" Genevieve screamed.

Knocked into violent motion just as it lurched out over the seemingly bottomless abyss, the car tilted terrifyingly. Everyone screamed.

"Jesus Christ, the pincer grip's come off the cable," Otto yelled as the car came down again, then went back up the other way.

"Hold on tight," Max roared over his shoulder. Sick with fear, Genevieve held on to him for dear life as the car rocked up into a wild, out-of-control swing that gained momentum as it came down again. For a seemingly endless moment at the top of the next arc, the car lay almost on its side in the air. Genevieve's heart shot into her throat as she found herself staring down into the sheer black drop below. If she hadn't been clinging to Max, she thought she might have fallen out. Emmy and Lillian, wrapped up together, their nails scraping metal as they scrabbled for any handhold they could find, screamed hysterically.

Berthe, still on her stomach, motionless since the explosion of the grenade, slid over the wall and into the void.

"Berthe." Torn from Genevieve's throat, it

was an agonized cry.

For what felt like an endless moment, Genevieve watched her fall into the bottomless blackness like a bird shot out of the sky.

Vivi. Pierre. The memories slammed into her. Her heart set up an endless shriek. She was paralyzed with horror, hurled back into the past.

"Maman!" The voice was Emmy's, raised in a terrified cry. Genevieve saw her sister, clinging to a roof strut, trying to keep their mother from sliding over the edge.

"Maman!" The past shattered in an instant. Hurling herself toward them, Genevieve grabbed her mother and the roof strut and held on.

The car swung the other way. She was flung to the floor with Emmy and Lillian. The three of them hung on, clinging together, and then when the car rocked up again, less wildly this time, a compulsive glance down into the vast emptiness below revealed nothing but dark.

Berthe was gone.

Heart pulsing with horror and grief, she said a silent prayer.

Max managed to pull Otto inside. Both men dropped to the floor, Max panting and Otto chalk white even in the gloom. His eyes fluttered. His lips parted, trembled.

The swinging slowed, but the car continued to rock erratically. It was tilted now, unstable, swaying with every gust of wind.

"What just happened?" Emmy's voice was tight with strain.

"Is this thing going to fall?" Genevieve added. They were all breathing hard. She could feel her mother trembling.

"No," Max said. But she knew him well enough to know that beneath the strong denial he wasn't quite so sure.

"The car rose with the force of the explosion, and the pincer grip came off the cable. When we came back down, it caught on the cable again, but it's not locked on. As long as nothing else goes wrong, we should be all right." Otto was sweating hard.

A pit opened in Genevieve's stomach as she registered just how precarious their position really was. Sick with horror over Berthe, terrified that something, anything might cause the car to fall, Genevieve made sure Emmy and Lillian were secure, then crawled carefully toward Max and Otto, who clutched his thigh as blood bubbled up between his fingers.

"Berthe was dead before she fell." Max's voice was rough with sympathy as she reached them. He was talking to her alone, Genevieve knew, and she could only imagine what her face must look like. "I've seen men fall on grenades before. She was killed the moment it detonated."

He was pulling his sweater over his head, and it took her a second before she understood that he was stripping off his undershirt.

She realized it was for Otto's leg as he pulled his sweater back on.

Max ripped the shirt into strips, and she tied them around Otto's leg. Otto leaned back against the wall and breathed.

No one said anything as the cable car reached another pylon and jerked upward again. The loss of Berthe was too raw, too shocking.

Her heart was heavy with sorrow, her eyes stung with tears but there was no time to grieve.

In the distance she saw the flaming torch that was Eber Schloss blazing bright against the night sky. Even as she watched, the highest, brightest flame, the east turret, broke off, plummeting hundreds of meters down the mountain while trailing fire like the tail of a kite.

Max said, "We can't ride this thing all the way down. You notice they quit shooting at the cable? For all they know, we might be dead from the grenade, but they'll want to make sure. They're going to be waiting for us at the other end. We have to get off right before we reach the next pylon. There's a hill there. After that, we're above a drop of hundreds of meters the rest of the way in." Max turned his head to look at Otto. "Did you park the truck where I told you?"

Otto nodded. Then he said, "Yes." He

sounded as if he was trying to gather his strength.

Max said, "When we reach the hill I was talking about, I'm going to drop you women over the side. There's a place where it's only about four meters, and the snow will cushion you. Otto, can you hang from your hands for a minute and drop? We need to be careful not to overbalance the car, but we have to do this fast. This particular spot's not that big, and if we miss it — well, we can't miss it."

Chapter Forty-Seven

"I can do it," Otto said.

"Did I hear you say something about a truck?" Emmy asked. It sounded as if her teeth were chattering. Genevieve didn't think it was entirely due to the cold wind that swirled around them all. Shocked by Berthe's death, frightened at the instability of the cable car, they were all struggling to stay strong, but the mood was grim and a pall hung over them all.

Max nodded. "I knew we'd have to get off where we're going to be getting off, so the truck's parked fairly close. We get to the truck, drive to the field where a plane is supposed to be waiting. If it's there, everybody's off to merry old England but me. I'm for France." He gave Otto a crooked smile. "Looks like you just bought yourself a ticket out of the war."

"I can't go to England," Lillian said. Her voice was breathy and weak, but there was no missing the determination in it. Like the rest of them, she was sitting on the floor of the cable car. Emmy was close by her side. "I have to go back to France. To Rocheford. I have to be there when the invasion comes. I have a mission."

"Maman, you can't," Emmy said. "That's over now."

Lillian shook her head. "There's no one else. I'm the only one who knows the way through the marsh. I have to do it."

"I know the way through the marsh," Genevieve said. "I can do whatever it is. Tell me."

Lillian looked at her. Their eyes met, and the memory of the many hours they'd spent together exploring the marsh, observing its creatures, harvesting its plants, learning its secrets, passed between them. Always, the marsh had been their shared bond, and it was still.

"You can," Lillian agreed, sounding as if the realization lifted a great weight from her shoulders. While the cable car slid through the night, creaking and groaning and rocking in the wind as it carried them over the seemingly bottomless crevasses that Genevieve refused to think about, Lillian told her, quickly but precisely, what she needed to do when the time came.

"She's not an agent," Max objected. "She's not trained."

"She's trained in what she needs to know," Lillian replied. "She's trained in the marsh.

She grew up in it."

"Maman's right. She can do it," Emmy said. "Genny always was a little swamp rat."

"I'm doing it," Genevieve told him, while narrowing her eyes at her sister.

The fact that Max didn't raise any more objections told her just how important this mission was.

Carefully Max stood up, grabbed the edge of the car to steady himself as the thing rocked, and looked below. "Just a few more minutes," he warned the rest of them. Equally careful, Otto hauled himself up beside him.

The uneasy feeling Genevieve had been experiencing ever since she'd heard she was getting ready to be dropped into nothingness intensified. Telling herself those four meters were no distance at all didn't help. Neither did the thought that she was probably safer out of the cable car than in it. Her pulse quickened, her stomach tightened and she sought a distraction. A glance at her mother, a flash of memory, and she had it.

"Maman, what did you mean when you said Wagner wasn't the first evil bastard you've killed?" She kept her voice low so the conversation couldn't be heard beyond the three of them. "You haven't been going around murdering people, have you?"

"Only for my daughters," Lillian replied, instantly riveting both daughters' attention.

"Maman —" Emmy sounded both appalled

and fascinated.

Lillian made an impatient gesture. "Alain — how do you think he died? It was the skullcaps. That night at dinner, in his beef bourguignonne."

Genevieve was struck dumb. She was shocked to the core, stunned, but the second she thought about it, it made perfect sense. She knew what skullcaps could do.

"You *poisoned* him?" Emmy gasped.

"He was violently abusive toward you. He killed Phillippe, leaving Genevra, heart-broken, to bear a child alone. When your papa came home, when he found out either of those things, he would have killed the bastard himself, then probably would have had to stand trial and maybe even be hanged for it. Alain had already damaged our family badly. I wasn't going to let him destroy us completely. So I did what I had to do." Lillian's voice was completely matter-of-fact.

Both girls gaped at her.

Then Emmy huffed a breath. "Maman. Well done."

"All right, it's almost time." Max turned to them, and the topic had to be abandoned. "Everybody on their feet. Hold on to the side and be careful how you move. Genevieve, since you're the only one who's uninjured, I'm going to drop you first, so you can help the others."

Genevieve's stomach clenched, but she

nodded and stood up.

"There it is," Max said. Standing beside him now, gripping the edge against the swaying of the car, Genevieve saw the snowy hill looming in the darkness. Beyond it, Stuttgart was in sight, its church steeples and tall buildings distant dark shapes in the moonlight. A quick glance back told her that Eber Schloss still burned ferociously. Glimpses of barely visible moving lights racing up and down the mountain made her think that multiple vehicles were coming and going on that narrow access road.

"It's time." As he'd told her he meant to do, Max gripped her around the waist and lifted her up so that she perched on the lip of the car. It rocked dangerously. Heart leaping, she grabbed onto his forearms for dear life. The night fell away below.

Terror leaped into full-blown life inside her, cramping her stomach, freezing her blood, paralyzing her.

"I've got you," Max said. While she clung to him, he shifted his grip so that his hands circled her wrists. She didn't dare look back, or down. Instead she kept her gaze fixed on him. He was all that kept her from falling — and soon she *would* fall. At the thought, she started to shake. He must have seen the panic in her face, felt the tremor in her hands, because, in full view of the others, he leaned close to press a quick, hard kiss on her lips.

Too terrified to close her eyes, she looked into his instead. Vivi, Pierre, now Berthe — all the memories, her horror of falling, the knowledge that she couldn't, *could not,* do this, was laid bare for him to read.

"Trust me, angel," he said, and she realized that she did, absolutely. Then, a command: "Swing your legs over."

It was just about the hardest thing she'd ever done in her life. But she did it, and for a horrifying moment, with the cable car rocking like a cradle, suspended over nothing until the hill appeared beneath them, she waited.

She slid off the lip when he told her to and hung terrified from his hands. Then he let go and she fell.

She hurtled downward, hit and found herself tumbling unhurt through deep snow.

Chapter Forty-Eight

The escape from the cable car was successful, the truck was where it was supposed to be and the Lysanders were waiting to carry them out of Germany. Max and Genevieve, the latter over Max's renewed objections, were dropped off in France. The others went on to England for medical treatment. Genevieve took up residence in a flat near Rocheford as she waited for the invasion to be launched. Thanks to Lillian's courage, the Germans were all but convinced now that the Allied attack would be launched in Pas-de-Calais, and as a result, Normandy and the area around Cherbourg were under slightly less pressure and scrutiny from the Germans. That benefited Genevieve, who was in hiding, with false identity papers, her hair cut short and dyed a nondescript brown, her face scrubbed clean, under the name Giselle Martine, supposedly a widow who sold soap. Word filtered through that after the devastating attack the German press was calling the

"Massacre at Eber Schloss," there was a price on her head. Only Max, who also had a price on his head and had also changed identities, and who stopped by as often as he could, although he was busy carrying out his assigned role in preparing for the invasion, and Emmy, who'd recovered and returned to France to resume her work as Merlin, knew who she really was. Lillian, safe in England, had told her that the signal for the invasion would be broadcast out of London through the BBC, which meant Genevieve spent endless hours listening to the radio. In the meantime, she harvested Lillian's mushrooms as her mother had directed and went for long walks that refreshed her knowledge of the marsh. When the time came, there would be no room for mistakes.

On one stormy afternoon — the invasion needed fair weather to launch, so she didn't fear being out of place when the signal came — she took the bus to Vère. The Sisters there operated an orphanage in a rambling, half-timbered house on ten hectares of land. Coming as a Good Samaritan with a contribution toward the upkeep of the children, she was welcomed. Anna — Anna Grangier now, her true identity erased by false papers — played happily with half a dozen other children in a large room in the rear. Watching her, Genevieve thought of Rachel, her mother, and felt a wave of sadness. But Anna was safe, and well, and protected, and that, Genevieve knew, was what Rachel would wish for her.

On June fifth, at around 9:00 p.m., not long after dusk had turned to full dark, she sat at the small table where she took her meals in the dismal, one-room flat that was all the person she was pretending to be could afford, listening to the radio that was turned down very low because possessing one was forbidden. As she listened, she methodically worked a mortar and pestle to grind the last of the mushrooms she had dried into powder.

The announcer cut away from an orchestra playing a cheerful medley of what they called "Swing Time Melodies." Another voice crackled over the tinny airwaves: "The carrots are cooked. Repeat, the carrots are cooked."

That was it: the signal.

Galvanized, she jumped up, scooped her freshly made mushroom powder into the bag with the rest, pulled on the dark shirt, trousers and flat-heeled shoes she'd scrounged up during the preceding days in anticipation of this moment, slipped out of the building, hopped onto her bicycle, and pedaled through the windy, overcast night to Rocheford.

She was terrified: anything could go wrong. She could run into a German patrol. The plan could have been betrayed.

Yet she felt exhilarated, too. Tomorrow the

free world rolled the dice, its survival on the line. Tonight, so did she.

The cellar cave at Rocheford was the rendezvous point. Already there, waiting for her, was the team she was to lead through the marsh.

"I've brought supplies," she greeted the men gathered around her mother's worktable as she let herself in. It was the agreed-upon code.

"I hope you brought dinner, too," came the looked-for response. The voice was familiar.

A single shuttered lantern in the middle of the table left most of the cave in darkness and cast leaping shadows everywhere. She peered through the uncertain light at the speaker and recognized him as the newcomer, the dark, wiry Basque whom she'd met the day she'd rushed to Rocheford looking for her mother. He was thinner now, gaunt, in fact. So were the other men. So was she, she knew. As Genevieve Dumont, she'd been privileged to partake of the same food as the German invaders. As Giselle Martine, she starved on Jerusalem artichokes, that food for cows, and turnips and greens. The edible mushrooms her mother had left behind were gone when she got back to the cave, consumed no doubt by members of the Resistance network once she was no longer there to protect them. The skullcaps, grown in a hidden, nearly inaccessible alcove, were all that had remained.

The newcomer didn't identify himself. No one did. Secrecy was their shield.

Instead he rose to his feet. "You," he said.

"You," she replied, equally rude, and looked past him at the others. She didn't know any of them. They didn't know her. There were five men in all. The team she was leading was supposed to consist only of four. One looked like a shopkeeper. The others were dressed all in dark clothes, with knit caps on their heads.

"If you are Rene —" it was a code name, told to her by Lillian "— this is for you."

She held the bag of powdered mushrooms out toward the shopkeeper. He stepped forward and took it, nodded his thanks, sent a look around the assembled men, said, "God keep us all," and was gone.

This was another, more personal contribution to the defeat of the Nazis that Lillian had planned to make, quite aside from her official assignment to act as a guide through the marsh, which she'd asked Genevieve to carry out in her stead: an arrangement with her friend the baker who prepared food each day for the German soldiers stationed at Fort du Roule.

"What's in the bag?" one of the men asked, ever suspicious. Genevieve didn't blame him. Suspicion, she had learned, was how they all survived.

"A special flour for the bread he bakes each morning for the German soldiers," the newcomer replied. "They will have it tomorrow with their breakfasts."

He didn't specify that the "special flour" was ground mushrooms. Specifically, ground skullcap mushrooms. It was, perhaps, better that the others didn't know.

What you don't know, you can't tell: she could almost hear Max saying it. And if tomorrow went wrong, they didn't want anyone knowing what she, Lillian and the baker had done. All those who ate that bread would, depending on the concentration of powder in it, either fall violently ill or die. One more small step toward the weakening of the German defensive line.

"Let's go," the newcomer said, precluding any more questions, and they did.

Theirs was a life-or-death mission to disable the equipment that worked the lock that controlled water levels along this westernmost section of the Normandy beaches. In the event of an attack, the Germans planned to flood the marshes behind the beach and the road that ran through them as soon as the invasion began, cutting off the beach so that landing Allied forces were unable to penetrate farther into the interior and would be trapped where they could easily be cut down by strategically placed German guns. Two coastal artillery batteries were in position to open fire on the beach for just that purpose.

The lock control mechanism was housed in a building that was heavily guarded to the front, toward the beach and the sea. As the marsh behind it was judged impassable, the back of the building was guarded only by a patrol that passed immediately behind it at set times. That made destroying the mechanism a stealth mission rather than a battle. Instead of blowing it up, which would attract unwanted attention and even, perhaps, send up a warning flag that the invasion was poised to begin, and in Normandy rather than Pas-de-Calais, where the bulk of the preparations were now taking place, they simply broke in and busted the thing.

The Germans wouldn't even realize it had been done until they tried to use it, and by then it would be too late.

Mission complete, Genevieve led the party back through the tall weeds and scrub trees that covered the thousands of hectares of brackish water and oozing silt. The night was dark but calm. The storms that had settled over the region for most of the previous week had finally blown themselves out. The temperature was cool rather than cold, but the water was icy. The faint rank smell of decaying vegetation lay over everything. The wind carried on it the salt smell of the sea along with the now ever-present burnt scent from the repeated firing of the Germans' defensive antiaircraft guns. Nevertheless, Genevieve was on edge: the sounds of the marsh — the lapping of the water, the plops of creatures going in, the cry of night birds — might be, she feared, enough to keep them from hearing any pursuit until it was upon them. And, too, there was the terrifying, exciting knowledge that the Allied invasion would soon begin.

The bombing started when they still had a fair distance to go before they were safely out of the marsh. The explosions were not too close, lighting up the sky farther to the east, but they were enough to make their small party hurry.

Moving with the men behind her along the invisible ribs of solid ground, no more noticeable, she hoped, than shifting shadows in the darkness, Genevieve heard the unmistakable growl of airplanes overhead.

Cold with dread, she looked up.

It was barely past midnight on June 6, 1944. The heavy cloud cover that still plagued the area in the aftermath of the storms had parted just enough to allow a glimpse of the full moon behind it. It was immediately blotted out again by a ceiling of dark shapes passing overhead, and, below that, a sky full of — something.

"What is that?" one of the men behind her whispered. A glance told her that he, too, was craning his neck to look skyward.

"I don't know," another replied, equally low.

At first she thought they looked like white moths. Then mushrooms in the air.

Genevieve's eyes widened and her lips parted as the shapes resolved into dozens of white domes swooping silently toward earth.

Chapter Forty-Nine

"Paratroopers," the newcomer breathed.

The men Genevieve could now see hanging from the domes that were their parachutes started to splash down in the water.

As they hit, their voices, quiet, startled, peppered the dark.

"What the hell?"

"Johnson, is that you?"

"Damn *water.* Wasn't supposed to be no damn water."

"Jesus, it's sucking me down!"

"It's cold as be-damned!"

They landed everywhere, in the water, in the weeds, in the eddies of silt that acted like quicksand. Their accents told her that they were Yanks: American paratroopers. Listening to them, watching them struggle as they landed, she realized that they were weighted down by their parachutes and packs and equipment. Many were trapped and sinking and would shortly drown in the murky waters and treacherous silt. Anyone who tried to go in after them would risk sharing their fate. Their only hope was to reach one of the paths that neither they nor anyone else could see. The paths that her childhood years in the marsh had indelibly imprinted on her brain.

Transfixed at the horror of the Americans' fate, she couldn't look away.

I have to help them.

If they could make it to her, to the path . . .

Cupping her hands around her mouth, she called to the closest of them, softly, in English. "Yank. This way."

An indistinct, but distinctly American, voice said, "Look there. Is that a dame?"

"This way." Careful to keep her voice low, she called again.

First one, then a second and a third started to flounder toward her. The silt sucked one of them down. He went under, resurfaced, splashed around.

"Help! I can't get my feet under me."

A buddy caught up to him, grabbed his arm. "Give me the Eureka!"

"Damned transponder's not more important than me."

"Sure is."

To the newcomer, who stood closest to her — single file was the only way to traverse most of the paths — Genevieve said, "We have to try to get them out. Don't step off the path, or you'll be sucked in, too. But we need to find a branch, or something we can reach out to them if they can get close, to pull them in."

He said, "Jacques has a rope." Turning to the man next to him, Jacques, he said something, and a moment later a rope was produced from the pack the man carried.

"Don't step off the path," she warned Jacques, who was coiling his rope in preparation for throwing it. To the newcomer she said, "I'll mark the paths. You start pulling them out."

She left the other two men from her group on another path. Using their coats and a branch, they were starting to haul more paratroopers in.

As one of the Yanks was pulled out, she heard him say, apparently in answer to a question she didn't hear: "Pathfinders. 101st Airborne. We're first. We show the way."

After that, more paratroopers came in waves. First by the dozens, then by the hundreds, then by the thousands, until they were falling out of the sky like a hard rain. The black marsh water looked like it was abloom with white water lilies as far as the eye could see. Gliders landed, too, towed in by aeroplanes and released to plow into the swamp like the unwieldy pieces of lumber they basically were. Their pilots and crews, too, floundered and risked drowning in the marsh. In the distance the relentless chatter of the German antiaircraft guns was answered by the ceaseless booming of the Allied bombs. But the Germans didn't appear to know the paratroopers were there.

Genevieve worked tirelessly, marking the paths with tall sticks and bits of cloth sliced from discarded parachutes, leading the paratroopers and the glider pilots and crews to the railroad tracks that were the marsh's high point and that, if followed, would take them to a road and their rendezvous point.

"Which way to Sainte-Mère-Église?"

"Have you seen the Eighty-Second?"

"The road's how far away?"

She answered questions until she was too exhausted to answer any more. By that time, she'd heard enough to know that the code name for this particular landing spot was Utah Beach.

As the night ground on, her original team was joined by more and more of the local partisans as word spread about what was happening. They formed human chains and used ropes and branches and ladders and anything else that was available to pull the Americans out.

Emmy arrived at some point, bringing members of her network to help. Genevieve had heard that Emmy had been working in the vicinity since she'd parachuted back into France, so she wasn't as shocked to see her as she might otherwise have been. The sisters, coming face-to-face on one of the marked paths, almost didn't recognize each other, as both were covered head to toe in mud. When they did, they exclaimed in surprise and exchanged a quick hug.

"You shouldn't be here! You shouldn't have come back at all," Genevieve scolded. "You've still got stitches. What happens if they break open and you start to bleed?"

"Don't be such a worrywart. They're coming out in two days. And what would Maman say if I let you do this by yourself?"

By 3:00 a.m. rumor had it that the Allied invasion force was massing off the beach.

As the hours ticked down toward dawn, huge waves of Allied bombers blanketed the sky overhead. The bombs spilling from their underbellies shook the ground, hurt the eardrums, lit up the night. At first Genevieve was alarmed, but they didn't target the marsh. They attacked the German defenses, not only around Utah Beach, but along the entire Cotentin Peninsula, and the Germans fired relentlessly back. The noise was deafening. Shells burst in the sky like fireworks, lighting up everything, filling the air with the smell of ordnance and enormous plumes of smoke.

By sunrise the last of the paratroopers and the glider pilots and their crews had been pulled from the marsh and were tramping along the railroad track and the road to join their units. The partisans were starting to melt away. The bombing had slacked off, along with the corresponding antiaircraft fire. Meeting up with Emmy on the railroad track, Genevieve was so tired she barely managed a smile. They were both filthy and limping and stooped with exhaustion.

"Look." Emmy took her arm, pointed toward the beach. Turning, Genevieve did.

It was low tide. Beyond the now scarred and broken concrete of the Atlantic Wall, three hundred meters or more of sandy beach were exposed, and the defenses the Germans had laid down in anticipation of what was coming were clearly visible. Farther in the distance, the invasion fleet floated offshore, stretching out along the horizon in a breathtaking, formidable lineup of gray and silver vessels. They glinted in the rising sun, which, despite the pall of smoke, still managed to shine through. Full squadrons of amphibious vehicles carrying tanks and other equipment bobbed in the surf along with landing craft loaded with infantry. They plunged up and down through the choppy waves as they headed toward shore.

The Germans opened fire with their big guns as the first of the landing craft neared the beach.

Emmy grabbed her hand. "We've done all we can. We need to go."

Together they turned and headed toward the road, jogging, which was the best they could manage because they were too tired to run.

They never saw or heard the German shell that hit only a few meters away.

Chapter Fifty

One moment they were fine, the next they were not.

When Genevieve regained consciousness, she didn't know if a second had passed or an hour. It was still near dawn: the mist rising from the marsh had that distinctive pinkish tinge that only came with the early morning light. She lay on her side on high, solid ground — the middle of the railroad tracks, she discovered as she felt the wooden ties beneath her and saw an iron rail. Her ears rang. Her head hurt. Lifting an unsteady hand to her forehead, she discovered she was bleeding. A cut above her eyebrow, a couple of centimeters long, from the feel of it. Pulling her hand back, looking at the blood on her fingers, she grimaced.

Somewhere not too far away, artillery boomed like thunder. Sharp barks of machine-gun fire punctuated the relentless *ack-ack* of the antiaircraft guns. The sky was thick with smoke. She could smell it, taste it.

She remembered looking out to sea, the dozens of landing craft riding the whitecaps, the lineup of battleships on the horizon . . .

Emmy.

Where was she?

"Emmy." She said it aloud. Despite her bleeding head, she didn't seem to be seriously injured. She could think, and see, and move and wasn't in terrible pain.

Dashing away the blood starting to trickle around her eye, she struggled up onto an elbow.

Emmy lay on the railroad track, too, sprawled motionless on her back not far away.

Genevieve half crawled, half scrambled toward her. Her sister's eyes were closed. Beneath the mud and grime on her face, her skin looked gray. There was no injury to Emmy's face that she could see; her blond curls, flung back against the weeds between the wooden ties and matted now with mud, showed no trace of blood.

Genevieve touched her cheek. "Emmy." She looked down at her sister's shiny dark shirt and gray trousers.

The shirt was tan, Genevieve realized with a thrill of horror, noting the light brown sleeves. The reason the middle looked dark and shiny was because the front of it was soaked with blood.

"Oh, no. Oh, no. Emmy." She unbuttoned her sister's blouse, stared aghast at the gaping wound in her chest. Blood everywhere. Exposed red muscle, the white of bone, the pink of an internal organ . . .

"Genny." Emmy's eyes opened. Her voice was scarcely louder than a breath.

"It's all right," Genevieve said, while her heart raced with terror. "I'm here."

Frantic, she looked around, spied a group of partisans not too far away, waved to signal she needed help. She had a length of parachute silk wound around her waist that she'd been cutting strips from to mark the paths. Snatching it loose, she pressed it gently, carefully, firmly over Emmy's wound.

"Uh." The sound Emmy made was full of pain, and it tore at Genevieve's heart.

"Lie still. Help's coming." She covered Emmy with her coat, slid her hands beneath to keep gentle pressure on the wound. The silk was already warm and wet with her sister's blood. A frantic glance told her that the partisans she'd signaled were moving carefully but quickly toward them along the marked paths.

Hurry. Hurry. But she couldn't scream it as she wanted to do. The last thing they needed was to attract the attention of more guns.

"I'm going to die, aren't I?" Emmy's tone was almost conversational. The eyes that were so like Genevieve's own seemed to be losing their brightness. Terror clutched at Genevieve's soul.

"No, you're not. Do you hear? You're not going to die." Genevieve leaned over her sister. "Emmy, do you hear me? You are not going to die."

"Bébé." Emmy's eyes found hers, focused. She smiled. Beneath the coat, one of her hands moved to cover Genevieve's. It felt cold as ice. "I'm glad you're here. *Je te tiens, tu me tiens.*"

"Je te tiens, tu me tiens," Genevieve repeated fiercely. Then her heart convulsed as Emmy closed her eyes.

Chapter Fifty-One

Emmy died at the home of a doctor in Montebourg without ever regaining consciousness. The partisans who'd carried her there had apparently known to get word to Max. He found Genevieve alone, in the examining room where Emmy had been taken.

She'd stopped crying some time before, for the simple reason that she had no more tears left to shed. She sat in an upright wooden chair beside her sister's dead body, tightly holding her cold and lifeless hand.

"Come on, we've got to get you out of here." Appearing in the doorway of the examining room, looking briefly unfamiliar in a scuffed leather flight jacket and loose trousers instead of his usual suit, Max took in the situation at a glance, then came over to put an arm around her shoulders, drop a kiss on her hair. Other than the cut on her forehead, which was bandaged now, she was unharmed.

She could barely stand the fact that she was unharmed.

"I can't leave," she told him as he pulled her to her feet. She gestured at her sister, gray in death and dirty from their exertions of the previous night and looking like a waxen image of herself as she lay lifeless on the doctor's table. "Emmy —"

"I'll come back and see that she's taken care of," he said. His voice was soothing. "You trust me to do that, don't you?"

She did. She would trust Max with anything.

Nodding, she rested her head on his chest and felt his arms come around her. He held her close, rocked her against him.

"It happened so fast," she said. "We were together and then —" Her voice choked. She took a deep breath.

"I know," he said. "I heard what happened. I know you're sad. But we've got to go now."

With a quiet word to the doctor, who'd entered to check on the identity of the new arrival, he hustled her out of the surgery, which was in a separate wing of the doctor's house.

"Where are we going?" she asked when they were outside.

They were on the outskirts of the village, she saw with a glance around, something that hadn't registered with her earlier. It was late afternoon now, and the sounds and signs of a raging battle were everywhere.

"I pulled every string I have and got you a spot on a plane going to RAF Tempsford. We don't have any time to spare." There was a motorbike parked in the street. Stopping beside it, Max swung a leg over it, started it up and yelled "Get on!" to her over the roar.

Genevieve did, wrapping her arms around his waist. The motorbike took off with a jolt, bouncing over streets that looked in places like they'd been chewed and spit out by a giant animal. More houses had been reduced to rubble than still stood. Gardens had been replaced by craters. Tall splinters were all that remained of trees. Tanks were stuck in hedgerows as their crews worked to get them out. Soldiers — Allies, Germans, a chaotic mix of the two — were everywhere, engaging in small, deadly skirmishes. On the road out of town, they skirted around dead bodies lying next to abandoned bombed-out vehicles. Bombers overhead, explosions, gunfire, smoke — the sights and sounds of war filled her senses.

A convoy of military trucks bristling with guns came over a rise, heading toward them.

Max turned off the road, bounced through a ditch and took the motorbike into a wood. Genevieve held on tight as they dodged trees, splashed through a creek, went up a hill, roared down the other side.

When he stopped abruptly, Genevieve was

surprised to see a small gray airplane sitting in the field in front of them. Its propeller was turning, its cockpit lid was open and it was obviously waiting.

The pilot, spotting them, waved.

Genevieve got off as Max shut down the engine.

"Come on." He grabbed her hand.

They ran to the plane. When they reached it, Max pulled her close, kissed her quick and hard, then let her go and pointed to a spot on the wing.

"Step there." He had to yell to be heard over the thrum of the engine.

"Wait." She was yelling, too. The cockpit looked like it would accommodate only one other person besides the pilot. "You're not coming?"

He shook his head. "I told you before. I'm a soldier. I stay."

"But —"

"Look, the Germans have ten thousand pounds on your head. For that price, even if they don't stumble across you themselves, lots of people will hand you over. Nobody knows how this fight's going to turn out. You're leaving while you can."

"Max, old sod, got to go," the pilot leaned out of the cockpit to shout. His leather helmet and the goggles pushed up to the top of his head made him look like some unknown species of giant bug.

"I can't go. I can't leave you." Her heart, still in shock over Emmy, trembled and shook at the idea of parting from Max. As she'd already learned to her cost, there were no guarantees in life, no guarantees that the person you loved would be there from one day to the next, no guarantees about anything at all. And this was war. Death waited around every corner. It came rocketing out of the sky, zipping through the air, blasting up from the ground. It came with no notice, no warning, no chance to say goodbye. "I'd rather take my chances and stay."

"You have to go," he said. She reached for him, and he caught her arms just above her elbows, holding her away from him, frowning down at her. His eyes were dark with strain. His mouth was tight with it. "Do you hear me? You have to go. I have a job to do, and I can't do it if I'm worried about you. And I'll worry about you every minute unless you get on this plane and go to England and I know you're safe."

"Max, I —" She broke off to look up at him, knowing that her heart was in her eyes and not caring. What he said made sense, she knew it did, she knew the only thing to do was get on that plane and fly away, but knowing that made no difference. To leave him now felt as impossible as flying to the moon. Her chest ached and her throat grew tight and tears stung her eyes. There was a catch in her voice as she said, "I'll go."

"Genevieve. You're breaking my heart here." His voice was rough, raw. His face tightened as his eyes moved over her face. She realized she was crying, realized that the hot tears had spilled over to slide down her cheeks, but there was absolutely nothing she could do about it. His hands tightened on her arms, his mouth twisted, and he pulled her against him and kissed her, a hot, hungry kiss that crushed her mouth, that invaded it, that had her pulling her arms free and going up on tiptoe to wrap them around his neck and kiss him back. He kissed her like he was never going to let her go, like he could never get enough of the taste of her mouth, like he was promising her forever, and she kissed him back the same way.

"Max, buddy, don't got all day." The voice of his pilot friend broke them apart.

"Go on." Max caught her arms again, pulled them down from around his neck, nodded toward the plane. "Get out of here."

Her smile was shaky, but it was a smile. "Don't get killed."

"I won't." It was a promise, but they both knew he couldn't promise that. She was still nestled against him, with her hands on his chest and her head thrown back so that she could look up into the hard, handsome face that was now dearer to her than anything in the world. She wasn't crying any longer, at least the tears had stopped, but she felt her poor broken heart throbbing in a way that let her know that, despite the losses, despite all the grief, despite all the pain, it was still fully functional, still fully alive. For him.

"I love you," she said.

His eyes blazed at her. "I love you, too."

Then he kissed her again, fierce and yet achingly tender. Knowing it was the last time for a long while at least and maybe forever, desperate at the thought of parting, she kissed him back with all the passion he'd awakened in her and all the love for him that burned inside her combined.

"Max." The pilot yelled in what was a clear warning as the plane started to move a little.

Max raised his head, put her away from him, pointed at that same spot on the wing. "Go. Step there."

She did, even though her eyes were stinging again and her throat was tight from the sobs she was holding back.

"I was going to say I'll write, but I don't even have an address. And you don't have one for me. How will we ever find each other?" Balanced on the wing, one hand hanging on to the edge of the open cockpit now as the wing jiggled and bounced beneath her, she turned to look back at Max.

"I'll find you," he said, and there was the ring of absolute certainty in his voice. "Count on it."

"Goodbye," she said, and turned away. Choking on the tears she could no longer hold back, feeling them spill down her face, she climbed into the cockpit and sank down in the tiny seat. The pilot handed her a helmet.

"Genevieve," Max yelled. He was standing where she'd left him, and she guessed he could see her tears. "Remember, angel, no regrets."

Her heart broke, even as she pulled the memory close.

"No regrets," she called back, and even managed a smile.

Then the pilot closed the cockpit and the plane started bumping forward in earnest.

Her last sight of Max as the plane rattled across the field and took off was of his tall figure lifting a hand in farewell.

Chapter Fifty-Two

May 8, 1945

Genevieve stepped out onstage for her final curtain call. She was in London, performing at the Savoy Theatre to sold-out crowds. This was the last night of her run before she took a well-deserved break. She had family things to take care of. And she was tired.

The war in Europe had ended days before. The city's mood was joyous, ebullient. The celebrations were ongoing. That giddiness was reflected in the enthusiasm of her audience. They'd been on their feet before the last note was sung. They were on their feet still. So many bouquets had been carried up to her that there weren't enough stagehands to cart them away and they were piling up in the wings.

The king and queen were in the audience. They were on their feet, too.

Even more important, her mother was there, in the front row. Lillian remained brokenhearted over Emmy's death — as did

Genevieve. Emmy's husband David had survived and returned home a few weeks before. Grief stricken at Emmy's fate, he had sought them out and they mourned with him. But Emmy would always be with them, just as Vivi would, and Paul and Berthe. One thing Genevieve had learned was that the people you loved were never lost. They became a permanent part of your soul.

Lillian was healing physically, and emotionally she was doing better lately, although she still had a long way to go on both fronts. Part of the reason for the improvement in her spirits was because she had fallen in love with Anna. After the Battle for Paris ran the Nazis out of France, Genevieve had arranged to have Anna rescued and brought to them. It hadn't been easy, but between Lillian's partisan connections and her own celebrity, she'd managed it. She'd been with them for six months now, in the comfortable house in Belgravia that Genevieve had leased until things settled down. Anna had been allowed to join them with the understanding that her stay with them might not be permanent — she would be restored to surviving family members if any could be found — but for now the three of them were a family. Genevieve caught herself being overprotective of the little girl sometimes, which was something she was working on, although she knew the tendency would probably follow her forever.

"Bravo!"

"Genevieve!"

"The Black Swan!"

They were shouting, whistling, clapping. It had been a good show, this final one. At least, final for a while. She would be back performing as soon as she had a rest, as soon as she got herself centered again.

Taking one more bow, she smiled into the blinding spotlights, waving and blowing kisses to the audience she could barely see.

She was happy the war was over. Of course she was. Ecstatic, really. But the many losses, the vast pain, could not be erased.

She was braced for more. She hadn't heard a word from Max in almost four months. When she wasn't onstage, she existed in what was starting to feel more and more like a permanent state of dread.

Which was why she was taking a break. The war, the losses she had endured, had taken an immeasurable toll. If Max didn't come back . . .

Another huge bouquet was on its way to her. A mass of roses, vivid red. She could see it being carried up the steps on the left side of the stage.

Picking up the full skirt of her white ball gown, cunningly sequined all over so that it glittered like a diamond in the lights when she moved, she walked toward stage left to take the flowers, smiling and waving to the audience all the while.

The lights were still in her eyes as she and the man carrying them drew close and she reached out for them.

She identified the uniform first: RAF. Then, as she accepted the flowers, which were heavy and redolent with perfume and just about the most beautiful bouquet she'd seen for a while, she saw the tall, lean, black-haired man who was handing them over. For a moment, the moment she took to process what she was seeing, her every sense suspended.

Then he smiled at her.

Max.

Roses and all, she flung herself into his arms as joy flooded her heart.

They closed tight around her. Laughing, crying, she wrapped her arms around his neck, and he lifted her up off her feet and whirled her around. In the auditorium, a spotlight hit a shock of white hair belonging to a man standing near the edge of the stage: Otto. He was there, safe as well. Beaming at her.

Her cup runneth over.

"Where have you *been*?" she said to Max.

"Did you think I wasn't coming? I told you I would. I just now got leave to come home."

"I've been so worried . . . I missed you so much."

His answer to that was to set her back on her feet and kiss her like she was the one thing he wanted most in this world. She kissed him back the same way.

The audience erupted into cheers. Not that either of them noticed or heard.

When at last he lifted his head, she leaned back against the strong arms that still circled her, looked up into the lean, dark face that had engraved itself on her heart and experienced the most profound sense of homecoming.

"It's over," she said. "Thank God, it's over."

"The war's over," he said, "but you and me, angel, we're just beginning."

AUTHOR'S NOTE

I researched this book to the point where I was muttering about the events leading up to D-Day in my sleep. Nevertheless, it's very possible that some factual errors have slipped in. If so, they are mine alone.

ACKNOWLEDGMENTS

I want to thank my husband, Doug, for putting up with me through the many long months I spent writing *The Black Swan of Paris.* My agent, Robert Gottlieb, possesses an encyclopedic knowledge of the events of World War II, which he generously shared with me. I thank him for that, as well as his tireless work on my behalf and unfailing support. My wonderful editor, Emily Ohanjanians, has done an absolutely fantastic job on this book. Thank you, Emily, for your patience, vision and hard work. I also want to thank Margaret Marbury for believing in this book and me, as well as the entire staff of MIRA Books. What a great team I have! Thank you all.

ABOUT THE AUTHOR

Karen Robards is the *New York Times, USA TODAY* and *Publishers Weekly* bestselling author of fifty novels and one novella. She is the winner of six Silver Pen awards and numerous other awards.

The employees of Thorndike Press hope you have enjoyed this Large Print book. All our Thorndike, Wheeler, and Kennebec Large Print titles are designed for easy reading, and all our books are made to last. Other Thorndike Press Large Print books are available at your library, through selected bookstores, or directly from us.

For information about titles, please call:
(800) 223-1244

or visit our website at:
gale.com/thorndike

To share your comments, please write:

Publisher
Thorndike Press
10 Water St., Suite 310
Waterville, ME 04901